PAPER RINGS

THE NEW ROMANTICS

BRITTANÉE NICOLE

BRITTANÉE NICOLE

This is a work of fiction. Names, characters, places, and incidents either are the product of the author's imagination or are used fictitiously. Any resemblance to actual persons, living or dead, events, or locales is entirely coincidental.

Boston Bolts Hockey: Snow © 2026 by Brittanée Nicole

First Edition June 2026

Cover Art: Classy Creeps

Formatting by Sara of Sara PA's Services

Editing by Beth at VB Edits

CONTENTS

Dedication

TO THE PEOPLE WHO SHOW UP: FOR THE CHILDREN WHO AREN'T THEIRS, BUT THEY LOVE THEM LIKE THEIR OWN; AND THE FRIENDS WHO AREN'T FAMILY, BUT ARE THERE FOR EVERY MOMENT, BIG AND SMALL.

AND FOR THE PEOPLE WHO DON'T ALWAYS FEEL CHOSEN.

YOU CAN DO HARD THINGS. BUT I HOPE YOU DON'T HAVE TO.

Foreword

Dear Reader,

Paper Rings is the first book of the New Romantics and can be read as a complete standalone. It is also the first book I've ever written in my second generation world. If you'd like to read the first generation, Adeline's parents' story can be found in Mother Faker, which is Book 1 of the Momcoms. If you'd like to read JJ's parent's epic duet, you can find it in Dirty Truths which is book 1 of the Extra Dirty Duet.

A suggested reading order for the rest of my books can be found on my website Brittaneenicole.com.

I hope you enjoy this world as much as I enjoy writing it.

xo,
Brittanée

PAPER RINGS - TAYLOR SWIFT
PLEASE DON'T BE - HAZLETT
18 - ONE DIRECTION
YELLOW - COLDPLAY
BAD IDEA RIGHT? - OLIVIA RODRIGO
YOU ARE IN LOVE - TAYLOR SWIFT
DO I EVER CROSS YOUR MIND - SOMBR
ETERNITY - ALEX WARREN, GIGI PEREZ
THAT WAY - TATE MCRAE
BABY STEPS - OLIVIA DEAN
ODE TO A COVERSATION STUCK IN YOUR
THROAT - DEL WATER GAP
MOVE ON FIRST - SADIE JEAN
FOREVER AGO - WOODLOCK
MY HOME - MYLES SMITH
FIRST TIME - VANCE JOY
HESITATE - HAZLETT, OSKA

Content Warnings

THIS BOOK CONTAINS SENSITIVE TOPICS INCLUDING DISCUSSIONS OF CANCER OF A NON-MAIN CHARACTER, SEXUAL ASSAULT (OFF PAGE), PHYSICAL ASSAULT (ON PAGE), INFIDELITY (NOT BETWEEN THE MAIN CHARACTERS), SEXUAL HARASSMENT, NON-CONSENSUAL DRUGGING AND PARENTAL ABANDONMENT.

Family Tree

THE LANGFIELDS

BECKETT LANGFIELD
& OLIVIA MAXWELL
(MOTHER FAKER)
↓
WINNIE LANGFIELD
FINN LANGFIELD
ADDIE LANGFIELD
JUNE LANGFIELD
MAGGIE LANGFIELD

GAVIN LANGFIELD
& MILLIE HALL
(A MAJOR PUCK UP)
↓
VIVI LANGFIELD
BOY 1

BROOKS LANGFIELD
& SARA CASE
(PUCKING REVENGE)
↓
TAYLOR LANGFIELD
BOY 1
BOY 2
BOY 3

AIDEN LANGFIELD
& LENNOX KENNEDY
(HOCKEY BOY)
↓
GIRL 1

SIENNA LANGFIELD
& NOAH HARRISON
(BEAUTY)
↓
OLLIE HARRISON
SARA HARRISON
KATE HARRISON

THE BOLTS

TYLER WARREN
& AVA ERICKSON
(WAR)
↓
BRAYDEN HAWKE
JOSIE WARREN
SCARLETT WARREN
BECKHAM WARREN

DANIEL HALL
& HANNAH PRESCOTT
(PLAYBOY)
↓
MAVERICK HALL
MONROE HALL

BOSTON BILLIONAIRES

CASH JAMES &
GRACE KENSINGTON
(FALLING FOR WHISKEY DUET)
↓
HOPE JAMES
THEO JAMES

JAY HANSON &
CAT BOUVIER (JAMES)
(EXTRA DIRTY DUET)
↓
CHLOE HANSON
JJ HANSON
JAMES HANSON

The Bouvier - Hansons

JAY HANSON **CATHERINE BOUVIER (JAMES)**

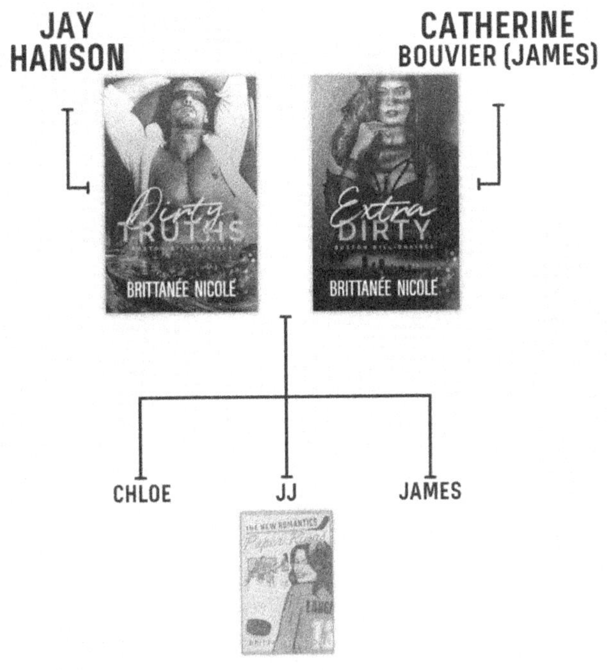

CHLOE JJ JAMES

The Langfields

BECKETT LANGFIELD **OLIVIA MAXWELL**

WINNIE FINN ADELINE MAGGIE JUNE

Prologue

Addie

Fourteen Years Old

"GIRLS DON'T BELONG in goalie gear."

I ignore Dirk's jabs and keep my focus forward just like Uncle Brooks taught me.

"Good job, Addie. Way to keep those eyes up," Coach yells.

"Such a good girl," Dirk says in an obnoxious high-pitched whisper.

What he doesn't understand is that I live in a house with seven people. It's constant chaos. I can tune anything out. And I'm not letting some prissy boy from New York who can't even properly shuffle get to me.

"Shut up, dickhead," JJ Hanson says from the other side of Dirk.

I ignore him too. Only twenty goalies nationwide got into this hockey camp. I won't let anyone distract me from soaking up every second of it. I'm the only girl, but I'm used to that. Since the day I started playing hockey, boys have been taunting me. I can handle it. I can deal with the sweet burn in my thighs after hours on the ice running drills, I can even handle the lack of a real locker room at camp and the solo dorm they've put me in.

What I can't handle is not being on the ice. Not making it onto Boston's roster this year. And JJ Hanson is my competition for that spot.

That's nothing new, though. He and I have been skating circles around each other for years. Our parents have been friends our whole lives, and from the time we were both old enough to play, they've had us training together.

"Good job, guys. Take a water break and then meet me at the net," Coach yells.

I've just taken a swig out of my water bottle when Dirk starts in again. He tosses his helmet onto the bench beside me and eyes JJ. "Are the rumors true? Is Addison Langfield that good on her knees?"

I'm more bothered by the way he treats his helmet than I am by his words, so I've already moved on from his comment when he goes flying backward.

"The fuck did you just say?" JJ pulls his own mask off and tosses it toward me.

I grit my teeth. God dammit. These boys have no freaking sense. These helmets are to be respected. Idiots.

"By the way you're always jumping in to protect her, she must be awfully good on her knees. And here you are, proving my point." Grinning, Dirk scans the other goalies, likely expecting a laugh.

Not a single one will even meet his eye.

He turns back to JJ, still wearing a cocky smirk, but JJ's fist is already flying. The hit is solid, colliding with Dirk's cheek with a loud crunch.

"Dammit JJ." I yank him back by his jersey.

Dirk cradles his face, screaming in shock. Stupid boys and stupid fights.

"He can't talk to you like that." JJ points at the asshole. "And her name is Adeline, dickhead."

The kid spits blood onto the ice and shakes his head. "What the fuck do I care what her name is?"

"Because," JJ seethes, "Adeline Langfield is going to be a legend in the NHL. You should ask her for her autograph now."

With a roll of my eyes, I hold JJ's helmet out to him. "He's not worth it. Come on, Hanson. I need you in tip top shape."

"You worried about me, Angles?" His unfairly beautiful blue eyes glimmer with amusement as he slips his helmet on, covering up his dark wavy hair.

Snorting, I slide my face mask into place. "Nah, just don't want you whining about how you wore yourself out defending my honor, and that's why I beat your ass for top spot on the team."

He chuckles and snags his stick. "I'm not going to make it *that* easy."

I pick mine up too, then follow him onto the ice.

"Two truths and a lie," he mutters as we skate toward the nets.

I nod. We've played this silly game for years. I don't remember how it started, but when one of us is spiraling out during practice or a game, we use it to rein ourselves back in, to get back to focusing on what truly matters—hockey.

"Dirk's dick is the size of my thumb, I'm gonna kick your ass in this drill, and you're going to be the best damn goalie the NHL has ever seen."

Frowning, I hold up my thumb. "Dirk's dick is this big?"

JJ spins, spraying ice as he comes to a quick stop in front of me. "Nah," he huffs out. "That's the lie. It's not even the size of my pinkie."

A loud laugh escapes me, echoing around the cavernous arena.

His face is lit up as I push past him, skating toward the net. "Nah, I'm totally gonna kick your ass."

He's chuckling when he catches up to me. As we approach our coaches, we slow. They're setting up for the next drill like they didn't see the altercation between JJ and Dirk or don't care.

"Did you mean it?" I say, my words quieter.

"That you're going to make it to the NHL?"

I give a jerky nod.

"Yeah, Addie, you're going to be a legend."

He can't see my smile behind my mask, but it's big enough to make my cheeks ache.

I believe him. One day I'll prove every one of those other assholes wrong and I can't wait.

CHAPTER 1

Addie

"HE SHOOTS, HE SCORES!" The mischievous voice bounces off the walls.

JJ's daughter Avery makes a whining sound, and then my sister is hollering from where she stands at the sink.

"Declan Langfield."

Her four-year-old son barely blinks, and he's already got his straw lined up to shoot another spit ball, this time at his brother Beckett. Winnie named her boys after the two men in our lives who never let us down, our stepdad, Beckett, and our uncle, Declan.

"Daddy, are you sure we have to stay here?" Avery asks in her sweet high-pitched voice.

JJ strides past me carrying another moving box. My father is right behind him, as is my brother Finn.

Apparently it's a damn family affair.

With a soft smile, JJ runs his free hand through her silky blond curls. A hand I have absolutely never dreamed about. I swear. Then those blue eyes of his land on me.

My stomach hits my throat, like it always does when he's around. I glance away. I'm not ready to deal with my ex-best friend or anything he has on his mind.

This is so not how I saw my first day in the NHL going.

Then again, this isn't how I saw my life going either. By now I should have an apartment in the city like the rest of my friends.

Okay, not all of my friends.

My best friend Savannah just moved out to the burbs with her fiancé, who's nearly twenty years older than we are.

But my other two best friends, Josie and Sutton, are both living my dream.

Or not exactly. Sutton is dating a Bolt, and I'd never date a hockey player. They're gross.

I digress. My point is that my dream always included the NHL, but I never would have imagined that at twenty-six, I'd be moving back into my childhood home to help my older sister raise her twin boys. And I never would have believed I'd be living with JJ Hanson.

Okay, that's also a lie. A long, long time ago, I might have wished that I'd share a home with this man, but those fantasies died a long, slow, murderous, torturous death.

And maybe I'm being a tiny bit dramatic this morning. Then again, who can blame me? I'm moving back into my childhood home with six kids under the age of four and the man who broke my heart.

My dad returns to the kitchen and greets the kids. Then he pauses in front of me and breaks into a smile. "Big day, Little One." He angles in and presses a kiss to my forehead, a box balanced against his hip. "You ready?"

At five ten, I'm almost as tall as he is, so the nickname doesn't make much sense to most people. But Beckett and I didn't meet until I was two, when he moved into a house a lot like this one with my mother and her friends and their many, many kids. He struggled keeping our names straight, so he gave us all nicknames.

At least that's what he let people believe. It's really because he's a total softy and that's just what he does. He gives everyone a nickname. He shows up for us too. I'm incredibly lucky.

Maybe I should do that. Not the showing up part—I do my fair share, even if I'm not soft like he is. The nickname thing might come in handy, though, once my brother's best friend Hope and her three kids move in as well.

I force a smile. "Ready as I'll ever be."

Stepping back, he nods. "If anyone gives you trouble—"

"*Beckett,*" my mother warns.

Head tipped back, I groan. Dad is so overprotective that I swear his picture is printed next to the word in the dictionary. He would do anything for his family—for me—but I've spent my life playing hockey with guys. I know how to take care of myself.

"I'm just saying, I still have pull." He winks at me.

With a roll of her eyes, Mom snatches the straw out of Dec's hand. "Your cousin should be here any minute."

The statement is directed at Winnie, because starting today, our cousin Vivi is the kids' nanny. All six of them.

She's also moving in with us. I feel for her. At least I'll leave the house for work every day. Then again, she brought it on herself when she dropped out of college. My uncle was having none of that, so he kicked her out and told her to get a job.

Uncle Gavin, who's the head coach of the Boston Bolts—my new team—is also normally a total softy like Dad, so this is probably killing him. But I can't deny that it's what twenty-one-year-old Vivi needs.

Winnie needs it too. While I'm moving in to support her, my schedule is packed. I'll be lucky if I can make dinner for the crew one night a week.

It's the only reason I agreed to this arrangement, honestly. The team travels to games for almost ten months out of the year, and it doesn't really matter where my stuff stays when I'm gone. Being here means that when I am in town, I can at least offer real conversation to my sister, who seriously needs another adult in her life.

"Thank god," Winnie says as she spins around and straightens her hair. "Do I have food on my shirt?"

Mom and I look her up and down, checking for evidence of the twins' breakfast on her clothing. Her light brown hair is pulled back in a tight bun, making her look so much like Mom used to, and she's in a navy-blue suit. She's self-conscious about her curves since having the twins, but they're incredible in my opinion.

I don't know how she is so put together at eight a.m. when she's spent half the morning wrangling two little monsters. I suppose she doesn't have much of a choice. Winnie is the CEO of the local baseball team. The team my brother plays for. The team the Langfield family owns—the Boston Revs.

Dad and his brothers have their hands in just about everything in Boston. It's always been a family affair.

"You look gorgeous," my mother says to her. "So for real," she adds, turning to me, "are you ready for today?"

I snort. "Mom, you just got after Dad for asking the same question."

She shrugs. "But I'm your mother. And he's unreasonable. I won't storm into the locker room and tell everyone to be nice to my little girl, but I will check in to make sure you're doing okay."

Warmth blooms in my chest. I truly do have the two best parents. My biological dad may have decided fatherhood wasn't for him, but Beckett more than makes up for his absence.

I don't remember a time when I wasn't a Langfield. The first time I really knew my name, that's the one I gave. I'm not sure when Dad officially adopted me and they changed it legally, but for as long as I remember, I've been Langfield.

I was the youngest when my parents got married, but when I was four, my twin sisters were born. Clearly twins run in the family. June and Maggie are just starting their senior year of college. So although I keep complaining about all the kids in this house, there were always five of us growing up. And then when JJ moved in, there were six.

"I think that's the last of it," my father says from the other room.

"I really appreciate this," JJ says, his voice a little quieter.

Ugh. I fight the urge to roll my eyes. Dad and Mom get to live by themselves in the Penthouse in Boston. JJ should be thanking me for this privilege. I'm the one stuck sharing a bathroom with him since he took Finn's old bedroom.

It's like déjà vu. The last time he lived with us, we shared that same bathroom, though Finn was still home, so the boys shared a room. We were fifteen and I had all sorts of feelings. Feelings I wish I could forget.

This is going to be so weird.

My parents ordered two sets of bunk beds and had them set up in the large playroom at the end of the hall. That's where JJ's daughter and Hope's oldest—Grace, who's four—will sleep, along with Winnie's boys.

Hope's other girls are little and will be staying in her bedroom.

It's not a perfect scenario, but it'll work.

With any luck, it'll be fun for the kids. I grew up in a house full of kids, too, and I have thousands of good memories of that time.

If not for one small detail, I wouldn't mind the situation at all.

And that small detail just stepped into the kitchen, his hands in his pockets. "Do you have to go?" Avery whines.

"Yeah, Avey girl, I do," JJ says, giving her a soft smile. He catches me staring at the two of them and smirks. "And so do you."

I tilt my head and focus on the counter in front of me. It's safer if we don't make eye contact. Easier. Though that's about to be nearly impossible, considering my new job. With that reminder, I force myself to meet his gaze.

It's annoying how beautiful JJ Hanson grew up to be. Yes, beautiful. He's got all these pretty lines on his face, a strong jaw, and long black lashes that most women would kill for. And then there are his eyes. They're a glacier blue, almost the dusty blue of the ice in Bolts Arena. The team color that just so happens to be my absolute favorite in the world.

I honestly can't say whether I love the color because I've always dreamed of being a Bolt or because it's the color of his eyes. I hate how much I've thought about this question. Despise it really.

And don't even get me started on his incredible body. It's not just that he's strong, with broad shoulders and thick thighs. Those traits are a necessity for all NHL goalies, and he's damn good at what he does. Not that I'd ever tell him that. But in my world, muscular guys are a dime a dozen. What I love about his body is that the man is built like a protector. Like a dad. That last part is the sexiest thing about him of all. How sweet he is to his daughter. He turns into complete mush for her. JJ Hanson is as incredible as a father as Beckett is. And damn if that isn't my kryptonite. As much as I despise this attraction to him, I'd never wish those traits away. I absolutely adore his daughter, and how could I not want him to be a great dad for her?

"I'm leaving shortly," I reply.

"We're going to the same place. Might as well ride together," he says.

I swear every eye in the room is on us, like they're all waiting for me to explode.

Avery peers up at me, her eyes the same glacier blue as her father's. "You should remind him he's not the boss of you." She gives me one of her signature saucy smiles. "*You're* the boss of him."

The room erupts into laughter, the tension breaking. Grinning, I pull Avery onto my lap, hugging her tight. Her mother disappeared recently, so I've made even more of an effort to show her love and affection since. I still don't know why she left, but that woman has caused more than enough grief for a lifetime. It serves me well not to think of her. I will, however, always have her little girl's back. Even if she happens to be JJ's daughter.

"Don't worry, I'll make sure to remind him repeatedly." I dart a look at JJ, who is wearing one of his many guarded expressions, his focus on us. "I'm driving."

His eyes instantly light up like he's surprised by my response. "Fine by me, Coach."

That's the other thing I got wrong when I pictured my future. I'm not the legend *in* the NHL. I'm just the legend's *coach*.

BOSTON
BOLTS

CHAPTER 2

JJ

I SHAKE my head as I sink into Adeline's Bolts blue Porsche. I'm pretty sure Beckett had it custom made for her. She's been obsessed with cars since she was sixteen. Probably because she's spent all her life hanging out with guys who are obsessed with three things: hockey, cars, and women.

Adeline doesn't give anyone even a second of her attention—male or female—but she could talk cars and hockey all day.

And sports cars have always been her favorite.

"What are you shaking your head at?" She grumbles as she revs the engine.

There's no stopping my smirk. "You showing off for me?"

She scoffs, keeping her focus fixed out the windshield. "Please, I don't do anything *for* you. Or anyone for that matter. I do what makes me happy, and what makes me happy is the sound of my pretty baby starting up."

Theo: We're playing in Boston in October. You
guys around?

I groan at my cousin's text messages. Dammit, he's waking the chat. In minutes, I'll have a dozen unread messages. He and Finn could go back and forth for hours. How is a mystery. Both are professional athletes like me with ridiculously busy schedules.

Finn is the Boston Revs' catcher, and Theo is the quarterback for Tennessee's NFL team. He's also Hope's overbearing younger brother who doesn't know what to do with himself now that she's moved back to Boston and he's the only one left in Nashville. I swear the kid is dying to move home.

Though I can't imagine he'd want to move into the brownstone with the rest of us. I still don't know how I got myself into this situation.

> Finn: Already in the calendar.
>
> Finn: and Hopie's good. Gracie and I are going shopping this afternoon. She wants to pick out decorations for Hope's room and surprise her. Says Mommy doesn't smile enough.
>
> Theo: I'm going to fucking murder her husband.

I'd like to get in on that, actually. What kind of spineless dick leaves his wife and three kids? Especially when his youngest isn't even a year old. Fucking kills me.

> Me: Let me know when and where.
>
> Bray: No one is murdering anyone. Also, where the fuck are you? The rest of the team is already here.

Brayden Hawke, my team captain, rarely participates in the chat. He's tried removing himself at least ten times, but Finn always adds him back. He's a more recent addition to our crew. The guys got him to come out with us one night, and Finn adopted him, probably against his will. He's a few years older than the rest of us, and for as long as

I've been with the Bolts, he's worked hard to maintain a professional relationship with his teammates. It's like he's scared to be friends with the guys he plays with. Though the last few years since he became captain he's loosened up a bit and now I'd consider him my best friend on the team.

I respond to Bray, then I sneak a few glances at my newest coach.

Adeline Langfield grew up fucking gorgeous. She's a knockout. I swear if she didn't play hockey, she'd be on a runway. Or maybe not, because I can't imagine her ever being interested in fashion. But she has the face and stature of a model.

Her long chestnut waves always smell like coconut, and she typically wears her hair pulled back from her pretty face. Her high cheekbones are brushed with the lightest of pink and her lush lips are always covered in a red gloss. She's never steered away from her femininity despite the shit she's gotten for it in this industry. Then there are the dimples so deep she can't hide them even when she's not smiling. I know because she rarely smiles at me. Not anymore. And then there are the prettiest brown eyes I've ever seen. She rarely looks my way, so I haven't had the opportunity to really study them in a long-ass time, but I remember many a night when those very eyes were the last thing I saw before I fell asleep.

She was my secret keeper and the only good thing in my life the year I lived with the Langfields. I wish I could work out why she hates me so much now.

And I wish it didn't bother me so much that she does.

"Stop staring at me," she grouses.

I smirk. I may hate that we aren't friends, but I do love engaging with her. Even if the only way I get to do it is by pissing her off.

"Now why would I do that?" I say with a forced smirk.

Finally, she looks at me, her expression making it clear that she thinks I'm the biggest idiot she's ever met. "You realize that I could make your season a living hell, right?"

Shifting in my seat, I turn her way. It's only polite to give her my full attention. So what if that also means I have an excuse to check out what she's wearing today? She looks gorgeous in the simple light blue Bolts zip up over what I'm guessing is a sports bra. I definitely shouldn't be picturing her in just that, but thanks to Josie's love for posting photos online, I know exactly what Adeline looks like in far less.

It's not like I've gone looking for the photos. We just move in the same circles. And I've seen photos of every woman in that circle in a bikini. And now we're living together. Sharing a fucking bathroom.

Shit, will she walk around in a tiny towel like she used to? She'd have full conversations like that, completely oblivious to the way my dick would immediately harden.

Probably not.

She's older. She knows better. Right?

She has to know the effect she'd have on a man were she to walk around like she used to. The effect she'd have on *me.*

She glares my way again.

Fuck. Of course she doesn't. The woman barely thinks of me. She's definitely not paying attention to the way I look at her.

I never should have agreed to move into the brownstone. The player-coach relationship the two of us have been forced into will be hard enough. I've spent the better part of a decade fighting this impossible crush. And for the past four years, I've put in extra effort. Even if my marriage has always been a farce, I tried for Avery. Giving up on Adeline and the future I thought we'd have almost killed me though.

And now I'll see her almost daily and travel with her weekly. We'll have to go over tape and work out together. There was a time when being on the ice with her felt like foreplay. Nothing, and I mean not a goddamn thing, has ever gotten me as hard as Adeline running drills with me. For years, she was my favorite distraction. Always the best player on the ice. Her tenacity and determination and her goddamn grit made her that way. She refused to give up. Refused to cut corners. Ignored the voices—and there were many—telling her that she didn't belong out there with us guys.

She's the reason I'm the best goalie in the NHL. The reason I won the Calder Trophy my rookie year and the Vezina the last two years.

If Adeline had signed with an NHL team, I'd bet anything that those awards would have been hers.

She's better than any of us. I'm lucky that she's back on the ice with me.

But between that and living with her, every moment of my life is about to be torture. A fucking disaster.

When my phone buzzes, I welcome the distraction, turning toward the window as I unlock it.

> Tabitha: I told you I needed time. Tell your
> attorney to stop harassing me.

I can't help the scoff that flies from my lips at my future ex-wife's demands.

Wife. Fuck, I hate that the woman ever held that title. That she still does. I guarantee the only reason she's holding on to it is because of the prenup. The one that states that if we stay married for five years, she walks away with a million dollars—and if we divorce before then, she doesn't get a dime.

My parents are stupidly rich, so by default, I'm stupidly rich. Not one of us was delusional enough to believe Tabitha actually loved me. She was a puck bunny and she didn't even try to hide it. But I never would have thought that she wouldn't love her daughter either.

That's the part that kills me. Avery deserves the world. And that's why I'm putting myself through this torture with Adeline. It's why I moved into the brownstone. My little girl deserves a family, and I've done a shit job providing that. So long as I play hockey, my schedule is intense and the planning is out of my hands.

With Tabitha disappearing completely two weeks ago, I'm in a bind. Though it's loosened a bit since Beckett Langfield swooped in and saved the day. Just like he did all those years ago when he brought me into his home at a time when I needed the support.

"Everything okay?"

I give a jerky nod, my phone squeezed tight in my hand.

"You sure?" Her voice is soft. So familiar and yet so foreign these days.

I refuse to let it comfort me. She's only being nice to me because of Tabitha. Since Avery was born and Tabitha became a true fixture in my life, Adeline has kept a professional distance from me. I'd do well to remember that and keep a healthy distance from her too.

"I'm fine."

There was a time that she would immediately know I was lying. When she wouldn't have allowed it. I have no idea if she believes me now because I no longer know her and she definitely doesn't know me. We aren't best friends anymore.

Hell, we aren't friends at all.

She's my coach and my roommate and nothing more.

CHAPTER 3

Addie

"YOU COMING?"

"Yeah," I say to JJ, frozen in front of the door to the arena. "Go get changed. I'll see you out on the ice."

He lets out a light laugh like it's really clicking for him, like it is for me, that I'm his coach. That I don't need to head to the locker room. That today is the beginning of a new era. "See ya out there."

I don't watch him step inside. Instead I focus on the words above the door.

Bolts Arena.

My cheeks grow warm and my chest expands. I did it. I'm really here.

"Big day."

I spin around and grin as my Uncle Cade approaches, his arms outstretched.

"So everyone keeps telling me," I say as I step into him and let him wrap me in a hug.

Like always, Cade is wearing a backward Bolts hat, a pair of black track pants, and a light blue Bolts long sleeved T-shirt.

"Thought you planned to actually enjoy retirement. Decide you want to keep tabs on me instead?"

He chuckles. "Nah, we all know you'll put the rest of the coaching staff, past and present, to shame."

Cade married my mother's brother Declan and became my uncle when I was young. I don't really have any memory of Uncle Declan without Cade. The two of them are also married to their wife Melina. Maybe their situation was scandalous at one point, but they've only ever been my aunt and uncles.

"Any last-minute words of wisdom?"

He reaches for the door and pulls it open. "Be on time."

Laughing, I step inside. The moment the air hits me, I stop and close my eyes, then breathe in deeply.

Ice. Cold. Rubber. Cleaner.

Home sweet home.

When I open my eyes, Cade is smiling at me. "Feels good, right?"

"I'm going to have to work on my game day face so it isn't obvious to everyone that I'm walking on a cloud today, huh?"

Chuckling, he drapes an arm over my shoulders. "Nah, it's good to be excited. Best job in the world."

It's not. Being on the ice as part of the team would be better. But Cade never played professionally, so I won't point that out. Already, I miss the rush of the game. As a goalie, I was usually on the ice through all three periods. It'll be an adjustment not being in the crease, but I made this choice when Gavin came to me and floated this idea. I was still playing in the PWHL at the time and until that day, I figured that's where I'd stay. The NHL has never seen a female goalie coach. Taking the job would allow me to blaze a trail along with the few other women holding assistant coaching positions. That detail alone made it impossible to say no.

It's not easy. It's mostly still a boys' club. Even in Bolts Arena, where my uncles and my father have worked hard to make all of their sports teams inclusive.

In a sport dominated by men, still watched mostly by men despite the increasing number of female spectators, I didn't take the offer lightly.

This is my opportunity.

Most assume nepotism got me here, I'm sure. And maybe there's some truth to it. Langfield Corp has employed the majority of our family members. That just means I have to work harder to prove that I deserve to be here because of my talent. That I can add value to the Bolts organization.

As we make our way around the rink, I take in every detail as if I didn't practically grow up here. The jagged lightning Bolts adorning the boards around the rink, the dusty blue seats, the *Langfield* scrawled across the score board. My uncles' jerseys hanging from the rafters alongside the banners for their Stanley Cup wins.

Aiden, my dad's youngest brother, is considered one of the best to ever play. He's an assistant coach now, but he played until he was forty, winning three Stanley Cups during his tenure. When he retired, the organization retired his number too.

"Guys should be out soon," Cade says as he guides me toward to the team bench. "While there will be a few goalies from the AHL and junior team here to practice with us for these first couple weeks, JJ and Sidney are our likely starters."

None of this is news to me. JJ and Sidney are our veteran goalies.

"But," he continues, "there's a chance that we'll have an undiscovered new hotshot in our midst, so don't rule them out."

I snort. "You're saying there's a chance I get to send Hanson back to the AHL?"

Cade side-eyes me, blue eyes sharp. "I know you two have a history, but I figured since he's living with you—"

"He's not living with me," I huff, the noise a little too loud in the empty arena. "You know how my father is. He offered him a room after I'd agreed to move in."

Cade's lips twitch like he's trying to hide a smile. "Yeah, your dad does shit like that." He chuckles. "Better watch out. He might be trying to set you up."

A short burst of laughter escapes me. "Yes, my dad is known as the weird matchmaker, but I assure you, he'd never set me up with a married man."

Cade isn't wrong. My father has a habit of claiming responsibility for the coupling of just about anyone he knows. He even took credit when Cade got together with Declan and Melina.

I frown. "Wait, how did he set you guys up again?"

Cade's blue eyes dance. "Mel needed a place to stay, and he offered her the guest room at Declan's house without asking first."

"Oh…" Eyes wide, I suddenly wish I hadn't asked. "I guess I… no—"

"No what?" a deep voice asks.

I turn at the sound, grateful for the interruption. When I meet Uncle Brooks's eye, I relax. "You guys are gonna give me a complex," I tease. "Are you all going to watch my every move?"

He rolls his eyes. Like Cade, he's dressed for practice in a long-sleeve Bolts T-shirt, though his is a darker blue. His athletic pants are dark gray and his signature long hair is pulled back in a low bun. "It's all hands on deck for the next few weeks, kid. Promise we're not hovering any more than usual."

My muscles loosen a little at his assurance. This position should be Brooks's. I always assumed this was the next step for him. Since he retired from the game, he's been working for the organization, though he hasn't settled into a single position. As the Bolts' most beloved goalie to date, it seemed logical that he'd be the next goalie coach. Instead he's continued to float. Sometimes he works with recruiting, sometimes he hangs with donors, and more often than not, he's here, at practice.

The man has four kids. Maybe he likes the freedom that comes with what he's doing now. It means he doesn't have to travel, and I imagine his family appreciates that. Regardless, his decision worked in my favor.

"Fine," I retort, "but call me kid in front of the team and I'll put you in the net without gear and give Aiden free rein."

Both my uncles let out raucous laughs.

"Understood." Brooks dips his chin. "And for the record, you're going to be just fine out there."

As the three of us sit on the bench to lace up our skates, a cacophony of voices echoes loudly through the space, and a heartbeat later, players filter in. The guys are loud, talking over one another, laughing, and joking around. The energy is electric.

Most of these guys are returning players, and from the excitement in the air, they're thrilled to be back at it. For people like us, hockey is so much more than a game or even a career. It's a lifestyle. It's an itch. Staying away from this rink is more difficult than showing up, even after brutal losses. These guys need the short break they get between seasons, but they don't want it. Neither did I.

This group includes a few rookies too. The guys from the AHL who are here hoping to prove themselves, eagerly awaiting the call that they've been moved up, and the draft picks. They could be put anywhere. They usually end up on a junior league or in the AHL. Very rarely do they get a shot at the show.

But this is where they want to be. Though the Bolts typically practice at the practice rink, day one is always held in the arena, on this ice. This way the rookies get a taste of what they could have. We show them how good it could be. And then we make them work their asses off for it. They'll be doing it for the next ten months.

I give myself a few seconds to imagine today through their eyes. To feel the hope that comes with the desperate desire to play for the Bolts, not a farm team. To see the kind of season that leads to the Cup. That's what we're working toward.

While this may not have been what I saw when I pictured myself in the NHL, I'm still here. I made it.

And it's a huge accomplishment.

Bobby Dean, our star center, is, of course, the first out. Because he's not in full gear, his hair is on display and styled to perfection. He's loud and obsessed with fashion, and he has an incredible slap shot. And his brown hair does this wave that makes women go wild. Or so he likes to claim.

Per NHL league rules, we can't actually practice on the ice today. We have dryland training for five days before on-ice practices begin. However, everyone's got their skates on so that we can meet here before we break up into smaller groups for the various workouts we've got planned. I'll be taking my guys to the yoga studio.

Bobby skates toward us, a big smile on his face, with Maxim Loob, a Russian defenseman, following. Maxim is huge, even without his gear. According to his stats, he's six seven.

Bobby rubs his hands together as he slides to a stop. "Big day, Addie baby."

Beside me, Brooks glares at him.

I shake my head, but it's Maxim who says what we're all thinking. "Idiot." His thick accent makes me smile, as always. He nods toward me then. "Welcome to team. Looking forward to having you, Coach."

"Was that so hard?" Brooks says.

Bobby shrugs. "Sorry, it's going to take a bit of getting used to after hanging out with you and Little Hawke all the time."

He's referring to Josie, and if her older brother Brayden heard him calling her that, he'd also call him an idiot. Before I can say as much, Maxim grabs the neck of Bobby's shirt and pulls him backward on the ice. "Say bye-bye."

He flaps his fingers up and down in a dramatic wave until Bobby does the same thing, making the three of us laugh.

A few more players make it out onto the ice, but I keep my eyes on the door, waiting for my guys.

Goalies are easily identifiable. They wear a hell of a lot more padding and a different helmet. Their sticks are different, and their gloves too.

My younger sisters used to call me the marshmallow girl, and for good reason.

I'm still smiling, relishing those memories, when I spot the first of the goalies.

My goalies.

They aren't dressed in their full gear today, but I'd recognize our veteran goalie anywhere. It's no surprise that Sidney Howe is the first one out. He's the most senior, at thirty-seven, though it's been a while since he's played on our first string. JJ was drafted out of high school and called up from the AHL after only one season. In his first season with the Bolts, he and Sidney played pretty equally. These days, JJ plays two games to every one of Howe's. While Sidney is a great goalie, JJ is phenomenal.

Not that I'll ever tell him that. As his coach, I have no intention of coddling him. I won't coddle any of the players or inflate their egos. If they're looking for someone to tell them how great they are, they can chat with the puck bunnies.

My goal is to help them become the best they can be. To study tapes so they're prepared for every opponent. To guide them in strength training and stretching, which I'm exceptionally qualified for since it's what I focused on in college. I incorporate a lot of yoga into my personal training, and in the next couple of weeks, every one of our goalies will be implementing it as well.

Sidney heads our way, saying hello to both Cade and Brooks and then giving me a friendly grin. "Welcome, Coach. Excited to have you."

This certainly isn't the first time we've met, but I appreciate the welcome.

He nods to the younger guy trailing him. "This is Jarred Kane. This is his third year on the AHL team. Jarred, this is our new coach, Adeline Langfield."

Jarred is shorter than Sidney yet still a little taller than I am. He gives me a crooked smile, showing off a chipped front tooth, and instantly, I find myself at ease. I typically have no trouble sensing a person's aura through their eyes, and Jarred's brown irises are calm.

As I shake his hand, it feels as though I'm being watched, so I covertly scan the guys around us. Over Jarred's shoulder, I find the blue eyes that seem to haunt me everywhere I go lately, and they're focused intently on me.

Just as I could sense Jarred's calm aura through his eyes, I can see the war in JJ's. And I have no idea what's caused it.

He stomps over to me, bypassing Cade and Brooks, who both try to say hello. "Can we talk?"

"Excuse me? *No.*" I brush him off.

Huffing, he clutches my arm. His hands are so big that his fingers touch, and I don't have twigs for forearms. I'm strong. I have muscles. Though they have nothing on his.

"JJ," I grit out in warning.

I can feel the scrutiny of every person in the arena. I don't know what the hell has gotten into him, but this is not how I want to start my tenure here. It's day one, and he's already making me look weak. From the outside, it might even look like we're having a lovers' quarrel. Women in sports have always gotten a bad rap. So many people believe that we're only here to bag ourselves a player. It's a stereotype I've worked hard to avoid my whole career, and within minutes of meeting my subordinates, this asshole is peeing all over me.

"We need to talk," he says, voice low. Deadly serious.

His tone and the way his jaw is clenched, all angles, hard and angry, put me on alert, and my annoyance drains away.

"Did something happen to Avery?"

He jolts back, horrified. "What? No. This isn't about me."

That's all it takes for the aggravation to rush back in. "Stop talking in riddles and let go of me."

A dark laugh floats around us. "Looks like some things never change."

I suck in a breath at the familiar and completely unwelcome voice. Meeting JJ's eyes, I finally understand the problem.

His blues are burning with rage. While a small part of me, buried deep, deep down, is desperate to soften, to give in and be thankful for the anger he feels on my behalf, I can't do that. I'm his coach. This is *my* problem.

So I force myself to steel my spine and look over his shoulder, where I meet the cocky smirk of a man I never wanted to see again. The man responsible for my current predicament. He's the sole reason I'm coaching rather than playing in the NHL.

Dirk Orr.

CHAPTER 4

JJ

I WILL KILL THIS MOTHERFUCKER.

While I hate Hopie's husband because he's an absolute douche, I despise this asshole because he's a predator.

Unfortunately, that trait isn't uncommon in hockey. I do my best to avoid dickheads like Dirk and put them in their place when I can. But if I went around beating every man who takes advantage of a woman, I wouldn't have time to play the game.

But Dirk? I would fucking love to put him in the ground.

"Derek, right?" Adeline says, her voice deceptively light, her expression completely neutral.

If not for the rage simmering in my blood right now, I'd laugh at the way the asshole scowls in response.

"Dirk," he grits out. He has the audacity to glance at Sidney with a sneer that says *Can you believe this chick?* My teammate ignores him completely, and the disgust on Jarred's face makes me hopeful that he's not going to offer him any camaraderie.

He doesn't bother looking at me. He knows better than to expect me to join in.

"Oh really? That's different." Adeline tilts her head. "Do you go by a nickname? One that might be easier to remember?"

Behind her, Brooks chokes, his face turning red. I'm pretty sure he's holding back a laugh.

Nicknames are a thing in hockey. We all have them. My whole life, the fans have called Brooks Saint. And he is a damn saint, both on and off the ice. The guy had more shutouts than any other goalie during his career.

Aiden was the Leprechaun. The nickname goes back to his high school days and stuck when he brought luck to the Bolts, scoring during his first pro game and later helping the team win those three Stanley Cups.

Personally, I always called the kid hovering beside us now Limp Dick, but the name that stuck in high school is so much worse. "He's the Muffin Man. Remember him now, Coach?"

Adeline Langfield hasn't aimed a real smile in my direction in nearly half a decade, but the one that splits her face wide open now is fucking spectacular.

"Oh, right," she says with a laugh. "Couldn't stop even the slowest of pucks back then if I'm remembering correctly. Hope you're better in my net this time around."

Cade is choking now too, he and Brooks turning away. Sidney has a gloved hand over his mouth, trying to stifle his own laugh.

"That's—I—" Dirk stutters.

He shouldn't even bother. He dug his grave a long time ago. No apology could ever make me like the man. And I'm positive he won't rise to a level that would incentivize the Bolts to keep him here for long. Still, his presence makes me itch.

"Time to get started," our coach calls from the ice.

The players all head for center ice and circle around Gavin. Addie doesn't give Dirk another second of her time. She lines up along with the other coaches, her head held high, though she garners more than a few stares. The guys aren't used to having a woman out here, and if I had to guess, more than a few of them are skeptical of her right to stand in that lineup. She's twenty-six, which is young for a coach. And she's a woman. Can't sugarcoat that. Then there's the family name.

But what most don't understand is how incredible she is. Sidney, thankfully, knows what she brings to the game like I do, and she'll spend most of her time with the two of us. Which means if anyone has a problem, they can deal with us.

"Hope you all had a nice, relaxing break," Gavin starts. He's been the Bolts' head coach for twenty years, and while there have been rumblings of a retirement after this season, I don't think he'll do it unless we make it to the finals.

It's possible. Last season was a good one, and if we can make the right tweaks and the young blood can keep up, we really have a shot.

With Addie's help, there's no way Sidney and I won't be ready.

I chew on my mouthguard, a bad habit, and stare daggers at Dirk. He can't possibly think he's going to impress anyone after he spent years torturing Adeline.

In any other position? Maybe. But as a goalie, the likelihood is diminished even further. The Bolts already have two goalies on the roster. We don't need another, and management sure as shit won't replace Sidney or me with the likes of the Muffin Man.

I chuckle to myself over the damn nickname. I had the honor of coming up with it. I whispered it to one of the kids at camp after Dirk had been a complete dickhead to Adeline, and the rest is history.

A slow puck is called a muffin shot, and after Dirk's slow as hell reaction when I punched him, the nickname came easy.

And damn if it hasn't stuck with him all these years. Fucker deserves nothing but misery.

Sidney and I both have a good rapport with management and the coaching staff and have remained in good physical health since I was drafted, mostly because Gavin and Cade are strategic about how they play us, allowing us to rest during long hauls because it doesn't really matter which of us is in the net. With either, the crease is protected.

Though that changed last year when Cade pushed for me to take on more of a front-line position. Sidney made it clear that he agreed with the tactic, and I expect it'll be more of the same this year.

I love the camaraderie here. And it feels incredible to be needed by the team like this. Yet I'm needed just as much, if not more, at home. I'm all Avery has. Even when Tabitha was still in the picture, she was barely involved.

Last season I was constantly scrambling to find someone to take care of Avery because Tabitha would just disappear on a whim.

Honestly, her absence is better in the long term. Having her pop in and out of Avery's life whenever she chose was brutal. Knowing that it's just the two of us now allows me to give Avery the structure she so needs at this age. Even if it's the chaotic structure of the brownstone.

Thank fuck Beckett offered this living situation as a solution. If not, I would have retired this year. I don't need this job or the money. I may love it, but no job is worth Avery's happiness and well-being. But once I found out my cousin Hope was moving into the brownstone as well, the decision was easy. Because starting now, when I travel, Avery will be surrounded by her cousins and a houseful of people who love her almost as much as I do. People I trust to have her best interests in mind.

"Aiden will be handling special teams," Gavin says as I force myself to focus on his instructions.

As Aiden steps forward, I expect him to break out in song like he does in almost any situation, but instead, he just gives a little wave.

"And I'd like to introduce Adeline Langfield, our new goaltender coach," Gavin continues. "We are incredibly lucky that Coach Langfield has joined us. Adeline is a two-time Olympic gold medalist and the former leading goaltender of the PWHL. And as most of you know, she's my niece." He smiles at her warmly.

In response, she offers him a simple nod, maintaining a professional air.

A rookie raises a hand, and with a sigh, Gavin nods at him.

"Permission to use nicknames, Coach? There are too many Langfields on staff to keep up with."

Several guys laugh, but Gavin, who is normally pretty laid-back, doesn't smile. "I'll let Coach Langfield inform you of what she prefers to be called, but if she's given a nickname, then I suggest you give Aiden and Brooks and me similar monikers too."

The warning is clear. Adeline should be treated with the same respect as any male coach in this room.

"I'm happy to go by Lep," Aiden says with an easy smile, breaking the tension.

The group breaks into quiet chatter, the guys discussing their own nicknames. Some are plays on last names, some are related to their positions, and some are throwbacks to stupid things the guys did when they were kids, like Dirk.

Adeline is the one who gave me my nickname.

Hansy is a play on Hanson, but it also refers to the way I used to stop so many goals with my hands. A terrible habit that resulted in me overstretching my back and did a number on my knees.

Addie Angles saved me, though. The girl could contort her body into angles not one of us could ever hope to mimic.

But fuck did we try.

The girl would do anything to stop a puck. That's why I still believe she should be out on that ice rather than standing on the sidelines training me.

Adeline gives the rookie the kind of smile that comes with teeth. She's not showing them, but damn is she about to bite. "You can call me Coach," she tells him over the loud chatter of the rest of the guys.

The noise dies at the sound of her voice, probably because we know that when any coach speaks, we shut the fuck up rather than because of her tone.

"And if that's too confusing for you," she coos with the deadliest of smiles, "I answer to Great One, Madam Hockey, and the devil. Take your pick."

Her uncles all chuckle, as does the majority of the first line. We all know that Adeline is pretty harmless, but we also know that in order to make it in this industry, she has to have one hell of a thick skin.

I gnaw on my mouth guard again, studying the only person in this room who didn't even crack a smile at her joke.

Dirk.

The guy is going to be a problem.

"Now that we've gotten introductions out of the way," Gavin says with a clap that echoes off the high ceiling, "let's have some fun."

As we disperse, I head to the boards, ready for instructions.

Sidney and Cade remain at center ice, talking, and Gavin asks Adeline to stay back for a second, so it's just me along with Jarred and

Dirk. Not wanting to make conversation with Dirk, I turn away from him and focus on retying my skates.

"Can you believe they put her in this position?" he grumbles to Jarred. "We'd probably be better off getting cut. Then maybe we'd get picked up by another team."

I roll my eyes. The kid doesn't have a shot at a spot on our roster regardless, but I doubt any NHL team will be knocking down his door in hopes of signing him.

"Door's right there," Addie says, skating toward the asshole.

She's put up with shit like this from bullies her whole life, and by now, it's clear she knows that she has to get in his face. That she can't cower.

I'm so fucking proud of her for the way she handles herself. She used to let him chirp. Ignore him. And I get the tactic. But now that she's the coach, she can't go on like that. She has to put him in his place. "Or you can get in the net and let me see if your reflexes are as fast as your mouth."

Dirk grumbles an apology, and she shakes her head like it's no big deal. "Go get sneakers on. I'll meet you in the gym," she tells us.

I shift closer to her as the guys skate toward the locker room. "You okay?"

She tenses, but only for only a second. Then she lets out a long sigh. "Yes. Why wouldn't I be?"

"It can't be easy seeing him again." I shouldn't push this, I know that, but I can't help myself. I can't help but remind her that there was a time when I knew just about everything about her. All her deep, dark secrets. Every insecurity. This must be hard, and I'm itching for her to acknowledge our past friendship even if only for a second. Why? I have no fucking clue.

She says nothing.

"You should talk to Gavin. Tell him—"

Her spine snaps straight and her head whips my way. "Are you planning on losing your spot on the team?"

"*No.*" I jolt back with a scowl.

She remains completely calm, her attention back on the net. "Has Sidney mentioned anything to you about retiring?"

A thread of uncertainty weaves its way through me. "No."

"Then I don't have to worry about Dirk. He'll be gone in a week."

I can't stop the irritated rumble deep in my chest. "You know what I mean."

"JJ."

I should feel bad for pushing her. Instead, I'm too caught up on my name coming from her mouth. Because for the last few years, she hasn't said my name. She stopped talking to me period. So for a moment I replay the way the two syllables sounded on her lips. It almost makes me smile, though the urge is extinguished quickly when her expression turns murderous.

"Mind your business."

CHAPTER 5

Addie

Hope: Finn's making dinner. Should be ready
at 6.

Winnie: Doesn't Finn have his own house?

Vivi: If he does, he hasn't gone to it yet...

Winnie: Were the boys okay today?

Vivi: They were fine.

Hope: She's being kind. Declan stuck a marble
up Beck's nose and Finn had to perform quite
a bit of gross work to get it out.

Vivi: Sorry, I should have been watching them
closer.

Winnie: LOL. Trust me, no one can stop them
from acting the way they do. I appreciate
you, Vi.

Hope: You coming home, Addie, or are you too
busy plotting JJ's murder?

I SNORT as I walk up the steps to the brownstone, inhaling deeply
and bracing myself. I'm not ready for the chaos. Fortunately JJ had

plans with the guys after practice, so I didn't have to chauffeur him home.

Damn, do I need a break from him and all his questions. And especially all the staring.

How dare he know that my bad bitch attitude wasn't helping my internal trembling at all?

Very few people have ever had the ability to shake me. Not because I think I'm better than the guys I trained with but because I grew up surrounded by women who constantly told me I could be anything I wanted to be and that I should be loud and proud about it. It was impossible to get a word in edge wise on this block unless it was spoken with my whole chest.

Even now that we're all grown, it's a miracle that I made it from my car to the steps without being stopped by a rogue aunt or uncle.

Aside from Aunt Sienna, they all live on this street. The only female Langfield of that generation was smart and put some distance between herself and the chaos, otherwise known as her brothers.

Chaos or not, I've always been fortunate that no matter what happens on the ice, this army will always have my back.

Early on, I learned to ignore the chirping. Hell, half the time I truly didn't even hear it. My ability to tune people out is beyond impressive.

But Dirk didn't chirp. He terrorized.

My body tenses as memories assault me, as the sound of his cruel laughter that morning plays in my head. I should be over it by now. It's absurd that I remember exactly how the room smelled—like sticky sweat—or the way my stomach rolled when I realized I was alone with him.

Blinking rapidly, I try like hell to focus on the singing of the birds in the tree above. On the smell of burgers on the grill—probably what Finn is making for dinner. On the black door and the yellow wreath in front of me. On the name spelled out above it. *The Langfields*.

Something I can hear, something I can smell, something I can see. Check. Check. Check.

Luckily, my pulse slows without too much work.

Dirk doesn't get to ruin anything else for me.

Inside, I find Hope in the kitchen talking to a raccoon.

We don't normally allow the raccoons in the house, but Junie (short for Junior, Jr.) gave birth a few months ago, and the twins insist that the babies need to be inside to be safe.

Raccoons may not be a traditional type of pet, but again, my dad is a softy. When Finn caught a raccoon stealing Mom's shoes many, many moons ago, he was horrified by the idea of the animal being removed from the house. And then we discovered that Junior—named, of course, by Finn—was pregnant, and suddenly we ended up with four pet raccoons.

The raccoons are apparently little sluts too, because they keep getting knocked up, despite the fact that we never breed them.

I mean, who the hell would breed a raccoon?

Hope looks like a grown-up Disney princess standing in our kitchen. She's always wearing flouncy dresses, her red hair styled like in those southern magazines, with big waves that only make her face look prettier. She inherited her mother's violet eyes, and she exudes kindness.

Along with her dress, she's wearing a pair of cowboy boots. She's always in boots. It makes me laugh, considering she's from Boston, but the James family has always split their time between Nashville and New England, and as a kid, Hope rode horses.

"You're so cute eating your grapes like that," she says to the raccoon. Again, total Disney princess. "God, I could stare at you all day. Oh wait. Don't jump up there." She twirls around and gently herds the other young raccoon away from the tomatoes she has set out on the cutting board.

Chuckling, I step into the kitchen. "They're experts at stealing food. You can't let them in the house." I open the back door and shoo them out.

On the patio, Finn is manning the grill. Beck is hanging on his leg while Declan chases a balloon on a string that is tied to Finn's wrist.

My brother has more energy than anyone I've ever met. He also has absolutely no reason to be here. He has his own place and his own life.

Hope hums and sways her hips to the melody as she slices the tomato, gentleness and warmth radiating from her.

I'd imagine *that's* the reason he's here.

Maybe if my brother hadn't been a little slut like our raccoons, he would have had a shot with Hope before she moved to Nashville.

Or maybe he became a slut after she left. I can't remember. But for years, my brother has spent his free time entertaining people, and most often they're of the female variety.

"Where are all the girls?" I ask, opening the silverware drawer. I might as well make myself useful. In a house as busy as ours was, we all had chores. We didn't have nannies or a cleaning staff because Mom and Dad wanted to be involved in our everyday lives. But there were a lot of us and our parents had demanding careers, so we all pitched in.

"JJ took the girls over to the park."

The forks I've just scooped out of the drawer clatter back into their spot. "JJ's home?"

Mid-slice, Hope peers at me over her shoulder. "Yeah, he got home around one and took us out for lunch."

"Oh." Swallowing, I go back to collecting utensils.

The rest of the team had plans to go to Ground Zero. When he told me he didn't need a ride, I assumed he was joining them. I should have known better, though. Avery is always JJ's first priority. As she should be.

Hope sets the knife on the white marble counter and turns to face me completely. "How was today?"

"Fine."

"JJ mentioned that a goalie he really hated growing up was there."

Grunting, I head for the cabinet and pull down plates. "I don't know why he won't drop it. Dirk will be gone by next week."

"My cousin doesn't know how to drop things when they involve people he cares about," Hope says evenly.

With my back to her, I roll my eyes. "If you're talking about me, you've got it all wrong. I'm his coach and nothing more."

"Right, but you used to be super close. I remember when—"

The front door slams and a tiny voice screams, "It's *not* a penis!"

Hope and I both startle, then rush into the foyer.

"It is a penis, and I want one." Gracie, who has her mother's red hair and eyes the color of whiskey, like so many other family members, stomps her little cowgirl boot against the hardwoods, face red and hands fisted at her hips like she's ready to throw down.

Avery has appeared too, her arms crossed like she couldn't be bothered by the tantrum her cousin is throwing.

JJ comes barreling through the door with the younger girls, looking all sorts of flustered. Two-year-old Mari is gripping his finger, her expression easy, like she's unaware of the fight that's about to occur, but it's the eight-month-old Emmy Lou who catches my eye. Because the infant is strapped to JJ's damn chest. Like he's a super uncle or something.

God, why is that so hot? I don't think I even want kids. Not after growing up surrounded by so many. But JJ Hanson wearing a baby is doing things to me. Things that he of all people should not have the ability to do.

He's married. He's married. He's married.

With a dip of my chin, I avert my attention from his strong baby-wearing chest and focus on the two angry four-year-olds. "What is happening?"

"*I want a penis,*" Gracie shouts.

"I've got a penis," another high-pitched voice yells from the kitchen. In a flash, Declan has joined the fray, jutting his hips wildly and waggling his pelvis in our direction. "I can even make it rain in here."

Before the words have even registered—and before the little boy has a chance to drop his pants—Finn is there, snatching him by the arms and tossing him over his shoulder.

Avery glares at her father, her blue eyes blazing. "This is really where you want to live?"

I swear that most of the words that come out of her mouth align perfectly with my thoughts. I love that little girl something fierce.

JJ sighs.

"I want a penis that rains," Gracie yells, her little eyes rimming red. "Momma, why can't I have a raining penis?"

"What is she talking about?" Hope growls, her voice low and her glare fixed on JJ.

Ha. Five minutes ago, she was singing his praises.

"Peonies, Gracie. You want a peony." JJ lifts Emmy Lou out of the baby-wearing contraption and sets the little chunk on the floor.

The little girl reaches for her toes and then falls backward with a laugh.

JJ kneels beside Avery, forcing a calm expression. "The only person you can control is yourself, Avey. Remember? Sometimes people get things wrong, and that's okay." His blue eyes flit in my direction, and he totally catches me staring.

My cheeks flame and the urge to disappear into the wall behind me flares to life.

With a deep breath in, JJ looks up at Hope. "She saw peonies on our way home. Pink ones. I told her we couldn't steal them from someone else's yard."

I snort. "Oh, Lennox's peonies. I get it now."

Uncle Aiden put in the most gorgeous flower bushes for my aunt. "How 'bout I take you over after dinner, Gracie? Auntie Lennox would love to cut a few of her pretty peonies for you."

Gracie's eyes go round. "Really?"

"Pretty sure you've just made a friend for life," Hope mutters, hand to her chest. "My god, living here isn't going to be for the faint of heart, is it?"

Finn, who has returned sans little boy terrors, wraps an arm around her, steering her toward the kitchen. "Don't worry, I'll be here every step of the way."

"Even though he doesn't live here," JJ grumbles.

"I wish we didn't live here," Avery mumbles, kicking at the floor.

"Maybe Addie would let you have a pink penis too if you were nicer," Gracie says with a saucy shake of her shoulders.

"It's not a *penis*," Avery yells.

"Okay, I'm getting her out of here." JJ tosses Avery over his shoulders and heads for the stairs. "Let's go wash our hands and change our attitude."

"She doesn't change her attitude," Gracie says to me with a laugh. "She changes her clothes. Uncky JJ is so funny."

I blink down at the three children I've somehow found myself alone with and mutter, "Yeah, Uncle JJ is a hoot."

The front door flies open, and Winnie steps in with a flourish. "Sorry I'm so late. What did I miss?"

CHAPTER 6

JJ

Theo: Any idea why Gracie was asking me to
bring her a penis when I come to visit?

I CHUCKLE as Finn picks up his phone, knowing he's about to read the same text.

Bray: Who is Gracie?

Finn: Hope's daughter. And she wants peonies.
Blame your cousin. He was in charge of her.

Scoffing, I point at the phone. "Dude, what the fuck?"

Finn clasps his phone to his chest, his head whipping from one side to the other, his eyes wide. "Watch your language. In this house, we use duck."

I scowl. "That's absurd."

"You'll see. Give it a couple of months, and you'll be making friendship bracelets and singing 'Duck, Duck, Goose.'"

I shake my head. What the fuck is he talking about? "Anyway," I sigh, "thanks for making dinner. It was a little less awkward with you here."

He roughs both hands through his curly brown hair. He wears it shaggy enough that it bounces as he moves, and the media in Boston goes nuts over it. "Awkward? How so? You mean because you and my sister do everything you can to *not* look at one another even though you can't look away?"

I give him the middle finger salute. "I'm gonna go help with bath time."

Grasping my shoulder, he squeezes. "I'm just kidding. This is going to be good for all of you. And who knows, maybe you'll actually learn to get along with each other again."

I let out a low huff of a breath. "You are really laying it on thick for a guy who refuses to tell the woman he's obsessed with how he feels."

With a step back, he turns and picks up a dish. Then he busies himself wiping down the counter, even though it's spotless. "I'm just being a good friend. She doesn't need anyone sniffing around her like that right now."

"Ah, so you're gonna play the role of her guard dog. Make sure no one else dates her rather than just telling her how you feel. Smart, smart."

My usually jovial friend scowls.

I glare back.

The two of us are hopeless. Neither of us can admit how we feel about the women in our lives.

Though saying Adeline is a woman in my life is a dramatic overstatement. Once upon a time she was my best friend. Maybe more. Now? She's my coach and my roommate. And if she had a choice, she'd be neither.

Our phones both buzz again.

> Theo: Weird. Is there a specific color she
> wanted?
>
> Finn: Pink. And don't worry, I'll get her some.

"Because you *love* her mother," I singsong as I head for the stairs. "See you tomorrow. Lock up when you leave."

Avery went upstairs a while ago with Hope and her girls. Since Hope is sharing a room with her two youngest, she moved into the owner's suite, and the girls begged all the way through dinner to use the jacuzzi tub in the connected bathroom. And because Hope is the sweetest, gentlest soul, who never says no, she took them all up for baths.

Figuring I have a little while before I have to put Avery to bed, I head toward my own room. I showered in the locker room after practice like I always do, but I usually take another at home. Showering with a bunch of grown, sweaty men doesn't leave me feeling clean.

I head into my room, yank a pair of sleep pants out of my dresser, then knock on the bathroom door. When I'm met with silence, I head inside, then turn the shower on. I've just grasped the collar of my shirt, ready to take it off, when Declan runs into the bathroom from my room. "I gotta poop."

"Don't you have a bathroom?" I ask.

The kid pushes down his pants and hops onto the toilet. "Get out, pervy old man. You can't look at my penis."

Eyes squeezed shut, I whip around and search blindly for the doorknob.

"Fuck." I slam the door and drop my head into my hands. "Why the fuck did we move in here again?"

"Why the hell are you in my room?"

I groan. "Shit, I must have gone out the wrong door, sorry." I straighten and drop my hands.

Instead of finding a pissed-off Adeline—*that*, I'm used to; she's always pissed off at me—I discover a sight that shocks the absolute hell out of me. While it's possible that her face is screwed up in its normally irritated way, I wouldn't know because Adeline Langfield is not wearing a lick of clothing. And my mouth has gone dry as I stare at her miles of creamy skin.

She slaps a hand over what I imagine is an absolutely delicious pussy and hisses. "*JJ*."

My focus jumps but still doesn't reach her face. No, there's no fucking way I'll make it there once I catch the swell of her breasts.

And her nipples. They're pink and pointed in my direction.

"Hello! Stop staring at me."

Finally I force myself to look at her face. Just as my attention lands on her lips, a pillow comes hurtling at my head.

"Get out," she shrieks.

Maybe the pillow knocked some sense into me because I finally stumble toward her door.

"Don't use that door," she hisses. "I'm naked."

Shaking my head, I point to the bathroom. "I'm not going back in there." A pissed off Adeline is scary, but I'm used to her. The angry four-year-old accusing me of staring at his private parts? Abso-fuck-ing-lutely not.

With a huffed *fine,* she stomps across the room to her closet. The entire time, I'm mesmerized by the way her ass sways. It doesn't jiggle because the woman is all fucking muscle. She has a six pack, toned thighs, and calves that could put any hockey player, regardless of sex, to shame. But it's the fucking curve of her hips when they meet her ass and the dimples at the small of her back that make my mouth water.

I want to bend her over and eat her from behind. I want to taste every inch of her until the fight has left her and she's a boneless mess. I want to kiss her lips and pull her into my arms and bury my head in the crook of her neck because for years that was my safe space.

Fuck.

Finally, I spin around and face the door, letting the shame and sadness wash over me.

"I'm dressed," she grouses. "You can go now."

Eyes closed, I drop my head to the door with a thud. "Adeline, I—"

"Daddy, can you come tuck me in?" Avery yells from down the hall.

As my shoulders fall, I shake my head. Now's not the time, apparently.

That seems to be the theme with Adeline Langfield and me.

It's never the time.

"I'm sorry." I ease the door open and disappear down the hall without waiting to see if she accepts my apology. I know better than to believe she ever will.

Before entering the room Avery is sharing with her cousin and the twins, I take a deep breath and force a smile onto my face. My little girl is far too perceptive, and the last thing I want is for her to worry.

"No, he walked in on me," Declan tells Winnie who is trying to get him to lie down on the bottom bunk. Beck is already resting on the top bunk, eyes closed and headphones on.

Pretty genius, actually. I might try it when I go to bed.

"Well, you were in his bathroom," Winnie says, patting the bed again. "Now go to sleep."

I turn away, not wanting to argue with a four-year-old, and head toward the girls' bunk. "Did you have a good tubby?" I ask them.

Avery is sitting on the mattress of the bottom bunk, setting up her row of Squishmallows. She's got an absurd number of them because my mother brings her a new one every time she sees her. Catherine Bouvier's philosophy on life is "What's money good for if I can't use it to spoil my grandbabies?" I suppose she's right. Still, Avery can barely fit on the twin mattress without being on top of one.

"Hey, short stuff," I say to Gracie, who's in the top bunk doodling in a notebook. "You almost ready for bed?"

The little girl giggles. "That's not my name, Uncky JJ."

Technically we're first cousins once removed or something like that, but she's always called me *Uncky* and I kind of love it.

"Can we call Mom?" Avery asks, voice soft but demanding.

Sighing, I pull out my phone. She asks every night, but Tabitha hasn't answered at all over the last two weeks. This is where the comment about harassing her comes in. Since she wouldn't answer calls or texts from my phone, my attorney stepped in, hoping to talk some sense into her and explain that her four-year-old misses her, but I'm not hopeful that she'll pick up. And when she doesn't, it'll crush Avery.

Still, I settle beside my little girl and hit Tab's number.

Avery stares at the screen as it rings five times. When it finally goes to voicemail, she hits the End button rather than leave a message. "Mimi next."

This is a nightly thing. Avery insists on saying good night to all the people she loves. It's sweet, of course, but I worry that it's because I travel so much and because Tabitha has never been a present parent.

My mother answers on the first ring. "Hi, my little angel. How was your day?"

Avery settles against my chest, smiling up at me. "It was good. Daddy took me to the park, and then Finn made burgers and we played with the raccoons."

"Sounds like a great day," Mom says.

"Is that Avey?" Dad asks, his voice muffled. There's a little rustling, and when he speaks again, he's louder and more clear. "Hey, blondie, when are we going for ice cream?"

Avery giggles. "My schedule's open. How 'bout yours?"

Dad hums, affection dripping from the simple sound. "For you? I've got all the time in the world. How about I pick you up tomorrow afternoon? We can drive around and sing and get ice cream."

"Okay, Pops," Avery says, yawning.

"All right, say good night to Pops and Mimi."

"Night, Pops. Night, Mimi. I love you." The second the call ends, she asks, "What about Uncle James?" Her eyes are getting heavy and she's burrowed deeper into me, minutes from drifting off.

"We'll call him and Aunt Chloe tomorrow night. We'll do it a little earlier so you aren't so tired."

She snuggles one of her many stuffed animals, burying her face in its plushness. "Okay, Daddy."

With gentle movements, I help her climb under the covers. Then I lean down and kiss her forehead. "I love you."

"Wait." Her eyes fly open. "What about Addie?"

I frown. "What about Addie?"

She nods toward the door. I follow her line of sight, and sure enough, Adeline's walking past.

My little girl sits up. "Can I say good night to Addie?"

"Why don't we just go to bed?"

Adeline is probably still pissed at me, and I don't want her to inadvertently take her anger out on my little girl.

"Addie," Avery yells. "Can you come say good night to me?"

We're met with silence, but a heartbeat later, Adeline shuffles back toward the door. She's in a pair of white shorts with light blue lines and a loose light blue T-shirt that matches. "Me?"

Avery nods.

My new boss pads into the room, pausing when she reaches the edge of the bed. I press another kiss to Avery's head and then shift out of the way so she can say good night.

"Good night, Avey girl," she says softly, her eyes full of affection as she looks at my daughter.

"Good night. I love you." With a smile on her face, Avery closes her eyes.

Sighing, Adeline brushes her fingers through Avery's silky blond hair. "Love you too, Avey girl."

My chest squeezes tight, and as I turn away, my eyes heat.

"Make sure you kick some hockey boy butt tomorrow," Avery mumbles.

Adeline's responding laugh is light. "I'll try."

"But go easy on my dad." Another yawn. "He's not as tough as he looks."

That comment has me turning back, my lips turned down.

Adeline peers at me, her big brown eyes seeing far more than they should.

Avery's right. When it comes to Adeline, I'm not nearly as strong as I should be.

CHAPTER 7

JJ

Fifteen Years Old

"I DON'T WANT to go to boarding school."

As my father weaves the car through the Back Bay of Boston, I glare at the dashboard. Why the hell is he so determined to make this my new home? I know nothing about this area.

"That's why this is the perfect solution. You can come home whenever you want, but this gives you the freedom to focus on school and hockey while your mother and I focus on her illness. You know her; if it weren't absolutely necessary, she wouldn't have agreed, but you can't miss this chance, and I—" His voice cracks.

I squeeze my eyes shut. I've looked up to my dad my entire life. He's a great businessman but an even better dad. And I've seen him break down more times than I can count in the last few weeks. He's always been emotional when it comes to us. He loves hard. Especially Mom. Their love story is an epic one. The kind that makes it impossible to believe it could ever come to an end.

He missed out on the first decade of my older sister's life and it's always killed him, so I understand that he isn't taking any of this lightly. My younger brother James left for boarding school last week.

It's in London, and Dad's brother Garreth will be nearby if James needs him.

And since Chloe is in Paris working for our family's magazine, it's just me they have to worry about.

Me and my hockey schedule.

It'd be impossible to keep up with it while Mom is in treatment.

If I went to boarding school, I would have to skip this season. And after all the work I've done to get here, my mother would be devastated if I gave it up.

This is the right answer. They're doing the best they can. I just wish I could be there for them *and* play hockey.

That I wasn't a chore. That I could help.

"I know. I'm sorry," I say, head hanging.

In my periphery, he swipes a stray tear and nods. "It's going to be okay. Finn is thrilled to have another boy in the house, and Beckett will get you to practice and games. It'll be easy since Addie has to be there too."

I plaster on a smile, not wanting to worry him more. "Yeah, it'll be cool hanging with Finn."

"And Addie?" He side-eyes me, his brows raised.

Frowning, I sit back. Why is he looking at me like that? Adeline is my friend. And a goalie like me. On the ice, she's my competition. And she's damn good. This season, there are three of us on the elite team. She's the only girl. Period. She's got to be used to it by now. All the other girls we played with as kids have either moved into girls' hockey or they've quit. At this level, it's hard for them to keep up. Adeline has never had that problem.

I shrug. "Sure."

Dad's responding chuckle is dry, but it's still good to see him smile. "Right."

Not understanding what he's insinuating, I turn toward the window and focus on the brick buildings we pass.

Soon we're easing down an unfamiliar street, passing brownstone after brownstone. Dad says that Brooks and Aiden Langfield live on the street too, so maybe it won't be so bad. Brooks is one of the best goalies to ever play, and now that he's retired, he's always down to train with Adeline—and me by extension. I guess I'll get even more of that now that I'm living with her. That certainly doesn't suck.

My father pulls into the driveway of a brownstone about five doors from the corner, and Beckett comes into view, with a massive dog at his side.

"If I don't get a chance to say it before leaving, I'm so incredibly proud of you, and I'm only a phone call away. If you need me, I'll be here." My father chokes on his words, his blue eyes glassy with tears. "And I'll come to as many games as I can."

Lips quivering, I suck in hard. I don't want to break down and give him something else to worry about. "I know, Dad."

He leans across the center console and pulls me in for a long hug. "I love you so much, Jonathan. You and your siblings are everything we ever wanted. I hope I'm not fucking you up too much."

I shake my head against my dad's shoulder, a strangled sob breaking free. "Never. Love you too."

As we pull apart, my father laughs. "Fuck, shit, I forgot to tell you —they don't curse here."

Frowning, I survey the large house. "What?"

"Beckett—" Dad shakes his head. "They use duck instead of cuss words. Just—" He rolls his eyes. "It's an expensive lesson, so try hard to use duck."

"I'll fucking watch my language before I use the word duck."

Dad chuckles, his laughter easing some of the tension in my chest. "Good idea."

I give him what I suppose could be considered a smile, then we both stare out at the lawn where Beckett stands, head down like he's talking to his dog, giving us space.

"You ready?"

I take a deep breath and will the tightness in my chest to abate. "Sure."

"Okay, let's do this."

As our doors slam shut, Beckett lifts his head and moves in our direction. "Morning, guys. Let me help you with your luggage."

He pulls my dad into a hug, but before I can get dragged into the greeting, I head to the back to grab a bag. If I'm going to walk into the house and hold it together after my father leaves, I can't take any more emotional moments. For now, I'll focus on getting through the next few months. I'll keep the sadness locked up from here on out. It's what my mother needs from me. My father too.

"All right, son," Beckett says.

He uses that word, son, in a way a lot of adults do when talking to kids and not like I'm his actual son because I'm moving in with him. Still, I bristle at the term.

"We're excited to have you here," he says, not picking up on my reaction. "This is Deogi."

"D-O-G? Did you just spell *dog*?"

I assess the massive dog. He's got shaggy brown fur, and his tail is wagging rapidly. With his mouth open and his tongue hanging out, I swear to god it looks like he's smiling. Then again, if this is the house an animal is lucky enough to be adopted into, of course he'd be smiling. The Langfields own two professional sports teams in Boston, and on top of that, they're generous as shit and fucking fun to be around. The dog is probably spoiled rotten.

I rub his head in greeting, and in response, he pushes his wet snout into my arm and licks me. Laughing, I pull back.

Beckett Langfield is about the same height as my dad, an inch or two over six foot. He's got green eyes, dark brown hair speckled with gray here and there, and laugh lines that crease around his eyes when he smiles.

He does that a lot. Smiles, I mean.

My family isn't unhappy by any sense of the word, but we don't fucking smile like this. It's like the guy is genuinely happy all the time.

Then again, why wouldn't he be? He's wealthy, with a big family and a beautiful wife. And his neighbors are all his brothers.

I guess that's the dream.

Who the fuck knows. My only dream is to make it to the NHL. And for my mother to live long enough to see it.

Shit. Fuck. My stomach rolls, causing me to step back. Why did I have to go and think about that?

"No," Beckett says, pulling me out of my spiraling thoughts. "That's his name. D-O-G."

My father chuckles. "Yeah, you spelled out the word dog."

Sighing, Beckett shakes his head. "You've been spending too much time with Gavin."

Gavin is his brother. And he's the head coach of the Boston Bolts. My dream team.

"Come on." He hefts a bag out of the trunk and heads for the house.

If I were to describe the Langfield home in one word, it would be loud. James and I can get rowdy sometimes, sure, but it's nothing like the level of noise in this place the second I walk in.

Beckett's oldest is already in college. Then there's Finn, he's seventeen and in love with baseball and the drums. That's where the loudness comes from, by the way. Jesus fuck. Pretty sure his drum kit is in the basement, but the sound reverberates through the whole house.

Finn's next sister Adeline is fifteen like me, then there are two more. Twins, Maggie and June, who are twelve.

While Finn is the loudest, Beckett and Deogi make a lot of noise too. And Liv, Beckett's wife. She's been yelling since I walked in. Not at anyone in particular but because she's trying to be heard over the goddamn drums.

By the time bedtime rolls around, I have a headache and want nothing more than to crash.

Beckett had two twin beds moved into the room, which I apologized to Finn for after he mentioned that he used to have a king.

"You kidding? This is awesome," was Finn's response.

Like Beckett, he's always smiling. He's got wild curly hair that is being held back with a pink headband at the moment. He swears the headband brings him good luck, so from what I gather, he wears it often.

He falls asleep quickly, like his battery has finally run out of juice. I, on the other hand, lie on my back and stare at the ceiling, begging sleep to come.

Finn starts humming in his sleep, random words slipping through.

Is he singing a Janet Jackson song in his sleep? Fuck.

When he dives into the chorus, I roll onto my side. "Finn?"

"All for you."

The kid's eyes are closed, yet the lyrics keep coming. Holy fuck. He's dead asleep.

I launch myself out of bed with a grunt. There's no fucking way I can sleep right now. Rather than locking myself in the bathroom we share with Adeline and risking waking her up, I head downstairs.

The light is on in the kitchen. Dammit. I really don't want to talk to anyone right now, but it feels weird to sneak around in order to avoid someone in their own home, so I blow out a breath and head that way.

That's when I see her. Bent over, ass up, searching the refrigerator.

Her shorts barely cover her peach of an ass. The ass she's spent years toning on the ice and through workouts by my side.

They're pink shorts. Hm, I never pictured Adeline wearing pink.

"Hey." I force the word out so that I don't scare her, but she jumps just the same.

"Fuck." Hissing, she straightens and whirls on me. "God dammit, JJ You scared the shit out of me."

I smirk, though the expression is hard to hold when I take in her tiny tank top. Shit. Holding my breath, I zero in on her face rather than the boobs I had no idea existed beneath Adeline's gear or the damn headlights poking against the thin baby pink fabric.

"Thought there was a no-cursing rule in this house," I say. "Aren't you supposed to say Duck. *Duck...*" Ah, shit, I can't say it with a straight face.

She growls. "If you say goose, I will mutilate you."

Coughing out a laugh, I hold up a hand. "I seriously almost did."

Her grumpy expression vanishes and she giggles. Fucking giggles. The light and airy sound makes an unfamiliar warmth inside my chest unfurl. "It's okay. My dad means well, but—" She shakes her head. "Yeah, that's all. He means well."

"Your dad's great."

She nods, and for a moment the two of us stand on opposite sides of the room, staring at one another. I've seen Adeline in workout clothes, but never anything revealing. She's always dressed in an oversized T-shirt and leggings. Never shorts. Probably because guys like me would ogle the shit out of her like I am right now.

I run a hand over my face, my stomach sinking. This is Adeline. *Stop acting fucking weird.*

"Can't sleep?" she asks.

I shake my head. "Did you know your brother sings in his sleep?"

Head tipped back, she groans. "Yeah."

"How do you get any sleep?"

She points at a pair of headphones lying on the counter. "They cancel out noise. You should get some."

Hand in my hair, tugging at the roots, I nod. "I'll order them tomorrow."

She gives me a soft smile. It's strange, really. She's always wearing a game face at practice. "You can bunk in my room for the night."

Scowling, I shake my head wildly. "That—no—your father—no."

"Oh my god, stop being weird. I'm like one of the guys."

The air leaves my lungs in a whoosh. That might have been true twenty minutes ago, but now that I've seen her in this goddamn little outfit? She doesn't even come close to being one of the guys. Fuck, her curves have my mouth watering. This is so fucking bad.

"Still," I say, pulling my shoulders back. "I don't think it's a good idea."

"Fine," she sighs, "be tired tomorrow for our game. I'll happily play goalie for all three periods."

I groan. She's right. We have to be out of the house by five a.m. "Can you set an alarm so I'm up and out of your bed before anyone catches us?"

A sly smirk creeps up her face. "Sounds so scandalous."

"*Adeline,*" I warn.

Smiling, she pads by me and brushes her hip against mine. "Yes, JJ I'll set an alarm. C'mon."

I stay where I am for a few seconds so I don't have to stare at her ass as we walk up the stairs. By the time I step into her room, she's already climbing into bed and pushing a pillow to the other side.

Hovering beside the king-size mattress, I ball my hands into fists. "You sure this is okay?"

"Yeah, just don't try to snuggle me in the middle of the night and make things weird."

"Ha." I cough out a laugh as I settle on the empty side of the bed. "Like I would ever."

With my head on the pillow, I inhale deeply. It smells like vanilla and coconut and a scent that's so very Adeline. It's rare that we spend time together when we're not sweaty messes, but even when she is, she still emits this sweet natural scent. She never smells bad, while the rest of us absolutely reek.

On our sides, we face one another. She's wearing another of those smiles, and with the way her brown hair cascades around her, I can honestly say she's the prettiest thing I've ever seen.

"You okay?" she asks.

I swallow the lump suddenly lodging itself in my throat. She's talking about my mom, about how my life has just been upended. "I guess."

"Two truths and lie," she whispers.

I roll onto my back and stare at the ceiling, heat gathering behind my eyes. "Um, your bed smells good, your brother's singing could use some work, and I'm okay."

The bed shifts, and then there's an arm wrapping around my waist. Closer now, Adeline squeezes me, offering me her warmth and comfort. It's weirdly natural to hug her back. To pull her so close that she's forced to rest her head on my chest.

When she does, she whispers, "My brother's singing could use more than a little work. But you will be okay, JJ, I'll make sure of it."

I'm not sure why, but I believe her.

CHAPTER 8

Addie

WHEN I HIT my second mile, I finally feel like myself again. This is what I needed. Since moving out of my apartment and leaving the team that I spent four years with, everything has felt off.

The consensus is that it will take time to get used to this new life. To not playing hockey professionally. To not living on my own. I'm not so sure. Maybe it's because all these changes occurred at the same time. Maybe it's because my old teammates have been texting constantly, always talking about their training camp, which started this week as well. Either way, it's all hitting me extra hard.

But with the fresh air filling my lungs, the rolling green hills as a backdrop, and a perfectly curated playlist on shuffle in my ears, the world seems a little brighter.

I make it around the park twice more, then head back to the brownstone situated a mere fifty feet from the park entrance. As I hit the front walk, I check my watch. Four miles in thirty-five minutes. Not too shabby.

Not professional hockey level, but I don't need to be in the same kind of shape as the players.

Still, I do ten sets of lunges, jumping jacks, and burpees before I call it a morning and head inside. I'll get an actual workout in after practice today, but I always feel better if I get my heart rate up and my muscles burning just a little first thing in the morning.

I sneak into the house, hoping like hell I don't wake any of the kids. The last thing I need is to be surrounded by chaos at five a.m. AirPods still in, I dance around the kitchen, filling a glass of water and taking my morning vitamins. Then I head upstairs for a shower. We've got to be at the practice rink by eight, but I'd like to relax and drink a cup of coffee after my shower and maybe do a little yoga and journal for a bit before I get dressed.

Honestly, since I have to deal with Dirk again—*and JJ*—I need to do more than journal, but with the time I've got, I'll have to settle for that.

With clothes in hand, I knock on the bathroom door, ensuring that JJ isn't on the other side. It's still so weird that he's sleeping in Finn's room. And it's even weirder that while he moved into that same room for an entire hockey season when we were teenagers, he didn't ever actually sleep there. Instead, he spent every night in my bed. Beside me.

My focus drifts to the king-size bed. The same bed I had back then. I can almost picture the two of us, fifteen and stupid, staying up way too late, talking, sharing secrets, laughing, crying.

That year was hell on his family. Even now, more than a decade later, I often think about how close they came to losing Cat.

But she's still here. Though I rarely see her anymore. Not since Avery was born, anyway.

Eyes falling shut, I shake my head. Why am I thinking about this? I thought I was over all of it. Over him.

I clench my jaw and chide myself. It's ridiculous to believe that I could be. That I ever will be. How could I get over the only man I've ever loved? The one person who knows every spot that elicits pleasure. The person who's caused me far more pain than anyone or anything else ever could.

Groaning, I turn the music up. I need to dance this out.

The bathroom is a few degrees warmer than my bedroom, like maybe JJ was in the shower not long ago. Good. That means we won't be late. I set my bundle of things on the closed toilet lid and strip as I dance, bouncing on my toes Meredith Grey style. My mom and her best friends forced all of us to watch every season of *Grey's Anatomy* in high school. And when I say forced, I mean we were all for it. Growing up the way I did, surrounded by so many honorary aunts and cousins, was incredible.

Shit. I stumble a little, realizing I forgot to turn the water on to heat up. I hate a cold shower, and I swear that's one thing Dad has never been able to fix about this house. It takes a good two minutes to warm up to the nearly scalding temperature I like.

Grasping the curtain, I tug it open. Rather than finding it empty, I discover a naked JJ standing before me, and a blood-curdling scream escapes me as my heart takes off at a gallop.

"Why are you naked?" I shout.

He barely reacts to my anger. Rather than covering up or yelling back, JJ stands under the spray with his cock dangling between his legs and a cool expression on his face.

I'm pretty sure something glistens on his cock. Is…is his penis pierced?

And is that a tattoo on his chest?

His mouth moves, but I don't hear a word.

Scowling, I holler, "I can't hear you!"

He points to his ears, a nonplussed look on his face.

Oh. Right. Lizzo is still singing, drowning out all other sound.

With a huff, I pull out an earbud. "Why are you just standing there? Why didn't you call out when I knocked?"

"I did. I've called your name at least twenty times since you ignored me when I shouted that I was in the shower."

"Well, I couldn't hear you," I say with far too much sass for someone who clearly carries some blame here.

He shrugs, his full body on display, making it hard to keep my thoughts straight. "Okay."

"So why didn't you get out when I came in?" I wave a hand wildly at the door.

"So you could see me naked?"

"I'm already seeing you naked," I shriek.

"I'm aware."

"Why aren't you covering yourself?" My heart is still racing, and by now, my face is on fire.

He shrugs, still wearing a smirk as the water beats down on his muscled body. He's truly a sight to behold. His form should be replicated and put in a museum. It's unfair that the world hasn't been blessed with this view. Because he's beautiful. A beautiful, cocky asshole.

"I've got nothing to hide, Adeline." His eyes dance. "Besides, nothing you haven't seen before."

I snatch a towel from the rod and whip it at him, then storm out. The cocky attitude and the sexy body are tangling up all my thoughts and emotions. "We need a better system!"

"Agreed," he yells. "Next time try listening for a response after you knock."

As I slam the door, he barks out a laugh.

Hands balled into fists, I roar. *Fuck.*

No amount of yoga, journaling, or running could settle my racing heart after the little interaction I had with JJ this morning. But a little time alone wouldn't hurt, so rather than wait for him to head to the rink, I sneak out the front door while the rest of the crew is in the kitchen talking over one another and banging pots and pans. I don't feel even a moment of remorse.

The silence on the way in was necessary, but hours later, I'm still off balance. And since it's a dryland training day, JJ's haughty smirk is on full display rather than covered by a freaking helmet. And my traitorous eyes can't focus on anything but his body. There are over sixty men in this room. I'm sure many women find the majority of them hot. They're all in incredible shape, obviously. I've just never given a hockey player a second glance.

Other than JJ.

Then again, I've never really given men attention period.

Again, other than JJ.

Ugh. I roll my eyes at myself. I hate this little crush I have. It's pathetic.

He's on the treadmill, laughing easily as he runs six fucking miles per hour. Beside him, Brayden Hawke, our team captain and JJ's best friend, grins.

I've known Brayden my whole life. Tyler Warren, former Bolts captain and close friend of my parents, was his guardian in high school and War and his wife Ava adopted my friend Josie and her younger sister during that time. So I know for certain that if there is one thing Brayden is not, it's funny. The man barely has a personality. All he cares about his hockey and his family. Kind of like me, I guess. I'm not funny either.

So why the fuck is JJ laughing so hard?

When his eyes meet mine in the mirror and he winks, my blood boils. The asshole has got to be doing this on purpose.

Patience snapping, I stalk over to the machine, pull the red cord to stop it, and glare at my roommate. "Since you seem more interested in talking than working when your friends are around, why don't you go run around the building five times?"

He coughs out a laugh, but he hops off the machine without challenging me. "Okay, Coach. Whatever you want." Winking *again,* he snags his towel and stalks toward the door.

Asshole.

Teeth gritted, I dig my phone out of my pocket. I need a girls' night and I need one pronto, so I type out a message to my best friends. Then I text the brownstone family chat.

> Me: I'm staying at Savannah's for the night. No need to save me a plate for dinner.

> Winnie: Okay, have fun!

> Hope: Ah, girls' night. I'm so jealous. We should do one of those soon!

I feel a twinge of guilt for ditching them, but it's not my fault they all have kids.

Before I can stash my phone, another text pops up, but this one is in a separate thread.

> Vivi: Oh my god, can I come for a few hours? I need a break.

> Me: Haha, it's been one day.

> Vivi: Two. Please, Addie. I've got no one.

My heart clenches a little at the desperation bleeding from her message.

> Me: What time are you off 'shift'?

> Vivi: Hope and Finn can watch the kids, so I'll be ready. Just let me know what time.

> Me: My brother is STILL there?

> Vivi: Yeah, he swung by after practice. He's got a few away games coming up, though, so he said he'll be gone for the next week or so.

> Me: Oh, whatever will he do without Hope?

> Vivi: LOL. So can I come?

> Me: Pack a bag. I can drop you off at home early tomorrow morning.

> Vivi: Thank you, Addie. You were always my favorite cousin.

I roll my eyes. She'd say that to any one of our cousins if they were the one springing her from her brownstone prison.

Once I've texted my girls to let them know I'm bringing Vivi, I take a deep breath and stuff my phone back into my pocket, then turn around. No JJ in sight. And no chance of running into him tonight.

Much better.

CHAPTER 9
Addie

SUTTON JONES HAS BEEN my best friend since we were eight. Only JJ has ever known more of my secrets than her, but that changed a long time ago. Sutton is in the middle of a Broadway run, so she's not around, but Josie and Savannah both answered my S.O.S. text with promises to take my mind off my problems.

Both women work for *Jolie* magazine, and JJ's mother is the editor in chief. I swear the connections between the people in my circle make my head spin sometimes.

Savannah is recently engaged. Her fiancé, Camden Snow—a former notorious bachelor who played hockey with my uncles—is old enough to be her father, but I've never seen a man so in love with a woman.

The two of them are so damn happy. As much as I can appreciate that, what I love even more is the beautiful house they recently purchased and the guest bedroom set up exclusively for me. Josie has one too, even though her parents' house on the opposite side of the pond is visible from the floor-to-ceiling windows in the living room.

I show Vivi the third guest room, and when she's dropped her bag on the bed, we head downstairs.

Savannah has the doors to the back deck open, letting the mild warmth of the September night in.

Damn, I wish I'd remembered to bring a swimsuit so I could do laps in the pool tomorrow morning.

"What smells so good?" I ask as I step onto the deck.

Smiling, Savannah motions to the dish on the table. "Whipped eggplant with focaccia for dipping. I've got garlic and oil as well if you'd prefer that."

Not only is my friend one hell of a writer, single-handedly increasing *Jolie*'s readership recently, but she's a fabulous cook.

She's also a knockout, with pinup-girl type curves, long red hair, green eyes, and a beauty mark above her lip. One I swear God placed himself before saying "There, now you're perfect."

Her life hasn't always been so luxurious. In fact, it's been pretty tough for the most part. Until she met Camden, I don't think she ever truly opened up to anyone, not even our close-knit group. Now that she's confided in us about her childhood and her family, the four of us are even closer.

"Looks amazing," Vivi says. "Thanks again for letting me tag along."

I drape an arm over my cousin's shoulders. It's an odd sensation, since I tower over her. She's tiny, with dark curly hair, big brown doe eyes, and the kind of energy that makes me think she's constantly ready to burst.

She's always been this way. While we're only four years apart, she seems so damn young.

"Of course. We're always excited to welcome new guests to girls' night," Savannah says.

Josie sashays through the open doorway carrying a bottle of red wine in one hand and white in the other. "Hell yeah, we are."

She has strawberry blond hair and freckles, and she's always wearing outfits that the rest of us could not pull off. Yet they look incredible on her. Not because of her figure but because of her style and confidence. Tonight's ensemble includes a floral boho-style top with a pair of blue chinos and strappy sandals.

She sets the bottles on the table, then pushes her sunglasses into her hair. "I'm just happy this week's get together doesn't involve a pole or ice skates or improv."

Vivi frowns. "Are those the things you normally do?"

"Oh yeah." Savannah picks up the bottle of red. "You should join us at pole dancing next time. We're up for another one in a couple of weeks."

I groan. For years, we've taken turns picking an activity for girls' night, and lately Savannah always picks pole dancing. At least we now have more privacy for the activity, since Camden's sister Cora kept his old house, which is outfitted with half a dozen permanent stripper poles in the basement. Cora also teaches classes. She's badass. Not that I'm interested in practicing any of those moves in front of anyone but my closest friends.

"Yup." Josie drops into a chair on the other side of the outdoor table, then scoots to one side, ensuring she's in the shade of the umbrella. "The one after is my choice, though, and I'm picking a rom-com and board game night."

Savannah lets out a throaty laugh. "Of course you are."

"You love it." Leaning back and lacing her fingers over her abdomen, Josie grins.

I nod. I certainly do.

Savannah hasn't even set the wine bottle down after filling our glasses before she eyes me. "You requested this little get-together. Do tell, how are things now that you're the coach instead of the goalie?"

With a sigh, I pick up my wine. "I requested this get-together specifically because I don't want to talk about any of that."

"Ha," Josie coughs out loudly. "As if."

Beside me, Vivi sips her wine, her eyes darting between the three of us. I'm pretty sure she's just happy to be here, which means she won't give me shit.

Too bad the two women across from us won't extend me the same courtesy.

"I heard from a little birdie that you walked in on JJ Hanson in the shower this morning," Josie says, wineglass dangling from her fingers.

Asshole.

Why are my friends all assholes?

Savannah sucks in a shocked breath while Vivi giggles beside me.

Eyes narrowed, I turn to her. "Glad you find my embarrassment amusing. Maybe we could trade rooms so you have to share a bathroom with JJ."

Her eyes light up. "Have you seen how hot JJ is?"

"He's also married," I remind them all.

It's annoying as hell how everyone forgets that crucial fact.

"To a woman who has disappeared," Josie snaps.

"So? She's Avery's mom and still his wife," I mutter into my drink. I hate both of those facts equally. More than four years later, my cheeks still heat in embarrassment when I think about it. It shouldn't bother me this much. I should be over the way it felt that day, all those years ago, when I found out about Tabitha. Back when I thought we were it. When I thought he was my forever.

Heat pricks the backs of my eyes, so I blink and straighten, keeping my emotions in check.

"So you saw him naked? How'd he look?" Savannah asks.

Irritation stirs to life inside me. "How do you know this?" I ask Josie, avoiding Savannah's ridiculous question.

He looked fantastic. Obviously.

My friend breaks into a wicked smirk. "He told Bray and Bray told me."

Assholes. Even Brayden. While I knew he had zero personality, I didn't realize he was *also* an asshole.

"He looked good, didn't he?" Savannah coos. "I could see JJ being a secret freak. God, I love my freak."

Josie groans. "We're so happy you're getting boned by Daddy Camden. Promise. But for those of us who call him Uncle Cam, could you keep the details to yourself?"

Cackling, Savannah leans back in her chair and kicks her feet up on the empty one next to her, wiggling her pretty pink toes. "Sorry. I think I'll keep it up until she tells us what JJ looks like naked. And I can go *all night long*. As can your Uncle Cam."

"Oh my god," I blurt out, slamming my eyes shut. "It was sparkly and there was ink and—"

Gasping, Josie lunges forward and smacks the table. "Are you telling me JJ Hanson has a pierced dick?"

Beside me, Vivi chokes on her wine.

"Little ears," I warn my friend as I smack my cousin's back. "You okay?"

She plucks a napkin from the small pile next to the food tray and wipes her mouth. "Yeah, I just didn't see the night going this way."

"Of course he does," Savannah says. "All the Bolts have glitter dicks."

"Please tell me my brother doesn't have a pierced penis," Josie whines, covering her face.

Savannah rubs her back. "It's okay, baby. It's tradition."

Vivi lurches upright, her chair scraping on the deck. "Are you for real?"

"Not your dad." Savannah shakes her head. "But Aiden, Brooks, Camden, Daniel, and War do. Well, and apparently, JJ," she adds with a grin.

Josie's head hits the table. "I hate my life." Poor girl has heard far more about her dad's sex life than any adult child ever should.

"Maybe Addie should survey the team. I bet eight out of ten of them are pierced," Savannah continues, unfazed by Josie's misery.

It's a common occurrence, really, so it's unsurprising. Savannah kind of bridges the gap between our friend group and the group of women married to the Bolts' last solid generation of players, since their husbands are Camden's close friends. And that group has told her many, many things about my uncles. Things I wish I didn't know. Like how they apparently like to pierce their appendages.

"I won't be taking any surveys," I promise. "Honestly, I'm considering just staying here for the rest of the season. That way I won't run into JJ or his possibly pierced dick or his cocky smirk or his annoyingly loud laugh."

There's no need to mention that JJ saw me naked less than twelve hours before I walked in on him in the shower. Or how his eyes heated as he perused every inch of me, just like they did once upon a time.

I don't like the games he's playing. Don't like them at all.

Savannah giggles, holding up her mostly empty glass. "You can stay here whenever you need to, shnookums."

Eyes closed, I take another swig of wine and do my best to forget what JJ looked like wet.

"Ah." Savannah gasps, perking up. "You know what you should do?"

My spine tingles in response to the look on her face. Dammit. I can tell already that I'm not going to like this. *"What?"* I whine.

"You should be our next New Romantics girl."

"What's a New Romantics girl?" Vivi asks before I can turn down the suggestion.

Dropping her feet to the deck, Savannah leans forward and clears her throat.

I can't help but smile. While I don't love where this is going, I do love that she's found such an intense passion.

"For my new column, I follow the dating life of one person at a time and document it. I write about all the fun parts and not so fun parts so the readers feel like they're on the journey with the subject as she lives out her love story—should she find one." Eyes glimmering, she looks at me.

Shoulders slumping, I let out an unintelligible noise. "I'm not looking for love."

"Because you have feelings for JJ?" Josie doesn't sound the least big sarcastic or judgmental this time.

Even so, I whip my head from side to side dramatically. *"No."*

When they all look at me like I'm full of shit, I expound, my chest instantly tight. "I mean I have feelings for him, sure. They range from annoyance to irritation. Even embarrassment after he saw me naked and then I saw him naked—"

"Wait," Josie screams. "He saw you naked too? Were the two of you naked at the same time?"

I blow out a breath. Dammit. I didn't mean to tell them that. "No. He walked in on me while I was changing last night."

Savannah cackles and Josie lets out a sound that's half scream, half laugh. Beside me, Vivi's jaw is unhinged. "I'm totally switching rooms with you."

"No you're not," Josie says with a finger in the air. "Because by the blush she's sporting, she didn't hate either of those situations the way she thinks she should have."

Huffing, I will the heat in my cheeks to subside. "Not true. The last thing I wanted was to see JJ naked. Swear."

That's the truth. Because it reminded me of all I once had. Before he was off limits. Completely forbidden.

"And need I remind you *again* that he's married?" I hold up a hand when each one of them leans forward, ready to interject. "And before you say he's not really married, that's not a thing. But even if it were a thing, or even if he were to get divorced, it wouldn't matter. He's a player and I'm his coach."

"Can you imagine how amazing that would be for my readers?" Savannah chirps.

Sighing, I slump back. "Cheating on one's spouse is not romantic."

"First of all it's not cheating!" she huffs. "They're separated. And she left her child! Also, I wasn't talking about JJ." She waves her hand with a *pfft*. "I'm talking about you. You're the prize. The NHL's first female goalie coach. You are a babe, babe. A total catch. A fucking inspiration. You deserve to be happy, and my readers would eat your story up."

"Her dad would kill me," I say, thumbing toward Vivi, going with another tactic. I've given up saying no for myself. They aren't listening. Besides, it's true. Vivi's dad, the Bolts' head coach and my boss, would not be happy to have that kind of attention on me at this time.

"Only because he's an overprotective ass," Vivi grumbles.

Josie frowns and pats her hand. "Your dad loves you."

"Ugh." She pulls away with a roll of her eyes. "Whatever."

"He does," I tell her.

"Can't say he did a very good job of showing it when he kicked me out." She goes for annoyed, but I swear her eyes are glassy before she turns away.

Savannah swigs her wine, then picks up the bottle and refills her glass. "My dad told me repeatedly that I was the worst thing that ever happened to him. Then he left. Believe me, if your dad is actually trying to get rid of you, you'd know it. Yours isn't. He's just scared that you're going to throw away all your opportunities without thinking about it first."

"Just because I don't want to finish college doesn't mean I'm throwing my life away. I just—" Vivi sighs, slumping. "I don't know what I want to do with my life and until I figure it out, school feels like a waste of time and money."

"Have you told *him* that? Or your mom?" I ask.

Vivi's eyes water in earnest this time. "They don't understand."

"Your dad may not get it; he's always known what he wanted. But I think if you sat your mom down and really tried, you'd be surprised by how much she understands."

"Doubt it. She's always known too. She wanted to write music, and she did it."

My Aunt Millie really is a wonderful songwriter and musician, but I'm pretty sure her story isn't as simple as Vivi is making it out to be. And Vivi's parents love her to death. They'd do anything for her. There's no way that Gavin's ultimatum came from anger. I imagine he did it because he's at a loss when it comes to getting through to her.

"Just promise me you'll talk to her," I plead, grasping her hand.

She only shrugs. "Can I have more wine?"

Laughing, Savannah pours her a generous amount.

From there the topic changes, thank god.

Because I have no interest in talking about JJ's possible glitter dick, or becoming the poster girl for Boston's next romantic comedy.

Tonight was good. We talked and laughed and drank and laughed some more. When Camden came home, he joined us for one more drink and Savannah snuggled on his lap. Witnessing the two of them so comfortably in love makes it hard not to wish for the same thing. Not now, of course. Between living with my sister and cousin and flying all over the country with the team, I have enough on my plate.

And honestly, the process is daunting. I'd kill to skip past the awkward get-to-know-you parts of dating and jump straight into feeling comfortable like Savannah does with Camden. Feeling loved.

I'm not sure I've ever had that.

Because that type of love only comes with time. When two people have been together for months or more. After many late nights spent delving into secrets. Sharing a life together.

And I've definitely never had that. I kind of wonder if I ever will.

When my phone lights up on the nightstand, I reach for it quickly, confused about who would text this late. While it's only ten thirty, most of my friends know that since my days start so early, I'm usually asleep by now.

Unknown number: Is it okay if Avery calls you?

I frown. Before I've figured out who's texting, another message comes through.

Unknown number: She can't fall asleep until she says good night to everyone who matters to her.

Oh my god. Is *JJ* texting me?

I navigate to the screen that details the caller information and tap the number. The last thing I want to do is make Avery wait.

"Hey." JJ's voice is quiet but surprised.

My stomach twists. I hate that I know him so well.

"Hi, is she there?"

"Yeah. Here, Avey, it's Adeline."

"Addie?" When her little voice fills the silent bedroom, my heart aches. "Are you coming home tomorrow?"

"Yeah, Avey girl. I'm just visiting some friends."

"Okay. I just wanted to say good night and I love you."

A sob threatens to burst its way out of me, but I bite my lip hard to keep it in. Dammit. Those simple words make me want to cry. *Hard.*

I was about her age when I finally began to understand that my biological father didn't care to make an effort with us. The ache still lives inside me too. While I had a loving dad in Beckett, the rejection still hurt. There's no pain like the kind that comes with realizing your own parent has chosen *not* to choose you. And that's what Avery is going through. Her mother has chosen to walk away. I don't know what's going on between Tabitha and JJ I try like hell to remain uninformed of their personal lives. But there isn't a world in which I would let my relationship with a man disrupt my relationship with my child.

Not that I ever plan on having one.

"I love you too, Avey girl. Why are you still awake?"

"Couldn't sleep," she grumbles, her breath ghosting over the microphone.

"How about you do me a favor? Try closing your eyes and thinking about good things."

"Like what?"

I hum. "What is one thing you really love?"

"My daddy," she says, her voice dripping with affection.

"Yeah, he's a good daddy, isn't he?" The words escape easily. JJ is as incredible with Avery as Beckett always has been with us. Regardless of my other feelings about him, I can acknowledge that.

"The best."

"Okay, anything else you love?" I ask her. "What's something you love to do?"

"I think I'd love skating, but it's hard."

I smile, understanding dawning. Little scam artist. "Would you like me to teach you?"

"You'd do that?" she asks in genuine awe.

A laugh bubbles out of me. "If your dad is okay with it, yeah. There's nothing I'd love more."

She yawns. "I'd like that."

"Okay. Why don't you close your eyes and picture the two of us on the ice, skating in pretty circles?"

"And my daddy?"

I bite down on my lip again. "Yeah, and your daddy." Those words come out a little harder. But I know JJ wouldn't miss Avery out on skates, so he'd be there.

"That sounds really fun. Thanks for talking to me."

"Always, Avey girl. You can call me anytime."

I won't be someone else who lets her down. "Now go to sleep, sweet girl."

"Night, Addie."

"Night, Avey."

I hang up and am still staring at the dark screen when it lights up and another message appears.

> Unknown number: Thanks for calling. It really meant a lot to her.

> Me: No problem. But how'd you get my number?

> Unknown number: I've always had it. Wait, you didn't know this was me?

I stare at the phone and blow out a breath before making the decision to add him as a contact again.

> Me: No, I didn't have your number.

> JJ: It's the same number I've always had.

> Me: Oh. Okay.

> JJ: You deleted my number?

> Me: I guess so.

I don't guess so. I remember the night I did it very distinctly. Knowing if I didn't, I'd be tempted to text him. It was before he got married but after she'd announced the engagement. He was no longer mine to text. He'd never really been mine.

Three dots appear, then disappear again and again. Still, I don't put the phone down. I can't. It's an addiction. To what, I don't know. Whatever it is we're doing is unhealthy. Just as unhealthy as it was before. And yet here we are again.

> JJ: I wish you'd tell me what I did to make you hate me.

I don't delete his number, but I don't respond. It's better this way.

CHAPTER 10

JJ

"HOW ARE things going with your coach?" Bray leans against the wall waiting while I finish dressing for practice.

I eye him, rolling my socks up. Adeline has managed to avoid being alone with me for almost a week. When I do see her, she's closed off. Shut down. Making it no fun to push her buttons.

She deleted my number. Maybe it shouldn't surprise me. She made a choice years ago and it wasn't me. I got angry, hurt, and what started as not speaking to one another for a few weeks morphed into months and then years of silence.

I was so busy with Avery and the NHL that I could almost forget she existed. At least for a few hours every day.

The truth is I thought about picking up that phone and calling her often. Or texting. Or just showing up at a game to support her.

I didn't. She hurt me. And I guess I took it harder than I wanted to admit at the time.

Still, knowing that she basically erased me from her life fucking stings.

And I don't know how to fix it.

But she matters to Avery, so I have to make an effort. Even if it's as nothing more than a casual friend.

"That good, huh?" Bray laughs, snapping me out of my thoughts.

I grunt. "You're the captain. You tell me. Did Coach say something?"

He shifts, standing straighter, then shakes his head. As far as captains go, he's the best. He makes sure he's always available for us. He's quiet and focused, and he'll do whatever is necessary to make sure we're all in the right headspace leading up to the puck drop.

Is that what he's doing now? I almost laugh. Definitely.

"No one's mentioned anything, but I have eyes. And yours never stray from her. Especially when she's talking to Dirk. They used to date or something?"

I grunt again. "No comment."

The decisions Adeline made after the day she stepped off that elevator and out of my life still confuse the hell out of me, but Dirk is the most difficult one to process.

"You're even grumpier than usual." Brayden studies me, seeing far more than I'd like.

The two of us don't spend a ton of time on the ice together. If he's doing his job, he's hanging with the other goalie, taunting our opponents, pissing them off, scoring. He's got his father's attitude. He's cocky as hell when he's in his gear, and he's got the talent to back it up. He's covered in tattoos and he's always trying to get the rest of us to let him ink us up. Because yeah, that's another of his talents. He's an incredible tattoo artist. I'm fortunate to have him in my life. He's an incredible friend, so I try not to be too much of a dick to him. I'd hate for him to trade me in for someone happier like our center, Bobby. He's always smiling and joking around.

"Just stressed. Haven't heard a fucking word from Tabitha, and Avery keeps asking for her. We're gonna be on the road soon, and what if she just fucking shows up? Could Vivi handle that?" I pull on my hair and slam my eyes shut. When I'm not thinking about the woman in the room next to me, these are the thoughts that haunt me at night.

Brayden squeezes my shoulder. "Sorry, man. I didn't realize how much you had on your plate. That fucking sucks. I get the whole parental disappearing act. I relate more to Avery in this situation than you, but you should talk to my dad. He certainly has experience there."

I offer him a tentative smile. "Thanks. Yeah. Maybe I will."

"As far as Vivi—" Brayden pushes a hand through his dark hair. "She's been good with Avery, right? I know Coach was worried about her dropping out of school…"

Strapping on one leg pad, I peer up at him, waiting for him to finish his sentence, but he almost appears lost. "She's a good kid," I assure him as much as myself. "And Finn's at the house more than I am at this point."

He laughs, the tension on his face easing. "Well, wherever Hopie is."

Lips pressed together, I dip my chin. "Exactly. And Hope's great. Winnie too."

"If you're worried about security while you're gone—"

I shake my head and stand. "Knowing Beckett and my father, that house is a fortress."

Bray coughs out a laugh. "So fucking true."

I breathe out, my chest relaxing a little. "Thanks. I needed that."

"Not sure I did anything."

"You checked in. You cared. And talking through it made me realize that Avery will be fine. She's in the best place she can be. The only way it would be better is if I was home with her instead of here."

Bray arches a brow. "That's not practical."

He might think that, but there are times when I lie awake and think that really is the answer. Avery needs me. The Bolts…they may be my team, and they mean a lot to me, but they aren't her. They don't need me in the way my four-year-old does.

"JJ." Brayden studies me, his expression searching, weighted this time.

"I know. She'll be fine." I shake off the thoughts. Now is not the time to ponder my life choices.

When we step out onto the ice, Dirk and Jarred Kane are already running drills. Addie has them coming an hour earlier than us. They need the extra training, and this shows that the Bolts are serious about the rookies and potential players, even if my spot on the team is secure and those guys will not see a day on the ice during regular season. Not this year.

"You're not moving with the puck," Addie yells as she pulls back her hockey stick and aims another shot at Dirk in the goal.

He grabs the puck before it goes into the net. She sent it sailing toward him slowly, giving him a chance to correct his technique, so the catch isn't much of a flex.

"Okay, Coach." His tone is mocking, full of disdain. "Why don't you show me?" Between one breath and another, he lifts the puck with his stick and whips it back at Addie.

In what feels like slow motion, she lifts her hand just like she would if she were geared up.

But she's not.

She's wearing regular gloves. The kind meant to protect her hands from the cold and nothing else.

She should dive out of the way. Or duck. But she does the thing we're all trained to do. It's in our blood. When the puck is coming at us, we block it. So she shifts her body and catches the goddamn biscuit in her hand. The second it makes contact, she lets out an ear-piercing scream that echoes off the walls of the cavernous space.

And in response, I don't see sense. I don't see reason. I just see *red*.

I toss my helmet at Brayden without giving him a heads-up. I'd never treat my gear like that if I wasn't so goddamn fucking angry, but right now, my only goal is to hurt this asshole the way he hurt Addie.

"What in the fuck is wrong with you?" I rush toward Dirk and slam the piece of shit into the net.

He doesn't expect it, so he goes down quickly. But I pull him right back to his feet, throwing my fist at his face. I make contact with his cheek and am rewarded with the satisfying crunch of his bones cracking.

"JJ what the fuck?" Adeline shouts as I'm tugged away from the asshole I'd like to murder with my bare hands.

"He's not worth it." Brayden yanks on my practice jersey, jostling me.

A guy I don't recognize—a rookie, maybe—nearby grabs Dirk before he can fall backward onto the ice.

Fucker would have deserved that too.

Panting and out of breath, I can't control this anger simmering inside me. "Did you see what he fucking did?" I yell.

Brayden's still at my side. Like always. "Yeah, I did. But you gotta calm down."

"Jesus Christ," Adeline mutters.

At the sound of her voice, I whip around and zero in on her.

She's a couple feet away, and one of the team trainers is inspecting her hand. Each time he pokes or prods, she winces and squeezes her eyes shut.

"What were you thinking?" she says in my general direction.

Heart in my throat, I skate over to her. "Is your hand okay?"

"Brayden, get him out of here," she says without even looking at me.

"*Adeline.*" I huff, my blood still boiling. "Look at me."

"If you don't get off my goddamn ice, Hanson," she says, focus fixed on her hand, "you'll be riding the bench for the first two weeks of the season."

Brayden pushes me back and I go without a fight.

With a long breath out, I deflate. "She's out of her mind if she thinks I'm the one in the wrong here."

"Yeah, fighter, you're not the problem at all," my best friend says.

The annoyance in his tone makes my spine snap straight.

"What the fuck?"

"I could say the same to you," he grouses, his face fixed in a glower. "I told you to settle this shit with Addie. Your head has never been on straight when it comes to her."

"He fucking rifled a hockey puck at her."

"And she's a coach. She should have known better than to catch it." He pushes me backward into the bench. "You didn't see anybody else rushing out onto the ice to defend her honor, did you? She's not your girlfriend," he yells, his face close to mine. "She's your goddamn coach."

The arena is deadly silent. I didn't notice that until now. As Brayden's voice reverberates around the facility, a single hiss comes from the ice. It's Adeline. I'd recognize any sound she makes anywhere. And we just made things worse.

When I inhale deeply and force myself to look up, only to find Brooks and Gavin staring at me, their eyes creased in concern, it really hits me.

I fucked up.

After I shower, I find Brooks waiting for me in the locker room. He's his usual soft-spoken self, full of genuine concern when he asks what the hell the incident was all about.

I don't lose my temper. I rarely show emotion. Goalies tend to be good at that. It's our superpower. If we allowed the shit that bothers us to fester, to get into our head during a game, one goal could easily turn into four.

I can't afford to spiral.

"I think I'm having a harder time than I thought I would," I admit as we sit side by side on the bench. "Adeline and I don't...we don't get along like we used to."

He stares at me for several seconds, disappointment radiating from him. Then he rests his forearms on his knees. "It's not your responsibility to protect her."

I nod and open my mouth to respond, but he shakes his head.

"We all appreciated the way you looked out for her when she was younger, and I'm sure you saw far more shit from the little assholes who thought they could pick on a girl, but JJ....she's not a girl anymore. She's your coach. Are you gonna be able to handle that?"

I nod, promising him I can, but long after he's gone, I sit in the locker room, rolling his words over in my head.

Can I handle this? Shit. Not like this. Something needs to change.

And it starts with an apology.

So rather than leaving like Brooks told me to, I bide my time, and when all the guys have left for the day, I make my way to her office. This can't wait until we get home. While we may be housemates, here, she's my coach. I should have respected that from the beginning.

I knock twice and when her "come in" filters through the closed door, I tentatively push it open and peek in, making sure she can see it's me before actually entering.

Adeline is seated at her desk, wearing the outfit from this morning, black leggings and a tight jacket with *Bolts* embroidered on the left breast. Her long brown hair is pulled back into a neat ponytail and her focus is fixed on her computer screen. Those big brown eyes of hers lift, and when she spots me, she sags with exhaustion. "JJ, can we do this later please."

I step inside and close the door behind me. With one hand still on the knob, I lean back against the solid wood. "I wanted to apologize."

With her tongue pressed into her cheek, she shakes her head. "I don't need your apology. What I need is for you to respect the roles here. I'm not one of your puck bunnies."

My jaw clenches as a sick ache pulses in my gut. "I know that."

"Then *act* like it," she grinds out.

Along with discomfort, my irritation flares to life again. Not wanting to escalate the situation, I reach for something we used to do, something that would always make her smile, no matter how pissed off she was. "Why don't we grab a slice of pizza at Antonio's? You can tell me all about how you're now my coach and I have to be better," I say, keeping my tone light. "I promise I won't interrupt or steal your pepperoni."

Her eyes widen for just a second.

Come on, Adeline. Meet me halfway here.

But then she turns back to her computer screen, dismissing both me and my idea. And maybe our shared past. That's what hurts the most.

"Go home, JJ I'll see you later."

So much for starting over.

CHAPTER 11
Addie

Sixteen Years Old

NOTHING but thirty seconds stands between me and this win. Maybe it's cocky to think it all rests on my shoulders, but we've got one goal on the board, and our opponent has none, so it's accurate.

Maine's center glides toward me, determination emanating from him. The kid is incredible on the ice. His movements are so smooth that it looks like he's flying, not skating, as he zig-zags around our defenders like they're merely mirages. If Sonic moved like him, he wouldn't even lose coins from brushing against the other guys. How could he when they can't keep up? Can't stop him?

Fuck.

He plays with the puck, tossing it back and forth with his stick using nothing but a flick of the wrist, taunting me.

I shuffle left to right, following his every move. When I expect him to come barreling into the net, he stops. The puck doesn't leave his stick as he scoops it into the air and slings it toward my left shoulder.

Had I been relying on him to use a snap shot, like most players would have if they were open the way he is, I'd be expecting it to my right. But JJ told me about this play. Warned me he'd probably try it. So as the buzzer sounds, indicating the end of the game, I flip the puck up from my gloved hand and smile.

Take that, motherfucker.

That's what they call a shutout.

My teammates rush me, jumping on top of me and knocking me over. I'm laughing and giddy. Effervescent, really. With that win, our team has earned a better spot in the finals, which means we'll have a bye week and some-much needed rest.

One by one, the guys pull themselves up. Then a set of gloved hands heaves me to my skates.

JJ.

"Fuck yeah! I told you he'd try it," JJ yells, pulling me into his arms and flinging me around like a rag doll.

Even beneath all this gear, I worry that he can feel my racing heart.

"You did," I respond, out of breath. "Though I doubt you coulda stopped that shot like I did."

He throws his head back and laughs. "Always so humble, Addie Angles."

I swallow the smile that tries to take over when he uses the nickname he gave me. They all use it now. This team is different from any I've played for. The guys seem to accept me even though I'm the only girl on the team. JJ and I play almost equal amounts of time, which is practically unheard of at our level. While I'm not the only girl in the league, I get a whole lot more ice time than the rest. And though I try not to pay attention to shit like that, JJ does. He constantly laments how unfair it is. He's sure there are other women who deserve the chance. He's my biggest champion. My biggest supporter.

Well, other than my dad. Right now, he's screaming his head off from the stands, louder than anyone else here. And when I get out of here, I'm guaranteed a giant hug from him. My uncles are with him, all wearing big smiles and letting out raucous cheers. My aunts and my mom sit with them too. Every single one of them is dressed in maroon, the team color, and they all have *Addie* bedazzled on the backs of their shirts. When Aunt Lennox is involved, the Bedazzler always comes out. She's fun like that.

With a wave to them, I head to the locker room. Well, my pseudo locker room. The individual handicapped bathroom is as good as it gets here. Honestly, it could be worse. This one has a shower, which means I don't have to go home sweaty and stinky. I've been to plenty of arenas where that's my only option.

I shower quickly, throwing my hair up in a thick bun on top of my head, and once I'm dressed, I head outside.

My entire family is waiting, but my Uncle Brooks grabs me first. "That was incredible. That center was something else. I honestly would not have stopped that goal."

I roll my eyes. "Of course you would have. You're the best goalie to ever play the game."

He drags me into his chest for a hug. "Proud of you kid. One day the commentators are going to say that about you. Best goalie to ever play the game."

His words send warmth rolling through me. Brooks is the kindest person on the planet. Soft spoken, even tempered, and oversized. He gives the best hugs and the greatest encouragement.

And most valuable of all, he gives me his time. On the ice, with yoga, workouts, watching tape. Uncle Brooks never tires of my questions or my requests to run a play one more time.

After I've hugged the whole crowd, my mom asks, "Are you hungry?"

I spot JJ hanging back, waiting for me, and shake my head. "Nah, I'll be okay. I'm going to catch a ride home with JJ if that's okay."

He's the only teenager I'm allowed to ride with. Naturally, my overprotective father doesn't trust anyone else. Not that it's an issue. He and Sutton are really my only friends.

My dad cranes his neck, and when he spots JJ, he smiles and waves him over. "Great game tonight."

JJ officially towers over my father. He's also bulked up a lot in the last six months—a detail I try not to think about. I also try not to notice how gorgeous his blue eyes are or how every time I see him, I find myself staring at his lips and wondering what they would feel like against my own.

"Can't say I had much to do with the result, but it was a great game, Mr. Langfield."

My dad glares at him. "How many times do I have to tell you to call me Beckett?"

JJ laughs. He's known Dad long enough to understand his bluster. "Maybe a few more."

"All right, take care of our baby girl," my mother says. "Come on, babe. I'm starving."

My father kisses my cheek, then winks. "Proud of you, Little One. Don't be too late."

The whole group disperses, and pretty soon, I'm left standing in the hall with JJ.

"I like what you did with your hair," he says, eyeing it.

I shove a hand against his chest. "Don't make fun of me."

"I'm not." Laughing, he drapes an arm around my shoulder and guides me toward the main hallway.

As we wander closer to the exit and approach a few of the guys, he drops his arm and high fives them.

They joke around, saying stupid shit. But none of it registers. I'm too busy focusing on the girl standing a few feet away, staring at JJ, to make anything out.

Her strawberry blond hair is done in waves, and her tight top exposes a bit too much cleavage considering how fucking cold it is in the arena. Her black leather skirt might be the shortest I've ever seen. She either didn't actually come into the game or she froze.

My guess is she only just got here.

I've seen her after a few of the games. And I've seen JJ talking to her. But I don't know her name.

"Hey, JJ.," she says, sauntering closer.

Grinning, he JJ swivels in her direction. "Hi, Tabitha. You see Addie's amazing save?"

The girl, Tabitha, frowns like she has no idea what that means, but she recovers quickly, smiling. "No, but I did see you do an amazing job. Best goalie ever."

JJ glances my way, covering a laugh with a cough. "Right."

"Any chance you want to grab something to eat to celebrate your big win?" she asks, stepping closer.

I hold my breath, waiting for him to blow me off. When he doesn't immediately, probably struggling after he promised my dad he'd keep me safe, I force a smile and take a step back. "You should go. I can catch a ride with one of the guys."

His spine snaps straight and his brow creases. "What? Who?"

I shrug, hoping the move looks unbothered. "Um, Peters. He offered last time."

"Did he, now?" he mutters, assessing our winger, his jaw flexing.

"Yeah, so you two should go," I chirp with another step back. "Have fun."

"Great," Tabitha says, eyes bright, as she reaches for JJ's hand.

He pulls it back before she can make contact. "Sorry, Tabs. I have plans."

"But she just said she can catch a ride with someone else."

Sweat breaks out on the back of my neck as he glances my way. Then he shakes his head. "Nah, it's not about the ride. We've got a date, right, Addie?"

My heart stutters. "A date?"

"Yeah, you, me, and a pepperoni pie."

In an instant, the anxiety dissipates. Snorting, I say, "Yeah. We do."

"Another time," he says to Tabitha with a lift of his chin.

Her jaw practically falls open, but I don't get to relish her reaction long because JJ immediately wraps an arm around me and guides me past her.

Rather than drop his arm once we're out of sight of her like I expect, he keeps it there. The warmth of it is comforting. He smells so fucking good too. Like soap and cologne and *JJ*. A hint of icy cold mixed with this woodsy whiskey scent I can never quite get enough of. "You could have gone with her. She was pretty," I say cautiously.

He hits the key fob, and his car lights flash. He finally drops his arm and pulls open the passenger door. "Was she?"

Shivering at the loss of his heat, I stand a little straighter. "You could have said yes, you know. I would have been fine."

The intensity in his stare makes me worry he can read my mind. "Right, with Peters."

I let out an awkward pfft. "Or by myself."

With a shake of his head, he steps back, giving me room to get in. "Well, you're stuck with me."

I shrug. "And you're stuck with me."

His lips hook to one side. "Sounds like the perfect night. Come on, I wasn't kidding. We're getting Antonio's."

CHAPTER 12
Addie

I STARE AT THE DOOR, keeping my expression neutral until I can no longer hear JJ's footsteps in the hall. Then I let out the longest breath and grip my hand. It's so fucking sore.

Stupid Addie. So fucking stupid.

I know better. I know not to catch a freaking puck like that. Not one being rifled as hard as that one was and especially not without gear. That's how a person breaks bones. That's how careers end.

I may not have a hockey career anymore, but I still need my hand.

Overwhelming emotions swirl inside me with nowhere to go. I want to tell JJ that yeah, I'd like to be friends. That I'd love that pizza. But too much has happened.

He chose Tabitha.

Or…whatever, it doesn't matter anymore. The point is, he's not my friend. We're…colleagues. I'm his damn coach. He can't go around defending my honor and acting like he's not the reason it needed to be defended in the first place.

If he hadn't…

No, I'm not going there. I refuse to look backward. Maybe Dirk wouldn't have happened if JJ had chosen me, but he didn't and Dirk did happen. And then my world blew up.

I can't let the two of them do that to me again.

I need this job to work out. More than that, I want it to.

When another knock makes the door rattle, I drop my head and groan.

"Go home, JJ."

The door swings open, and Uncle Brooks steps in. "Can we talk?"

I nod. I should have expected he'd be here. He sees too much. This day keeps getting better and better.

Settling in the chair across from me, he folds his arms over his chest. "How's the hand?"

I glance down at it, trying to ignore the way it throbs. "Fine."

His face darkens, his usually even expression slipping. "Have you had it looked at?"

"Yeah, nothing's broken."

"Luckily," he growls in a tone that makes him sound like my dad.

Shit. I've never seen him so upset.

"It's just bruised. And I know it was stupid. I shouldn't have caught the puck."

Head hung, he shakes it. "You know better, Addie. You could have been really hurt."

I suck in a breath to keep my emotions in check. Knowing I've disappointed him makes me want to cry. "I know. I swear, I—" I blow out a breath. "Sometimes I still feel like that fourteen-year-old girl again. Like I have to prove myself to these guys."

"Is it Dirk? Is there something I should know about him?" His voice has softened again, reminding me that he wouldn't judge me if I told him the truth.

But I can't.

I can't go back to that time. Can't go back to that night.

Keeping my focus on my desk, I straighten the small stack of papers to my left. "Just old training stuff. He can be a dick on the ice, but I can handle him."

"Addie, I want to step in but it's not my place. If the guys are going to respect you, then the punishment, the leadership, all of that *has* to come from you."

I angle forward and can't help but let my frustration bleed into my words. *"I know."*

"And JJ…"

"What about him?"

Brooks blows out a breath. "Is something going on between the two of you?"

"What?" I say as a strained laugh escapes me.

"Are you sleeping together, Addie?"

My face heats. Talk about awkward. "Uncle Brooks."

"I can't help you if you aren't honest with me. He's a player, you're his coach."

"He's married." I can't even believe we're having this conversation.

He rolls his eyes like that's irrelevant.

Why does no one get how that part matters? A lot.

"On paper only."

"And that paper is pretty freaking important. I'm sure Aunt Sara would agree."

"Our marriage is nothing like his."

I cross my arms and push back in my chair. "How so?"

"Because we married for love, Addie, and we all know why JJ married Tabitha."

I look away. I can't think about that day. Can't think about any of this. "Nothing is going on."

"*Addie.*"

I snap straight again. "I swear. Blame your brother for inviting him to move in with us. I'm trying to keep the lines professional, but it's hard when he's *everywhere.*"

My uncle tilts his head, those deep green eyes seeing far too much. "Because you have feelings for him."

"*No.*" I reel back. "God, why does everyone keep saying that?"

"Because you aren't rational when it comes to him and you're the most rational goalie I've ever known."

I huff out a breath. "Stop blowing smoke up my a—"

"Duck."

I snort. I can't help it. My uncle knows precisely how to make me smile.

"We're at work. I can surely say a—"

"Duck."

"Oh my god, Uncle Brooks." Falling back against my chair, I laugh. He does too, the tension in the air dissipating.

Then I blow out a breath. "I'm trying. It's just not easy."

He hums thoughtfully. "I know that. I had a major issue with my coach back in the day. I didn't handle it well. It wasn't good for me, and it wasn't good for the team. You need to figure this out, Addie girl. Because this job, it's yours to win, but it's also yours to lose. And if you can't get those guys to respect you—" He motions toward the door. "Then we're going to have a different conversation next time."

Stomach sinking, I nod. "I get it. And I'm coming up with a plan."

He smiles as he stands. "That doesn't surprise me. If anyone can do this, it's you."

When the door shuts behind him, I realize I actually do need to come up with a plan. And soon.

CHAPTER 13

JJ

Bray: How's the fist, tough guy?

Finn: Who's fist? Did someone get in a fight? Dammit, I miss all the fun stuff when I'm traveling.

Theo: Not me. Can't put this pretty face in jeopardy by fighting.

Bray: Lover boy JJ He punched another goalie defending Addie's honor.

Finn: Who are we beating up?

Theo: I suppose I can risk my face for Addie girl.

I GROAN as the texts roll in. Fucking Bray is a bigger gossip than all the girls in this house combined. It's always the quiet ones.

Me: My fist is fine and there's no one to beat up. I took care of it.

Finn: Course you did. Thanks, man.

Me: Always.

Bray: And there won't ever be again because we're not fighting our own teammates to protect our COACH.

Me: Dirk will NEVER be our teammate. I promise you that.

Theo: I feel like drinks are in order when I get to town. I'm definitely missing a story.

Bray: I'm down.

Finn: Always.

Me: Let us know when you're coming, cousin.

"I'm starving." Avery throws her body onto my lap on the couch with a dramatic groan.

"Me too," Declan says, falling to the floor.

Lips turned down, Beck assesses me. "I'm hungry, but I'm not doing that."

"Addie is bringing dinner. She'll be here soon," Winnie calls as she descends the stairs, having swapped her work clothes for sweats and a T-shirt. We tagged Vivi out a few minutes ago, and she beelined for the door immediately. Can't blame her. I can't imagine being stuck with six kids all day long by myself.

Hope is home too. The baby is sleeping, and she and her older girls are out back feeding and playing with the raccoons.

Raccoons. I shake my head. The Langfields have had them for as long as I've known them. Doesn't make it any less weird.

A car door slams out front, and Winnie heads to the foyer. "There's your auntie now."

Nerves swamp me, making my stomach clench. Is she still pissed? It's been a few hours, so if I'm lucky, she's cooled down.

"Oh my god, that smells so good. Also, did you buy out the joint?" Winnie's voice floats down the hallway.

When a wall of pizza boxes with legs marches into the room, I jump up and take them. To my surprise, Adeline lets me without biting my head off.

"Where's Antonio's?" Winnie asks, squinting at the name on top of the boxes.

Adeline's eyes go to mine when she answers. "Off Commonwealth."

My heart is suddenly in my throat again. She went to Antonio's? Why?

"Isn't that across town?" Winnie says with a frown.

Adeline frowns back, the resemblance between the two easy to spot. "Um yeah?"

"Why would you go so far out of the way?" Winnie grumbles.

"They make good pizza," Adeline retorts.

"It's my daddy's favorite," Avery chirps.

I peek over my shoulder, pizza boxes in hand, and smile at my girl, who's still sprawled out on the couch. The way she looks up at me, like she adores everything about me, has my heart swelling.

"See? Told you it's good." Addie sticks out her tongue at her sister.

"I want pizza," Declan shouts.

"Me too," Beck joins in.

The door to the kitchen opens and Hope appears with Gracie and Mari in tow.

"We got pizza," Avery tells her cousin, her voice unnecessarily loud.

"Go sit at the counter and we'll bring your pizza to you," Hope tells them with her sunshiny smile. She guides the girls and the twins into the kitchen while I follow Addie over to the counter to set the pizzas down. "You got a lot of pizza."

She glances at me, practically expressionless. "Hadn't been there in a while. I might have gone a little overboard."

"Ya think?" The ache in my chest eases, allowing me to laugh.

Adeline pushes a box my way. "I got the hero his favorite."

"Hero, huh?" Smirking, I open the pizza box, and at the sight of the extra pepperoni, my mouth waters.

"So the rumor is true?" Hope asks, suddenly standing a couple of feet behind us. "You beat up one of the other goalies for looking at Addie?"

"How do you know that?" Winnie asks, taking the words right out of my mouth.

Hope's lips twitch. "Your brother."

"Traitor," I groan. "And that's not what happened."

Adeline smirks. "Nope, he defended my honor after one of the players was being a di—" She slams her mouth shut, her eyes going wide.

"What a di?" Beck asks.

"A duck is what she meant." Winnie doesn't miss a beat, and she doesn't turn around. She's too busy glaring at her sister.

"Oh, those are no good," Declan tells us. "Grandpa only says that word when he's really mad."

"Well, I was really mad," Adeline explains. "He was being a total duck."

"I really don't love the duck thing," I mutter.

"Just go with it," Winnie prods as she picks up the cheese pie and shuffles over to the kids. "It'll get easier."

Adeline leans in, eyeing my pizza. "You going to share some of that with me?"

Her scent washes over me, making my chest constrict. "Is this like an apology pizza?"

She tilts her head back and forth. "More like an olive branch."

Nodding, I smile at her. "I can work with that."

She dips her chin. "Good."

"Good."

With her lip caught between her teeth, she lifts those big brown eyes to mine. "Any chance we can talk after the kids go to bed?"

"Of course."

"Daddy, where's my pepperoni?" Avery calls. The rest of the kids have slices of cheese on their plates, but she's my girl through and through, so she must have what I have. God, I love her.

"You gotta share with Avery too," I tell Adeline.

She laughs softly. "My kinda girl." She snags the box from in front of me and walks away. "Look what I got, Avey girl. Extra pepperoni just for you and me."

"Hey," I call, feigning annoyance. In reality, I wouldn't care if they ate every freaking slice. Because Adeline isn't ignoring me anymore. And Avery is smiling.

It takes longer than I'd like to get through our bedtime routine. The kids are wired and Avery once again can't get ahold of Tabitha. When we FaceTime my brother, he cheers her up by doing impressions of every animal known to man. I love him and he's a great uncle, but I'm dying to talk to Adeline, and as the time ticks closer to ten, my chances dwindle. The woman's bedtime routine is stricter than the kids'. I don't blame her, since she gets up so early every morning, but I need to hear what she has to say. And maybe say a few things of my own.

Like *I'm sorry. What the hell happened between the two of us? How did we get here and how the hell do we fix it?*

When Avery finally closes her eyes, I quietly tiptoe out of the room.

"Night, JJ," one of the twins calls as I'm pulling the door closed.

I chuckle. Of course they're still awake. "Night, boys."

My pulse thumps as I head to Adeline's bedroom. I pause outside the closed door and take in a couple of deep breaths. Then I knock. When there's no response, my heart free falls. Dammit. She's already asleep.

I rub my face, trying to fight off a wave of aggravation. The time I spend with Avery, giving her what she needs, is never wasted. I was where I needed to be. But it still stings that once again I've missed out on an opportunity with Adeline, small as it could have been, because my daughter needed me.

That will never change, though. I'll never not pick Avery. She'll always be the priority. Not that I think Adeline expects anything different.

It's exactly what she pushed me to realize years ago. What she knew would happen the moment I met my daughter.

I stare at her door for a few more seconds, my shoulders slumping, then give up. There's always tomorrow.

As I reach my bedroom door, a little blue sticky note snags my attention. And when I recognize the writing on it, my mood lifts.

Meet me on the roof—A

It's probably really bad that my heart trips over itself over a little note. I shouldn't feel this way. Shouldn't allow this hope to grow. Shouldn't get so excited about having even a few minutes with the one woman I've never stopped thinking about.

But for years, I lived for our moments. Sometimes I think maybe that's why I loved hockey so much. Because during the season, we saw each other just about every damn day. Summer was brutal. She traveled with her family. I traveled with mine. After we graduated, those moments became even more infrequent. But our talks continued.

I could spend hours on the phone with her, talking about absolutely nothing. Sometimes just listening to her breathe was enough for me.

Hands fisted, I remind myself not to run as I take the steps up to the roof.

The rooftop is just as impressive as the rest of the house, with a canopy of twinkling lights over several outdoor couches. The oversized fireplace is lit, and Adeline sits on the edge of it, eyes on the sky, like she's making a wish. For a moment I just stare at her. At the woman who's owned me for at least half my life.

I wish I hadn't wasted so many years trying to fight my feelings for her. Wish I hadn't been so scared to ruin our friendship. Fucking happened anyway. Dating other women only taught me that she was the only one I wanted. I should have told her that sooner. Should have risked it all before I got drafted and found myself a world away from her while she continued her own life in college.

I'd give anything to change our story. Or at least the ending. Maybe there's still a chance I can. Maybe we're not over.

She's in an oversized Bolts sweatshirt that falls off one shoulder, exposing her smooth skin, her tiny sleep shorts dotted with little stars. Her long hair is down, the soft breeze blowing several strands into her face. She runs her hands through it, pushing it back again. That's when she spots me, a tentative smile hitting her lips as she waves me over.

I consider the setup. A bottle of Hanson whiskey. Nice touch. And two tumblers. "You mean business, huh?" I tease.

She grins. "Well, this is about our careers, right?"

A pit opens up in my gut. Right. This is about work.

I temper my expectations and settle on the hearth beside her.

Adeline reaches for one of the glasses, and when she wraps her hand around it, she winces.

"Still hurt?"

She shakes her head. "I'll be fine. Just need a little medicine." She dangles the whiskey bottle between her fingers.

"Allow me," I say, taking it from her.

Rather than opening it, I reach for her hand. "Can I see?"

She sucks on her bottom lip but nods and sets her hand in mine.

I flip it over and lean in closer. The red mark in the center of her palm sends fury through my veins again. "Fucking Dirk," I mutter.

"I shouldn't have caught it. But it was instinct."

"He shouldn't have flung a puck at you in the first place."

She shrugs. "No, he shouldn't have."

"This needs ice." Very gently, I run a finger over the spot.

"Yeah." The single syllable is a little breathless.

I don't take my eyes off her as I pluck a piece of ice out of the tumbler closest to me.

When I set it to her palm, she hisses.

My gaze roams over her. Over this pretty girl that has me wanting to do anything I can to ease her pain. I can't ease the ache in my own chest that comes from seeing her in pain, but I can do something about her hand. I slip the ice into my mouth and hold it in place with my teeth. Then I bring my mouth to her palm and roll it across the angry red skin for a handful of seconds before pulling it back and brushing my lips against her cool skin.

Eyes meeting hers, I silently ask her if this is okay.

She gives me a quick nod, holding my gaze even as I slip the ice out again, this time just past my lips. I repeat the process, this time stroking her skin with my mouth, the ice a mere excuse.

She hisses a surprised breath. "*JJ.*" It comes out as the most beautiful whine. A whimper. It's a sound I've memorized. A memory that has lulled me to sleep and awoken me more nights than I can count.

I slide the ice to one side of my mouth, but I don't release her. "Is it helping?"

She shakes her head.

She doesn't have to speak to tell me she doesn't mean the pain in her hand. This isn't helping us.

Looking away, I bite into the ice, breaking it up and swallowing it down.

She pulls her hand back, and I pick up the whiskey and pour us each a generous amount. Then I take a quick swig.

"So you wanted to talk?"

Her eyes fly to mine like she's shocked that I've switched topics so easily.

But I can't just sit here and stare at her. If I do, I'll tell her everything in my head—everything in my heart. And that's far too dangerous.

"We need to figure out how to act around one another now that..." She sighs.

Now that Tabitha's gone? Is that what she wants to talk about?

"Now that I'm your coach," she finishes.

Right. Of course. Jesus. What the fuck is wrong with me? Bray is right; I need to stop looking at her this way.

"Okay." I dip my chin. "I'm open to whatever you think will work."

"That's kind of why I wanted to do this," she murmurs, head down. "I have no idea how to even talk to you anymore. It's been so long and there's so much baggage."

A lump forms in my throat, and I have to fight the urge to move closer to her. "Two truths and a lie."

She tilts her head, frowning. "Huh?"

"Covering everything that happened when we weren't speaking would take a long, long time," I explain.

She arches a brow.

"But we could cover some things." I shrug, going for nonchalant. "Keeping it professional, of course."

"Of course," she agrees. "It's just, we haven't done that since..." She looks away, bringing her whiskey glass to her lips.

No. We haven't done it since that night. The night that everything changed. And then it changed again.

"Fine." She interrupts my thoughts, and with a deep breath, she says, "Working and living with you is harder than I thought it would be. I want to be there for Avery, but I don't know how to do that without stepping on toes. I'm a better goalie than you ever were."

I chuckle, a little levity flowing through me. "Well, we know the last one is true."

She shakes her head. "No. That was the lie."

Before I can wrap my head around what she said about Avery, she clears her throat.

"Now you go."

I examine her in the moonlight. She's rushing through this, but fuck do I want to slow us down. I don't want to just get through things with Adeline. I want to know her again. I want her to know me. I want us to be friends. At the very least.

"You're a better goalie than anyone in this league. I'm lucky you're my coach. It's impossible to not tell you my every thought."

She snorts. "All lies, really?"

All truths, actually. But I don't tell her that. "The coach thing was a lie," I fib. "Because right now I'm a shitty goalie and you're a shitty coach."

With a hand to her heart, she says, "Ouch." She takes another healthy sip of her whiskey and looks out over the skyline. "But you're not wrong. I have been a shitty coach. But that changes tonight."

I raise my brows. "Really?"

Tongue in her cheek, she nods. "It's up to me not to blow this for myself. No one else can do that for me. So I need to get over this rivalry I have with you and Dirk." She shakes her head. "You guys won, right?"

Fire flares inside me, and not from the alcohol. "Fuck him. That piece of shit doesn't deserve to be on the same ice as you."

She gives me a wobbly smile. "Thanks."

I shake my head. "I'm serious."

"So, um, truce?" Her brown eyes lock on mine, wary.

"One condition?"

She lets out a sarcastic laugh. "Jeez, you act like I'm the only one responsible for this little rift."

Little rift. Like the jagged canyon that has existed between us for the last four years could ever be categorized as something so minuscule. But she needs us to figure out this working relationship, and I do want to move forward—need it, in fact—so I don't press on that sore point. "We promised Avery that we'd teach her how to skate. Do that with me?"

Her eyes light up. "I will always keep my promises to Avery."

I nod, my heart settling again. "Then I think you and I will be just fine."

CHAPTER 14

Addie

I WAKE up earlier than usual to give myself time to get in the right headspace. While I focused on righting things with JJ last night, I need to deal with Dirk today.

The problem is, my head is still a mess.

I'd like to say that the two truths and a lie exercise helped get JJ and me back on track. But there's no forgetting what he did with that piece of ice.

Is it reasonable to be jealous of a piece of ice? Because the way JJ sucked it into his mouth will probably play on repeat in my mind for the rest of my life.

Then there was the way he held eye contact while he brushed the ice—and by default his lips—against my palm. I shiver now just thinking about it.

Those blue eyes of his were so deep. I wanted to jump in and swim. I wanted to grab him by the neck and pull his lips to mine. I wanted to kiss him and never stop. I wanted his lips everywhere.

If only I didn't know how good they felt pressed against mine. If only I couldn't remember his exact taste—

"You wanted to see me." Dirk's voice pulls me from my thoughts.

Not necessarily a bad thing.

I'm sitting in the stands, right where I told him to meet me, behind the net. I glance toward the man who used to be nothing but a tormentor and a bully to me.

Actually, he was so much worse than that. Even now, being alone with him makes my skin crawl. I should have asked someone I trust to be here with me. Not Uncle Brooks. Then I'd have to explain why I'm uncomfortable being alone with a player. But maybe Sidney.

Definitely not JJ. I doubt he could be alone with Dirk either.

And he doesn't even know the truth. Or at least not all of it.

"Sit down." I nod at the spot beside me.

Unsurprisingly, the asshole chooses to stand, arms crossed, towering over me.

"I'm good right where I am."

I shake my head. God, he's still such a dick. Standing—fuck him and his effort to intimidate me—I lift my chin and zero in on him. "Fine. We need to talk about yesterday."

His brows lift. "What's there to talk about? I didn't expect you to try to catch the puck. Figured you knew better."

I swallow thickly but steel my spine. "Right, well, I was trying to show you how you should block."

He scoffs, his lip curling. "I know how to block."

Dammit. This isn't helping. I summon every ounce of patience I possess and say, "Listen, with Hanson and Howe on the roster, we both know the likelihood of you getting a spot on this team is low."

Jaw flexing, he only glares.

Still, I continue, unwilling to let him rattle me. "But there's still a chance."

Another scoff. "Right, like you'd ever actually go to bat for me with your uncle."

"In this space, he's not my uncle. He's the head coach of this team. A team I love and want to see succeed. So yeah, Dirk, if I thought you were better for this team than either of them, despite how much I despise you, I'd do just that."

He snorts like he doesn't believe me.

"Point is," I grit out, reminding myself that I expected this and that as his coach, I have to be the bigger person, "it's my job to make you the best player you can be."

His lips tip down thoughtfully. Or maybe skeptically. *"Okay…"*

"So if you're game to move on, so am I."

Eyes wide, he jolts back. "You're telling me you'd actually let the past go?"

I ignore the way anxiety crawls through me having him this close and take a deep breath. "Yes."

He stares at me for a few seconds, like he's mulling it all over. Then he must realize that this feud will do him no good, and he nods. "Okay. I'm game. What's your plan?"

"I realize my coaching style may be different from others. Maybe it's because I'm still fresh from the game." I shrug. "Either way, we might as well use that to our advantage."

He kicks at the concrete floor. "Meaning?"

"I'm going to run drills with you today."

Another frown. More skepticism. "What?"

"Yup." I dip my chin. "And tomorrow morning you'll join me for my yoga session at six. We're going to train like I did when I was a player. It's the way I've always done it and I think that's why I was hired."

Dirk's tongue goes to his cheek like he's trying to keep his words in. I imagine he wants to argue, to tell me I was hired because I'm a Langfield. But like Brooks said, that's an issue I'll have to deal with. Probably repeatedly. So I'm leaning in. Playing the cards I've been dealt.

"Got it?" I grind out, my tone letting him know this isn't really up for debate.

"Yes."

"Yes, what?"

His nostrils flare, and for a second he doesn't respond. But finally, he mutters, "Yes, Coach."

I give him my fakest smile. "All right, I'm going to get my gear on. Get dressed and meet me on the ice in twenty."

I forgot how much I loved doing this. Or maybe I just swallowed the longing down, telling myself that coaching NHL goalies was as close as I'd ever come to performing at the highest level in the sport I've dedicated my whole life to.

Playing in the PWHL was incredible, but—and I mean this in the most diplomatic way—it's not the NHL.

The NHL comes with a level of prestige, a level of respect, that isn't given to the women's version of this sport.

Seeking validation from a man goes against every single fiber of my being. I've spent years in therapy dealing with my biological father's choice to walk away. Eventually I came to understand that no matter how successful I am, at the end of the day, it doesn't matter. He didn't abandon me because I wasn't good enough, but because he wasn't.

Logically, I recognize that I don't need a male to validate my existence, and yet, when it comes to this sport, I've done it time and again.

Needless to say, while I love being out on the ice, doing the drills with the rest of the goalies, I love the praise I'm getting almost as much.

I block a low shot on the right, then have to immediately stop a slap shot on my left, holding back a grin the whole time.

"Jesus fuck, Addie, do that again," Sidney says.

One of the hardest skills to master as a goalie is the ability to predict when a player is going to fake a shot one way, only to switch at the last second and aim for a spot out of our reach.

Goaltending is as challenging mentally as it is physically. This is why we study tape. So we can pinpoint the tells of our opponents. I could watch hockey all hours of the day, so reviewing tape, studying every offensive player prior to a game, isn't even close to a hardship.

"No one does it better," JJ mutters to him.

While my cheeks go hot behind my mask, I don't let my reaction show. Instead, I deflect.

"You should do it better."

I straighten, ready to leave the crease so one of them can take my spot and practice the technique, but before I get more than a foot or two away, Aiden calls out, stopping me.

"Hey Ads, can you stay there for a second?"

He signals the offensive line to follow, and as they make their way over, I snag the water bottle from above the net and pull my mask up.

"I wanna show the rookies how we do our drills." There's no missing the signature sparkle in his eye.

People tend to give Brooks the most credit for coaching me when I was a kid, and while his guidance has been absolutely invaluable, they forget that a goalie is only as good as the person they play against.

And I learned to play against the greatest center of all time: Aiden Langfield.

"Sure." I drop the bottle and pull down my mask.

While I settle into position, Aiden glides backward, stick in hand, cocky smirk on his face. He won't be wearing that expression for long. Because Aiden has a tell. I've never told him that I discovered it, but after watching him play hundreds of games by the time he retired when I was a teenager, it's obvious to me. For years, he dazzled crowds and destroyed defenseman and goalies. He could skate literal circles around the biggest and best players, and it wasn't always the goals he scored that were his best plays. It was how he knew precisely when to pass. A goalie would be preparing for him to take that direct shot. He had it most of the time. The goal was his to score. But then he'd pass it at the last second, and the shot would come from a completely different angle.

And his tongue always, *always*, gives him away. Though I seem to be the only person in the world who's discovered this. Because my uncle can't help but press his tongue against the corner of his lip, just for an instant, as he prepares to shoot. If he goes right, that tongue darts out on the right side of his mouth. If he's going left, his tongue goes to the left as well.

It's such a fucking easy thing to miss. It's barely a lick. I'm not even sure he knows he's doing it.

He skates toward me, his stick work as impeccable as ever. That's where my attention is supposed to be. Goalies are trained to never take their eyes off the puck. But doing that means they miss other details.

Which is why Brooks drilled into me the importance of taking in *everything*. During a game, I've got to keep track of what five opponents are doing and be ready for anything, but practice, with only one opponent, should be much easier.

And it would be if that opponent weren't Aiden Langfield.

Being one-on-one with such a skilled center is the stuff of nightmares for most goalies.

But I've been doing this my whole life. As he gets closer, I survey the whole scene. Aiden gliding toward me, playing with the puck, the slice of his blades as he quickens his pace, the sound they make when he comes to a stop quickly. His arm flies back, his position giving me every indication that he's going for a wrist shot toward my right shoulder. A split second before he moves that arm forward, his tongue pokes left, and I'm there, catching the biscuit, a smile on my face.

"Kid's still got it." Aiden skates backward, grinning and pointing at me. "Okay, let's let—"

"Again," Gavin calls from the other side of the ice, an arm sweeping out, signaling the guys he's working with to move closer to us. "Show us that again."

With a shrug, Aiden goes back to his spot. "I'm not going to go as easy on you this time."

I laugh as I drop into position. "Do your worst, Lep," I tease, using the nickname the crowds used to chant at games. They called him Leprechaun because they believed he was the Bolts lucky charm. Before Uncle Aiden, the Bolts had never won the Cup. With him on the roster, they won three

It's silent except for the sound of the puck smacking against his stick as he glides straight for me. He doesn't play with the puck this time. No, he picks up speed like he's on a breakaway. He doesn't stop or even slow as he moves into position to shoot at the low left corner of the net. I wait another fraction of a second, and when his tongue goes to the right, I'm ready to go that way too. And when I block it smoothly, a thrill goes through me.

"Jesus," one of the rookies mutters.

"Fucking incredible," another says.

"Again," Gavin yells.

We do this five more times before Gavin instructs the offensive line to take turns doing the same. Eventually, I bow out and head to the side of the rink where Aiden and Gavin have gathered while the goalies take turns blocking.

Ten minutes before practice is set to end, Gavin calls me over. "Go shower and get changed. I'll keep the guys here until you're done."

"Thanks." I really do need a shower, and since our practice arena only has one locker room, this is the only way that'll happen.

I collect my gear and turn away, but Gavin calls me back.

"Addie," he says, his tone serious. "It's a sin you don't still play. It was damn fun to watch you today."

"Thank you." I duck to hide my smile and the way my cheeks heat at the praise. But as I glide off the ice, I stand a little taller. Because for a little while, I didn't just keep up with players in the NHL, I fucking dominated them.

CHAPTER 15

JJ

"FUCKING UNFAIR," Sidney grumbles.

"You want in?" I turn to him, frowning. I've been focused on Adeline, so I don't know what his problem is, but now that's she's disappeared, I pull myself together.

Dirk's taking hits from the offensive line now, and he's handling himself okay. He's nowhere near as good as Adeline, but not a single person in this room could do what she just did—including myself.

"I'm talking about Addie. It's a damn shame she can't play." He blows out a breath. "She's better than most of the goalies in the NHL."

Grinning, I turn his way. I shouldn't feel this sense of pride; I don't have any claim over her and I'm not responsible for a lick of her talent, but it's hard not to swell when someone else recognizes it too.

And he's right. It's a damn shame she doesn't get to compete at this level.

"Kane," Gavin hollers. "Go watch the showers for Coach Langfield. Make sure no one goes in there."

I dart forward. "He hasn't gotten a chance in the net yet. I'll go."

"Fine. Just make sure no one goes in that locker room."

I dip my chin. As if there's a world in which I let a single one of these fuckers see Adeline naked. While I'll defend them like my brothers on the ice, I'd cut my own brother's eyes out if he tried to get a look at Adeline without her consent.

Fuck, I'd cut his eyes out if he did it *with* her consent.

Groaning, I double time it off the ice. I'm such a fucking goner.

When I reach the door to the locker room, I give it two hard knocks.

"I'm in here," she calls loudly.

"It's JJ. I'm just standing guard."

"Thanks," she yells. "I'll be quick."

I lean against the wall and huff out a breath. "Take your time. No one is getting through me."

Her chuckle echoes off the cinderblock walls. "Okay, tough guy."

She's probably rolling her eyes in there. How many times has she done this dance? How often has she had to rush through a shower or skip one altogether because of a lack of facilities?

Maybe it's because the two of us played together for years, or maybe it's because I'm a girl dad, but the unfairness of it gets under my skin.

In general, yeah, most women don't have the strength and power to play at the level the NHL requires. Hell, most men don't either. But there are exceptions, and there should be space on rosters for those exceptions.

And there should be accommodations for them too. Like a place to take a fucking shower.

I'm still chewing on my annoyance when Adeline calls out, "All good. You can come in."

I enter, and when the door closes behind me, I turn the lock. I don't want those guys barreling in and stripping down while she's still here.

Stomping over to my own locker, I yank off my practice jersey. I'm working on my pads when Adeline heads my way, braiding her hair.

Nostalgia washes over me, and for a second, I forget to breathe. Suddenly, I'm seventeen again, living for the few moments I had with her alone. When she let her guard down. Back then, she knew that if there was one person in this world who had her back, it was me. At least I hope she knew that.

"What are you thinking?" she asks, a tentative smile on her face.

"Huh?"

"You're looking at me weird. Do I have deodorant on my shirt or something?" She ducks, studying the fabric, her fingers still rhythmically moving through her hair. When she gets to the bottom, she loops an elastic around four times. Then she eyes me again. "What?"

"Two truths and a lie."

She coughs out a laugh. It's a little forced. "Okay, weirdo. Um, the water pressure in that bathroom is better than some of the best hotels I've stayed at. Even though the cleaning staff here is incredible, the showers still feel gross. And I'm slightly offended that you didn't try to sneak a peek."

I hold her gaze, a thread of excitement running through me. "The water pressure sucks, the showers are gross, and how do you know I didn't?"

That laugh again. It goes straight to my heart. "Obviously the last one was a lie. Gavin would have your head if you did."

I shrug. I'm not worried about what Gavin or any of her uncles or even her father have to say on the matter. I'll always protect her.

"Your turn." Tilting to one side, she peers at the door.

"I locked it." I toss a leg pad to the floor.

With a sharp intake of breath, she stomps toward the door. "*JJ.*"

A chuckle rolls out of me. "I didn't want anyone to come in while you were in here."

"People will think we're—" She whips around, her eyes going comically wide.

The chuckle turns into a full-on laugh. "No one is going to think a goddamn thing because I'll have their head if they do."

Huffing, she rolls her eyes. "Right because you can police the thoughts of others. You men are all the same."

I pull down my pants, exposing my compression shorts.

With a hiss, she spins around again, giving me her back. "Stop getting undressed. I'm leaving, Jesus."

"It's not like you haven't seen it all before," I murmur as I slide off my shorts and cup. "Besides, I haven't told you mine yet."

"Oh my god, you can tell me later," she mutters, but she doesn't make a move to leave.

I snag a towel and saunter past her, headed for the showers. "I'll never look at a piece of ice the same. I didn't sleep a wink last night. And your talent is wasted on coaching."

"Obviously it's the third one," she hedges, her tone uneasy, even if she tries to hide it.

I glance over my shoulder and catch her staring at my ass. "Nah, the lie was number two, Angles. I slept like a fucking baby last night."

CHAPTER 16

Addie

A FEW HOURS later we're back at the rink but this time it's not for practice.

"But what if I fall?" Avery assesses the ice warily, then tips her head back, her blue eyes on mine.

She looks absolutely adorable all bundled up like this, though the weight of the snow pants and helmet might actually cause her to fall, so her concern is legitimate.

"You might," I tell her honestly. "But you've got plenty of padding, so it won't hurt. Plus, and this is the important part, your dad and I will be right next to you. We'll help you get back up."

She frowns like she was expecting a different response. But I'm not a liar and I won't fib to get her onto the ice. The most important thing for a child is their ability to trust you, and once you fuck with that, you fuck with their confidence and trust for life.

Ask me how I know.

JJ steps onto the ice, does a little spin, and skates backward.

I inhale, ready to tell him he's not helping, showing off like that, but before I can, he trips and falls flat on his butt.

"Daddy." Avery looks up at me with the sweetest expression of concern. "Help him."

Before I can react, JJ pops up, arms wobbly, and smiles at her. "Look at that. I fell and I'm okay."

I flatten my lips to keep from laughing. He looks ridiculous, pretending he's having trouble staying on his skates. He scissors his legs back and forth dramatically and then falls again.

Avery giggles this time. "Daddy!"

I snort. "Hmm, it's wild to think we pay you so much to play on the ice."

He shoots me a devilish grin, his brows dancing. "Why don't you show us how it's done then, Adeline?"

With a roll of my eyes, I shuffle to the opening in the rink. Before I can step out, Avery tugs on my hand. "Can I come?"

A bolt of surprise hits me, but I tamp it down, only giving her a gentle smile. I was sure it'd take all kinds of coaxing to get her out there.

Instead, when I get in position and hold out my hand to her, she puts one little white skate onto the ice, gripping my hand with one of her own and the board with the other.

At the feel of her tiny mittened hand in mine, the gravity of this moment hits me. I peer over at JJ. He's got his phone out, already recording. When he catches me looking, he gives me the warmest smile he's probably ever shot my way. His eyes are so blue and happy, they make my heart skip.

I force myself to focus on Avery, who, like most kids when they step onto the ice for the first time, slips. She catches herself, throwing her tiny body forward, and I hang on tight, making sure she doesn't go down.

"Look at that," I cheer as I guide her upright again. "You're on the ice."

Her focus remains on her feet, her expression serious. "Now what?"

"March," I remind her. I've taught plenty of kids how to skate, and this is how we start. Once she's steadier, we'll work on gliding and shuffling.

She tries, and her legs almost go out from under her tiny body, but I catch her before she goes down.

"How 'bout you hold both my hands?"

She nibbles on her lip, brows furrowed in determination. "Okay."

Skating backward, I guide her slowly, mostly pulling her along. JJ follows, camera aimed at Avery, beaming.

He looks at her the same way Beckett has always looked at me. Not just when my skills have impressed him, either. Or when I've been recognized for my talent. He's been there for all the little things. Hell, Beckett isn't even a big fan of hockey. Yet he taught me how to skate. He came to every game that didn't coincide with his team's schedule. And he always, *always*, made sure that I knew how proud he was of me.

That's the thing about men like JJ and Beckett. They're proud of their children for who they are, not what they can do. Early on, when I'd tumble on the ice, my dad would smile and make an encouraging comment. And I have no doubt JJ would do the same for Avery.

But she doesn't fall. And as we go around the rink for a third time, she gets a little more daring. "Can I try it myself?"

I glance at JJ "What do you think? Is she ready?"

He bends at the knees so he's at her level and skates by. "She's a Hanson. She was born ready."

Despite his statement, he gets in front of her so he can catch her if she goes down. But he doesn't make a big deal out of it. God, he's good.

"Okay, Avey girl. Let's try this." I drop one of her hands.

With her other hand, she squeezes tighter, her little body wobbling as she struggles to stay up.

"You've got this," I tell her. "Just march those feet."

With a deep breath, she releases me, and then she glides forward. "Oh," she squeals. "Daddy, I'm skating!"

She makes it four entire steps before she falls forward.

JJ is right there, catching her, lifting her and zooming around, making her fly like an airplane, as if that was his plan all along. "Yeah you are."

"Did you see that, Addie?" she yells.

I laugh. "I did. You were great."

As they glide back my way, her smile is wide. Mine is too, if the ache in my cheeks is any indication.

"Can we get ice cream to celebrate?" she asks as they slow.

Chuckling, JJ heads for the bench. "After dinner."

"Oh man," she whines, still in his arms. "I worked so hard. I was hoping you'd feel bad for me and I could have ice cream."

A full laugh rumbles out of JJ as he sets her down. "I don't feel bad for you at all. You just skated."

She zeroes in on me as I catch up to them. "Can Addie come for ice cream too?"

Kneeling in front of her, unlacing her skates, he peers up at me. "Can you?"

I shrug. "Only if I eat all my vegetables first. I need extra protein and veggies after kicking everybody's butts at practice today."

Avery's eyes go wide. "Did you kick my dad's butt too?"

"Nope, but she was definitely staring at it," JJ mutters, his neck craned so he's facing me and not his daughter.

I knee him in the back, making him tip forward.

He steadies himself with one hand on the bench beside Avery. "What?"

I shake my head at him and his cocky smirk.

"You shouldn't use your hands or your legs when you get mad, Addie. Right, Dad?"

JJ gives me a ridiculously fake serious face, nodding. "Absolutely right, Avey. We never use our hands or legs to express our anger. We use our words. Adeline, do you want to tell us how you *feel* about seeing my butt today?"

I snort. "I hate you."

Avery tuts. "We use our words, but we don't say that. Right, Daddy?"

JJ glances back at his daughter, a real affectionate smile on his face again. "You're right, Aves. We don't tell people we love that we hate them."

"And you love my daddy, right, Addie?"

Oh, he got me good with that one.

JJ drops to his ass on the floor and hangs his head, hiding a smile.

I inhale deeply and nod. "Yup, I love you guys *so* much."

She smiles. "I love you too. Now let's go get ice cream."

"Nice try, tiny skater," JJ says with a laugh. "*After* dinner."

I sit next to Avery and get to work removing my skates while JJ does the same thing from the floor.

"Can I see my video?" Avery asks.

JJ digs his phone out of his pocket and pulls up the video, then hands the device to her.

Her eyes are wide, as she watches, and I swear to god she's studying her every movement carefully. It's the way I watch game tape. I can practically see her wheels turning, like she's working out what she should do differently next time.

For a moment, I forget that she isn't mine. Suddenly, I understand how Beckett must have felt all those years. This kinship. This pride. This feeling that maybe she could be a little like me. It doesn't matter that we aren't related by blood. I'm here for this moment. And I want to be here for as many moments as JJ will allow me to be.

Because Avery deserves people in her life who show up.

And the more of us, the better.

CHAPTER 17

JJ

Eighteen Years Old

"I'VE GOT orange soda for you, Twizzlers for me, three kinds of chips, *and*, don't get too excited, but they had Ding Dongs too."

Adeline snorts as she pulls her hotel room door open wider.

I step inside and almost stumble when I discover how much skin she's got on display. Damn. There may be pieces of fabric covering some parts of her body, but I don't know that I'd categorize them as clothes.

Her tank top is tiny, her shorts tinier, though she's wearing absurd socks that come up to her knees that have Aiden Langfield's face all over them.

"Nice socks." I stride past her, ignoring her sweet scent. She goes back to braiding her wet hair, something I've seen her do a hundred times, as she follows me toward the—fuck, there's no table. "Where's your table?"

She snorts. "Damn, hot shot, way to point out that your room is nicer than mine."

I eye her. "They really gave you a standard room?"

"They gave us all standard rooms. You're just bougie. Your parents probably upgraded you without you knowing."

I drop my head forward and sigh. I could totally see my dad doing that. He's still trying to make up for how many games he and Mom have missed the last few years.

Like I'd ever hold my mother's cancer diagnosis and treatment against them.

She's in remission, thankfully, and her hair is finally long enough for a short bob, which she seems very excited about.

Sometimes I catch my dad watching her with fear in his eyes, like he's scared she'll disappear. It's a reminder that we're not in the clear just yet.

I force a smile to my face. "I like nice things. I deserve them, Angles."

She laughs. "And he's modest too. Also, Twizzlers taste like plastic. I wouldn't consider them a nice thing."

"Yeah, but they're my mom's favorite, so I've been addicted since I was a kid."

Her brow creases a little. "You never told me that."

I shrug. "Well, now you know."

"Give me one," she says, holding out a hand.

I drop the goods onto the bed closest to the door. This room has two beds, even though she doesn't have a roommate, and she always sleeps in the one farthest from the door because she claims it's safest.

Like somehow the extra ten seconds she'd have if someone broke in would do her much good.

That weird pinch in my chest hits when I imagine something bad happening to Adeline. Before I can think too much about it, she's standing beside me, that sweet scent surrounding me. With her this close, it takes all my brain power to focus on how to open the Twizzler package.

I fail epically, because of course I do, and rip the bag completely down one side. The contents spill onto the bed, and because they're basically plastic like she said, they fall in one big clump.

With a light laugh, she picks it up, pulls one off, and throws it at me. Then she does the same for herself and takes a big bite.

"Yup, still tastes like plastic," she says, chomping on it. She takes another bite, ripping at the candy with her teeth. "I kinda like them, though."

Chuckling, I pick up the soda I brought for her and shuffle to the bathroom.

"Where are you going with that?" she yells.

I open it over the sink, taking the brunt of the spray I knew was coming, then clean it—and myself—off before bringing it back to her, top off. "Opening your drink."

Her teeth glide over her bottom lip and those pretty brown eyes of hers rise to mine. "Oh, thanks."

I settle on the bed with a sigh. "You upset about missing prom?"

We signed up for this goalie camp last year, before we knew it was the same weekend as the dance. Even if I'd known, I would have been here. Though maybe that's because I knew Adeline would be here too. After sneaking into her room and sleeping beside her every night for almost a year, talking with her and confiding in her, I miss her. Sure, we still play and practice and travel together and we go to school together, but it's not the same. We don't get many moments like this.

Adeline settles on the bed beside me and grabs another Twizzler. "Eh, it's not like anyone asked me to go."

I frown, studying her. "Was there someone you wanted to ask you?"

She rolls her eyes. "No. But who wouldn't want to at least be asked? I'm not like you, JJ."

"I have no idea what that means."

She scoffs. "For guys, playing hockey ups your level of hotness. For me, it only makes me intimidating."

I sigh. She's not wrong. Girls are happy to drop to their knees the second they find out I play hockey. Not that I take anyone up on the offer.

Still, I work not to swallow my tongue imagining someone else asking Adeline out. "Who's intimidated by you?" I ask, managing to keep my tone aloof.

She smacks me.

Without my permission, my eyes dip down, taking in her body

again. "It's just because they don't see you in these short shorts and tank top."

"Shut up. These are my pajamas."

I laugh. "What's the excuse for the socks?"

She shoves me again and I fall over onto our snacks. As I go down, I snag her hand. "Stop being so violent. All I'm saying is I don't think anyone would remember that you play hockey if they saw you right now."

She stares down at me. "I'm not sure if that's a compliment or not."

I'm not sure either. Would she appreciate the idea that I'll probably be using the image of her in this exact outfit many a night going forward? Probably not.

I shrug it off and sit up, snagging my iPod. Head down, definitely not looking at her again, I find the playlist I want. Then I connect it to the little speaker in my pocket, and we've got music.

"It's so weird that you have one of those," she teases, folding her legs into a pretzel shape.

I pluck one of the bags of chips off the mattress and pull it open, then hold it out to her.

"It's my dad's," I tell her. "Well, actually…" I can't help but smile. "It was my mom's, but my dad stole it."

Shifting, Adeline exhales loudly through her nose. "What?"

"She used to listen to it on the train from Providence to Boston. She mostly did it so she could ignore my dad, who was trying really hard to get her to go out with him."

"Really?" She breaks into a big smile, the expression sending a warm rush through me.

"Yup. And since he's never been one to play fair, he hacked into her iTunes account and wiped out her playlist."

Her mouth drops open and she lets out a breath. "Shut up."

I chuckle. "Yeah, my dad was down bad."

"God, I can't imagine what that would be like. To have someone try so hard to get your attention." Her eyes widen in this dreamy way for a second, though she quickly catches herself and sits straighter. "I'm sure you've had women do crazier things to get your attention."

I laugh. "Nah, my dad was definitely the craziest. Anyway, he would add a song a day. And then you know how they were separated for a long time—"

She nods.

"He kept adding songs. She had no clue. And when he proposed, there was a ridiculous number of them. Like thousands. One for every day since he first met her."

Her jaw drops. "Even when they were apart?"

"Yup."

"Wow. That's quite the story. Your mom was in Paris when they were separated, right?"

"Yeah, for some of the time. She loved it so much that they moved there about the time I was born."

"Oh god, I can't imagine moving to another country and not knowing the language."

"My dad learned it so he could flirt with my mom."

Head tipped back, she lets out a loud laugh. "Your dad has some major game. And he doesn't even need it."

This time I'm the one gaping. "Are you saying you think my dad is hot?"

"Yes. And everyone within a one-hundred-mile radius of your father would agree."

I scowl.

She rolls her eyes. "Like you didn't benefit from that. You look just like him."

"You trying to tell me you think *I'm* hot, Angles?"

There's that eye roll again. My dick twitches. Fuck.

"Do you know any French?"

As if by divine design, "Yellow" by Coldplay starts.

I hold out a hand. "Tradition in my house is that when this song comes on, everyone stops what they're doing and dances."

She stares at my outstretched hand, lips tugged down.

With a huff, I snag her wrist and yank her up. She falls into my chest, laughing, then wraps her arms around my neck. "Smooth, JJ, so very smooth."

As I settle my hands on her hips, I struggle to catch my breath. When she's this close, I lose even the ability to breathe.

We move, and her tank top rides up a fraction, my thumb burning at the feel of her skin beneath it. Eyes locked with hers, I say, "I'm not smooth, Adeline." Though I say it in French. "Not with you," I continue, thankful she doesn't understand. "I look at you and think *fuck it, I should kiss you*. But then I remember that I'm scared to death of losing you."

"What does that mean?" she murmurs, her face tipped up.

"You were leaning too far to the left in the goal today," I say calmly. "If you keep doing that, I'm gonna take the top spot this week."

She scoffs, but she's smiling. "God, it sounded more like a declaration of love than you being an asshole." She shakes her head, eyes shining. "I should have known." Sighing, she settles her head against my chest. "Your parents' love story is really beautiful."

The warmth of her steals my breath once again. Resting my cheek against her head, I close my eyes and wish I had the balls to tell her she's the most beautiful thing in the world.

Instead, I mumble, "Thanks, Angles."

CHAPTER 18

Addie

"WHEN WILL YOU BE BACK?" Gracie asks.

Finn, who made dinner yet again, sits across from her, forking a giant bite of chicken and fried rice into his mouth. While he cooked, the kids sat at the counter, watching him like he was performing at one of those teppanyaki restaurants, chopping up food and tossing the vegetables into the air so the kids could try to catch them in their mouths. It was a whole experience.

"Finn is in the playoffs," Hope explains. "He's got to be fully focused from now until the World Series."

"Can I come to the World Series?" Declan asks as a hunk of carrot flies off Beck's fork and smacks him in the face.

"See what you started?" Winnie glares at our brother as she snatches Beck's fork from his hand. "You don't get to use utensils if you use them to throw food."

Beck beams at her. "So I can eat with my hands?"

I bite back a cackle as Winnie groans. "No."

Vivi, who's sitting beside Beck, hands him a spoon, her lips twitching. "Don't throw food or we're not going to watch the first preseason game."

Beck's face grows serious and he focuses on his plate. My nephew loves hockey, much to his grandfather and namesake's chagrin. The little troublemaker would rather behave than miss a game, even if it's only on TV.

Well played, Vivi. Seems like she's taking to this position better than we expected.

"Of course you can come to the World Series," Finn says, bringing us back to the conversation.

"You sound pretty sure you'll be in it," I tease.

He looks at me, wearing a bewildered frown. "Of course I'm sure. Have you seen the Revs this year? We're on fire."

I laugh. My brother has always been the most positive person I know. He's genuinely a happy guy, and he's right, his team is primed for this.

"You know who else is on fire?" JJ prods.

Avery, who's seated next to him on the long bench on one side of the enormous table, shifts, giving him her full attention.

The benches were my mom's genius idea. Makes it easier to squeeze kids around the table, and they're not upholstered, meaning no stains on expensive fabric. Pretty important now that we've got six preschoolers living here.

"My sister?" Finn grins, dark eyes twinkling. "I heard."

Vivi nods. "Me too. Dad was going on and on about how amazing she's been."

My cheeks burn in response to the praise. It's been a full week since I first stepped into the net, and every day since, we've run similar drills. The team is looking really good, and preseason games start next week.

That, thank god, means it's almost time to say goodbye to Dirk. He's still an asshole, though he's done a better job of hiding it since our talk. But luckily, he hasn't performed well enough to threaten JJ's or Sidney's spots on the team. In a matter of days, he and the other rookie will be heading back to their own teams.

"Nah, though she's done well." JJ winks at me, the look making my heart stumble. "I was talking about Avery."

"*Daddy*." Avery's giggle floats around us.

I nod at her from across the table. "It's true. She even did a little spin today."

We've been out on the ice with her three times so far. It's the least I can do since JJ has shown up to every extra practice with the rookies and every early-morning yoga session.

And I love spending time with her. I want so desperately to be a constant positive force in her life, but those feelings I used to have, the ones that were always so impossible to ignore, are getting louder.

"I want to go skating," Beck yells. "Why haven't you taken me skating?"

Winnie picks up her wine and takes a long swig. "Not everything is about you, bud."

"You can come next time," I promise him, "if it's okay with your mom."

"Can I go to the baseball field with Uncle Finn, then?" Dec whines.

"Maybe I can take you and my girls down there one day when they're practicing," Hope offers, eyes darting to Winnie. "If that's okay with the big boss."

My sister huffs out a laugh. "Are you saying that because I'm their mom or because I'm the CEO of the Revs organization?"

"The CEO part," Hope says with a laugh. "They don't care that you're their mom."

Winnie snorts. "Yeah."

"Mommy's not the boss of the Revs, Grandpa is," Dec argues.

"So he continues to think," Winnie grumbles into her glass. She is the official CEO of the baseball division of our family company, but as COO of the entirety of Langfield Corp—including both the Revs organization and the Bolts—Dad has had a tough time letting go of control.

Mari, Hope's two-year-old, flings a piece of chicken across the table, hitting Finn in the face.

From there, the room falls into complete chaos. In unison, the twins scream *food fight!* and we're all pelted with rice. Once the chicken and veggies start flying, parents scoop up their children, putting an end to the madness and dinner.

"I'll clean this up after bath time." Winnie nods at the mess on the table as she pushes her boys toward the stairs.

Finn and Hope have already taken her girls upstairs to get cleaned up.

"Don't worry about it. Get the kids taken care of. I can handle this."

"I'd stay and help," Vivi says, "but I promised Willow I'd watch a movie with her and I'm already late."

Not only is Willow Vivi's best friend, but her Dad, Cortney, is Dad's best friend. Even if the two men act more like an old married couple.

Cortney and his wife live next door, and if Willow is in town, that means she's home from college for the weekend.

"I'm fine. I promise," I say as I stack plates.

JJ follows me, his hands full of cutlery. "I'll help her."

My jaw clenches. Why can't he give me five fucking minutes alone? He's everywhere lately. Home and practice and workouts. I can't even shower without thinking of him because his damn body wash taunts me from its spot next to mine.

I put the dishes in the sink and when JJ reaches around my shoulder to add the silverware to the pile, I growl.

"I'll wash them. I'm not leaving them for you to do." His breath is warm as he teases me, his chest to my back.

I flex my shoulders, forcing him back and giving myself some space.

"I'm just putting them in the dishwasher. I don't need your help for that," I snap.

I should feel bad about my reaction. I would, truly, if I could get five fucking seconds to myself.

"Right, of course." His heat disappears instantly, and then he's gone, hustling out of the kitchen.

Head hanging, I growl again. Dammit, Addie. Way to be an asshole.

I scrub each plate before loading it into the dishwasher, working out my frustration. Then I add soap and hit start.

Still feeling like I'm bursting from within, I decide to go for a run, so I rush up the steps, change, and head out.

The moment I step back inside, Finn mutters an "Oh duck!" from the kitchen. It's followed by an "Oh shit, what happened in here?" from JJ.

I rush into the kitchen, only to slip the second I hit the first tile. "Holy duck," I squeal as I cling to the kitchen counter.

"Bubbles!" Dec rushes in, sliding just like I did, though he goes down, landing on his butt with a thunk.

"What the—"

"Winnie, no," I warn, as my sister rushes in. Fortunately she grabs the wall before her feet go out from under her.

"Where is it coming from?" she asks, her face twisted in confusion.

Laughing, Finn points at the dishwasher and the bubbles pouring out from either side and the top of it.

JJ smirks, his focus landing on me. "Thought you said you could handle the dishwasher, Angles."

I groan, my stomach dropping. "This is so embarrassing."

Winnie shuffles along the wall. "Did you use dishwashing detergent?"

"I don't know," I say, the words a little too high-pitched. "I used the one on the sink."

"That's dish soap, Addie. *Not for machines,*" she groans.

"How do we make it stop?" I ask, my cheeks hot with embarrassment.

JJ glides over to the dishwasher with ease, like he's skating on the ice, and presses a button on the front. The machine goes quiet.

"At least we don't have to wash the floors," I say meekly.

The way Winnie rolls her eyes makes her look so much like Mom.

"True." JJ snags a towel from the counter near the sink and throws it at me.

"Rude." Laughing, I catch it, then assess the soapy mess surrounding me. "How in god's name are we going to get this all wiped up?"

He reaches into the drawer and produces a few more towels, throwing one at each of my siblings. "We're going to have a dance party."

"A what?" Winnie asks, eyes narrowed.

"Dance party!" he howls, throwing his head back like a lunatic.

Upstairs, Avery screams, "Did you say dance party?"

A thundering rush sounds above us, then two little girls come flying into the kitchen.

My siblings and I shout "Wait!" at the same time, but JJ is already sliding over to them and snagging them each around the waist. "You heard that right, Avey girl," he says, hauling them up on either side of him. "What do you say? Should we show them how it's done?"

"How what's done, Uncky JJ?" Gracie asks with a giggle.

"Dad, get out the iPod," Avery squeals, bouncing in his arm.

He sets her on the counter and pulls that damn iPod from all those years ago out of his pocket, then scoops her up again.

Seriously? Does he still keep that on him at all times?

Peering over Avery's head, he presses a few buttons. A second later, music blasts through the speakers my dad had installed in the kitchen years ago.

Why am I not surprised that JJ is already hooked up to system?

"What's happening?" Winnie asks as Taylor Swift's "Shake It Off" starts playing.

The girls go wild in his arms, making it hard to hear even the music. The song may be decades old, but it's still a hit.

JJ drops his towel to the ground, steps on it, and shimmies, cleaning up the mess while dancing.

Finn does the same, holding out a hand to Gracie, who jumps from JJ's arm into his.

JJ spins toward me with Avery in his arms, the two of them wearing matching bright smiles. "You going to join us, Angles?"

"You're ridiculous." But I do. Winnie and the boys do too. Eventually Hope comes down with Mari in her arms—the baby presumably asleep—and dances too.

When the song switches to "Yellow," my eyes dart to JJ without my permission and my heart jumps.

"This is my Mimi and Pops's song," Avery, who's now dancing on her own towel, tells everyone. She grasps Gracie's hand. "Come on. We dance like this to this song." She wraps her arms around Gracie's neck, and the two of them sway adorably.

After a few bars, she looks up at me. "Why aren't you dancing?"

I cough out laugh. "I like watching you."

"Daddy," she says, using the tone that means she's annoyed. Avery never hides her disappointment.

JJ shrugs and holds out a hand, like this is an everyday thing. Like the last time we danced to this song doesn't even register to him. Like it didn't mean a thing.

Of course it didn't. Why would it have? I was one of many girls that he's danced with. It's not his fault that I've only ever danced with him.

Still, it'd be weird if I said no. And I can feel eyes on me. If I refuse, everyone will think I care or something, which I totally don't.

So I take his hand. When he pulls me flush to his body, I can't hide my surprised intake of breath. And when he presses one hand to my back and holds the other to his heart, it takes effort to keep my knees from wobbling.

Head bowed, focused on me, he murmurs in French, "Right back where you belong."

My heart flutters in my chest. Does he mean it? Is it possible he feels this? The pull that's always existed between us? That even after all this time, just like me, he realizes we just somehow fit?

He's got a wife, Adeline. A wife.

Reminder in place, I smirk and in French, I reply, "Sweeping up the floor with you? Yeah, I'd agree."

His mouth falls open. "You speak French?"

With a *pfft*, I say, "Oh, I wasn't taking a chance on not knowing what you were saying ever again."

I only wish I could remember what he said all those years ago so I could translate it properly. Because I'm starting to believe that I had things all wrong back then.

JJ smiles down at me while Chris Martin sings about the stars.

Mouth at my ear, he murmurs, again in French. "Oh what a thing to do…You're never not taking me by surprise, Adeline."

Hours later, while I'm lying in bed still thinking about tonight, a knock sounds on my door, then a tiny voice calls, "Addie."

I jump out of bed and throw the door open, finding Avery

standing in the hall in her pink pjs, carrying her teddy bear, her face stained with tears. "I c-can't sleep," she hiccups. "I h-had a bad dream."

I scoop her up, squeezing her tight. "I'm sorry, Avey girl. Do you want to tell me about it?"

She shakes her head. "N-no. I want my daddy."

I frown. She knows where her dad's room is, so why did she come here?

Now is not the time to ask, so I head for the door to the bathroom. "Okay, want me to take you to him?"

She nods, sniffling against my chest.

I knock on the door connecting the bathroom to JJ's room, quietly calling out, "It's Avery. She's upset."

The door swings open seconds later and he appears, blinking rapidly, his face scrunched in confusion and concern.

And he's in nothing but a pair of shorts.

There's ink covering his chest. So much ink. And muscles. And the shorts hang so low, I can see the divots in his abdomen and where a trail of dark hair follows the deep V.

When I come dangerously close to choking on my own saliva, I decide to avert my eyes. Quickly. *Shit.*

"What's wrong, Avey girl?" he asks as he reaches for her.

She digs her fingers into my pajamas and buries her face again. "No, I want Addie."

My heart thumps off beat, and JJ steps back. "Okay."

"Can you lay with us?" Avery asks me, voice pleading.

"Lay with you and your dad?" I croak. No. She can't mean that.

"Yes please. I'm scared. I want you both."

JJ eyes me, a pleading look on his face, like he actually believes I could say no to his little girl.

"Of course," I say quickly, shuffling for the bed. When my knees bump the mattress, I inhale deeply. *This isn't a big deal. We've laid in a bed together plenty of times and nothing's happened. And his daughter is here. This is about Avery.*

The covers on the side closest to the wall are pulled down, but JJ pads to the other side.

"What are you doing? Isn't this your pillow?" I say as I lay Avery in the middle of the bed. She curls up with her bear and turns to face JJ.

"I'll sleep by the door. Ya know, in case someone breaks in." He winks, then he pulls down the covers on that side and slides in.

My traitorous heart skips a beat. He remembers.

I try not to make a big deal of this moment.

So what if I'm getting into bed with a man I once loved? So what if he remembers that I'm a big baby when it comes to my sleeping arrangements and I always sleep farthest from the door? So what if his daughter is looking at me like I belong in their little world? With their little family.

This isn't a big deal.

I climb into bed, and immediately, I know it's a mistake. The spot is warm, the sheets creased, evidence that only moments ago, JJ was lying here. And the second my head hits his pillow, I wish I could go back in time thirty seconds. He's everywhere. I can't even close my eyes to avoid him because his scent clings to the bedding, and it's heavenly.

"Can you hold me?" Avery sniffles.

JJ drapes an arm over her, ready to pull her close, but she throws out a hand and shakes her head. "Addie."

He lets out a huff, and I can't be sure in the dark, but I think he rolls his eyes.

Holding in a little laugh, I place my hand on her back, rubbing gently.

"I love you, Addie," Avery says. "Love you, Daddy. Good night."

JJ's eyes fall shut, a look that's half pain, half affection on his face. Like it physically breaks him when his daughter is that sweet.

It does the same to me.

He leans forward and pushes her hair back, stroking gently. "I love you too, Avey girl." He presses a kiss to her forehead and snuggles a little closer, stroking her hair. The third or fourth time he does it, I'm moving my hand up as he's moving his down, and when our fingers accidentally brush against one another, I suck in a breath.

Over Avery's head, he stares at me. Then he twists his pinky around my own.

My heart beats like a drum, warning me that this is a terrible idea. But I don't look away. Even when Avery's breaths even out and my eyes start to droop.

And when I wake up, the sun not yet peeking over the horizon, Avery is snuggled between us and he's still holding my hand.

I pull away, flexing my fingers to get blood flowing again. But I don't think that's what's caused the tingling.

Tossing the covers off, I suck in a shaky breath.

I can't do this with him. No matter how much I want to, I can't play house. I'm not Avery's mother and I'm not JJ's wife.

With those words replaying like a mantra in my mind, I rush out of the bedroom and snag my phone from the charger on my nightstand.

Then I type out a quick message to Savannah.

Me: Fine. I'll be your New Romantics girl. Just tell me what to do.

CHAPTER 19

Addie

Twenty-One Years Old

THE MOMENT I get the news, there's only one person I want to call. I'm pacing my dorm as I pull out my phone, trying to remember where he is tonight. Does he have a game?

JJ signed with the Bolts last year and this is his first full season on the team. Their veteran goalie, Sidney Howe, gets far more ice time, but JJ still plays, and getting any time during his first year is a huge deal. And he's playing for our hometown team. Honestly, that's just about every hockey player's dream.

I was there the day he got drafted, and like we always do, we celebrated with pizza from Antonio's. Just the two of us.

While he's living it up, I'm still in college. Even if I was brave enough to enter the draft, my parents were adamant that I wait until after I graduate. I've been telling myself that when that time comes, maybe I'll be ready. After the news I just got, I'm starting to believe it.

I'm pretty sure the Bolts are in Michigan, so Antonio's is likely out of the question. But I still need to hear his voice.

I pull up his contact info and put the phone on speaker, then drop it onto my bed and pace.

"Hello?" A female voice crackles through my room, stealing the air from my lungs. "Hello, JJ's phone. Is someone there?"

I work to clear my throat and snatch the device off the mattress. "Yeah, um, hi. It's Adeline. He can just call me back."

"JJ, baby, someone's on the phone," the woman coos.

There's a jostling and then another hello. This time the voice is familiar, making my heart stutter, even as it sinks.

"Hi, uh…" I bite my lip. God, why do I want to cry right now?

"Adeline?" JJ asks. "Is that you?"

"Yeah."

"Are you okay?"

"Baby, who is Adeline?" the woman asks.

He huffs. "Can you give me a minute?"

I shake my head. "Yeah, of course. Just call me another time."

"Not you," he says into the phone. A second later, a door clicks shut, and he murmurs, "What's up?"

"Where are you?" I ask, unable to stop myself.

"In a hotel in Michigan?" he answers, his pitch rising at the end like it's a question.

"Baby?" I say, my mouth really getting away from me.

"Huh?"

"She called you *baby*."

He sighs. "Is that why you called? To ask about what some girl called me?"

My stomach rolls. "She's in your hotel room."

"And?" he asks, his tone shorter than usual. "Do you have a problem with that?"

"No." I shake my head. "Why should I have a problem with that? Just because we're best friends doesn't mean you owe it to me not to sleep with anyone else…and we're not sleeping together so, like, yay," I say in the fakest of squeals which ends with a stupid clap of my hands.

"Did you just clap?"

I tap my forehead with the edge of the phone a little too hard. *Seriously, Addie? Could you get more embarrassing?* "Maybe?"

He chuckles. "Fuck, I miss you."

"I miss you too." I deflate. I hate how much I mean that. And I hate that the sentiment means something completely different to him. God, I'm pathetic.

"So what's going on?" JJ asks.

"I, um…just wanted to tell you that…" My throat tightens, making it hard to speak. Eyes closed, I take a deep breath. Why am I acting weird? Let the man get back to his random hookup. "I made the Olympic team."

"Adeline! Holy shit that's incredible." He barks out a laugh. "I'm getting on a plane."

An incredulous sound escapes me. "What?"

"We need to celebrate."

"I'm pretty sure you're celebrating enough for the two of us," I mutter, that envy seeping back in.

"I'm coming home."

"JJ."

"Adeline. You've been working toward this your entire life. I need to hug you. Need to—*fuck*."

"You need to play in Michigan tomorrow night," I remind him.

He sighs like it physically pains him. "I know."

"When will you be home?"

"Um…" He's quiet for a minute, like he's looking at his calendar. Then he grunts. "Not until next week."

My heart drops. "I'll be in Minnesota then."

"What?"

"I have to report for Olympic training on Sunday. It's in Minnesota."

"Fuck it, I'm coming home."

I roll my eyes, even as butterflies erupt in my belly. "JJ, stop."

"Adeline, I can't not see you for four fucking months. We need to celebrate."

I smile, tears pricking at the backs of my eyes. "We will, when my team wins the gold medal."

His exhale gusts over the microphone, sounding staticky. "That's months away."

"And you'll be busy kicking ass during that time. We'll talk between my training and your games," I promise, forcing myself to sound upbeat, though I feel anything but. It's what we've been doing for the last three years though since we both went our separate ways after graduation. We try to see each other whenever we're both in town but he's busy so sometimes we'll go months where our only communication is Facetimes. And it's not like we're dating. JJ does enough of that for the both of us though.

"I hate this," he mumbles.

"I know, but we're doing what we both dreamed of..." I sigh. "JJ, I'm going to the Olympics." When the words are out, excitement rushes through me again.

"Yeah, you are. I'm so fucking proud of you."

I smile. "Me too. I'll let you get back to your date."

"It's not a date."

"Ew, I was trying to be PC about it."

"I'll have her out of here in ten. I'm ordering you a pizza, then we can FaceTime and celebrate our way. Okay?"

I hate how my heart skips a beat. I hate the stupid bout of hope I feel that maybe one day JJ will feel the same. "You sure?"

"Yeah, Adeline. I'm sure. Ten minutes."

CHAPTER 20

JJ

"ENJOY your last weekend of freedom. See you on Sunday for game one," Aiden calls as he heads out of the locker room.

"Who's coming out tonight?" Bobby rubs his hands together, his lips kicked up on one side.

Royal Bombardier, a winger, nods as he tugs a clean shirt out of his locker. "I'm down."

One of our defensemen, Maxim Loob shrugs and says "I go" in a thick Russian accent.

When all eyes turn to me, I hold up my hands. "Sorry, I've got Aves."

"Don't you have a sitter for her?" Bobby whines. For a grown man, he can be such a child.

"Yeah, who watches her all day. And when the season starts will be with her more than I will be. So yeah, I'm going home to my kid."

Bray saunters out of the showers with a towel wrapped around his waist, his tattoos on display.

"What about you, Cap? Gonna come out with us? Or do you have some lame excuse about another tattoo client?"

Bray looks my way, the lack of interest in going out there in his eyes.

So I clear my throat and take a step forward. "Bray's hanging with Aves and me. Sorry, guys."

Bray shrugs. That's as close as he gets to smiling. "Yeah. Sorry, guys."

"You suck," Bobby says. "Come on, boys. Let's go enjoy our last weekend of freedom."

The three of them disappear, rounding up other teammates as they go. Fuck, I don't envy our head of PR. I'm sure she works overtime cleaning up their messes.

"I'll, uh, see you Sunday?" Bray says as he tugs on a pair of boxers.

Chuckling, I close my locker and turn around. "Nope."

He stares at me, mouth turned down. "What?"

"You're coming to my place. You know I never lie."

He scoffs. "Terrible habit of yours."

"Absolutely awful." I zip my bag up and sling it over my shoulder.

"Fine, I'll hang with you and Aves, but only because she's so much cooler than you."

"Obviously." I pull my phone out of my pocket and check the time, wondering if Adeline has already left. She's been avoiding me since I fell asleep with my pinky linked around hers.

Fuck, my heart trips over itself at the damn thought of the innocent moment. How is it that holding her pinky is now the highlight of my fucking love life?

It's been three days, and I can't wait any longer to talk to her. We missed our chance years ago, and I won't let that happen again. If there's even the slightest possibility that she feels the same, that she could ever be interested in a relationship with me, then I can't let fear keep me from speaking up. Not again.

"Meet you at your house?" Bray asks.

"Yeah, you going to ride that ridiculous death rocket over?"

Letting out a low laugh, he snags his wallet and his keys from his stall. "It's called a Harley. You seriously need to stop being such a dad."

"I am a dad." I flip my phone in my hand with a chuckle, then head for the door.

"We're all aware," he mutters.

Adeline's office is empty when I pass it on the way to the garage, so I head home. There's a good chance I'll see her there at some point tonight. As my phone connects to the Bluetooth in my car, I discover I have a text from Vivi.

> Vivi: is it okay if Winnie and I take Avery to dinner and a movie tonight?

Hmm. A little thrill zips through me at the prospect. This could definitely work to my advantage. Maybe it'll give me a chance to talk to Adeline alone. And if I show up with Brayden, she's less likely to hide from me. Then, when I find a convenient way to get rid of Bray, I can invite her to dinner.

Yeah. This could totally work.

I dig my phone from my pocket and respond.

> Me: If you're sure you don't mind. I know she'd love it. I'll Venmo you for the tickets etc.

> Vivi: Stop! Winnie's paying anyway.

I laugh. Of course she is. I'll Venmo her, then.

> Me: Thanks, Vivi. I appreciate it. Tell Avey girl if she needs me to just give me a call. I'll be around.

> Vivi: Take the night off. You don't always have to be such a dad.

I huff out a laugh. I'm seeing a pattern here. But Jesus, I'm the only parent Avery's got at the moment. I haven't heard a word from her mother in weeks. For me, that's a positive thing. The less I have to do with Tabitha, the better. But for Avery, it's awful.

Still, maybe I should take their advice. Maybe, just for a few hours, I can focus on the other most important woman in my life.

I pull up to the brownstone as Bray is parking his motorcycle.

"Good news," I tell him as he sets his helmet on the back of his bike.

Bray runs a hand through his dark hair, shaking it out. "What's that?"

I clap once, the sound loud on the quiet street. "I'm kid free for a few hours."

With a laugh, he shakes his head. "Fuck, maybe we should meet the guys out for a drink."

I head for the door, pulling my house key from my pocket. "Let's see if Adeline is home. Maybe she wants to join us."

"You mean Coach Langfield?"

I scoff as I unlock the door. "Here, she's Adeline."

"Right, but to you, she should always be Coach Langfield," he says, voice low and full of warning.

"Oh my gosh, do not check that box," Adeline screams, the sound reverberating off the walls.

Brayden and I share a confused look, then stride to the kitchen.

"Whatever." The tease is followed by a loud, raspy laugh. "If you're going to answer this thing, at least answer it honestly. You can't tell me you don't want to get boned at least twice a week."

"Boned?" Brayden scowls as we discover Josie, Adeline, and Savannah hanging in the kitchen.

"What are you doing here?" Josie shrieks and rushes toward her brother. Her strawberry blond hair sways and her face is lit up with joy. She's wearing a long purple fringy dress with beading that makes clicking sounds with every step she takes and as she throws her arms around her brother's neck.

Sighing, Brayden pats her back. It's as close as he gets to excitement. "JJ conned me into a night in."

"*Oh*, I always knew you'd find your way to the other side," she teases. "I can't believe Tabitha turned you off women completely, though," she says to me. "Then again, if there was ever a woman who'd send a man running for dick—"

"Oh my god." Adeline huffs. "Could you at least try to go five freaking seconds without talking about sex?"

Savannah sidles up next to Josie and pulls her in for a hug. "No, and that's why we love her so very much."

Savannah is a shit stirrer. I've only met her a few times, but the more time I spend with her, the more I like her. She's good for Adeline. She's outgoing and loud and not at all concerned about what others think.

Josie winks at her. "Right back at you, babe."

Brayden pulls out a stool and scans the papers laid out on the counter. "What are you guys doing?"

Adeline scoops them up quickly, shuffling them together. "Nothing."

A hint of unease seeps into my veins. "Why are you acting weird?"

"I'm not acting weird. You're acting weird."

I cough out a laugh. "Okay." I study her again quickly, then the girls to her left who are both doing a terrible job hiding their smiles. "Bray and I were going to grab dinner. You want to come?"

Savannah and Josie shake their heads. "No can do."

"Sure we can," Adeline says.

"No, I need these answers by tonight so we can enter them," Savannah says, snatching the papers from her. "And we still have"— she riffles through them, her long red hair falling forward—"ten pages to get through."

Adeline groans. "Why do you need seven thousand questions to set me up on a date?"

My stomach bottoms out. *A what, now?*

Brayden's the one who asks the question, though. "A date?"

Josie's eyes flick my way, and then she grins at her big brother. "Yup, Adeline is the next girl for our New Romantics campaign."

"The what?" I frown at Adeline, who refuses to meet my eye.

"It's the column I write for *Jolie*," Savannah tells me.

"You know, the magazine your mother runs," Bray deadpans.

I glare at him. "I'm aware. I just—"

How do I diplomatically explain that I don't read my mother's magazine because while I am extremely proud of her, she's always popping in with editor's columns, and I've learned far too much about my parents' sex life that way.

I fight a shudder and focus instead on the questionnaire Adeline is holding. "So what's the role?"

"The point of the column," Josie explains, "is to follow our leading lady, *Adeline*, on dates until she meets *the one*. Then Savannah will tell the love story all the way through a happily ever after."

Lungs seizing up, I blink at Adeline. "And you signed up for this?"

For maybe the first time since I walked into the kitchen, her dark eyes land on mine. "Yeah, I'm not getting any younger." It's a quiet admission, but a pointed one. Like she wants me to accept this without question. Like she's telling me it's none of my business.

I might have an aneurysm.

I hold her gaze, trying to figure out what this is about, but Savannah claps once, stealing her attention. "Let's get these questions answered. You really don't want to say four or five times a week? Camden works me over at least that many times a *day*."

Bray scowls. "What kind of questions are these?"

I grind my teeth hard, grasping for all the control I possess.

"Important ones," Josie says. "Sex is an important component of any relationship, and though our little Addie is quite virginal, we don't want her to stay that way forever."

"I'm not a virgin," Adeline grits out.

"Christ," I mutter, clutching the back of my neck. I'm going to throw up. "Can I talk to you alone?" I ask her.

"No," all three of the women say at the same time.

"Come on." Brayden grasps my arm. "We're going to grab dinner. Girls, have a great time. Jose, I'll see you at Mom and Dad's tomorrow?"

She blows him a kiss. "Wouldn't miss it."

"Coach," Bray says with a dip of his head. "This is cool. Good luck."

Adeline's eyes light up. "Thanks, Bray."

My best friend drags me out of the kitchen.

The second we step out into the fresh air and the door shuts behind us, I turn on him. "What the fuck was that?"

"What the fuck was what?" he parrots, brow arched.

"You just told Adeline that you think what she's doing is a good idea. It's an awful idea."

Jaw working, he gives me a pointed look. "You can't be with her. What about that don't you understand? She's your coach and *you're married*. It doesn't get more off limits than that."

I can barely catch my breath. I'm too angry. And so damn scared. Because it's happening again. I'm going to lose her if I don't stop this. I *can't* lose her.

CHAPTER 21

Addie

"JJ SEEMED PISSED," Josie says.

"More like stressed," Savannah muses, sliding a wineglass her way.

I grab the one she pushes in front of me and take a sip, buying myself time to think. He was surprised, yes. And overprotective. But that's JJ I don't think of him as a brother. That'd be gross. But to a degree, that's how he's always treated me. Like a little sister he has to watch out for.

I set my glass down on the counter and grab the questionnaire. I have no interest in discussing JJ or his feelings, so I might as well get to it. "Where do you see yourself in five years?" I say aloud.

"Head coach of the Boston Bolts, of course," Josie says with a smirk.

Exhaling loudly, I shake my head. "A female head coach in the NHL? Even my family isn't that open-minded."

And it's not what I want. I like being a goalie coach. In my current position, I still have the freedom to coach the way I want. To get on the ice with the guys and run drills. A head coach has to oversee practice, control the staff, and do all sorts of other bureaucratic bullshit that I don't have the stomach for.

"Okay, then where do you see yourself?" Savannah asks.

My mind betrays me, and it makes my heart twist. Because my

instinct is to say that I'll be playing hockey. Running drills with the guys has been good for the team, but it's also wreaking havoc on me mentally. Making it difficult not to doubt the decision I made when I left the PWHL.

While keeping up with them during practice is one thing, playing in an actual NHL game would be another. I doubt I could cut it. Which is why I'm coaching.

"Still coaching. Hopefully not living here." I look up at the ceiling and huff.

"Not loving living with six kids?" Josie asks.

"They're fine," I admit, a little smile playing on my lips. "But I never wanted kids and I definitely didn't expect to be living with six of them at my age."

"You don't want kids?" Savannah asks, her brow furrowed in surprise. "You're so good with Avery and your nephews."

"Don't get me wrong, I love them all. But—" I sigh. It's hard not to feel selfish or like there is something wrong with me when this topic comes up. So many people can't fathom a world in which a woman wouldn't want to procreate. But Savannah and Josie aren't like that, so I go with the truth. "I've just never had the itch. You know how some kids walk around with dolls mothering them?"

Both of my friends nod.

"I carried around a hockey stick."

Josie snorts. "Yeah, you did."

Savannah hums as she swigs her wine. Then she sets it down and leans forward. "There's no right or wrong way to live your life. If you don't want kids, you don't want kids. So no single dads, I'm guessing? You should probably put that on the form."

I bite on my lip. Probably. Because there's only one single dad I'd ever risk falling for, and I'm doing this precisely so I won't.

And Avery will still be in my life no matter what. I don't have to be a mother to care about the children in my life. There are plenty of them around.

This is the right decision.

No single dads, I write in big letters at the top of the form. "There." I underline it for emphasis.

"Okay, next question," Josie sings.

It takes us hours to get through the questionnaire. Afterward, Savannah promises that she'll be in touch regarding it next week. First she'll write an article that will introduce me to her readers, so I'll need to come in for a photoshoot.

Looks like I need to talk to Gavin soon. He is my boss, and I don't want to bring any negative press to the Bolts organization, but I can't imagine he'll give me too much shit. Honestly, I think my family will get a kick out of this.

Savannah plans to put together a list of potential dates and promises I can have input. Josie was super excited. She says this is like reality television tinder. I'm not sure how she made that leap but I'm trying not to freak out at the thought of the public being all up in my business.

I may not be a virgin, but I haven't actually ever dated.

Which is…well, slightly pathetic.

But being a female hockey player, and Beckett Langfield's little girl, is beyond intimidating. And that's before my uncles are factored in.

Men don't even go after me in hopes of meeting my family. The moment they find out I play hockey, the conversation dies.

Though now that I'm coaching instead, maybe that will change.

At least in this scenario, the men Savannah sets me up with will know who I am and what I do before I have to come face to face with them. That means I'll only go out with men who are genuinely interested.

In theory.

Head tipped back, I take in the dazzling stars and wonder if I'll ever be able to do it again without thinking of JJ.

Him and his parents' damn song.

When Winnie and Vivi came home with the kids half an hour ago and the chaos returned, I retreated to the roof. Hope took her girls to her parents' place for the weekend, so we're down to three children, but the twins are louder than all four girls combined, so it's not a whole lot quieter.

The door opens, startling me, and I hold my breath, wrapping the soft blanket tighter around my body. When JJ comes into view, I have to bite back a groan. Of all the people I'm hiding from, he's number one on that list.

"There you are," he says.

"Yup, it's almost like I want to be alone," I mutter.

Ignoring the comment, he saunters my way, eyeing the bottle of wine and the glass on the table.

That's another thing I won't feel bad about. I'm a single twenty-six-year-old woman. I can have a glass—or bottle—of wine if I want.

"Wasn't sure if the girls were still here," he says as he sits beside me.

"Oh, so you came up to hang with Savannah and Josie?"

His blue eyes remain locked on mine for a beat too long, like he's trying to figure out where the attitude is coming from.

But I'm past the point of being diplomatic.

"No, I wanted to talk to you, actually."

"Avery already asleep?"

With a hum, he nods. "She could barely keep her eyes open through her bath. She wanted to say good night to you, but I told her you were busy."

"I'm never too busy for Aves."

"You sure? It seems like you've been running in the opposite direction when she and I are around."

"I have not." I take offense to the idea that I'd want to take any space from her.

He arches a brow. "So you haven't been avoiding me since Avery begged us to sleep with her?"

"No, JJ, I've been avoiding you since—" I snap my mouth shut. I can't even put into words what happened between us, and summing it up to Avery begging us to sleep together is so infuriatingly wrong.

"Since I held your hand? Is that what this is about? Is that why you've now agreed to be the poster child for dating?"

My body ignites with annoyance. "Jesus, you really are full of yourself."

He pulls on his dark hair, clearly as aggravated as I am. "No, what I am is confused. We had a moment, Adeline, and rather than discussing it, rather than talking about where we go from here, you go off and become *Boston's Bachelorette*." He says the last few words with a scowl, like it disgusts him.

"I'm not doing this with you." I snatch the bottle of wine off the table. Then because I can't help myself, I go on. "Before Avery was born, you dated any woman you wanted. I had to sit on the sidelines and watch as you slept with one puck bunny after another, and then you *married* one of them. I never so much as went on a single date, and you damn well know why." Tears sting my nose, but I inhale deeply. I will not cry. "I'm sorry if your life with Tabitha didn't pan out like you hoped, but don't I deserve to find someone too? Or am I just supposed to sit here and watch from the sidelines again? I already have to do that as your coach. Don't ask me to do that in any other facet of my life."

JJ opens his mouth and then slams it shut. Then with a simple nod, he breaks my heart. "Right. Of course. I'm sorry."

Eyes falling closed, I let out a quick laugh. "You always are."

CHAPTER 22

JJ

Twenty-One Years Old

Salt Lake City Winter Olympics

"I APPRECIATE you letting me tag along," I say to Beckett as we make our way through the crowd.

I have a game tomorrow, but I couldn't miss opening ceremonies. I need to see Adeline. It's been months since I laid eyes on her in person. Between her training and the Bolts' schedule, we're never in the same place at the same time.

"She'll be thrilled to see you." He wraps an arm around my shoulders and jostles me around a little. "Besides, you're family. You're always invited."

"Tell me there's a bar near our meetup spot," Finn says, bouncing as he walks, peering over the heads around us.

"Addie probably won't drink. But I say let's go wherever she wants," Winnie says.

"And we aren't taking your sisters to a bar," Liv tells Finn, giving him the mom look.

The twins, who are seventeen, don't bother chiming in. They're too busy documenting their every move on social media, even after Beckett has told them to put their phones away at least twenty times.

Finn nudges me. "Want to go find a bar while they find Addie?"

I fight back a grimace. "Uh. No. I actually want to see your sister."

He rolls his eyes. "Come on, there are female athletes everywhere. When they find out that you play for the Bolts and I play for the Revs, they'll be lining up."

Winnie smacks him. "One: that is sexist. And two: you're an idiot. JJ only cares about one female athlete."

I shrug. "She's not wrong."

"Fine. But once we find her, you are grabbing a drink with me."

I'm not, but I won't waste my breath arguing with him.

My pulse goes haywire every time I even think about wrapping my arms around Adeline again. I don't know what to expect. Has she been as out of her mind as I have the last few months? Probably not. Her focus has been 100 percent on these games. Like mine should have been on my own. It's my first goddamn season in the NHL, and the only thing I can think about is when I'll see Adeline again.

"There she is," Beckett says, pure affection and excitement in his voice.

I whip around and immediately zero in on my best friend's big smile. Those brown eyes of hers look straight at me, shimmering. Then she's launching herself into my arms.

"Ah. You made it," she squeals.

I spin her around, then set her on her feet and pull back so I can look at her again. "Of course I did. I wouldn't be anywhere else."

"I'm here too, ya know," Finn grumbles. "Missing a preseason game for this. Do I get a big hug too?"

Laughing, she makes the rounds, hugging her family. As she steps to one side, sidling up to a guy I don't recognize, my stomach sinks.

She shakes her head, still beaming, and turns to the guy. "Ah, sorry. This is Ryan Hobbs, he's the goalie coach for Team USA. Ryan, this is my family."

Beckett is the first to step up and shake his hand. Ryan is the same height as Beckett—*so not as tall as me*—and he's got dirty blond hair tied back in a ponytail. He looks like he's in his late twenties, but it's hard to tell since he's in the Team USA sweats, which make everyone seem younger than they really are. But he's muscular, and he's wearing a perma-smile. One he keeps directing at Adeline.

"His family couldn't make it for the ceremony, so I told him he could join us for dinner. You guys don't mind, right?" Adeline peers around the group, only stopping when she gets to me.

Finn nudges me. "How 'bout that drink?"

"Of course he can," Liv says. "I'd love to hear all about your time working as a coach for the Olympic team."

Ryan answers a few of her questions as the group follows Beckett.

Lagging behind a little, I snag Adeline's hand. "Hey."

"Hi," she says with a big smile. "God, it's so good to see you."

"You too." I let out a breath. "I was hoping we'd have a little time by ourselves to catch up. Maybe skip out after dinner?"

She glances at Ryan, her teeth sinking into her lip. "Strict curfew," she mumbles. "I've only got an hour."

"Fuck," I mutter.

She winces, her dark eyes sympathetic. "I'm sorry. You traveled all this way, and all I have is a free hour."

"Worth it." I lock eyes with her, hoping she can see in them that I'd travel anywhere for her. "I was just hoping we could talk."

She nods. "Of course. You can tell me anything."

I'd thought of this conversation hundreds of times over the last few months. Every time it ended with her and I together. There definitely wasn't another man in the picture, that's for damn sure.

I look her coach up and down. "Alone."

Lips folding in on themselves, she sighs. "Oh."

"Is there—" My gut twists, but I force myself to ask. "Is there something going on between you two?"

She lets out an uncomfortable laugh. "What? No. He's my coach."

Ryan glances back, and when he sees she's looking his way, he winks.

Immediately, a flush works its way up her cheeks. Fuck. Shit. *No.*

"Right," I grit out. "And that would be totally inappropriate."

Her brow creases. "Yeah, I'm aware. Stop being weird."

"I just want five minutes alone with you. Can we do that? Ditch everyone for a few?"

I sound pathetic begging like this, but I don't care.

"Sure. How about we sneak off for a few after we order?" She squeezes my hand like she's trying to settle my nerves, like she can sense my internal freak-out.

I don't even care, because for five fucking seconds with her hand in mine, I relax.

Forty-five minutes later, Adeline and Ryan are still regaling us with stories of training, discussing the upcoming games, and sharing inside jokes they've amassed during their months together.

And I lose my shit.

Desperate for fresh air and concerned that if I stay here any longer, I'll launch myself across the table and strangle him, I excuse myself, holding up my phone, pretending I'm getting a call.

I'm pacing back and forth, trying not to pull my hair out when the door opens and Adeline appears.

"What are you doing? Is everything okay?"

Pulling up short, I frown. "Huh?"

"Your phone call? Is it your mom? Is that what you wanted to talk to me about?"

"What?" I'm so off-kilter after tonight that I can't make heads or tails of the conversation.

When she steps up and presses her hand to my racing heart, she does me no favors, but like hell will I back away.

"JJ, it's me. You can tell me anything. What's going on?"

"I just wanted to see you," I admit, my voice rough.

Her eyes warm as her lips curl up. "Well, hi."

I blow out a breath, shoving my hands into my pockets. "Hi."

"What's going on?"

I shake my head. Where do I even start?

"Fine, I'll go first," she says, still smiling. "I'm scared that I'm going to miss every shot and cost our team the win. I'm insanely excited to see you. *And* you're kind of freaking me out."

That lightens the weight pressing on my chest a little. "We both know you aren't scared, Adeline."

She grins. "You're correct. Now you go. Like I said, you're freaking me out."

Licking my lips, I take a step closer. The ground beneath us is cobblestone, and the light coming from the old kerosene streetlamp makes Adeline's brown eyes twinkle as she assesses me.

I press my hand to her cheek, stroking her warm skin gently with my thumb. "I haven't gone a day without thinking about you. I'm crazy jealous of that Ryan guy because he's gotten all this time with you. And if I don't find out what your lips feel like right the fuck now, I'm going to lose my goddamn mind."

Adeline's smile falls and her eyes rove over my face. "What?"

I inch closer. So close her breath mingles with mine. "Guess the lie, Angles."

"Um—" Her voice wobbles and I swear she stops breathing.

My heart races. Does she want this as much as I do? Has she wondered what would happen if we threw caution to the wind? Does she hate the air between us, and the distance too?

"Maybe I should just show you," I murmur, my mouth ghosting over hers.

"Addie, we gotta go."

Adeline jumps back, her eyes going wide. "Oh, shit." She glances at Ryan, who's standing just outside the restaurant. "Can you, um, just give me one minute?"

I don't look away from her. Every muscle in my body is rigid. Why the fuck didn't I just kiss her the moment she walked outside?

"Hey," she says, slightly breathless. "Can we—can we talk about this when the Olympics are over?"

I nod, my mouth dry.

She throws her arms around my neck and squeezes me tight. "Mine were all true too," she whispers. "Wish me luck."

I hold her close, inhaling her scent. "You don't need luck, Angles. You're going to kick ass." I press a kiss to her shoulder and then let her go. When I turn around, Beckett is standing a few feet away, attention locked on us.

"Run in and say goodbye to your mom."

Adeline takes a step forward, then pauses and glances back at me.

With one final smile, she steps into the restaurant with Ryan on her heels.

Beckett doesn't move. "It's hard being away from her," he says.

I'm not sure if he's talking about how I feel or how he feels, but I nod anyway. "Yeah."

"Did you know I met Liv before she met Adeline's biological father?"

Frowning, I study him. He's watching me just as closely, this serious look on his face, like he's about to impart wisdom.

With a sharp inhale, I shake my head. "I didn't know that."

"Only a few seconds before, really. We got on the elevator and struck up a conversation. Drake got on a floor or two up." Beckett shakes his head. "My point is, I saw her first. I was immediately intrigued by her, yet he asked her out before I got the chance. Seconds, JJ. That's all it took. I hesitated for mere seconds, and I lost a decade with the woman who makes my life worth living."

I slip my hands into my pocket, a weight tugging at my gut. "Why are you telling me this?"

"Time isn't guaranteed. I'd hate to see you standing on the outside like I was while Adeline finds her forever with someone else. All because you waited a few seconds—*or years*—too long to speak up."

A strangled chuckle works its way out of me. "And you'd be okay with me—" I duck my head, my face going hot. "With me saying something?"

Beckett wraps an arm around me and guides me toward the restaurant. "Son, nothing would make me happier."

CHAPTER 23

JJ

"I DON'T CARE what you have to do. I want this done by the end of the month."

Annoyed, I hit the End button on my cell. It's not nearly as satisfying as slamming down a phone, but it's something. At least I'm headed to work out next.

We've made it through two weeks of preseason games and we're set for our season opener in five days. Though there's no practice on the schedule today, I never take a day off in season.

Working out is as important for me mentally as it is physically, and right now my mental state is a fucking disaster.

When I pull into the garage beneath the arena and spot my dad's car, I frown. What's he doing here?

Gavin's car is here too, which isn't all that strange, but so is Beckett's. Hell, I think all of Addie's uncles are here.

What are all the old guys doing at the arena?

My phone lights up with a text as I shift into park.

Finn: I think it's awesome.

He thinks it's awesome?

His message is in response to the one I sent just before leaving the house. The one that read *Addie is going on her first date tonight with those weirdos from the magazine thing*.

Annoyed again, I type out a quick reply.

> Me: What do you mean it's awesome? They could be complete freaks.

> Bray: First of all, Josie has worked really hard to vet these guys. Savannah too. So let's give her best friends a little credit.

> Bray: Second, it's none of your goddamn business.

> Finn: Sorry, JJ I'm with Bray on this one.

I scowl. Seriously? Has everyone lost their goddamn minds?

> Theo: Catch me up to speed. What dating app is she using? I can check out the matches if ya want.

> Me: It's not a dating app. It's some magazine article that Savannah is writing for Jolie. They had her fill out this ridiculously long questionnaire, and they're going to set her up on dates, then document them all in the magazine over the next few months.

> Theo: Oh, that sounds pretty cool. Go, Addie.

Growling, I slam the back of my head against the seat. What the fuck is wrong with my friends?

I turn off my phone, irritated by their nonchalance, and head for the door. Inside, the familiar sound of sticks clacking against the ice is like a siren's song, calling me to the rink rather than the gym.

When the group of old guys comes into view, I chuckle. The whole lot is on the ice, playing their version of beer league hockey.

Brooks is in one goal, and my Uncle Hayden is in the other.

Gavin, Beckett, and Aiden are on one team, and Uncle Garreth, Uncle Cash, and my father are on the other.

The Langfields versus the James/Hanson crew. There was a time when my dad and uncle were arch enemies. But then my mom married my dad, and by some miracle, the guys figured their shit out, and now they're best friends.

Every man on the ice is over the age of fifty. Hell, most of them are in their sixties. Yet they're skating around like guys half their age.

When my dad pushes Cash into the net, knocking Brooks over in the process and scoring, Beckett grouses, "That was a cheap shot."

A bark of a laugh bursts out of me. They should take all the cheap shots they can get when they're up against Brooks fucking Langfield. I'm actually pretty impressed with my dad's moves.

The sound of my laughter echoes in the empty arena, and all heads snap my way.

"JJ," my dad calls.

The group of them skate toward the bench, and I wander that way too. By the time I get there, they're pulling their helmets off.

"I didn't know you guys still did this." When I was a kid, my dad would meet up with the guys, but I guess I stopped paying attention somewhere along the way.

He never stopped taking me out on the ice. It's where he told me my mom had cancer. It's where he brought me to share that she was in remission. It's where I told him about Avery and where the two of us had our biggest blowout. The day I informed him that I was getting married. And it's where he helped me figure out how my life was going to work after I became a father.

Honestly, I could really use a shift on the ice with him right about now. I could use his input about what the hell happens next. I know what I want. Fuck, I don't remember a time in my life when I haven't wanted this—*her*—but she's right. It's not fair of me to ask her to pause her life while I figure out my own.

And in our current situations, yeah, we can't be together.

She's barely spoken to me since she gave me that hard truth on the roof. While we're at the arena, she keeps things professional; she doesn't ice me out. But she hasn't joined us for a single family dinner since that night. She's always conveniently busy with Savannah or Josie. I'm pretty sure she's even been sleeping at Savannah's.

But she makes sure to say good night to my girl every evening. She texts, letting me know she's ready for Avery's call, and the two of them talk on the phone while I strain to listen to her side of the conversation. I'm on the outside, but I'm nothing but grateful, because if I can't have Adeline in the way I want her, at least my daughter can have her in the way she needs her.

But Adeline has always been good at showing up for those who need her, me included.

"Thirty years and counting," Gavin says with a laugh. "It's good for these old guys."

He smacks Uncle Garreth on the back.

Garreth, who's quiet and a little broody most of the time, glares in response. "I'm two years older than you."

"And we"—Aiden points to himself, then Brooks—"definitely weren't playing with you thirty years ago."

"Jesus," Gavin mutters. "Everyone's so fucking sensitive."

"Ducking," Beckett grumbles.

"There's not a fucking child in a mile radius." My dad pins me with a look. "Please tell me you aren't using that stupid word now that you're living in the brownstone."

Beckett nudges him in the ribs, and he bends at the waist dramatically, groaning.

"What are you doing here?" Brooks asks me, ignoring their antics.

"Just working off some steam."

"Wanna join us?" Beckett asks.

Gavin glares at his older brother. "He's got a game tomorrow."

Taking a step back, I hold up my hands. "I'm not trying to play with you old men."

My dad laughs. "Why you working off steam? Something you want to talk about?"

I glance at Beckett, then each of his brothers, then huff. What the fuck do I have to lose? Brayden tells me I'm out of my mind. Finn thinks I'm being absurd. But there's no way Beckett isn't concerned about Adeline going on dates with a bunch of strange men.

I run my hands through my hair, grimacing. "I'm nervous about Adeline's date tonight."

Every single eye widens. Not one of them expected that. I guarantee it. Maybe I've danced around my feelings with my dad, and I all but told Beckett about them years ago, but the rest of these men haven't pushed me into admitting something I never could.

That Adeline Langfield has always been the only woman I want.

Even when I married someone else.

Admitting that to myself is a step in the right direction. For so long I was so goddamn mad at her that I refused to admit my marriage was a reaction to my anger.

Even if I've always sworn I did it for Avery. So I wouldn't have to split custody, so I could always be with my little girl.

That was a perk, sure, but I never would have married Tabitha if Adeline hadn't hurt me so deeply.

Fuck, I'm an idiot.

"Why are you nervous about it?" Dad is the first to risk asking the question.

My gaze goes to Beckett. "Because she's going out with a complete stranger. What if he's a serial killer?"

My dad laughs. "He's not a serial killer."

"No, he definitely isn't," Beckett says, eyes wary.

"So you're okay with this? And you," I look at Gavin, "You don't think it looks bad to have our coach traipsing around town with different men—"

"Watch it." Beckett's voice is cold, his tone sharp.

My face heats. "You know what I'm saying. I care about Adeline just as much as you do—"

He arches his brows. "Do you? Would you give up everything for that girl? Because I would. Don't play a game of chicken with me."

Frowning, my dad scrutinizes me, probably trying to figure out how I'm going to handle this.

That's a good question.

Eventually I let out a long breath, willing my anger to settle. Beckett doesn't deserve my wrath. Neither does Adeline. I do. I'm the idiot who fucked up. "I just want to know she's safe," I say, not bothering to hide the desperation in my voice.

"Addie's got a good head on her shoulders." Aiden dips his chin. "She'll be good."

"And I already looked into every man on the list," Beckett adds, throwing me a bone.

Dad scowls. "You what?"

"Like you wouldn't do anything to keep Chloe from getting hurt," he throws back.

Lips tugged down thoughtfully, my dad nods. "You're right."

"Anyway," Beckett says, eyeing me again. "Everyone on the list seems legit. No problematic men."

"Okay, but what if you missed something?" I point out.

"What would you like us to do?" Brooks asks, always the calmest man in the room.

I throw my arms out wide. "I don't know. Maybe we should follow her? Just be nearby in case something goes wrong?"

Uncle Hayden laughs, then lets out an *oof* when my dad hits him in the stomach.

"No, maybe he's onto something," Beckett muses, scratching at his jaw. "What would it hurt if we all went out to dinner and just happened to be in the same restaurant? If anything goes wrong—"

"Which it won't," my father says, looking from Beckett to me. "This is your mother's magazine. She'd never risk Addie's safety. She loves her like her own."

"Still," I grumble, squeezing my hands into fists.

Beckett nods. "Yeah, still."

Gavin laughs. He's much more relaxed when he's hanging out with his brothers than when he's playing the role of coach. "You're just agreeing with him because you think it'll let you work around Liv's no meddling in your children's dating lives rule. You realize we see right through you, right?"

Beckett shrugs, unbothered. "I'm just watching out for my little girl."

"Yeah, he's just watching out for his little girl," I agree.

"So what time's dinner?" Uncle Garreth asks.

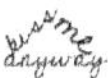

The stress has already begun to fade when I start my workout, and by the time I'm done, I feel lighter than I have in days. This will be good. I can watch out for Adeline, and once all my bullshit is settled, I'll finally make my move.

When the door to the gym opens and Beckett strolls in, I smile, wiping sweat from my forehead. "Enjoy your game?"

"Yeah, we beat your family, so I'm feeling better about myself."

I laugh. "You did have two professional hockey players on your team, so I wouldn't get too excited."

He lifts both shoulders, scanning the facility. When he looks at me again, his expression is stony. "Listen, I'm only going to say this once and then I'll drop it."

My insides twist into knots, but I nod and give him my full attention.

"Five years ago, I explained what to do when it came to Adeline. I told you what regret feels like. Watching the person I wanted most start a family with someone else? I wouldn't wish it on my worst enemy. And JJ, you did that to my daughter." He lets those words hang between us, and all the lightness I'd found only moments ago is gone in an instant. I did do that to Adeline. And I can't even imagine what it must have felt like for her. Probably a little like I'm feeling now. Beckett steps closer. "So be very sure that your concern is real and not just jealousy. Because Adeline deserves to be loved. Maybe it won't be this guy, but it will be someone, and you're going to have to get on board with that."

My heart thrashes wildly at the thought of anyone else with her. At the idea that any other man could love her the way I could. But somehow I remain completely calm as I say, "I just want her to be safe."

Beckett nods. "Then we're good."

CHAPTER 24

Addie

Twenty-One Years Old

Salt Lake City, Utah, Olympics

JJ: Not that you need it, but good luck today.

Me: Thank you again for coming yesterday. It meant a lot to me.

JJ: You mean a lot to me. We'll talk soon. Go focus.

JJ: Holy shit, Addie Angles! A goddamn shutout!

Me: Ahhh! It was wild!

JJ: Call me when you can.

> Me: Tried calling but it went to voicemail. Heading to bed.

> JJ: Sorry, I forgot to charge my phone. Game tonight, but I'll call you after.

> Me: Ah, sorry I missed your call. Was super loud in the Olympic village. Tomorrow?

> JJ: Sorry I was short on the phone. I'm irritated. Not at you. At this situation. I miss you. I'm proud of you. And I hate that I'm not there to watch you kicking ass. Adeline, your photo is everywhere! There are grumbles in locker rooms. Two fucking shutouts during the Olympic games? You are incredible and I'm a dick.

> Me: you're not a dick. I'll be home in a week. Is it bad that I can't wait? I want to enjoy this. I've been working toward it for my whole life, and now…I feel like…

> JJ: I know. But I'm not going anywhere. Promise. Enjoy this.

"TIME TO GO." My roommate's voice sounds in one ear as the familiar robotic voice telling me to leave a message plays in the other.

Shit. Yet another day without talking to JJ. These two weeks should be the most joyful time in my life, yet I'm nothing more than a pathetic girl wondering if the boy she likes really likes her.

It's disturbing.

But it's JJ.

And two weeks ago, he almost kissed me.

It was the first time he's ever truly surprised me. I'd given up hoping that one day he would see me the way I see him. That one day he would want me.

And I'm so damn nervous that he only did it because he was jealous. That it was an irrational reaction to the idea that Ryan—my freaking coach—had any interest in me.

He should know by now that men don't see me like that.

JJ friend-zoned me years ago, and in all these years, no one else has interested me.

But hockey has always interested me. And right now, I'm about to head into the biggest game of my career—the final game in the Olympics. If we win this, we win the gold medal.

I owe it to my teammates to focus.

I owe it to myself too.

At the sound of the beep, I sigh. "Hey, it's me. Headed to the game. Just wanted to say hi and hear your voice. But, um, hopefully I'll talk to you after. Tag, you're it."

With that, I power down my phone. It's time to win a medal.

Sometimes, if we're lucky, goalies have this moment when we can sense what'll happen next. I've played enough to recognize when this sense overtakes me, so when the Russian center is on a breakaway, I lean into the instinct. By every indication, she's about to take a slap shot. Instead, she flips the puck with her stick, tossing it in the air, with the intent to send it toward the net, past my shoulder. I shouldn't have enough time to correct, and if I hadn't anticipated it, I wouldn't.

But I've been playing against Aiden Langfield all my life, and that's a move right out of his playbook.

So while it's not a pretty stop, I fling my body upward like a damn starfish. The puck hits my chest, and as it bounces back, the buzzer sounds.

And we win the fucking gold medal.

Immediately, my teammates are on me, hugging and cheering and laughing.

We win, 2-0. Another freaking shutout.

On the way to the locker rooms, a microphone is shoved in front of my face.

"Addie Langfield," the reporter says, "you just pulled off quite the hat trick."

I give him a polite smile. "Not quite what a hat trick means, and it was a team effort."

"Right, but no goalie in Olympic history has ever completed three shutouts."

A burst of pride shoots through me. It's not new information. There were murmurs about it going into the game. Still, I tried to ignore it. My mission was to win today. Not allowing a single goal is more than a freaking cherry on top.

"I'm very proud to be part of Team USA."

"What's next for you? Word on the street is that Las Vegas has an open goalie position."

I frown. "The Las Vegas Lions?"

He lets out a deep laugh. "No, not the PWHL. The Las Vegas Vices. Can you confirm whether you'll be a free agent after this?"

I shake my head. The question is ridiculous. Only one woman has ever played goaltender in the NHL, and she lasted a single game.

"I'll be returning to college."

"But—"

"Adeline," a familiar voice calls.

A thrill shoots up my spine. There's only person who calls me Adeline, so when he shouts my name again, my heart flips over on itself. I push past the reporter, and when I spot JJ rushing my way, it all hits me.

This moment, everything I've worked for, everything I've dreamed of, didn't feel nearly as satisfying as it should. Until now. Until the boy who worked by my side helping me chase this goal all along appears.

"What are you doing here?" I say as he approaches, big smile spread across that handsome face, dimple popping, and blue eyes blazing with a wild heat in them.

He wraps me up in a hug, squeezing me tight, and I inhale the familiar scent of him. "You won the gold medal, Adeline. Where the fuck else would I be?"

Laughing, I push back so I can see him properly. He's wearing a Team USA jersey, a team USA hat, and the biggest smile.

"I see someone went shopping today."

Scoffing, he holds out his arms and turns in a circle. When I see *Langfield* on his back, my heart stutters. "I had this made. Though after today, I have a feeling everyone is going to want a Langfield Team USA jersey."

I roll my eyes, even as excitement floods me. "Right."

With a huge smile on his face, he shakes his head. "You still don't get it. Adeline. The whole country isn't just proud of you, they're in awe. Just wait. You're the talk of Salt Lake."

I bite my lip, my face, which has only begun cooling after the game, heating. "I can't believe you're here. Aren't you supposed to be playing tonight?"

His expression turns sheepish. "Sidney's playing."

I smack him and gasp. "JJ."

Chuckling, he pulls me back into his chest. "Like there was a shot in hell I'd miss this." He peers down at me and cups my jaw. "I've been waiting too damn long to do this. Can I finally kiss you, baby?"

"I'm a sweaty mess," I mumble, my insides quaking more than they have during a single Olympic game.

He shrugs. "Kiss me anyway."

"Everyone's watching."

He grins. "Kiss me anyway."

My heart is lodged in my throat, making it hard to breathe. "This is going to change everything."

JJ ghosts his mouth against mine. "Kiss. Me. Anyway."

So I do. I wrap my arms around him and press my lips to his, and finally, after what feels like a lifetime of waiting. I kiss JJ Hanson.

It's not like fireworks. Those would be shocking and loud. Something for others, a show. This is slow. JJ takes his time. It's gentle, not exactly tentative because I don't think the man has a tentative bone in his body, but it's reverent. And when I get greedy and slip my tongue into his mouth, he growls and buries his hand in my hair, and then he ravages me. Gone is the softness and in its place is this fire. It consumes me. It's like he threw gasoline on top the kindling that had been burning for years beneath the surface, and now an inferno has overtaken me. My heart races as I wrap my arms around him, pulling him closer. "I want," I mumble, breathless. "I need."

His blue eyes are fathomless as he pulls my mouth to his again. "I need to get you alone."

"Oh my god, I'm gonna be sick," Finn groans from somewhere off to the side.

I pull back from JJ, eyes wide. We're surrounded by reporters, my family, and about a hundred thousand spectators. Fuck.

JJ doesn't spare anyone else a glance. His focus remains on me. Cautious. Waiting. Like he expects me to push him away. Or disappear right in front of his eyes. Silly man. I've been waiting my entire life for him to look at me this way. There isn't a chance I'm going to let him go. Though I do need to do something. "I need to shower," I say with a smile.

JJ groans, his hands fisting my jersey. "Fine. Shower. Then you're mine."

If only he realized that I always have been.

"So this is your room," I mumble as he leads me into the fancy suite.

"Yup."

I doubt JJ has felt awkward a day in his life, so as he removes layer after layer, tossing his hat, gloves, scarf, and jacket onto a nearby chair, he does it like a fucking model. Smoldering at me the entire time.

I, on the other hand, take an awkward step back and trip over my own two feet, landing on the couch, still in full winter clothes.

A smirk plays on his lips. "You okay there?"

Cheeks burning, I roll my eyes. "Yeah. Obviously I meant to do that. I'm tired." I'm rambling, but I can't stop as nerves sweep through me. "I just won an Olympic medal and dealt with my parents, not so subtly trying to avoid the topic that is now trending online—*you kissing me*—while we had, like, a ten-course meal."

He chuckles like he finds me endearing. It's infuriating. "I thought dinner would never end."

"*Seriously.*"

He meanders my way, and with every step closer, my insides burn hotter.

"What—um, what are you doing?" I ask.

"I'm going to take your jacket." Chuckling, he holds out a hand.

He waits like that while I not so sexily pull off my many layers. I toss my jacket and all my warm gear his way. With a content hum, he takes it over to the table, folding it nicely and setting it on top. Then he turns around, crosses his arms over his very inviting chest, and leans against the table.

"What are you doing now?" I ask.

"Giving you a minute to get used to me."

"I'm used to you," I scoff. "I'm, like, *so* used to you."

"Oh yeah?" Eyes dancing, he takes a step my way. "So you won't freak out if I do this?"

"Do what?" I panic as he gets closer.

He stops halfway across the room, brows raised. "Sit next to you?"

"Oh, yeah," I breathe, patting the spot beside me like he's a dog. "Make yourself comfortable."

The cushion dips under his weight as he settles beside me. When he turns my way, my spine snaps straight.

"Adeline, breathe," he says softly. "Nothing has to happen tonight."

I whimper. "I don't know why I'm being so weird. It's just—"

Nodding, he pushes my hair behind my ear. "Hey," he says, his tone soothing. "It's a lot. I know. But it's also just us, you and me. Always."

"Yeah, just you and me," I repeat, willing my muscles to relax.

He smiles at me, leaning in close. "Can I kiss you again?"

My lungs constrict, making my response hoarse. "Um, yeah?"

An uneasy laugh passes his lips. "Maybe we should try something different."

"I've never tried anything, so whatever it is it will be different for me," I ramble.

Brows tugged together, he pulls back and searches my face. "Wait… never?"

Head lowered, I shake it.

He rumbles something in French, the sexy sound lighting up my nerve endings.

"What did you just say?"

"I said…" He presses his lips gently against my neck, sending shivers through my body. "This is going to be so much fun."

"I don't think that's what you said," I murmur.

He chuckles. "Then you should probably learn French, mon trésor." He nips and sucks at my neck gently.

Electricity races through me, pulling a moan from deep inside my chest and making my nipples stand at attention. "This doesn't feel real," I whisper.

"Two truths and a lie," he coaxes, never taking his mouth off my body. "I can't tell you how many times I've wondered what it would be like to have you like this. It might be your first time but this is the first time it's ever mattered for me. And I'm scared that tomorrow, you'll change your mind."

None of them are lies, but the seriousness in his tone keeps me from calling him on it. Shifting so I can look at him, I place my hand against his cheek.

Eye to eye like this, I realize he's just as nervous as I am. He's just better at hiding it.

"You were my first crush," I tell him. "I'll probably be awkward all night. And there's nothing you could do to make me not want you."

He huffs. "Dammit, your first crush was Dominic Hasek, wasn't it?"

I laugh at the mention of the champion goalie. "So was yours."

He shakes his head. "Nah, Brooks has him beat in my book."

A familiar sense of ease seeps in. This is us. JJ and me. Always.

"I can't believe you really put my name on a jersey and wore it tonight."

He scowls. "You've done it for me plenty of times. Why wouldn't I want to have my favorite player's name on my back?"

I roll my eyes, but internally, I'm swooning. "*JJ.*"

"Yeah?"

"Will you kiss me again?"

His entire face lights up. "I thought you would never ask."

He eases me into the kiss, coaxing me with soft lips and a curious tongue. My body grows warmer the longer we play, and when his hand drifts to the hem of my shirt, I don't wait for him to ask if it's okay, I beg him to touch me.

"Please, JJ, I need this. Need you."

He slips beneath my bra, and when he cups my breast, he lets out a groan that vibrates through me.

It's still not enough.

I pull off my shirt and straddle him, grinding against his lap. Lips tingling and blood heating, I beg him to take me to bed. He stands easily, guiding my legs around his waist without breaking the kiss. We drown in one another, forgoing breathing for just another moment of touching.

I can't get enough. Of him. Of this sensation. I've always enjoyed spending time with JJ. Playing hockey, practicing, working out, talking —they're my favorite things to do. Anything that involves him is on that list. But not a goddamn thing has ever compared to doing this with him.

When he settles me on the bed, placing his hand behind my head and easing me beneath him, I feel like the most cherished person in the entire world.

He whispers something else in French, the sound of the words on his lips making the warmth in my core build.

"This is better than every dream I've ever had," he says. "Adeline, I —" He sucks in a breath. "I love you."

Instantly, tears spring to my eyes. The words aren't caused by the heat of the moment. They're genuine. We may never have done this before, but we've built this friendship, this trust, and this love, for years. So I don't even think before responding. "I love you too. So much."

"We don't have to do anything else tonight, but—"

I shake my head. "I want to. I want to know what it feels like. With you. I want more of you than anyone else has ever had."

Hovering over me, he smiles, then presses another kiss to my lips. "You already have it, mon trésor. You have my heart. And you're the only one who ever will."

"Then show me." The words rasp out of me. "Make love to me, JJ. Make me yours."

He searches my face again. Like he's looking for evidence that I'll change my mind. But I won't. I want this. I want him. More than I've ever wanted anything.

Sitting back, he tugs his shirt over his head with one hand like one of the sexy characters from Aunt Hannah's books.

That thought makes me giggle.

JJ smirks down at me, his face cast in shadow. "What?"

I roll my lips to temper my laughter, but it's no use.

He looms closer and presses his finger into my side, where he knows I'm most ticklish.

"JJ." I squeal.

His laughter is throaty. "Tell me."

I suck in a breath and push him back. "Fine, I was thinking that the way you took your shirt off was like a move straight out of a romance novel."

He jolts back. "You read romance books?"

"No," I say, embarrassed.

"What kind of books, Adeline?" he says, his tone both knowing and teasing. A singsong of sorts.

I suck on my bottom lip and shake my head.

He pokes the spot that makes me squirm again. "Tell me."

I huff. "Fine. Sexy, slutty, steamy, delicious books."

His eyes dance. "And do you picture me when you read these books?"

"Oh my god," I groan, covering my face with both hands.

"You do, don't you?"

"I hate you."

He tugs at my wrist, and when I drop my hands, he kisses me. "No you don't." His words are soft against my lips. "Do you touch yourself while you read these books and think of me?"

A gust of air escapes me without my permission.

His pupils blow wide. "Fuck, I need to see that."

"What?" I squirm beneath him, shyness and need and confusion warring inside me.

He rocks back on his knees and smirks. "Come on, I'll play if you do?"

"Why don't we just play with each other?" I whine. The thought of touching myself in front of him sends a wave of mortification through me. By now, my whole body is probably beet red.

But he doesn't squirm. He doesn't blush. The man just slips off the bed and shoves his pants off. He pushes his boxers down a second later, and I lose my breath.

"Holy fuck," I mutter.

He eyes himself, then meets my gaze, a shyness in his expression I didn't expect. "Is this okay?"

"Um, that—" I point, searching for a term to describe the enormity of the extremity hanging from his body. "It's supposed to go in here?" I point between my legs.

He leans forward, lips twitching, and presses his thumb to my bottom lip. "Or here, or—"

"If you point to my ass, we're going to have a problem."

He chuckles. "We've got all the time in the world, Adeline."

His words send relief through me, and when he kisses me again, the sensation is joined with heat. I'm pretty sure he could get me to agree to anything.

"Can I take off your pants?" he mumbles against my lips.

I nod, a shiver rolling through me.

Without taking his mouth off mine, he pulls them down. I shimmy, helping him until they're at my ankles.

"Fuck." He groans as he teases the waistband of my underwear. "This is a big moment," he murmurs, slipping beneath the fabric.

Pulling back, he assesses me. "Are we rushing this? I don't want to rush this."

An exasperated groan surges from me. "JJ, I've waited years for you to touch me. If you stop, I will literally kill you."

He chuckles. "Okay, baby. No more stopping."

It's that baby that does me in. And when he tugs my panties down and settles his weight over me, I forget everything else. I forget about all the years I've longed for this. When I was on the sidelines, hoping he'd look my way. When we were friends sharing a pizza or teammates vying for the same coveted spot. When we were bed mates who wouldn't cross the pillowed line. All of that time slips away and the inevitability of us shifts into place.

He slides his hand between my legs, groaning like what he's discovering feels just as good for him as it does for me. Pressure builds inside me quickly, its power uncontrollable. My skin feels tight, like a ball of energy has formed inside me and is threatening to explode.

I'm nervous about what will happen when it does, but JJ talks me through it.

His tone is sweet as he mumbles against my mouth. "That's it, Adeline, come for me. Let me feel you break."

My toes curl and my muscles tense. Then my eyes fall shut and a wave rushes over me. He kisses me through it. Tells me I'm beautiful. That he's obsessed. Addicted.

"Can I taste you?" He whimpers against my lips.

My mind can't make sense of the words for a moment. Maybe it's the orgasm. Maybe it's the way his voice goes soft and high when he begs.

Eventually, it clicks, and my breath stutters. "Um, yes."

He licks my lips, groaning. "I've dreamed about this." He kisses down my neck, then rolls his tongue over one of my nipples.

I arch in surprise, a moan rolling out of me.

"Oh, my girl likes having her nipples played with. Fuck, I love that." He puts his mouth on me again, rolling his tongue in circles, not touching the tip. When he tweaks the other, a bolt of electricity shoots straight to my core. In seconds, I'm a mess, begging and whining and panting.

He chuckles, moving to my other breast. When the cool air hits me, I feel like I might combust. What is this sensation? How is he doing this with just his tongue?

"How?" I babble. "I—oh my god, your tongue."

With his teeth gently clamped around my nipple, he grins up at me, his blue eyes devious. He flicks the sensitive bud with his tongue over and over, and I swear I see stars.

"Just wait until you feel it against your clit. I am going to love eating your pussy, baby."

My pulse spikes. Holy shit. "You're going to—" I glance down.

He nods, though he lifts up a little, his brows furrowed. "Has no one ever tasted this pussy?" He finds my clit and plays with it lazily.

I squirm, digging my heels into the bed. "JJ—"

"Oh, baby, you are so fucking special." Working his way down my body, he presses a kiss to my stomach. "I love that you're giving me this. That I'm your first. Shit, it's fucking with my head." He lifts up, his face going serious. "Thank you."

It's so sweet. So unlike JJ. Not that he isn't sweet, but it's different now. We're different now.

I sigh, a smile breaking across my lips. "Thank you."

His expression turns wicked. "I haven't done anything yet."

With that, he shifts even lower and returns his focus to the spot between my legs.

I hold my breath, not sure what to expect.

When he presses his mouth to my clit and gives me the most intimate of kisses, pleasure rocks through me.

"Oh my god," I pant, my eyes rolling back.

"It's JJ, but I'll answer to that too."

A laugh bubbles out of me. I inhale sharply, ready to mock him for his cocky attitude, but he slips his tongue inside me, and I lose my words.

He adds a finger, gently working it in and out of me, then another. "Just stretching you out." He sucks on my clit again, this time while fucking me with his fingers, and everything I knew about pleasure before this moment is erased. Every sensation I've ever experienced is rewritten.

When I come again, I chant his name.

He doesn't stop licking and humming until I'm begging him to stop. Begging him to fuck me.

He crawls up my body and kisses me, ravenously. "You are my favorite person in the world, Adeline. My best friend. And the absolute best meal I've ever had."

I laugh. He's always so fucking ridiculous. That hasn't changed. But at the same time as the amusement registers, warmth rolls through me.

Eyes locked with his, I say, "You are that for me too, JJ. The person I always want with me. The one I look for in every room. Every time something big happens, I want to tell you, but I'm tired of telling you things. I want you there for it all. I want all of it. You and me and this and…"

He kisses the rest of the confession from my lips. "Shh, baby. I know. And it's you and me from here on out. No more sharing stories. We're living them."

I nod, my breath stuttering and tears pricking at my eyes.

He presses one more kiss to my mouth, then sits up and reaches for his jeans. He pulls a condom from his pocket, and his eyes don't leave mine as he rolls the latex over himself.

I lick my lips, nervous but ready.

When he settles back over me and drags his cock against me, teasing the places he's already set on fire with his tongue, I shudder.

"We're going to go slow," he says. "Okay?"

I nod, my breaths coming quickly.

As he presses into me, those catastrophic blue eyes hold mine. "I love you," he says, and it sounds like a promise. The sentiment holds so much more meaning than three simple words should. Because what we're doing is so much more than a physical act. It's the beginning of something new. And as I cry out in pain, he holds me and kisses me through it, only releasing my mouth when that pain bleeds into pleasure.

From this moment on, there's no way we'll ever be the same.

CHAPTER 25
Addie

"ARE YOU SURE I LOOK OKAY?" I eye my sister, Vivi, and Hope in the mirror. Before they can reply, I snag a hair tie from my bureau, the instinct to put my hair up overwhelming.

"No," Winnie yells from my bed. "Your hair looks great the way it is."

"It really does," Hope agrees.

"God, what I'd do to have hair like yours" Vivi mumbles.

The three of them are snuggled up in my bed, already in pajamas, while I'm dressed up and about to go out on my first date. Ever.

I spin, unable to look at myself any longer. "Please, people would kill for your hair," I say.

Vivi's got naturally bouncy curls that women spend thousands to replicate. It's wild, really, that she and Aunt Millie have the same gorgeous curls since she isn't her biological daughter.

"You wouldn't say that if you had to take care of them." She tugs on a curl and sighs. "But you look gorgeous. Don't touch a thing."

Chin tucked, I take in the skin-tight black leather pants Josie picked up while thrifting and the low-cut shirt Vivi lent me. She's like a miniature doll in comparison to me, so it's nearly a crop top. Still, it's all black, which is not exactly my style. Then again my style is workout clothes and sports bras. Not exactly date appropriate.

"You sure I don't look like I'm going to a funeral?"

Winnie snorts. "I can see your boobs."

"What she's saying is you look hot." Hope gives me and encouraging smile.

I tug at the shirt. I barely have boobs. "And the shoes? I'm too tall for heels. What if this guy is shorter than me? I'm like six foot in these things."

I couldn't borrow shoes from any of them because my feet are so damn big. Tall girl problems. But Aunt Sienna gifted me these Louboutins a few Christmases ago. This is the first time I've pulled them out of the closet, because where in god's name would I wear them?

"Savannah knows how tall you are," Winnie says, breaking out the older-sister tone. "She's not going to set you up with a man you aren't comfortable with."

But what if I'm uncomfortable with all men? What if I'm awkward and I've never gone on a date because men don't find me attractive? What then?

What if the only man who's ever shown the slightest interest in me is the one man I can't be with? The one who's hurt me the most.

"You're going to be late." Vivi clambers off the bed and pushes me toward the door. "Come on, I already ordered you an Uber."

I pull up short. "Why can't I drive?"

She sighs like I'm exhausting. "Because if things are going well, then you have an excuse to let him drive you home. Or, you know, to go to his place."

My stomach rolls. "You think he's expecting that? Is that what people do after dates? They *sleep* together?" I whisper hiss.

Winnie snorts. "Oh my god. As your big sister, I clearly failed at my duties. You can't even say sex?"

Hope swats her arm. "Be nice."

Head dropped back, I groan. "I'm so nervous. What if he hates me? What if he's only doing this because of the magazine? What if—"

"What if you just take a deep breath and have fun?" Hope prods softly. Like a ray of sunshine, she practically glows as she grasps my arms and smiles. "He doesn't have to be the one. Even if he's a total dud, tonight will be a success because you put yourself out there." She releases me and takes a step back. "Have fun, Addie. You deserve this."

I blow out a breath and nod. "Yeah, okay." Without my permission, my attention darts to JJ's door. I haven't seen him since he stormed out this morning, mumbling something about the gym.

The girls and I were in the kitchen making breakfast. I have no idea what got his panties in a wad, but I can't keep worrying about him.

"He's not here," Hope says.

"Hmm?" I hum, my chest pinching when I realize they're all looking at me.

Hope's tongue goes to her cheek as she stares at his door too. "I think he might have a date tonight."

My stomach drops.

"So his marriage is really over?" Vivi asks, oblivious to my reaction.

"I think it's been over for a while, but her disappearing on Avery was the last nail in the coffin." Hope shrugs. "But he left with a smile on his face, dressed like he was going out on a date. So maybe he's moving on."

I snort. So fucking typical. Here I am spinning out over a goddamn pinky brush, and he's already dating.

Well, fuck him. I'm going to do it better. I'm going to date the fuck out of this guy.

Okay, yeah, that sounded ridiculous, but still…

I straighten and lift my chin. "All right, I'm going."

"Yay." Hope claps, bouncing on her toes.

Winnie smiles proudly. "Have the best time."

"Hope we don't see you tonight," Vivi sings.

I huff out a laugh. "You definitely will." My focus roams to JJ's door again. Judging by the way he used to *date*, I doubt we'll see him before tomorrow, though.

I wish that thought didn't make me want to throw up.

Scott is not short. He's also surprisingly funny. And hot.

I should have trusted my friends. If there's one thing Savannah likes, it's to start with a bang. She literally did that the night she met Camden, so starting with one of the hottest men I've ever seen, who has a personality to boot, tracks.

His green eyes are strikingly bright, especially against his jet-black hair. He's got a deep voice and large hands that look very capable of enjoyable things. He also towers over me.

We're at the bar having a drink. The area is crowded, but that's not the reason I move closer to Scott. I'm genuinely comfortable. I think I might like him.

"Can I be honest?" he asks, his tone dropping even farther, if that's possible.

I give him a little nod, then nibble on my straw, studying his face.

I ordered a vodka soda because it felt cool. Don't ask me why. All my aunts drink gross dirty martinis. I never could stomach them, even if holding one automatically makes a person seem infinitely more sophisticated. "As opposed to lie?"

Chuckling, he presses a little closer, like he's being forced into me from behind, one of those large hands grazing my hip. When I don't pull back, he gets a bit more daring, gripping my waist gently. "I wasn't sure how tonight would go. So I suggested a drink first in case it got awkward."

An amused huff escapes me. "Let me guess. You told one of your friends to call you in thirty minutes with a fake emergency just in case?"

"That what you did?"

I pick up my drink again. "My friends don't need to be told." I slip my phone from my clutch and show him the three calls I've ignored so far. Josie. Savannah. Josie. Every ten minutes like clock-work. "My guess is they'll give it a rest for an hour, then check again."

He throws his head back, his laughter booming. The sound sends a shot of adrenaline through me. "Those are some good friends."

I nod. "Truly."

"So when they call again, are you going to answer, then dip out on me with some fake emergency, or are you ready to agree that we'll be honest tonight? No excuses." His eyes hold mine in challenge.

I can't stop the giddy smile from hitting my lips. "I'm game if you are."

He pulls out his phone and types out a quick message, then turns the device to show me.

No saving needed tonight. She's gorgeous AND funny.

My heart trips over itself. Even if I wanted to hide my smile, it would be impossible.

I navigate to the text thread that includes both Savannah and Josie and type out a message of my own.

You can call off the guard dogs, Savy. I think you picked a good one.

He smirks. "Think?"

Lips twitching, I shrug. "We'll see how the rest of the night goes."

He chuckles, scanning our surroundings. "So are there really guard dogs?"

I make a sweep of the bar, playing along, but my stomach plummets when I spot JJ across the room. I can't see who he's sitting with because of the crowd, but I'd know his profile anywhere.

Scott follows my gaze, frowning. "Wait, did they really send guards?"

I huff out a laugh, trying for casual. "No. I just—" I shake my head. "I—" Eyes closed, I give myself a second to just breathe. "Can I be honest?"

His brows lift. "Thought we already agreed to that?"

"Right. Well, I've never been on a date before. So I might be awkward."

He jolts back, his mouth dropping open. "Like never?"

I press my lips together, my cheeks heating, and shake my head. "Nope."

I'm not sure how I expected Scott to act, but it didn't involve a warm smile. "Then I guess I really do have to make a good first impression, huh? Let's grab a table, Addie."

I nod and pick up my drink. I just hope the table is nowhere near JJ and his date.

CHAPTER 26

JJ

"HAVE YOU SPOTTED THEM YET?" Dad looks up from his menu and peruses the place.

"They're at the bar. Don't be obvious," Beckett grumbles, though he glances over his shoulder, being exactly that.

Aiden rubs his hands together, his dark eyes flashing. "I can't wait to see Addie's reaction."

Brooks huffs. "Why am I here?"

I nudge his foot and frown. "To support me."

He scrutinizes me. "Support you in what? Stalking the woman you consider *just a coach*?"

I sigh. Looks like the jig is up. But that doesn't mean I'm ready to admit it.

At least Garreth and Hayden aren't here to witness this. Gavin either. He said he wanted nothing to do with pissing off his assistant coach. He suggested the rest of us follow his example, but Beckett was having none of that. Neither was I.

And thank god I didn't listen, because the guy Savannah chose is huge. There's no way Adeline isn't uncomfortable. He's standing too close and towering over her. Probably talking down to her too. While she keeps laughing, it's probably because she's nervous.

The guy can't be that funny.

Not that she has ever laughed at a man's jokes just to make him feel better.

Fuck. It's like the Adeline I've known for more than half my life is disappearing right in front of my eyes.

Aiden clears his throat and sets his menu down. "What's good here?"

"It's a steakhouse," Brooks grumbles.

"So? Maybe the porterhouse is better than the filet. Or maybe they have a really good fish option on the menu. Don't be so closed-minded."

With a sigh, Brooks downs his whiskey. The second he sets it on the table, he holds up his hand, signaling to the server to bring him another.

My father sets his menu down. "I always get the filet here. They have a good garlic butter rub."

Beckett sets his menu down as well. "I prefer the porterhouse."

"Shit. Now what?" Aiden says, focus once again on the menu. "You want to get one and I'll get the other?" he asks, peering over at Brooks.

"Are we five?" his brother huffs.

"Jeez. With that attitude, you'd think Sara was the one on a date with another man. Not even JJ is biting my head off, and his girl is the one who's with someone else."

"She's not his girl," both my father and Beckett growl.

Tongue pressed to my cheek, I fight the urge to tell them the fuck she's not.

That's not why we're here, though. Tonight we're just watching out for Adeline. Making sure this oversized creep doesn't take advantage of her.

Aiden chuckles like we're all idiots and when the server comes around to take Brooks's drink order, he grins at her. "What's the best thing on the menu?"

"Most people order the filet but the porterhouse is fantastic as well."

Nostrils flaring, Brooks hands her his menu. "We'll take one of each."

Aiden bounces in his seat. "And the lobster mac and cheese for the table too."

I place my order for a steak and am quickly distracted by Adeline's laugh again. "What in god's name could be so funny?" I grumble.

My father tilts closer. "Maybe he's got a good sense of humor."

"What do we know about him?" Aiden asks.

Beckett leans back in his chair, his whiskey glass dangling from his fingers. A Hanson gold blend, of course. "Thirty-two," he says, "hedge fund manager. Oldest of three, two younger sisters, family lives in Newburyport. He talks to his father daily, mother twice a week," His lip curls on one side in displeasure. "Went to college at Notre Dame and played football—defense."

"Fuck, did you get his social security number too?" Dad chuckles.

"Zero-three-two—"

Jaw dropping, Dad lurches forward.

Beckett's green eyes sparkle with mischief. "I'm kidding. No. But I do know he owns his apartment, has no kids, and has no divorces under his belt."

That wasn't meant to be a jab in my direction, but it hits me in my gut anyway.

I never wanted kids. Adeline's words from years ago plague me.

"Thirty-two and single," Brooks mumbles. "I wonder why?"

Aiden coughs out a laugh. "Maybe he's been saving himself for the perfect woman."

Brooks gives him a surly look I don't understand and don't have the energy to dig into.

"He's not wrong," my father agrees. "Why is someone so seemingly perfect on paper still single?"

"Look at Adeline," Beckett counters. "The same could be said for her." He lifts his chin, his focus landing on me. "Maybe someone strung him along for a while and he's just now realizing it's time to start fresh."

Okay, that was definitely aimed at me. Clearly, Beckett is still pissed about what went down four years ago. Can't blame him, I guess. But I never got the impression that he held a grudge. No one knows what really happened anyway. And on top of that, he invited me to live in his damn home with his daughter. But fuck, there's really no other way to take what he's saying.

"I'm going to run to the bathroom." I heave myself up and stride away without waiting for anyone else to acknowledge me. I don't even look toward Adeline's table. I just get the fuck out. I need a little quiet so I can breathe and figure out how the fuck I'm going to convince Beckett that I'm good for his daughter. Because it seems that convincing him might be just as hard as convincing her.

My foot hits the tile in the hallway outside the bathroom half a second before a fist slams into my chest, pushing me against the wall.

"What the hell are you doing here?"

Breath held, I take in Adeline. A very pissed off, very beautiful, Adeline.

Her lips are painted a gorgeous red, her cheeks are flushed—probably from all that laughing she's done tonight—and her brown eyes are wild.

And then there's the goddamn outfit.

The black blouse has the thinnest of strings for straps, showing off her incredibly toned arms, with a neckline that dips low, exposing cleavage she never shows off. That's as far as I make it before she hits me again. "Eyes up here, asshole."

With a groan, I roll my neck. "Sorry, I'm just, thrown by—" I shake my head and motion toward her top.

She bites down on her tongue and huffs. "I told the girls it looked ridiculous."

"You don't—" I sputter, squeezing my fists. "You don't look ridiculous."

Her expression goes stony again. "What are you doing here? Could you really not go somewhere else for your little date?"

My heart lurches. "My what?"

Eyes shut, she shakes her head. "This is the first date I've ever been on. *First.* Do you get that? Do you understand how hard it is for me that you're here? Why *here*?" Her voice warbles, but she pulls her shoulders back and goes on. "Did you ask the girls where I'd be so you could show up for dinner at the same place and really rub it in? Why are you doing this to me?"

I blink. First date? And what the hell is she talking about me being on a date?

A woman appears, neck craning so she can look around us. "'Scuse me, is there a line?"

I grasp Adeline's arm and pull her down the hall. When I come to a door with no sign on it, I wiggle the knob, and when it opens to a small closet, I pull her inside.

"What are you doing?" she hisses, tugging against my hold.

I turn, putting one hand on her hip, and glower at the infuriating woman I adore. "I'm making a few things very clear, because last time we tried this, I didn't."

Her brows furrow.

"I'm not here on a date. I came with our dads and your uncles to make sure you're okay."

Her jaw drops. "What? Why?"

"Because your first date shouldn't be with that guy. It should be with me."

Eyes turning glassy, she tips her chin up, her lips a breath from mime. "You had *all* of my firsts. *Every one of them.* While I don't even get seconds when it comes to you."

I angle in, my nose brushing hers, and clutch her other hip, tugging her against me. "I'll give you every second I have. Every minute will be yours, Adeline."

Pulling back, she searches my face, a confused frown marring hers. "*Why* are you doing this *now*?" Her voice cracks, and my heart does too.

Like last time, I give her all my truths. Only this time, I won't blow it the way I did back then. "Because I haven't gone a day without thinking about you. I'm crazy jealous of that Scott guy. And if I don't find out what your lips feel like right the fuck now, I'm going to lose my goddamn mind."

She sucks in a surprised breath. Unlike four years ago, I don't hesitate after that declaration. I press my mouth to hers, telling her with a brush of my lips that she's the only woman I've ever wanted to date. That she's the girl of my dreams. That I'd risk everything for her. That dating isn't worth it if it's not the two of us.

A soft whimper escapes her, spurring me on. I slide my tongue against her lips, holding her tighter, so damn relieved that she doesn't push me away.

Until she does.

She shoves me.

Hard.

"*No.*"

Panting, eyes heavy, I beg. "Please, Adeline."

"No." She shakes her head and holds up a hand. "I can't do this."

"Yes you can." Refusing to give up, I step into her space, and when she keeps her focus averted, I press my hand to her cheek and guide her face until we're eye to eye. "You and I both know this is inevitable. *We're inevitable.* Stop fighting me and help me figure out a way to make this work. To make us work."

Her face sags with exhaustion. "I hate you."

I press a kiss to the side of her mouth. "Lie. Now tell me a truth."

"I hate how much I want you."

Smiling, I stroke her cheek. "Better, but still a lie. You love this as much as I do."

"This is never going to work, JJ." A tear slips down her cheek.

I kiss it away. "Another lie. Come on, baby, try harder."

"We're wrong for each other," she whispers.

"We're meant for each other," I murmur against her lips. "Try again."

She shakes her head, her mouth softly brushing mine, and she whines. "I'm so tired of fighting these feelings."

I smile, my forehead resting against hers. "There's my girl. Now stop fighting and let me take care of you for a minute."

When she doesn't argue, I lick into her mouth. She moans, wrapping her arms around my neck. And for the first time in years, I feel like I'm home.

"I need," she pants against my mouth, her hands traveling down my chest to my belt.

"Slow down, baby."

She pulls her head back, taking that delicious mouth away from me. "No, I need you." Those brown eyes of hers hold mine. "Please, JJ. It's been too long."

It's been an eternity since I had her, and I'm not strong enough to say no. Not when this is all I've ever wanted. So when she reaches for my belt again, I don't stop her. Instead, I match her enthusiasm, tugging her leather pants down.

"Shit," she hisses as she wraps her hand around my hard cock.

I suck air between my teeth. Nothing has felt as good as this simple touch in years.

"I forgot," she mumbles, stroking once, twice.

I squeeze my eyes shut. *Do not fucking come, JJ. Hold it the fuck together.*

"Adeline," I grunt.

"I forgot how big, and holy fuck—"

I slide my middle finger inside her, all the way to my knuckle.

"You're…" She drops her head back against the door.

"Pierced," I finish for her. Then I take her mouth, relishing the way she strangles my finger with her tight pussy. "Remember how good it feels, mon trésor? How many times you came all over it. It'll be even better with the piercing. You gonna do that for me now, Adeline? You gonna come again and again?" I roll my thumb over her clit and curl my finger inside her.

With a cry, she detonates. It's the most beautiful sound. And her expression, pure pleasure, is my undoing.

"That's my girl," I murmur.

"Fuck me," she begs against my lips.

My already racing heart thunders in my ears. "Are you sure?"

She grips my cheeks, looking me in the eye. "Now is not the time to pull back. I need that cock inside me. Please."

I chuckle. "Bend over, Angles."

Without hesitation, she spins and pops her fantastic ass out. With a single stroke, I notch myself at her entrance. I lean over her, press my mouth to her ear, and admit, "I fucking missed you." Then I thrust deep inside her.

"Holy shit," she whimpers.

I don't go slow and I can't stifle the groans escaping me. It's been too long and she feels too goddamn good. I fuck her for the years we missed out on. I fuck her for all the times she ignored me. For the moments when I thought I hated her.

But mostly, I fuck her like I love her. Because I do. Because over the last four years, no matter the time or the place, had Adeline Langfield shown an ounce of interest, I would have had her bent over like this. I would have been inside her. Beside her. Spending my life with her. And now, finally, I can.

"I'm going to come," she cries.

I wrap my arm around her throat and press myself against her back, my heart beating wildly and her pussy spasming, pulling my own orgasm from deep within me.

I'm still breathless, panting, when a knock rattles the door.

"Shit," Adeline whispers.

"Shh." I grip her upper arms and spin so I'm standing between her and the door.

"Um, guys…"

Her eyes widen as my stomach sinks.

"If that's you in there," Aiden says, "just, um, your dads are getting anxious. I said I'd come check on you, JJ, but you weren't in the bathroom and—"

"Um—" I start.

"Don't. Don't make a sound," he rushes out, panicked. "I don't want to know if Addie's in there with you because then I'd have to lie. I'm terrible at lying. But maybe just come back to the table."

He falls silent.

I listen for his footsteps but can barely hear over the blood rushing in my ears.

When I think he's gone, I tuck myself back into my pants, only to startle when he yells again. "Soon. Please."

Addie drops her head to my chest. "Holy fuck," she whispers.

"It's okay." I squeeze her upper arms. "I'll talk to him."

"No." She snaps up straight, her face a mask of anger. "There's nothing to talk about. This—this didn't happen."

Dread swirls inside me. "Adeline—"

She shakes her head, yanking up her pants. "Oh my god, how could we have done this? I have a date out there. A very lovely man who's funny and has said nice things about me and you—you're… nope." She straightens her top and fluffs her hair. "He's going to know. Oh my god, my dad is going to know I fucked a married man."

"Adeline—"

"And I'm your coach. Dammit. Now I'm just another cliché—"

"Adeline."

"Stop saying my name," she begs. "This is my career, JJ. Maybe this isn't a big deal for you, but for me…*this is my career*," she whispers, desperate. "It's hard enough being taken seriously as a woman in sports without a scandal. The NHL was my dream. Please, JJ. Please just…let it go. Let me go."

My heart thrashes wildly. I want to fight her on this. She's still dripping with my cum and she's about to run out and give up on us.

But I can't argue with a damn thing she's saying. Like hell would I ever let her give up her career for me.

So I cup her cheek and lean in, brushing my lips against hers. "I'm going to figure this out for us. I'm letting you go right now, but make no mistake, I'm not letting *you* go."

I press my mouth to hers and soak in the feel of her, knowing it will have to last me for a while.

"We'll see about that," she murmurs, turning for the door.

And then she's gone.

Again.

CHAPTER 27
Addie

I'M GOING to throw up. In two minutes, I have to head to the locker room. Okay, the hallway outside the locker room. It's night one of the NHL season.

As I pace, shallow breaths are all I can manage. Stopping in the middle of the room, I blow out a long breath and will my heart and my muscles to relax. This is absurd. I'm not even playing.

Still, thousands of eyes will be on me. The first female goalie coach in the NHL. A Langfield. Boston—hell, North America—is waiting to see if I have the chops or have been given a handout.

Regardless of what the talking heads say, not a goddamn thing has been handed to me in my entire life. I've worked hard and bled for every accomplishment, every win. Even Beckett's affection. While he absolutely gave it freely, I never could fight the need to make him proud. Didn't ever want him to regret all he'd given to us. Without him our lives would be very different. And despite knowing better, I've never been able to silence that little voice in my head. The one that often said *If my own father didn't want me, why would Beckett? There's nothing in it for him.*

Yet he's never let me down. He's the *only* man to never let me down. Okay, my uncles too. The Langfield family really is incredible. Not one of them has ever made me question their love for me.

I squeeze my eyes shut and suck in another deep breath. *They didn't give this to you. You did this all on your own. You deserve to be here.*

Straightening my shoulders, I give myself one last look in the mirror, confirming that the red stain on my lips hasn't bled onto my skin or my teeth. Then I adjust my Bolts blue suit and smooth back the flyaway or two that has escaped my low ponytail.

Then, head down and hands clenched at my sides, I head for the door.

I'm reaching for the handle when there's a knock.

I inhale sharply, startled. *Please, for the love of God, don't let it be JJ.*

He's respected my wishes and given me space for the last sixteen-ish hours, and now is not the time to change that.

I open the door, and when I come face to face with Uncle Aiden, my stomach drops.

He's wearing a blue suit as well, though his is a bit brighter. His brown eyes warm when he sets his sights on me, and he hums. "Big day, kiddo."

Though affection runs through me, I roll my eyes. "Please don't call me that in front of the press."

Laughing, he points inside my office. "Can I come in for a second?"

"A second? Yeah. That's about all we have."

"I know. And I'll be quick, promise." He saunters in, his hands in his pockets.

I examine him, my pulse thumping with nerves. I know why he's here, and I'd like to avoid getting into it, if possible. "Did you enjoy your dinner last night?"

He shuts the door behind him and leans against it. "The lobster mac and cheese was incredible. Did you have it?"

I shake my head, giving him an annoyed look. "Scott and I decided to grab a burger instead. When I pointed out the table of bodyguards, he paid for our drinks and took me to a dive bar. The food was great."

Aiden smiles. "Good. I'm glad."

What I don't mention is how I forced a smile and made conversation, feeling like shit the entire time. Because I fucked another man while on a date with him. Who does that? I never would have believed

I could be capable of that, and I don't want to be that kind of person. It's not sexy, it's not kind. It's just...awful.

"I know what you're going to say," I start. I can't just stand here smiling and making fake conversation.

He arches a brow. "Do you?"

I nod, my jaw clamped shut. "He's a player, and I'm his coach."

His response is a simple shrug. "Yeah."

"So, I'm aware of that and...nothing will happen between us."

The smile he gives me is sympathetic. "Okay. Like I said last night, I know nothing."

Relief washes over me. He's letting me off the hook. And it's true. Nothing is going on. JJ and I may have a past, and at one time I thought he might be my future, but that isn't possible anymore. Life doesn't always turn out the way we thought it would. Hell, for a long time I even thought I'd be on this team, not coaching it. But here I am. And this isn't a bad alternative.

And Scott isn't a bad alternative either. Not that he deserves an asshole like me.

"But Addie?"

His serious tone instantly has my attention. He's the fun-loving uncle, the goofy one, so this is out of character. I brace myself, waiting for him to impart wisdom I might not be ready to hear.

"If your Aunt Lennox had been my coach or my boss. If she'd held any position that made her unavailable to me, I would have moved heaven and earth to figure it out. Because there was no way in hell I wasn't getting my second chance with her."

"She was your wedding planner," I rasp, words suddenly hard to find.

Expression softening, he squeezes my hand. "And I dumped my fiancée the moment I found out." He holds eye contact, letting that sink in. "Anyway, I just wanted to say I'm proud of you. I know how hard it is to give up those skates and be on this side of the boards during games, but we're damn lucky to have you. So enjoy tonight. You've fucking earned it."

Emotion clogs my throat, but I can't help but snort. "Don't you mean ducking?"

He wraps an arm around my shoulder, guiding me out of my office. "You're in the NHL now, Addie. It's fucking."

I was very clear with my family before my first game. I made sure they understood that I did not want any type of ceremony or party to celebrate after. While they've assured me they have nothing planned, the entire crew is here, seated right behind the players' bench, screaming their heads off when I come out. At the ridiculous hooting and hollering, I turn and glare at them, holding up a finger to quiet them. Naturally, that only makes Aunt Lennox and Aunt Sara scream even louder.

Winnie and Hope are laughing hysterically at my distress. I'd be annoyed, if not for the little girl holding up a sign and wearing the biggest smile. "Kick some hockey player butt, Coach Addie. I love you."

I point to my chest, make a heart sign and point to Avery. "I love you too," I mouth.

She dances on Vivi's lap, and when she spots JJ on the ice, she perks up and screams, "Hi, Daddy. You kick hockey butt too."

JJ skates over to the bench and waves at her. When he turns, he's grinning. "She's proud of you," he says, voice low so only I can hear him.

"Thank you for letting her be here tonight," I say, internally reminding myself not to stare into those blue eyes of his. Trying to hold back memories of last night, of the way he made me feel when they were fixed on me, telling me how beautiful I was as I came.

"She wouldn't have been anywhere else."

"All right, enough emotional stuff." I take a step back and scan the ice. "Go warm up."

His eyes warm and he smirks. "Okay, Coach."

And there goes my stomach flipping over again.

After the game, Bobby insists that I join the team for a drink to celebrate our 3-0 victory. Fortunately, the bar they frequent is not only owned by my family, but it's also on site, located underground beneath Langfield Corp. It sits between the hockey arena and the baseball stadium in an area that can't be accessed without a code.

I give in easily when Josie and Vivi agree to join in too. One drink to celebrate is warranted.

I assumed since Vivi was off duty tonight, JJ would go straight home. It's rare that he goes out. I've learned that over the last few months. Maybe I knew that even before then. He's always put Avery first. But tonight, he walks into the bar with Brayden and Sidney a few minutes after we arrive.

Beside me, Josie asks a question, but I only catch the tail end of it.

"What?" I ask, still watching JJ.

How is it possible for a man to look that pretty after playing three periods of rough hockey? After games, I'd braid my hair and swipe on a little lip gloss. He's in a navy suit, the top of his dusty blue shirt undone, exposing a gorgeous neck that I'd really like to rest my head against.

Fucking him was such a bad idea.

It's awakened a beast inside me. That feral part of me is desperate for him and I can't go there again.

He laughs at Sidney, and then his gaze is on me, making my heart thump wildly. The laughter dies and his smile falls into a warmer one. He gives me a small nod, then his focus returns to the guys. As it should. Just like I should be paying attention to Josie, who is now waving her hand in front of my face dramatically.

"Huh, I really thought you'd have made it until at least a home game." With a shake of her head, she glares at Vivi.

My cousin laughs, tossing her head back. "Told you it was only a matter of time."

"But she was on a date with someone else last night. When was there time?" Josie sighs.

Blinking, I force myself to turn so JJ is out of sight. "What are you guys talking about?"

Vivi bites on her bottom lip, eyes dancing. "How long it would take you and JJ to finally bang."

Lunging forward, I cover her mouth. "Shut up." I dart a look around, confirming no one was close enough to hear her. Shit. Fortunately, we're at the end of the bar and most of the guys have ordered their drinks and moved over to the pool tables. Because apparently they haven't experienced enough competition yet tonight.

Josie groans. "I am just…" She shakes her head. "I have no words. No words, Adeline Marie Langfield."

I roll my eyes. "That's not my middle name."

She pushes her strawberry blond hair behind her shoulder, her chin lifted. "Whatever. You get the point."

In one quick move, I down my drink. Then I hold up a hand, ordering another. "I have no idea what you're talking about."

"Okay, then how was the date last night?" she asks, her words snippy. "Did you kiss? Do you plan to see each other again? At approximately what time did you fuck JJ Hanson?" The questions roll off her tongue like she thinks I'll answer them rapid-fire.

"I didn't," I lie.

She examines him where he's still standing by the pool tables.

Shit. I'm beginning to wonder if there's any chance of getting Josie out of here before she corners him and blows up my career.

"Please." I settle my hand on hers and squeeze, hoping she can understand the severity of the situation. "I wouldn't jeopardize my career." Again. I definitely won't do it again.

No matter how good he looks. Or how good he is at doling out orgasms. And sex. And all the things that involve orgasms and sex.

My best friend studies me, then shakes her head. "It's a bad idea, Adeline."

"I think it's a great idea," Vivi argues.

I sigh. "It's a bad idea."

Josie takes a deep breath and dips her chin, like she's satisfied with my response. Like she believes I won't totally fuck up my life.

She may have more confidence than I do, but relief rushes over me when she finally drops it.

And the timing couldn't be better, because not even five seconds later, Bobby Dean pops up out of nowhere, yelling about a celebratory shot. In less than a minute, the entire team is congregated at the bar. One shot turns into three, and they don't let me skip out. When I set that third shot glass down, I'm feeling mighty buzzed and beyond tired. Between the emotional Olympics I was subject to last night, the excitement of today, and the late hour, I'm done.

"I'm going to head out," I tell Josie. "You ready?"

She's deep in conversation with Sidney and Vivi has disappeared.

She shakes her head. "I'm going to hang for a bit longer. I'll make sure Vivi gets home."

"You sure?"

She grins. "Yup. Congrats, babe. As always, you're a total inspiration and a knockout while doing it." She scoops me into a hug. When her chin hits my shoulder, she adds, "Don't fuck it all up. He's pretty, but you're a badass, and badasses deserve to be loved out loud, not in secret."

I squeeze her tighter. She's right, even if it's hard to hear.

I'm headed toward the door when JJ steps into my path. "Leaving?"

I nod.

"Any chance you have one more in you?"

"One more drink?" I frown, my knees wobbling.

JJ smirks. "Nah, I was thinking a different kind of celebration."

A smile tugs at my lips. "Antonio's?"

He breaks into a matching expression. "It's tradition."

My damn traitorous heart flutters. "Yeah, it is."

An hour later, we sneak into the house, a pie between us, and tiptoe up to the roof. Still tipsy, moving through the house silently is not an easy feat. The moment we hit the cool October night, we burst into laughter.

"Made it." I rush to the couch, ravenous, the smell of the greasy pizza making my stomach rumble.

JJ snags a blanket from the bench seat and hands it to me, then he settles at my side, and when I open the box, we both lean in, inhaling.

"*God,*" I groan. "Why does it smell so good?"

Chuckling, he picks up a slice and takes a huge bite.

I snag my own piece and close my eyes, letting the taste really hit me. Suddenly we're sixteen again, celebrating after our first win on the same team. Or eighteen, when JJ was drafted to the Bolts and rather than going out with his friends or celebrating with a puck bunny, he wrapped an arm around me and said we had plans. Or the night of his twenty-first birthday when he ditched everyone at midnight so the two of us could spend it together.

So many memories, so many moments I've tried so hard to forget.

I swipe a finger against my lip, wiping at the grease, and set the pizza back in the box. "Thank you."

He arches a brow. "For what?"

"For letting it go. I would have been sad if we couldn't celebrate like this tonight."

He drops his slice next to mine and shifts so he's angled my way. "No matter what happens between us, I never want to go back to the way things were. I can't miss another four years of your life."

I nod, my throat thick. "Then let's make a deal. No more icing each other out."

"I never wanted that," he says. "I never wanted to lose you."

I know. Unfortunately, neither of us could have anticipated what happened the morning after Team USA won gold.

CHAPTER 28

JJ

Twenty-One Years Old

WHEN I WAKE up with Adeline's warm body pressed against mine, I swear I must be dreaming. For almost a year, I slept by her side, and I can't count how many mornings I'd wake up at three thirty so her family wouldn't catch us. After my alarm went off, I'd give myself a few minutes to watch her sleep, wondering what she would do if I pulled her into me. Wondering how soft her lips would be. Wondering what she'd taste like.

Now I know.

Unable to resist, I press my lips to hers. Her mouth slants into a smile. "Morning."

"Good morning, baby." I press another kiss to her lips.

She sighs. It's this soft, sweet sound. Her eyes are still closed, but she looks so damn happy. Just like I feel. Content. Like we can breathe easy for the very first time. For so long I held my breath around her or tempered my words, hoping like hell I wouldn't admit how I felt and screw it all up.

She was my best friend. The only person I could be honest with when everything in my life felt so precarious. I was too scared to rock that boat. Even after my mom was in remission. We'd only just celebrated five years cancer free. We'd already done this dance before though. We'd made it years without a recurrence and then they'd found another mass. My mother was the center of our family's universe. I couldn't voice how it felt like my chest was being squeezed tight at the thought of losing her to anyone else. But Adeline knew. She knew it without me even having to say it. She'd see me spiraling and hit me with a round of two truths and a lie. Or she'd link our pinkies and squeeze. Or she'd challenge me to a round on the ice. She just always knew when I needed that distraction. When I needed her.

And when I was younger the thought of risking that type of bond for the chance at something more felt selfish. It felt like taking the one thing the universe had given me to deal with my mom's diagnosis and saying, *this is great, but it's not enough.*

Adeline was always enough. Even when she wasn't completely mine.

But the day she called about the Olympics, the way she sounded on learning there was a woman in my room—someone who meant absolutely nothing—it was the first time I thought she might just want more.

And I realized that me being scared was hurting her. I never wanted to hurt her. And I'd risk losing everything to avoid that.

Thank fuck it didn't come to that though. Thank god those days are over. She wants me. She *loves* me.

"You're so warm," she says, her beautiful eyes finally open. This close, they're so dark. Chocolate swirls with slight golden sparkles, even as sleepy as she is.

I tug her closer. "You're so perfect."

Her body quakes as she laughs. "You're just saying that because I made you come three times last night."

Smiling, I kiss her again. I can't stop. "No, I'm saying that because I love you. Because I can finally kiss you whenever I want."

She presses her lips together, one brow cocked.

I cough out a laugh. "And you made me come three times last night."

Her resounding laugh is loud. Joyful. Delicious.

"I love you too," she says, her eyes dancing over my face. "I still can't believe this happened." She nuzzles into my chest, embarrassed maybe.

I press a kiss to the top of her head. "Believe it. I'm yours, baby, and you are most certainly mine."

"I feel like I could run a marathon right now. I have all this excited energy." She grins up at me. "This is the best morning of my life."

"You won the damn gold yesterday. You had a goddamn shutout."

"And I made you come three times," she teases.

Damn, this girl. I've been awake for mere minutes, and I can't stop laughing.

"Yeah, baby, and you made me come."

Her cheeks are pink with heat, but her eyes are full of delight. "I'm rather proud of that fact."

"So it seems."

"I was thinking." She presses a kiss to my bare chest and peers up at me from beneath her lashes.

"Hm?"

"Maybe I can do it again." She pulls back, then with a wicked smile, she eases herself down the bed, dragging her mouth over my stomach, peppering kisses along the way.

"Adeline," I breathe out. Her name is a goddamn prayer on my lips.

This woman is my everything. And knowing she wants me this way…it's fucking with my ability to speak.

"Yes, Jonathan Francis?"

"Oh." The sound is rough, full of surprise. "I didn't know you knew my real name."

"Your real name is JJ," she says with an eye roll. "But you always call me Adeline, even though everyone else calls me Addie, so I thought I'd try it."

"And?" I raise a brow.

"If you react like this." She drags her fist up and down my erection. "I'll call you whatever you want."

Pleasure shoots down my spine and my eyes roll back in my head. "Adeline, you do that to me, not some goddamn name, I assure you."

She gives me a secretive smile, the look piquing my curiosity.

"What?"

"I used to wonder why you called me that. Drove me nuts, actually."

My heart thuds at the sincerity there. "Adeline?"

She nods from where she's perched between my thighs, her mouth so close I could roll my hips and stroke her lips if I focused.

"It felt like…" I sigh, forcing my mind to focus on the conversation, not my dick and the way she just licked her lips. "It felt like you were mine when I used that name," I finally say. "Everyone else got Addie. I wanted a little piece of you all to myself, even if I couldn't claim you completely."

She shakes her head, releasing a breath of a laugh. "JJ, I was always yours. Didn't matter what you called me."

Warmth rushes through me. I think I always knew that too. Fuck, I wish there had never been anyone before her. I wish I'd been smart enough to make my move years ago. Or to wait for her. Because now I know how special this is. How good it can be with the right person. And I should have known that all along.

I don't get a chance to tell her that, though, because she slides her mouth over me and my eyes roll into the back of my head. "Jesus fuck." The sound is stolen from my throat. Dragged from my lungs.

There is nothing sexier than a naked Adeline, hair mussed from sleep, skin soft and warm, taking my cock into her mouth, dark eyes studying my every reaction. Like she wants to know that I'm enjoying it. That she's pleasing me. "Fuck, Adeline."

Lashes fluttering, she sucks me deeper.

I toss the covers, desperate to see all of her. Kneeling between my thighs, she grips me, pumping with her hand and her mouth.

A whimper escapes me, snagging her attention immediately.

Her eyes burn as she watches me watch her. "Oh, you like that," I say. "You like knowing you're doing a good job, don't you?"

She hums around me.

"Fuck, I'm going to think of you like this every time I jack off from now until eternity."

She pulls off me slowly, a string of saliva stretching between my crown and her lips. "What if—" she says slowly.

I narrow my eyes, too damn turned on to guess where she's going with this. "What if what?"

"What if you don't just have to think about it?" She reaches for her phone and taps at the screen. Then she hands it to me. "Record me sucking you off, JJ. You can keep this handy when you're away for all those games…I don't want you thinking anyone else—"

I press a finger to her lips. "Adeline. It's you and me. I swear to you I would never."

She gives me a soft smile. "I know that. But now you'll have something to watch." Without waiting for me to respond, she goes back to her task, wrapping her mouth around my swollen cock.

I don't know where to look, at the screen of the camera that's filming her or around the side of it, at the real thing.

She's so goddamn perfect. So good at this. Cupping her jaw, I stroke her cheek. "My beautiful girl. You are doing such a good job. Fuck, baby, you're a dream."

My balls tighten, but I don't want this to end. It's been sixty seconds, and already, I'm close to exploding. "Addie baby, come here."

Her eyes jump to mine.

"I need to be inside you. Please, let me make you come."

She pops her lips off me and shrugs, wearing a cheeky grin. "Okay, if you must."

Chuckling, I prop the phone up against the lamp so it can capture the two of us. Then I pull her up my body. When I've got my head between her thighs, she grips the headboard and rides my face.

"Oh, JJ," she cries, grinding down on me.

Fuck, she tastes so good like this, wet and excited from sucking me off. Without slowing, I fondle her tits, touching them the way that pulled the deepest moans from her last night.

She slows, peering down at me, watching me eat.

"You're such a good boy," she murmurs.

Holy. Fuck. I didn't think I could get any harder, but I swear I'm leaking, making a mess between my thighs.

My hips roll of their own accord, humping the air. Needy and excited.

I need her to come. So I double down. I suck her clit into my mouth, eliciting a breathy wine. Then I flick it with my tongue. Her head falls back and she rolls her hips. When she starts to pulse, I drag her down my body and thrust into her, wanting to feel her orgasm from the inside.

"Oh god," she babbles.

"I know, baby," I rasp against her mouth, kissing her through her first orgasm.

"How?" she whines.

"How what?" I press a kiss to her jaw, her neck. Sucking her sweet skin.

"How does it feel so good. Like—" Eyes wild, she shakes her head, like she can't find the words.

"Because it's us, Adeline. Because this is how it's supposed to be. Me inside you. Always."

Smiling down at me, she swivels her hips in a way that has my balls tugging tight again.

"Fuck, baby, I'm going to come."

She moans, back arched. "Come on my tits."

"That dirty mouth." I pull out, then make room for her to lie on the mattress.

When she's on her back, her hair splayed out around her, I drop between her thighs. But I want her to come one more time before we're finished.

So I bury my face between her legs, and when my mouth meets her clit and I suck, she cries out. I add two fingers and press on the inside wall in a way that made her shatter quickly last night. Within seconds she's clenching around me, her thighs squeezing around my shoulders as she comes in waves.

I press kiss after kiss to her sensitive sex, only stopping when she sighs out a soft sound. Then I lean back and jack myself until I come all over her gorgeous tits.

"That's gonna be one hell of a video," I say, collapsing beside her.

She surveys the sticky mess across her chest and then glares at me. "You're going to clean this up, right?"

I smirk. "One second." I pick up the phone, stop the recording, then switch over to the photo option. "Smile for me, baby," I tease.

She tries not to, but the scowl slips quickly. We're both too damn happy for that. The second it morphs into the smile I love so much, I snap a picture of my beautiful mess. Then I toss the phone onto the bed and rush to the bathroom so I can get her cleaned up.

After showers, we get back into bed, snuggling and ordering breakfast.

"What time do you have to get back?" she asks.

"I'm supposed to meet the team in Chicago tonight. We play tomorrow."

I hate leaving her. Damn, I'd give just about anything to have a week alone with her in a bedroom. We deserve at least that.

But there's nothing I can do about that now, so I move on. "What's on your agenda now that the Olympics are over?"

Her lips twist, her cheeks going pink, like she has a secret.

I turn to face her completely, eager to know everything.

"There's a spot in Vegas."

"A spot?" I parrot.

"A goalie spot."

"On the women's team?"

She shakes her head, her smile growing. "I checked my email while you were in the bathroom. They want me to fly out tomorrow to practice with the team."

"The Vegas Vices?" I ask, my mind blown.

She bounces on the mattress, her expression brighter than I've ever seen it. "Yes."

I clutch her to my chest and squeeze. "Adeline, this is huge."

She nods, burying her face in the crook of my neck. "I know."

"Fuck, baby, the NHL."

"I know," she says again. "But it's just practice. I might not get the spot."

"But they called you. They wouldn't call you if they didn't think you could do this."

She presses her lips together, her dark eyes holding mine. "I know," she whispers. "JJ, I might play in the NHL."

"Oh, baby, you definitely will. I can feel it."

Laughing, she holds me tighter. "I'm gonna kick your ass when we play the Bolts."

I nod. "Probably."

The wave of excitement I'm riding suddenly disappears. Because this means she'll be on another team. On the other side of the country. We just got this, and now we'll be apart for ten months out of the year. Fuck, I don't want to be selfish, but this…well, it sucks.

"I know," she whispers, like she can read my mind.

I'm an asshole. She shouldn't have to deal with my mixed emotions about this. This is a huge opportunity for her. We'll figure it out. I didn't go out on a limb and finally get everything I wanted just to lose it twenty-four hours later. We're us. We'll figure it out.

"We aren't going to focus on anything but the good right now."

"Okay," she whispers against my chest.

"I love you, baby." I run my hands through her hair, stroking softly.

"I love you too."

When there's a knock on the door, I release her. "That must be the food."

She leans back against the pillows, and I press one more kiss to her lips before jumping out of bed.

My phone rings as I reach for the doorknob, so I holler over my shoulder, "Can you get that?" With a wide smile, I pull the door open and smile at the waiter. "I can grab that," I tell him, stepping over the threshold.

There's no way he's coming into the bedroom, not when Adeline is practically naked. I hand him a twenty and pull the cart inside.

"The food smells delicious."

When she doesn't respond, I peer over at her.

She's staring down at the phone, her face ashen. And all that joy and peace coursing through me moments ago drains from my body.

"What's wrong?"

She shakes her head and lets out a sardonic laugh. Then she holds out my phone. "It's Tabitha. She, uh, she said she needs to talk to you. She's in the hospital. She said she just had your baby."

CHAPTER 29
Addie

Twenty-One Years Old

DESPITE THE WINTER CHILL, I feel nothing. Generally, I like the cold. I've yet to meet a hockey player who doesn't. We kind of have to, since we spend hours in frigid arenas. Of course, I'm normally sweating under all my gear, so I'm not actually cold.

Still, I always soak in the first moment that the sensation hits me. It's invigorating. Thrilling.

Right now the nip in the air is doing nothing for me. It's not comforting and it's not troublesome. It's just there. JJ squeezes my fingers as we walk hand in hand toward the hospital. Twelve hours ago, we were in a hotel room, in our bubble of perfection. Cozy. Making plans for the future.

Now we're minutes from meeting his daughter.

JJ has a daughter.

I'm going to be sick.

Yanking my hand from his, I pull up short on the sidewalk just outside the entrance. "You should go in without me."

Frowning, he examines my face. His dark hair is mussed from pulling at it the entire flight and there are dark circles around his eyes. "Adeline, I can't do this without you."

My heart cracks. I want to be here for him. I know he needs me. But what about me? This isn't…this wasn't. Dammit, I don't want to be angry, but I can't help it.

JJ had a baby with someone else. With Tabitha. My stomach rolls.

It was no secret that JJ dated women over the last few years. I tried to ignore that little fact of course. We were barely ever in the same place over the last three years because of our opposite schedules and he never took anyone home when I was around. If anything he always wanted to leave and just hang out the two of us whenever we'd be out with friends. Women would flock to him, flirt, and it was like he didn't see them. And Tabitha was one of those women who just seemed to always be around the bars where the hockey players would frequent. When they weren't at the one beneath the arena that is. I just thought he was smart enough to stay away from the likes of her.

And now she's had his child.

A baby.

Still, he's JJ. I buried my feelings for him for years so I could support him. I can do it for one more hour.

Nodding, I slip my hand into his again. "Okay, let's go."

Rather than continue on, he holds still, studying my face like he's memorizing every feature. "I love you, Adeline. And I know this isn't —" Eyes falling shut, he sighs. "I'm so fucking pissed at myself for doing this to you. Truly. And asking you to be here for me—"

"Hey." I place my hands on his shoulders and squeeze. "Look at me."

His blue eyes are watery as they hold mine, full of fear and desperation and maybe a little hope. Like I'm his salvation. So I straighten, digging deep for some version of confidence. "I love you. We'll figure this out. Now let's go meet your little girl."

His eyes fall shut and he sags in relief. "I don't deserve you," he rasps. Then his lips are on mine, taking me in a sweet kiss. He pulls away quicker than I'd like, and as he links his fingers with mine, I tell myself that that kiss won't be the last one we'll ever share.

Still, I wish I'd savored it more.

Hand in hand, we walk inside, and after JJ gives his name to the receptionist, we're given name tags and directed to the elevators.

We're silent as the stainless-steel box climbs. When we hit the tenth floor, we step off and walk silently down the hall, following the signs on the walls. I pause when we get to room 1021, my breath stalling out.

This is the room where he'll meet his child. She's in there. But so is Tabitha. And I just—I don't know how to do this.

"It was once," he murmurs, staring at the closed door. "Before—" He shakes his head and then looks at me, expression pleading. "When you called me about the Olympics, when that girl answered…that was the first time you'd ever given me any indication that it bothered you that I was with a woman."

Pain and frustration clash inside me. "So had I brought it up sooner, you'd have kept it in your pants?"

Eyes widening, he wavers, like he's on the verge of losing his balance.

I slap my hand over my mouth, mortification shrouding me. "I'm sorry."

He shakes his head. "You have nothing to apologize for."

"We don't have to do this right now," I tell him. "This isn't about me."

"I need you to know this," he says quickly. "When I hung up the phone that night, I promised myself that I'd find a way to have you. I hated myself for how you sounded and I hated that I wasn't with you. There has been no one since then and there never will be anyone but you. I'm sorry that this is happening. It kills me that I put us in this situation, but Adeline, I need you." His eyes go glassy, like he's fighting tears. "Tabitha means absolutely nothing to me—"

"She's the mother of your child," I say softly. "I had a really shitty father. One who was never around. Who never put me first, or even second or third. I won't let any child, especially yours, experience that kind of pain."

He scowls, the look anguished. "I can be a father without being anyone to Tabitha."

I shrug. "Maybe."

I say the word, but I don't believe it. I know women like Tabitha well. They're everywhere hockey players tend to be. I've watched them work their charm for years. And they all have one goal. Tabitha got her wish. She's not going to make this easy.

Still, I force a smile. "We'll figure it out. Let's just…go meet your daughter."

"You're the most important person in the world to me, Adeline."

I smile sadly, my lips wobbling. "Not anymore. And I shouldn't be."

JJ blinks at me, like he's considering denying it. But he's a good guy. The best. The moment we walk in there, his heart is going to shift. As it should. I wouldn't love him the way I do if he didn't fall absolutely in love the second he sees his little girl.

So I smile when he leads me into the dimly lit room. I smile as he goes quiet, taking in his daughter for the first time. And I stand back, allowing him to choose her. Thankful he chooses her. It's the right thing to do. Even if my heart is breaking, I stand tall, silently watching him settle on the bed beside Tabitha so he can hold his daughter.

"Does she have a name?" His voice cracks on the last word.

Tabitha, who looks annoyingly gorgeous twenty-four hours after a c-section, nods. "Her name is Avery Catherine Hanson."

I have to bite back a spiteful laugh. She's good. I'll give her that. Naming her after JJ's mom is diabolical, really.

JJ turns to me. "Hey, baby, come meet my daughter."

Tabitha's face falls. She shifts, her strawberry blond hair hiding her eyes, but I swear she's shooting daggers at me as I take a step closer.

I ignore her for a moment, focusing instead on the soft smile on JJ's face as he studies his little girl. She's so tiny, six pounds, two ounces according to the weight on the board. Seventeen inches. She's got fuzzy blond hair and rosy cheeks. She lets out a big yawn, and when she opens her eyes, my heart stutters. They're the same color as JJ's. Ice blue. If there was ever any question about paternity, we've got our answer. "Avery, this is Adeline. She's my bestest friend in the whole world and I know she'll be yours too."

Tabitha makes a squeaky sound. I ignore that too, instead focusing on the small hand wrapped around his pointer finger.

She squeezes and he laughs, his gaze flying to mine. "She's got a good grip."

"Hi, Avery," I say. My voice sounds rough against my own ears. "It's so nice to meet you." I run my finger gently against her hand, a strange affection blooming inside me as the softness of her skin registers. "She's perfect."

He nods. "She really is."

"Could you get me ice?" Tabitha asks. "And water?"

Stepping back, I glance at her. "Sure."

"Not you," she says. "JJ, can you?"

He silently defers to me. Not wanting to overstep or get involved, I nod quickly.

With a kiss to Avery's forehead, he stands and faces Tabitha. "Do you want to hold her?"

"Put her in the bassinet," she says with a wave of her hand. "They told me not to coddle her. Better that she gets used to being in a crib now."

I frown. I've been surrounded by children my whole life, and never once has anyone warned against coddling a newborn.

"Oh, okay," JJ says, sounding a little thrown too. He settles Avery in the clear plastic bassinet.

She makes a little whimpering noise, though she quiets quickly. Sweet baby. "Want to come with me?" JJ asks as he heads my way.

"I'm sure she'll be fine without you for a few minutes," Tabitha says. "Plus, it would be good for us to get acquainted."

I give JJ another silent nod. I'll be fine.

With a shrug, he pads out into the hall. He's been gone a total of five seconds when Tabitha clears her throat and sits a little straighter in bed. "How long have you two been together?"

I want to look anywhere but at her, but I hold her stare, determined not to back down. "It's new."

She nods. "Right. Listen, I never wanted to be a mother."

A shocked breath escapes me at her candor. "Okay."

She doesn't even look at the baby to her left. "I already found a couple to adopt. That was the plan when I thought she was my ex-boyfriend's, but the second she came out, I realized that was highly unlikely."

My stomach drops. "What?"

"My ex has very dark features. Olive skin, dark eyes. He's Dominican. There's no chance in hell that baby isn't JJ's."

I want to argue with her, but Avery really does look like JJ. She has his eyes, and honestly, there's this strange sixth sense inside me that tells me that this little girl belongs to him.

"The second I realized that, I made the call," Tabitha continues.

"Made what call?" I'm having a hard time following this conversation, my head spinning.

Tabitha has an agenda. It's clear as day, but I haven't quite worked it out.

"I told the couple that I'd decided to keep her. But—" She holds up a finger. "And this is the important part, Adeline. My daughter and I won't play second fiddle to you."

Jaw slack, I shake my head. "I would never ask JJ to pick me over his child."

She settles back against the pillow. "Good, then we're in agreement."

"What are we agreeing to?"

"You dump him. Tonight."

My stomach rolls. This fucking bitch. And yet I'm not even a little surprised.

"Are you out of your mind?"

"No. I'm protective. And with you in the picture, JJ will never put me and our daughter first. So the choice is yours. You stay with him, and I'll push for the adoption. His name's not on the birth certificate yet. He'll have to fight it if he really wants her. It'll be a mess. Or you break up with him and give him the chance to be a father to his daughter. Give us a chance to be a family."

My heart crumples in on itself. Family. God, had she used any other word, I might consider fighting back. But she's right. Avery deserves to have her father in her life. JJ will be an incredible dad. And I...I never wanted to be a mother. This will get messy. No matter what. With a woman like Tabitha in his life, JJ will never have peace. And my presence will only make it worse.

JJ returns, a cup of ice in one hand and a pitcher of water in the other.

Tabitha's smile turns sugary sweet as she thanks him.

He barely looks at her, instead focusing on the baby, picking her up and snapping a few pictures of her.

By the time we leave, it feels like I've been trapped in one of those twirly upside-down rides. I can't catch my breath or find my footing. Every scenario I consider ends the same way. JJ and I will be over. It's only a matter of time. But he'll have his daughter. I won't get in the way. My whole life, my own father has wanted nothing to do with me, and that has shaped me into who I am now. A woman who's always a little chipped, a little broken. I won't do that to JJ's daughter. I won't do that to him.

"She's so perfect," he says as we get into the elevator. "My mom is going to lose it when she sees her."

I force a smile. "Yeah, she is."

"And my dad, oh my god, I can't wait for them to meet her. Do you think Tabitha would let us to take her over there to meet them once she's out of the hospital?"

I shrug. "Maybe?"

"And your parents," he rambles. "Can you imagine your dad's reaction? And—"

I hit the emergency button and the elevator jolts. "JJ stop."

Eyes widening, he runs a hand over his face. "I'm so sorry."

"Stop apologizing," I say, aggravation bleeding into my tone. "You have a beautiful daughter. Don't apologize for that. I'm happy for you. And your parents are going to love her, one thousand percent. But my dad," I stare up at the ceiling and shake my head. "She can't be in his life."

"What?" The single word is dripping with confusion.

I flatten my lips together and sigh, forcing myself to look at him.

"I don't want to be a mother."

Confusion turns to pain. "What are you saying?"

I keep my shoulders back and my head high. I won't waver. Because even though Tabitha forced my hand, it's the truth. "I'm saying that I need to focus on my career, and you should focus on that little girl. She needs you."

He stumbles back like I hit him. "And you don't?" he asks, this time with shock and a decent dose of disdain.

It hurts, the way he's looking at me now, but I shake my head, holding back the tears. "No JJ, I don't."

CHAPTER 30

Present

LAST NIGHT WAS A TURNING point of sorts. Sitting on the roof with Adeline, celebrating in the way we used to, brought me clarity.

I respect that she doesn't want to risk her career for a relationship. The issue is similar to the one we faced that night four years ago. But back then, I didn't see it from her perspective. I was so angry. So pissed. So goddamn hurt. I did things I never should have done and I reacted in ways I'm not proud of. Yet she took it all. She held her head high, walked away, and chased her dream. And she was right to do so.

I, on the other hand, sought revenge, married the revenge, and destroyed the last vestiges of our friendship.

I punch the pillow beside me. None of that matters anymore. I'll do things differently this time. I'll listen when she asks for space. I'll be her friend and support her both at work and at home. And while I'm doing that, I'll get my life sorted. That way when I go to her the next time, when I beg her to give us a shot once again, we'll actually have a chance.

I jump out of bed, determined. The team is flying out this afternoon and then we'll be on the road for three games. Then we've got a full week in Boston. Thank god. I hate leaving Avery. If Vivi wasn't also taking care of Hope's and Winnie's kids, I'd have her traveling with us so my little girl could come as well. But this is better for her. She needs routine, and it's why I moved into the brownstone to begin with.

I snag a shirt from the dresser and throw it over my head, then I step into the hallway.

The house is quiet. Luckily, the kids all seem to be pretty good sleepers. The big ones, at least, and since they share a room, they often end up playing first thing in the morning rather than coming out in search of food.

Warmth blooms in my chest. That's not a terrible way to grow up. Maybe I'm not doing such an awful job after all. I wish I could give her the mother she deserves, but we're doing the best we can, and that has to count for something.

The floor creaks down the hall, catching my attention, and when I turn, Brayden is peeking out the door that leads to Vivi's loft wearing last night's suit, sans jacket. The white button-down shirt is open, his sleeves rolled up. And there's a backward Bolts hat on his head. That's standard. The only time he's not wearing a cap like that is when he's on the ice. His shoes are in one hand and his phone is in the other. He's typing away, head down, oblivious to my presence.

I lean against the wall, smirking. "Going somewhere?"

Cursing, he drops his phone. "Fucking A, JJ. Why the hell are you standing in the hall like a creep?"

I laugh. Loud. "Me? A creep? Did you or did you not just step out of the bedroom that belongs to our coach's *daughter*? That's much more creepy than sleeping with the coach."

He scowls. "One, saying it like that implies said coach is Gavin. Gross. He's sixty and like a second dad to me. Two, I didn't sleep with anyone last night."

Pushing off the wall, I open my mouth to retort.

Before I can, he shakes his head. "I'm not finished. Three, I'm here because I'm a good guy. I made sure our coach's very young, very drunk daughter got home last night. Don't compare that to you trying to romance your goalie coach." He shakes his head. "We are not the same."

"Fuck, you're in a foul mood."

"I didn't sleep well. I was too busy watching a twenty-two-year-old breathe all night."

I scratch my neck. "She was that drunk?" I eye the stairs, unease swirling inside me. Vivi has been really good with Avery. I'd hate to think I can't trust her. Especially since I'm leaving in a matter of hours.

Sighing, Bray drops his shoes. "Fucking Bobby was feeding her shots," he grouses as he shoves one foot in. "The girl didn't know heads from tails by the end of the night. It wasn't her fault."

"So you drove her home?" I'm still confused about how he ended up being the one to take care of her.

"Bobby tried to leave with her. Something they'd both regret. Coach would literally skin him alive."

I nod. He's not wrong. "You need a ride home?"

He holds up his phone. "Just ordered an Uber."

"Okay, I'll walk you out."

Halfway down the stairs, his phone blares loudly.

"Jesus," I mutter.

Wincing, he answers.

So much for the kids sleeping in.

"Hey—"

"Why the fuck am I looking at a picture on my ring camera of you carrying my daughter into her goddamn house last night?"

Coach's voice is so loud I can hear it from here. *Shit.*

Brayden's eyes slide shut and he sighs. "It's not what you think—"

"Good, because right now I'm thinking that my goddamn captain was carrying my intoxicated daughter into her home. So if that's not what it looks like, then please enlighten me."

"Well, I mean yes, that is exactly what it was, but—"

"Hawke, so help me god," he grits out, "if you tell me you didn't sleep with my daughter—"

"Sir, I didn't," Bray stammers.

"You shouldn't even have to fucking say it. Why the fuck did you allow her to get that drunk?"

Rather than tell Coach that it was Bobby, rather than stick up for himself, Brayden swallows and ducks his head. "I'm sorry, sir."

"Where is she now?" Gavin grits out.

"She's asleep."

"You're still in her goddamn room?"

"Nope," I say, unable to stop myself. "Hawke's with me. He stayed on the couch. Found him myself."

My best friend shakes his head, jaw tight.

"Oh, hi, JJ," Coach says, sounding a bit caught off guard. "Were you there when my daughter got obliterated?"

Brayden and I eye one another. Gavin is normally pretty rational, but right now I think he'd like to castrate us both. "No, sir. I left to get pizza with Adeline."

"At least someone has some goddamn sense. Do me a favor, when my daughter wakes up, tell her to call me."

"Of course," I say quickly.

"And Hawke?"

"Yes, sir," Brayden says, sounding tired.

"I'm really fucking disappointed in you."

"I'm sorry, sir."

"A lot of good that does me," he snaps. "Stay away from my daughter. She's twenty-one. And how old are you? Thirty-three? Thirty-four?" He doesn't give Brayden a chance to answer. "She's off limits. Do you understand?"

Brayden nods like Gavin can see him. "Of course."

When the line goes dead, I stare at him. "That was so not good."

He shakes his head. "Just make sure she takes the pain reliever I left beside her bed. And, uh, I'll call Josie. See if she can come over and help with the kids before you have to leave."

I blow out a breath. "Thanks, man. You better tell Bobby he owes you."

"Yeah, he fucking does." Grumbling, he slips his phone into his pocket. "Uber's here. I'll see you later."

Three hours later, Vivi is cuddled up on the couch with all the monsters watching a movie. She looks like shit, and she winces every time the music gets loud. More than once, she's muttered, "Fucking A, Uncle Beckett just had to spring for the best surround system."

Chuckling, I drop my suitcase by my feet. Then I hold out my arms. "Come on, Avey girl. I gotta head out."

My little girl runs toward me, throwing her arms around my neck and hugging me tight. "You're going to call before bed, right?" Her sweet voice is insistent as she snuggles into me.

I pull back and look her in the eye. "Every night. And you're going to be extra good for your aunties, right?"

She nods aggressively, making her blond hair float around her head.

Before I can ask her what she wants me to bring home—it's a trick question because I bring her a key chain from every place I go; every airport, every arena, every city, if I see a keychain I bring it to her, the sparklier the better— my girl squeals in my ear and shoves away from me.

"Addie! You're going with Daddy too?"

Adeline appears at the bottom of the stairs, suitcase in hand. Today's red suit makes my tongue feel heavy. It's form fitting and dips low between her breasts. It's sexy yet classy. Her chestnut hair is down and wavy against her shoulders and her lips are the same color as that suit. Sinful red. Fuck me.

"I am, Avey girl." She crouches to Avery's level.

She's wearing black heels with the red bottoms. The same shoes she wore that night at the restaurant. Shit. I cannot have visions of those shoes on either side of my head right now, while my four-year-old grins up at her.

I'll save those thoughts for later.

"Kick some hockey player butt like always."

Avery launches herself into Adeline's arms and hugs her just as tight as she did me. I have to look away. It's painful, seeing what we could have had. What we could have been. If only Tabitha hadn't been Avery's mother. If only Adeline was.

Then again, Adeline didn't want kids. Just the thought makes my chest burn.

"And you promise to call me every night?" Avery asks.

Head snapping up, I step forward, ready to explain to my daughter why she can't ask for stuff like that. But before I can, Adeline nods, that soft smile she only gives my daughter on her lips. "Of course I will."

"You can call with my dad." She beams up at me like we're in on a secret. If I'd thought of it, I'd have helped with the scheme, but this is all Avery.

Adeline peers at me over my little girl's head wearing a wary look. "You can call me on my phone," she says.

"I'll call you with Daddy. I like it when you sleep in the same bed. Then my daddy isn't lonely."

Still curled up on the couch, Vivi squeaks out a "what?"

I glare at her. The girl has no room to talk. "We only did that because you were between us and having a bad dream, right?"

Avery shrugs her little shoulders.

This girl. Regardless of her motives, I'm not mad about it. I'd happily sleep with these two in my bed every night. God, it'd be a damn dream come true.

"We should go," Adeline says, probably ready to put a stop to Avery's off-the-cuff comments.

"Wait," my daughter yells.

"What's the matter?" Adeline says, always patient with her.

"You didn't say I love you." Her voice is so small, so sad. Fuck. I swear if I could pull my heart out of my chest and hand it to her, I would.

Adeline drops down again and takes her hands. "I love you always. And I'll call you tonight. With your daddy."

Beaming, Avery throws her arms around her.

I'm done for.

Before I can get my wits about me, Adeline strides out the door. She insists we take separate cars, saying she has to make a stop, though she's vague about where and why I can't come with her.

Maybe it's for the best anyway. The solo drive, with only music for company, should settle me.

And it should help me wrap my head around what I need to do to make what just happened in that house more of a reality. Avery and Adeline and me.

If we could find a way to be together, would she really want that?

I get so lost in my thoughts that I miss the exit for the airport. When I realize, I take my time, continuing in the wrong direction for several more minutes before circling back. By the time I pull into the reserved parking lot, Adeline's car is parked and she's nowhere in sight.

Bag in hand, I head for the private terminal where the reporters traveling with the team have congregated. I spot Bobby first. He's sporting sunglasses inside—clearly feeling like shit after all those shots last night. Then Bray, who is leaning in really close, probably giving him an earful. I take a step in their direction so I can witness the smack down, but I pull up short when Adeline's voice rings out behind me.

"Why, Savannah? Why here?"

I whip around, finding Savannah hovering around Adeline, fixing her makeup.

And my girl looks absolutely miserable.

"Because he was going to be late, and you can't waste this gorgeous outfit." Savannah motions to Adeline's hot as fuck suit.

"I'm at work, Sav. I need these guys to respect me, not look at me like I'm a contestant on *The Bachelorette*."

Her redheaded friend snaps a hand to her hip. "You're the damn lead, not a contestant. Own it."

Adeline whines. "You know what I mean."

"Smile," Savannah commands. "It'll be over in a few. Oh, look. The *contestant* is here."

I frown. The contestant?

"Adeline." The sound of her name—my fucking name—on someone else's lips makes anger flare to life in my veins.

"Scott," she says to the man she went on a date with two nights ago.

I glare at him. He's dressed in a navy suit, his black hair slicked back, and I swear to god he's wearing blush. He's also got a bouquet of roses. Red ones.

My lips tip up in a smirk without my permission.

While many girls would love that, Adeline isn't one of them. She hates roses. They make her sneeze.

As if on cue, he holds them out, and she sniffles. Sneezing, she takes a step back. "Allergic," she gets out before another sneeze overtakes her.

I chuckle, the sound catching her attention, and she glowers at me.

"I'll take those." Savannah plucks the bouquet from his hand and steps out of the shot the photographer is clearly trying to capture.

"Shit, I'm sorry," Scott says.

Adeline gives him a kind smile. "It was really sweet of you to bring them. But I'm kind of surprised to see you here."

Slipping his hands into his pockets, he nods. "You mentioned you'd be traveling for the next two weeks, and I wanted to see you before you left. I tried to get tickets for yesterday's game, only to discover they were sold out. I didn't realize that would happen."

I roll my eyes. It was our season opener. Does this guy know anything about Boston hockey? Our fans are ruthless and dedicated. There's never an empty seat.

"That's very sweet. Had I known, I would have gotten you a ticket. I kind of have a connection."

He laughs like she's said something funny when all she's done is state the obvious.

Idiot.

The thought was supposed to stay inside my head, but when Adeline's gaze cuts to mine again, I wonder if I've said it out loud.

I smirk.

"Maybe you can get me one in the future. After our second date." He gives her a hopeful smile.

I hold my breath, my hands clenched into fists. *Come on, Adeline. Tell him to take a hike.*

"Oh. You want to go out. With me?" she stutters awkwardly. "Again?"

He steps closer. "I had a really good time the other night. I thought you had a good time too."

Yeah, with me in the closet, buddy. Now back the fuck away from my girl.

Adeline gives him a smile I don't recognize. It's almost…shy.

What the hell? She doesn't do shy. Why the fuck is she acting like that? Does she have a thing for him? No. She fucked me. And even though we can't be more than friends right now, we're going to figure it the fuck out.

She doesn't know that, but she will.

Fuck.

What if she really likes him?

"I had a great time." Her words are so soft I almost miss them.

Scott leans in, and I swear to god my throat closes. "I really want to kiss you," he says, voice low, gaze roaming over her face.

Pain radiates through my chest. I'll die if she kisses him. I'll fucking die.

Adeline sets her hand against his chest, pushing him back a fraction. "I'd prefer it if our first kiss wasn't in public." Finally, she stands a little taller, her confidence returning. "I'm kind of at work."

I blow out a relieved breath.

"Oh shit, sorry," Scott mutters. "First the flowers, now this."

Popping up on her toes, she presses a kiss to his cheek.

I swear it's like a sucker punch. Ducking, I stare at the floor. I can't watch their goodbye.

I'm lost in my tangled thoughts, trying to catch my breath, when Adeline steps up next to me.

"JJ," she hisses.

With a look over my shoulder, I note that Savannah and the camera crew are following Scott out of the terminal. Good.

"Yeah?" I say, focusing on Adeline.

"What are you doing?" she whispers.

"Standing here," I say, my words clipped, my frustration threatening to bubble over.

"You can't look at me like that."

I frown. "Now I'm even looking at you wrong?"

"You know what I mean." She sighs heavily.

Jaw clenched, I stare her down. "He called you Adeline."

She shrugs. "It is my name."

"No one calls you that."

"You do," she says haughtily.

"*Adeline.*"

"See? You just did it right there," she snaps.

"You know damn well *why* I call you that," I growl out, voice low, shoulders so tense I know I'll need a massage before the game tomorrow.

Her body sags, and for a moment she looks so goddamn broken. Fuck. "I'm sorry," I say quickly, my chest aching.

Her eyes meet mine. "JJ, I—we—" She shakes her head.

"I know, okay." I scan our surroundings to make sure no one is watching or listening. When I confirm it's just us, I give it to her straight. "But Adeline, that's *mine.*" It's desperately ridiculous to claim a goddamn name. *Her name.* But I do it anyway.

She rolls her lips, the anger draining from her expression. "I'll tell him to call me Addie."

The relief is brief, but it hits hard. "Thank you."

"We should get on the plane," she says, nodding at the line of men who are doing just that.

As we walk toward the gate, bags in tow, I can't help but pry a little. "So you guys really didn't kiss the other night?"

Her eyes go wide. "I was still flush from your orgasm...I wouldn't..."

I nod, biting down on a smile. "Good."

"It doesn't mean—"

"I know. Just give me this one thing to be happy about for a moment."

A long breath escapes her, but she dips her chin. "Okay."

"JJ. Addie."

We turn, and when I notice Gavin rushing down the hall toward us wearing a panicked look, dread pools in my gut.

"Jesus," he says as he stops. "This day has been a goddamn nightmare."

"What's wrong?" Adeline asks.

As far as I know, she doesn't know about Bray and Vivi, whatever was going on there, but I wouldn't have expected Gavin to bring it up to her, not here. Then again, he did sound extra pissed this morning.

"Sidney was in an accident on the way home last night."

Heart dropping, I dig my phone out of my pocket. "Is he okay?"

Gavin shakes his head. "Yeah. Except he's got a broken leg. He's out…for at least the season."

"Fuck," I mutter, navigating to his contact. Sidney and I have been playing together for six years. He's like my older brother.

"I wouldn't," Gavin says, nodding at my phone. "I stopped by the hospital on the way here. He's on lots of pain meds and sleeping now. His wife's there."

"Good. I should tell her if she needs anything—"

"Beckett's on top of it already, as is Sara."

"What do you need from us?" Adeline asks.

"You'll be playing for this series," Gavin tells me.

No surprise there. "Not a problem."

"And we'll have to call Dirk up," he says to Adeline. "Do you want to make the call, or do you want me to?"

An instant wave of disgust hits me. No fucking way.

I wait for Adeline to say the same thing, but she just nods. "Of course. I'll make the call."

Gavin blows out a long breath. "Fuck this day. Thanks."

Adeline smiles in response, but the moment Gavin steps away, her expression falls.

"Are you going to tell them what happened," I grit out, "or am I?"

Avoiding my gaze, she shakes her head. "Please just drop it."

I lean in close, anger getting the best of me. "He's not playing with us, Adeline. You're not coaching him. Not a fucking chance. So are you going to tell them, or am I?"

CHAPTER 31

Twenty-Two Years Old

I NEVER COULD HAVE IMAGINED it would be so hard saying goodbye to a person I just met, but getting in the car and driving away, knowing Avery was inside and I wouldn't see her for two weeks, was damn near impossible.

Seven days. I've only known her for a week, and I'm head over heels in love with her. She's perfect. I spent the week staying in Tabitha's guest room so I could help out and so I didn't have to miss any more time than necessary.

The two of us are awkward around each other. Tabitha and me. Or maybe it's just me. Because when I'm not focused on my daughter, I'm staring into space thinking of what I could have done differently with Adeline. What I should have said. How I should have handled the bomb dropped on us.

I shouldn't have asked her to come to the hospital. It was too much, too fast. Of course she wasn't ready to deal with this long term. We'd barely gotten out of bed for the first time when we found out that I'm a father.

But in that moment, I needed Adeline my friend, not my girlfriend. *Girlfriend.* Was she even that for those brief perfect moments? We never defined anything. She's certainly not that right now. We haven't spoken since the elevator. She got off and told me she'd call an Uber. I let her. I left her there like a complete dick. Angry and shocked.

But I'm going to fix this. Over the last few days, I've worked out a plan. We're playing Vegas tonight and Adeline will be there. I'll knock on her door at the hotel and beg her to talk to me before morning skate. I want to be with her. Even if we only see each other for eight weeks out of the year. Even if we have to FaceTime every night just to spend time together. When I'm not with Avery, I'll do everything I can to show her I can make this work. That I *will* make this work.

She doesn't have to be Avery's mom. She just needs to want to be with me.

I love her. We've got to figure this out.

With a very large tip, I convince an employee to give me her room number. My hands tremble the whole way up to her floor, and outside her door, I stop and take a deep breath before knocking.

There's a commotion inside. Multiple voices.

"Just get out of here," she hisses.

A second later, the door swings open and Dirk fucking barrels into me.

I stumble back, frowning. "Dirk?"

"Hey, JJ, see you tonight." Winking, he smacks my chest. Then he saunters away, whistling.

"JJ?" Adeline's voice sounds off.

Vision going red, I step over the threshold. "Fucking Dirk?"

She pulls her robe tighter, her fingers white as she squeezes the fabric together. "It's not what you think," she mumbles, barely looking at me. Her hair is a mess. Her lipstick smudged.

My stomach rolls.

"It's not what I think? Seriously Adeline? I—we—" I shake my head. How the hell could she do this? "You know what? Forget it. You made your choice." I spin, fury engulfing me, and step into the hall again.

"Wait, JJ, please, he—*please.*"

"I loved you," I shout, whipping around again. "I fucking loved you, and you…how could you do this to me?"

With tears streaming down her cheeks, she shakes her head. "I hate you," she whispers. "I needed you, and you…I *hate* you," she sobs out.

She slams the door, the sound startling me out of my blind rage. Holy fuck, what did I just do?

All day, my stomach rolls. What I saw this morning? Something was off. Something…it's not right. I need to see her. Confirm she's okay. Then I can go back to being mad. Because right now, I'm too confused to be angry. Her eyes, they were…glassy. Sad. Scared.

That's what haunts me. The emptiness in those deep, dark eyes. Like she didn't expect anything but for me to walk away. Like I did exactly what she anticipated.

She begged me and I walked away. But not until after I yelled at her.

Fuck.

I do a lap around the ice, looking for her. Even with gear on, I can always pick her out. She wears her hair in a braid. She uses a bright pink mouthguard. Even without all that, I know Adeline better than anyone in the world. But she's not here. Not on the ice or on the bench.

I skate up to the closest Vegas player and stop quickly. "Adeline Langfield playing tonight?"

The guy looks over his shoulder, glancing at his coach, and grimaces. "You didn't hear it from me, but there were pictures of her naked everywhere in the locker room. Taped to all the stalls, in the shower, all over the floor."

"What?" My stomach bottoms out. I glance around. This can't be… *fuck*.

"And then she never showed," he goes on, oblivious to the way I'm spiraling. "Coach was pissed. I'm pretty sure she's done."

Without another word to him, I dig my skates into the ice and power toward Dirk, who's warming up in front of Vegas's net.

"What the fuck did you do?" I say before I've even reached him.

He looks up, his eyes wide with surprise, though a smirk quickly slides across his face. Cocky fucker pulls off his mask and settles it against the net, then reaches for his water. "You were right. She was pretty good on her kn—"

My fist meets his mouth before the last word leaves it.

CHAPTER 32

Addie

SOMEHOW I HOLD it together through the plane ride to Chicago, through the bus ride to the hotel, and through practice.

Only when we're finally released for the night, do I sneak away while JJ is talking to Brayden and Bobby and rush to my hotel room. The moment I shut the door, I collapse against it and slide to the floor.

It's been four years since it happened and I still feel dirty when I think of Dirk. Dirty because somehow he ended up in my room. Dirty because I wasn't dressed when I woke up and found him sitting in a chair, staring at me, like he'd been waiting for that moment. Waiting to humiliate me just a bit more.

I'd barely opened my eyes when JJ had knocked on the door. I saw Dirk. Told him to leave. He went pretty quickly, but when the door swung open, there was JJ, looking like I had betrayed him in the worst way.

I close my eyes and will my breathing to steady. It's a routine I've fallen into far too many times since that morning after the Olympics. Everything was perfect and then it wasn't.

I couldn't face the team after Dirk plastered photos of me all over the locker room.

Pictures that came from my phone.

Stills from the video JJ and I had taken together.

Dirk took my most intimate moment, with a man I thought I could trust, and plastered images of it all over the locker room.

A friend on the team alerted me to it while I was getting dressed in the bathroom. Yeah, the bathroom. Not a locker room. The Vices only had one. He took a picture and sent it to me.

I couldn't face it.

I'd put up with a lot through the years playing with men, but if that kind of harassment was what it took to stand in an NHL locker room, if that's what it took to set foot on that ice, they could keep it.

At the time, that felt like my only option. I'm older and wiser and I have thicker skin now. And I'm angry. I should have faced it. *I* didn't do *anything* wrong.

But between JJ's betrayal and the way he lashed out, I'd been drained of all my drive. I was still reeling, shocked by how easily he walked away when I was so fragile. Time and again, I'd stood by his side when he needed me, and yet he didn't even give me the opportunity to explain.

I didn't know why Dirk was there. And I absolutely didn't want him in that room.

The time between when I sat down in the bar the night before and when I woke up was missing from my mind. Nine hours completely unaccounted for.

I never have more than two drinks now.

I never allow a man to buy one for me.

He did that to me.

Shaking, teeth chattering, I stare at the hotel bed.

I can't coach him. I can't travel to countless hotels wondering if I'll wake up not knowing again.

I was tested. Pregnancy tests. STD tests. A rape kit.

We found nothing.

It was bullying. I'm almost positive. Mind games. He wanted the position and he couldn't stand on his own damn skates and prove himself. I would have had that position. It was mine.

But I didn't report it. Not to the NHL, not to the cops, and definitely not to my family.

I don't even know what JJ knows and what he assumes. Maybe he thinks Dirk took advantage of a sad girl. He doesn't know the whole truth. That, I'm sure of. If he did, he'd have killed him on day one of practice. He wouldn't have waited until Dirk pulled that stupid stunt with the puck to go after him.

But JJ isn't who I'm worried about right now. No, today I'm choosing me. I deserve to be here. I don't deserve to have to coach Dirk. To face him every day for an entire season.

I can't. I won't.

Before I can chicken out, I pull out my phone and text my uncles.

Me: Can we talk?

Gavin, Brooks and Aiden are seated at a round table in the back when I walk into the restaurant. I made a reservation at a place a few blocks from our hotel and asked them to meet me here.

Not one of them questioned it.

And here they are. God, I should have gone to them years ago. I should have spoken up.

Seeing them here now, I can't believe I ever thought I couldn't.

But my best friend, the person I trusted most in the world, didn't believe me when I tried to tell him back then, so why would they?

Brooks is sitting against the wall, so he spots me first. Eyes lighting up, he waves me over.

Both Aiden and Gavin smile when they see me as well.

And there goes the fluttering of nerves again. Because now I have to talk. I have to do what I should have done before.

"Thank you for meeting me here," I say past the lump in my throat.

Aiden gives me a funny look. "Why are you being so formal? It's just dinner." He stands and pulls me in for a hug. Wrapping my arms around him, I close my eyes and settle my head against his chest. And for a moment, I just breathe.

He shifts, looking down at me. "You okay?"

His voice is soft. Too soft. If things continue like this, I might cry.

Pulling back, I nod. Then I slide into the empty seat, sitting before my other uncles can soften me with more hugs. "It's actually not just dinner," I say, placing my hands flat on top of each other on the table.

Gavin frowns. "What's up?"

I take a deep breath and dig deep for the words. "I don't want to call Dirk up."

Brooks eyes Gavin, brow creased. "You think the rookie would be a better fit?"

Gavin shakes his head. "Nah, he's too green. Dirk isn't the best, but with Addie coaching—"

"That's just it," I say. "I don't want to coach."

All three sets of eyes snap to me.

"What?" Brooks asks.

"I want to play."

The moment the words come out, a giggle breaks free. "I would make the better second goalie. *I* want to play."

When they're all silent, expressions stunned, I launch into my stats. I list off every record I broke in the PWHL. Every record I broke the second time I played for the Olympic team. A complete shutout. The entire series. Unheard of.

"Camden had been begging me to consider playing. Even if it wasn't for the Bolts."

Gavin's smile is blinding. "You don't have to convince us of your abilities. We've seen you play more than any of the guys on the team. It's all we've wanted for a long time. You were meant to wear this uniform. But you didn't want it."

Head lowered, I swallow. Then I meet his eye and then tell the truth. "I was scared." I shrug. "I didn't think I would be accepted."

Brooks frowns. "You might not be. But you can't run from that."

"Who gives a shit what other people think?" Aiden says. "Every single one of us dealt with shit talk. We were handed our positions because of the last name. Brought in to work for the team because of connections. We were losing our touch on the ice. Brooks was getting slow—"

"Fuck you very much," Brooks says with a soft laugh.

Aiden grins. "My point is, that guy is the best damn goalie we ever had. Arguably the best to ever play."

Brooks huffs, "Now you're just sucking up."

"He's not wrong," I tell my biggest, gentlest uncle.

"And this one," Gavin says, squeezing Aiden's shoulder, "is a hall-of-famer. But the pundits said I should have moved him down so Keegan could play more."

I roll my eyes. The damn media put so much stress on my Uncle Aiden. It got so bad that one season he had a panic attack on the ice.

"And everyone said he was just a rich boy who took a job meant for a real coach," Brooks says, thumbing toward Gavin.

Our head coach nods and leans forward. "Our point is, people are always going to talk shit. You just have to learn to tune them out."

"And if you can't, use it. Work harder, practice longer, prove them fucking wrong," Aiden says, lighting up.

"So you want to be goalie?" Gavin leans back in his chair like he's really considering it.

Could he be? Could this actually happen?

I dip my head once. "Yes."

"We'd still need to call Dirk up until Sidney hits IR."

I figured he'd say that. We're at cap, so we can't add another player to our roster until Sidney is out for seven days. But after that, he's considered injured reserve and that opens up a spot to either bring a player up on waiver or sign a free agent. Me, hopefully. In the meantime, we'll have to bring someone up from our AHL team, since they're under our cap.

Could I handle coaching Dirk for a week? Yes. Obviously. I handled him during preseason just fine. Mostly.

But since JJ and I have grown closer over the last few weeks, memories from that time have resurfaced more and more, and now I can't look at Dirk without thinking of that night. Of the way I felt when I woke up and couldn't remember what had happened.

I felt helpless. Used.

I never want to feel that way again.

"About that," I start.

All eyes turn to me again.

"What if we bring up the rookie? It's only seven days. And I think it might be worth bringing him up and keeping him on the bench after the week is up. He should be practicing with us in case anything happens to JJ or me."

"Why not Dirk?" Gavin asks, his tone one of genuine curiosity.

"Honestly," I say, going with part of the truth, "because I don't like him."

Brooks nods. "Me neither. He's an ass with a bone to pick when it comes to Addie. And while I wouldn't normally put too much stock in shit like that, it's not good for the team. And right now, at the beginning of the season, after losing our other goaltender, it's best if we stick with team players."

I breathe a huge sigh of relief and meet my uncle's eye. "Thank you."

Gavin frowns thoughtfully. "We'd need you to take over for her."

Brooks nods. "I'm aware."

Tongue pressed to his cheek, Gavin sits back. "I actually have someone who might be able to help you," he says to Brooks.

"And you're sure about this?" Aiden asks.

"Are you guys sure?" I ask, my heart hammering.

It can't be this easy. God, I asked them not to bring up Dirk, and they just…agreed. They just believed me. It's…freeing.

"I know you tried to convince me to become a free agent last year, but—"

"Addie, you're the best goalie I've seen in a long fucking time," Brooks says. "It would be my honor to coach you. And the only reason I'm agreeing to step into that role is because I'd get to work with you. Understand?"

My eyes heat. Dammit. I sniff, holding myself together, and eye Gavin. "And you?"

"We're going to have so much fun. And I gotta be honest, I'm hoping this is my last year, so I'd really like to enjoy it."

Elated, I throw myself across the table and finally hug them both, knocking over the salt and pepper and maybe a glass of water or two. "Okay, let's have some fun."

CHAPTER 33

JJ

Theo: Who's excited to see me this weekend?

Finn: You better get me the best seats in the house, Cowboy Quarterback.

Bray: LOL, cause you can't get your own tickets to a BOSTON football game?

Theo: Um, Tennessee.

Bray: You're playing in Boston. And sports outside of Boston don't count.

Theo: That's not how it works.

Finn: Says the kid who is crying over not playing for Boston.

Theo: I hate you all right now. How's my sister?

Me: She's good. I think she's getting used to the whole single mom thing. Especially since she's not doing it alone.

Theo: I really appreciate you and the girls helping her out.

Me: I wasn't referring to myself. I'm talking about Daddy Finn.

Finn: Duck you very much.

Bray: It's duck. It will never be duck.

Bray: Duck.

Bray: Duck.

Finn: Okay, this was too easy. GOOSE

Bray: Jesus fucking Christ.

Me: Now it works! Ha.

Me: Also, don't worry, Finn. Turns out you're not the only one helping out women in the house.

Finn: What's that supposed to mean? Who the fuck is helping my sisters out?

Me: Not your sister.

Bray: I'd be very careful what you say next. We ALL know you're holding a very LARGE, very flammable candle for SOMEONE'S sister.

Theo: Will someone just tell me what's going on? And Finn, I love you, man, but a: she's too good for you. b: she's vulnerable. And c: stay the fuck away from my sister.

Me: Okay, let's all take it down a goddamn notch. I MEANT Bray.

Theo: Bray slept with my sister?

Bray: Holy fuck, everyone calm the fuck down. JJ I'm going to kill you.

Finn: Answer the goddamn FaceTime, Bray!

Bray: I didn't sleep with your girlfriend. Calm the fuck down.

Finn: Pick up the goddamn phone.

Theo: Wait, Finn, why aren't you refuting that
my sister is your girlfriend?

CHUCKLING, I drop my phone. That's what Bray gets for being a shit stirrer and a judgmental prick.

He won't get a moment of sleep until he talks to Finn and convinces him that he and Hope are not fucking.

I shiver. Okay, definitely don't want to think about my cousin fucking anyone.

When there's a heavy pounding sound on my door, the excitement fades a little.

"Don't get your panties in a wad," I say as I stomp to the door. "I'll tell Finn I was fucking with him."

I throw it open, and rather than finding Bray on the other side, ready to beat my ass, I come face to face with Adeline.

Adeline in an old Bolts sweatshirt that swallows her figure and falls off one shoulder, exposing her soft bare skin. Adeline with her hair up in a messy ponytail, face glistening and free of makeup like she just washed it. Adeline, looking at me like I've lost my damn mind.

"What's this about fucking with Finn?" she questions.

I shake my head and swipe a hand over my face. Fuck, every time I see her, she scrambles my damn brain cells. Everything goes soft inside me.

Okay, not *everything*, I guess.

Grasping the doorframe, I grin. "I thought you were Bray."

With her tongue pressed to her cheek, she looks me up and down, gaze heating. "So this is how you answer the door for Bray?" Her lips twist, mischief flashing in her eyes. "I can see it."

I duck, assessing myself, and chuckle. I'm wearing a pair of shorts and nothing else. "I just got out of the shower."

"Ah," she says, lips twitching. "I'll get out of your way so you can wait for Bray."

She turns, that bare shoulder taunting me.

Before she can walk away, I snag her by the elbow, spinning her back. "Why did you come by?"

Her brow creases. "Isn't it time to call Avery?"

I slide my phone out of my pocket and check the time. Fuck, she's right. Motioning her in, I head for the bed and get settled. As I hit the FaceTime icon, I pat the spot beside me.

She hesitates, though not for long, before easing herself onto the mattress.

I offer a smile, but Avery's face appears quickly, and the two of us focus on her.

"Hey, Avey girl," Adeline says.

"I told you they'd call," Vivi says in the background. "She was nervous that she'd miss the call, so we've been staring at her iPad for the past half hour."

I chuckle, my heart squeezing. "Avey, you know we said nine. If we couldn't get a hold of you, we'd have called Vivi."

"I told her that too," Vivi says.

Avery nibbles on her lip. "I wish you were here," she says quietly, her eyes filling with tears.

Dammit. My heart fucking breaks.

"I wish I was there too." It's the hardest goddamn thing about this job. I'm not around enough to be the parent I want to be for Avery. She deserves to have at least one parent who's present.

"But you know what's exciting?" Adeline says, squeezing my knee like she knows I'm struggling for words.

"What?" Avery asks, voice cracking.

"Your daddy and I will be home this weekend, and your Uncle Theo is coming to town. We're all going to watch him play football on Sunday."

Avery's little brows tug together. "He's not my uncle; he's my cousin."

Adeline coughs out a laugh and nods. "You're right. I heard that your cousin Theo is bringing cowboy hats for everyone and he wants us all to wear them to the game. What do you think? Should we ask for pink ones?"

Avery's lips part in surprise. "We could match?"

With a big smile on her face, Adeline nods.

"Can we wear pink jerseys too?"

Her responding laugh is light. "I'll see what I can do."

My heart lights up at the way they interact. It eases so much of my worry knowing how good Adeline is at calming Avery's anxiety. She has no idea how much it means to my daughter, but I'll make sure she knows how much it means to me.

"Can I call Mimi and Pops after this?"

I nod. "I'm sure they'd love to hear from you."

"And Auntie Chloe and Uncle James?"

A low chuckle rolls out of me. "I'll text them and let them know you'll be calling."

"Yay," she says with a clap.

"And Mommy?" she asks.

Adeline glances away from the screen and I clear my throat. "I'll text her too. If she's around I'll let Vivi know, and you can call her. Okay?"

Avery sighs, her little shoulders sinking like she knows her mother won't be around. "That's okay. It's getting late. Maybe she'll call me tomorrow."

I've hated Tabitha for a lot of things over the years, but lately, with these conversations coming up nightly, I've come to despise the woman in a way I didn't know was possible. The pain that comes with watching my daughter come to terms with the fact that her mother doesn't care is unlike anything else.

"I love you, Avey girl," Adeline says, her soft voice pulling me from my spiraling thoughts. "Thank you for letting me FaceTime with you tonight."

Avery's blues lights up. "I love you too. And you can FaceTime whenever you want. Sometimes I get sad when I'm away from my daddy, so I'm guessing you get sad when you're away from your mommy and daddy."

Adeline smiles, and I swear there are tears in her eyes. "I'm sad when I'm away from you."

"My daddy always says he's right here." She points to her chest with one tiny finger. "So you can be right there too, and then you won't be sad, okay? I'll keep you right there." She pats her chest with her whole hand this time, and now I'm blinking back tears.

Mimicking her, Adeline presses her hand to her heart. "And I'll keep you right here."

Avery nods. "I like that. Oh, and remember, sleep with my daddy tonight. I don't want him to be lonely."

I bark out a laugh. Adeline chuckles too, and Vivi is giggling in the background of the call.

"What's so funny?" Avery asks, her little face scrunched in confusion.

I shake my head, smiling so wide my cheeks hurt. "Nothing, Avey girl. Go make your phone calls. I love you."

"I love you too. Bye, Addie."

"Bye, Avey."

The screen goes blank, and for a long moment, we're both silent, just staring at the device.

Interacting with Adeline isn't awkward, but I know if I speak now, she'll say she should go. And I'm not ready for that. It's nice to just sit by her side, even if only for a few seconds. Like this, I can pretend a little longer that life could ever be that easy. The two of us, together, raising Avery.

When she blows out a breath, I decide I can't ignore her any longer just for the sake of keeping her here.

I turn, the bed creaking beneath me. "What's the heavy sigh for?"

She gives me a wary look, studying my features. "I'm just waiting for you to ask."

Confused, I frown. "Ask what?"

"What my plan is."

"Oh." I lean back on my hands. "I'm not pushing."

Her face contorts in response, making my stomach twist. Fuck. She's not happy.

"But you gave me an ultimatum."

The twisting sharpens as regret seeps in. "That was shitty of me."

She blows out a breath, her body relaxing a little. "Yeah, it was."

"Listen, I know you don't trust me, and I know that's my fault—"

"JJ—"

I force an uneasy smile. "Just let me finish, please."

She nods

"I love you."

Eyes widening, she sucks in a harsh breath.

"I don't want to wait and tell you that when I'm deep inside you because I don't want you to think I use the words lightly. I don't want you to think my love is contingent on getting yours in return or any kind of commitment from you. *I love you.* That's it. And that's what I should have told you four years ago. You were right. I shouldn't have pushed back then. I should have given you space to figure out how you felt." Head lowered, I close my eyes and inhale deeply. "And if you were sure you didn't want to be a stepmom, then I should have taken friendship. I'm not going to make that mistake again. I love you and you deserve my support. It's that simple. So I trust you to do what's best for you."

Her eyes well and her lip quivers. "I don't know what to say."

"Just tell me we can be friends, Adeline. Tell me you trust that I have your back."

Looking away, she swipes at her tears with the back of her hand. "I'm trying to. I really am."

With a deep sigh, I nod. That's the most I can ask. "I have a lot to prove when it comes to you, but I've never been afraid of putting in the work. Especially with something so precious. And that's what you are to me. The most precious person."

She rolls her tear-filled eyes and, voice wobbly says, "No, that's Avery."

I shrug. "It's different. She's my daughter. I'll do anything for her and I love that little girl more than life itself. But I choose you, Adeline. I love you. Loving Avery doesn't change that. I have room for you both."

With her lip clamped between her teeth, she nods. "I think I'm beginning to understand that."

"Do you…" I shake my head. Why am I pushing my luck here? "Never mind."

"Do I what?" Her voice is soft, her eyes warm. It's enough to make me just a little brave. Hell, maybe a lot.

I swallow thickly, my anxiety ratcheting up. "Do you still not want kids?"

She shakes her head. It's quick. Too quick. Like she wishes it weren't the case.

My stomach rolls, but I manage to croak, "Okay."

I don't like it, but I'll respect it. She didn't ask for this. Avery may have been a surprise for me, but she was never an unwelcome one. I have to accept that this may be the issue we can't overcome. I can fix many things—my career, my marital status—but Avery and I are a package deal, and I can't change that. I wouldn't. My daughter is part of me. And if Adeline doesn't want that, then friendship it is.

Brows knit together, she searches my face. "Okay?"

Grasping her hand, I squeeze it. "Yes. Okay. I may wish things were different, but I'd never push this on you. Friends no matter what, right?"

She's searching my face again, this time frowning, like she's puzzling something out. "JJ," she breathes, "Avery doesn't count."

I jolt, certain I'm not understanding her, despite how simple the words are. "What?"

"I don't want my own kids. That's the truth. But Avery doesn't count. She's—she's part of you. She's Avery." An affectionate smile plays at her lips. "I love her and I'll always be there for her. In whatever capacity I can be."

A rush of hope floods me, and though I try to temper it, it swamps me completely. "Meaning if things were different with everything else, Avery wouldn't be a deal-breaker?"

Her cheeks go this pretty rose color. "Avery sweetens any deal, JJ. But—" That smile turns into a grin. "This is all hypothetical because we're just friends, right?"

I smile back stupidly. "Right."

"Then hypothetically speaking, if things were different, when I say I don't want kids, I mean I don't want other kids. I'd want your kid,

JJ." With tears in her eyes and her fingers pressed to her lips, she whispers, "I *want* your kid."

The room brightens. Hell, the world does.

All that anxiety and worry fade, the stress lightens, and I swear I'm floating. She wants my kid. She loves Avery. And I can't help but believe deep down that she still loves me too.

CHAPTER 34

Addie

MY FIRST OFFICIAL week as an NHL coach coincides with my last. Never would have seen that coming.

When Jarred Kane arrives, his excitement over being called up, especially over Dirk, is something to behold. JJ immediately takes him under his wing. They're together constantly, talking strategy, running plays, watching tape. JJ works out with him. Prepares him. It's impressive and I appreciate it.

Until I sign my deal, I'm not telling a soul, including JJ. But I can't lie to him, so I avoid instead. If we're not preparing for a game or playing, I spend most of my time in the gym. Fortunately, since I've been training with the guys during practice already, it's not tough to slip back into my regular routine.

Still, this is the NHL, and I don't just want to play, I want to dominate.

So despite how late we got in from D.C. last night, I'm up early to use our home gym. It's in the basement and has every piece of fitness equipment imaginable. My favorite part, though, is the long-mirrored wall and cushioned rubber floor. It's perfect for yoga.

I'm just settling in to stretch when my phone pings. Normally I ignore it while working out, but since I haven't officially started, I swipe it up.

> Savannah: Happy Sunday. Can't wait to see
> you at the game tonight. Invite Scott!

I sigh. I have zero interest in inviting the man I went on one date with to an event where my entire family and basically everyone I've ever met will be. Theo James does nothing without a show. Even if the cowboy boots and hat aren't an act.

Growing up, Theo spent as much time with the horses on his dad's property in Bristol, Rhode Island, as he did playing football. And once he was drafted by Tennessee six years ago, he went all in. There's not an ounce of city boy left in him. But he doesn't need to be so loud about it. Though I can appreciate his love for his sport. And coming home to play in Boston for the night means he wants everyone he knows to come watch.

I'm pretty sure my father bought about 25 percent of the seats in the stadium. That's about what it takes to fit all our family members—blood-related and otherwise.

It's weird, really. Yes, my dad is over-the-top in all aspects, but he's never really been into football. Then again, since Brooks's sons play, he has taken more of an interest.

And he loves all his friends' kids, and that includes Theo.

I tap the link Savannah sent, and when it opens to the next installment of the New Romantics article, which includes quotes from both Scott and me about our first date, I try not to wince.

He called me beautiful. Funny. Engaging. And kind. I was definitely not kind when I snuck into a closet and got carried away with my…uh, how would I even describe JJ? He's not my ex. That is so… well, it doesn't encapsulate who he is to me. Besides, we barely dated. Actually, we didn't date at all. We were best friends. We were teammates. And for one perfect night, he was mine and I was his.

How does one sum that up?

"What are you reading?"

With a shriek, I drop my phone.

Chuckling, JJ saunters closer. "To be fair, I said hi when I came down. You were just so invested in whatever you were looking at."

I huff, trying to ignore the very large, very fit man above me. He's wearing a shirt with the sleeves torn off. The fabric is ragged, like his biceps didn't fit into it, so the sleeves evaporated to make it easier for him to move.

More likely, he cut them so he could show off his muscles. Either way, I'm irritated. I find myself feeling that way a lot around him. Being in his presence is like being near chocolate when I'm on my period. I want all of the chocolate, but I know I'll feel worse if I have the chocolate, so instead I just drool and get hangry.

That's what I am right now. I'm hangry for JJ freaking Hanson.

I pick up my phone, but before I can turn it off, his eyes are locked on it. The picture above the article is one of Scott and me. I've got to hand it to Savannah, her camera crew is good. It was taken the moment I placed my palm on his chest to push him back, but the photographer made it look like I'm about to kiss Scott rather than stop him from kissing me.

A rumble rolls out of JJ, and when I tip my head up, I'm treated to a view of his throat flexing as he growls. The dusting of dark hair across his chin makes him seem gruffer. A little possessive. Dangerous. It's… annoyingly hot.

"You were there. Nothing happened," I remind him.

He steps in, lowering his head, his mouth an inch from mine.

I suck in a breath and lick my lips. I swear I can taste his minty mouthwash.

"Doesn't mean I have to like it," he says, voice rough, the sound dragging between us.

"No, I guess you don't," I say. I'm actually not sure what the fuck I'm even saying. All I can do is stare at his lips.

JJ drags his tongue slowly across the top of his lips before swiping against his bottom.

Before I can stop myself, I whimper. I goddamn whimper.

He smirks.

Asshole.

With both hands, I push him away by his shoulders.

He stumbles back, laughing. "Jesus, Adeline, I forgot how vicious you could be."

I grin at him in the mirror as I lower myself to the cushioned floor. "Happy to remind you."

"What are you doing in here anyway?" he asks, settling beside me.

I don't turn to face him, choosing to engage with him through the mirror. "Yoga."

"All right, I'm game."

I blow a frustrated breath, making that childish flappy sound. "*JJ*," I whine.

He chuckles. "Yes?"

"I was hoping to work out by myself."

He shakes his head, his eyes sparkling. "Too bad. You are my coach, aren't you?"

I glare at him.

He grins. "So teach me, Coach, I'll be a good boy, I promise."

The space between my legs tightens in response. Dammit. I glare down at the offending body part. Traitorous hussy. She's been hanging out with Josie and Savannah too much lately.

Head dropping back, JJ lets out a laugh that ricochets around the room. "Did you just tell your pussy to stand down?"

"*JJ.*" I hiss between my teeth. "You can't talk like that to me."

Focus fixed on my reflection, he pinches his thumb and index finger and drags them across his lips like he's zipping them. Then he pretends to throw away a key. All the while, his eyes dance with amusement. Shit. I can practically hear him promising to be a good boy again.

And dammit, I grin. Thank god I'm only his coach for a little while longer. This is fucking torture.

While JJ's in the shower, I sneak out of the house and head to Langfield Corp, where I'm set to meet with the GM.

The Bolts' general manager also happens to be my uncle. Noah married my dad's sister Sienna when I was young. He also played for the Bolts back then, and he might be the most down-to-earth of my uncles.

"We've talked to Sidney."

I'm seated across from him at his desk with Brooks on my left and Gavin on my right. Like this, I feel like I'm part of the mafia.

"How's he doing?" I ask. We've been traveling, so I haven't had a chance to visit him.

Noah frowns. "He's unlikely to come back this season. That means he'll be on the LTIR, which gives us room in the cap to negotiate. You should have your agent review our offer." He slides a piece of paper across the desk.

I stare at it, awkwardness taking over. "Uncle Noah—"

"In here," he says, scanning the office that once belonged to my father, "I'm only your GM. I can't look out for you like I would if you were going to play with any other team, Adeline. My loyalty is to the Bolts."

"Mine isn't." Brooks heaves himself forward and snatches the paper from the desk.

Gavin groans. "We shouldn't be in here."

"Oh, will you stop it?" I say to them. "Whatever you offer, I'm sure it'll be fair. I probably shouldn't say this, but I'd play for my PWHL salary."

Noah coughs. "Adeline, we're offering you more than the PWHL has in their annual salary cap."

Eyes bugging out, I tug the paper out of Brooks's hands. "Two million dollars?" I gasp. "You're offering me two million dollars to suit up as goalie for my favorite team?"

Brooks sighs and tilts my way. "Ask for two point five."

"Three," Gavin demands.

Noah rolls his neck and pulls the black frames from his face, then squeezes his eyes shut.

I can't imagine how exhausting it is to work with the Langfield brothers like this. Every one of them is a master at steamrolling. Then again, he can probably handle it. He married their baby sister, and Sienna is definitely not a pushover.

"Like I said," he grinds out, "I think an agent would be a good resource right now."

I shrug. "I don't know. Three sounds good to me."

Noah laughs. "I didn't offer three."

The men on either side of me glare. One pair of green eyes and one pair of brown narrow on him.

Shifting closer, he takes the paper from me and crosses off the two. In one quick movement, he draws a big three, then pushes the sheet back at me. "Fine. Three million dollars for one season. We can only offer you a one-year contract for now. We still have two goalies under contract for next year, both with *very high* salaries." He zeroes in on Gavin when he says it.

Gavin just glowers back.

"How much does JJ make?" I ask Brooks.

He smirks. "Thatta girl."

I laugh. "I'm not asking because I expect to make the same."

"Why not?" Gavin prods. "You telling me he's better than you?"

My natural instinct is to say yes, but that's not true. He may be more experienced in the NHL, but better? That remains to be seen, I suppose.

"JJ makes more than Sidney. We don't have the cap to match their salaries," Noah explains.

Gavin grunts. "Make room."

I shake my head. "Three million is good. Grand, actually. I was making forty-five thousand in the PWHL."

Brooks drops his head back and growls. "Motherfuckers. Does Beckett know that?"

Gavin yanks out his phone. "I'm texting him now."

"Guys," I grit out.

All three look at me.

"He can't change the cap in the PWHL."

All three let out incredulous noises.

"Have you met your father?" Brooks asks.

Eyes falling shut, I sigh. They're right. Where there's a will, Beckett Langfield will find a way. And in this case, it isn't a bad thing. Female players deserve more, and if getting my father hot under the collar gets that done, then that's better for everyone, I suppose.

"Can I sign now?" I ask, my knee bouncing. I want to make this official before they take it back.

Noah straightens. "Are you sure you don't want to have your agent look this over?"

"I trust you guys." I roll my eyes. "Obviously."

"Still, the boss will want this all done in a press conference. This is a big moment," he reminds me. "You're the first female goalie ever in the NHL."

"The boss, as in his wife." I hitch a thumb at Brooks.

Brooks shakes his head, the look on his face half exasperation and half affection. It's the look he most often wears when Aunt Sara is involved. "She'll be pissed if we don't make it happen. And I don't want to hear about it. Take the contract home. Share it with your agent. Negotiate if you must, and then we'll schedule the presser."

"Ugh, you sound like such a suit," I tease him.

He groans. "I know. But don't worry, I'll kick your ass during practice this week."

A thrill courses through me. "I can't wait."

CHAPTER 35

JJ

"MIMI," Avery yells, darting into the family suite and straight into my mother's arms.

My dad grins down at her. "Doesn't Pops get a hug?"

Head thrown back, Avery giggles. "You have to wait your turn, Pops. Don't you know the rules?"

My parents are laughing and loving on my little girl as I stroll in with Adeline by my side. As promised, she and Avery are wearing matching pink Tennessee jerseys with Theo's name and number on the back. I'm not sure how she got them on such short notice, but if anyone in Boston has connections, it's the Langfield crew.

Everyone we know is here. Adeline's parents, mine, her aunts and uncles, my aunts and uncles, and too many cousins to name.

Though my sister couldn't make the trek, she will be in town for Thanksgiving, and Avery is ecstatic to see her.

"Aw, look at you and Addie," my mother says to Avery, a knowing glint in her eye as she peers up at me. "You match perfectly."

"That's because Addie is my best friend. She even sleeps with Daddy so he isn't lonely."

Three feet away, Beckett whips around, glowering. "Excuse me." As he stalks toward us, my mind scrambles for a response.

Adeline shuffles forward. "Dad, that's not—"

"She literally means sleep," I choke out, pretty damn certain I'm about to die.

Behind me, Gracie yells, "Uncky JJ is the best to Addie. He gave her a pink penis. Lots of them."

Adeline groans and Hope slaps a hand over Grace's mouth.

"Pink *peonies*," I annunciate.

My father's eyes are dancing with amusement and my mother is trying to hold in a laugh, but Beckett is red. So fucking red.

"Why are you giving my daughter flowers, JJ?"

"Dad," Adeline grinds out.

Beckett's attention doesn't leave my face.

"I gave them to all the girls in the house. Moms and kids alike. Gracie discovered them in Aiden's yard and wanted them, so I asked him if I could bring one for Gracie, and he cut me an entire bushel."

"What about me?" Aiden asks, popping up right when I need him.

Adeline recounts the story for Aiden, and everyone else seems to move on when Aiden confirms that he in fact did cut all those flowers for everyone and I didn't just give Adeline peonies, *or my goddamn penis.*

But Beckett still stares like he knows there's more to the story.

Of course there is. He knows Adeline is it for me. Hell, probably every person in this room does.

Doesn't change our situation. Nothing can happen.

Not until the end of the season, at least.

Adeline takes Avery's hand. "Hey, Avey, want to grab a cookie with me?"

My little girl bounces on her toes. "Can I, Daddy?"

"Just one, then I want you to eat some real food."

She nods seriously. "I'll even eat my broccoli."

My mother laughs. "I'm pretty sure you're safe from broccoli today, my girl. But I think I saw some carrots over there. I'll join you."

With one hand in Adeline's, Avery reaches for my mom. Then the three of them walk away. I can't take my eyes off them. Especially when Adeline and my mother lift Avery between them, swinging her, and my daughter lets out the happiest laugh. This is what she deserves. A room full of people who love that laugh. My mother and Adeline showing her the love a mother and grandmother should.

My heart pinches. Adeline's *not* her mother.

My father steps into my side, his arm brushing mine as we watch the scene unfold. Knowing my dad, he's swooning internally. He always does when he looks at my mother. And he's the best damn grandfather there ever was. He's so good with Avery.

"Have you heard from Tabitha?"

Without turning away from the beauty in front of me, I shake my head. Regardless of the depressing topic, my mood doesn't dip. How could it when Adeline is smiling warmly at my little girl and pointing out every kind of cookie so she can pick which one she wants?

"But she's been served?"

That question hits me, sobering my mood. "No. She's working hard to avoid the sheriff."

His jaw flexes. "You never should have married that woman."

The familiar defense flares in my chest. My father and I fought a lot when I told him I was marrying Tabitha.

Just because you had a baby together doesn't mean you have to marry her. You don't love her. What are you thinking? She was a puck bunny. She is going to ruin your life.

He was right. About all of it.

My shoulders deflate. "I know."

My father's blue eyes, the same exact icy shade as mine, widen.

I've never admitted as much. Through all these years, all her affairs, all the misery she put us through, I've always told him to mind his own business. That I had it handled.

Truth is, I never wanted to touch Tabitha. I gave her free rein, permission to do whatever the fuck she wanted so long as she was a good mother to Avery. I told her when I proposed that I was doing it for Avery.

I wasn't the good guy. I didn't give a relationship with her a shot. I was still in love with Adeline. Of course I was. I still am.

But I was hurt after finding Dirk in her room and I couldn't find my way past the pain, instead becoming destructive. Marrying a woman I despised in a huge wedding that Adeline couldn't avoid hearing all about or seeing pictures of all over the internet.

I was cruel. I deserve everything that has happened to me. But Avery doesn't.

"We'll get her served." Dad squeezes my shoulder. "Have I told you how proud I am of how you've handled all of this? What a good father you are?"

Throat tightening, I force out a jerky response. "Learned from the best."

He pulls me into his chest, hugging me tight. "Love you, son."

I wrap my arms around him, and for a moment, I allow myself to take the comfort I need from the strongest man I know. "I love you too, Dad."

"They're taking the field," Hope squeals.

Releasing me, Dad pats my shoulder, then the two of us head over to the glass. Uncle Cash and Beckett are standing side by side, watching as Tennessee's players rush the field.

And keeping with the schtick my cousin is famous for, he runs out wearing a cowboy hat.

The crowd cheers wildly. Even though Theo plays for the opposing team, the people of Boston still consider him one of their own. He's like a damn celebrity everywhere he goes. Everyone loves Theo James.

When he gets to the sidelines, he takes off his hat and snags the helmet a member of the staff holds out to him.

"He going to do that in Boston too?" Beckett asks.

"I don't think you'll get him to stop that."

Beckett laughs. "Nah, and the crowd likes it. I think they'll be even happier when he's playing for the home team."

I frown, looking from one man to the other. "Theo's being traded to Boston?" I scan the Boston sidelines. In most professional sports, New England teams dominate, but that's not true when it comes to football. They're awful. I can't imagine my cousin wanting to come here, even if it meant coming home.

"Not exactly," Uncle Cash says with a grin.

Beckett eyes me, distrust still swimming there. "I made a bid for the team."

I suck in a breath. "You're *buying* a football team?"

My dad nudges me, a silent reminder of who I'm talking to. He's one of the most powerful men in Boston and he's one of my dad's closest friends, but more than that, he's Adeline's father. If there was ever a person I should act respectfully toward, it's him. I swallow. "I mean, good for you."

Smirking, he surveys the field. "I've never been a huge fan of the sport, but considering all of Brooks's sons play, I figure we should build them a team. Ya know, family tradition."

My dad nods like it makes perfect sense. Like buying a football team for his nephews is like buying them a car. No big deal. Perfectly sensible.

"And Theo is part of that deal?" I ask.

Uncle Cash beams. "It'll be good to have both my kids back in New England. Grace is ecstatic."

"It's not a done deal," Beckett reminds him.

But I know Beckett. If he wants it, he'll make happen.

On the sideline, Theo looks up and waves.

I've got to admit, it will be nice to have him home for good.

By halftime, Tennessee is up twenty-one to nothing. Theo is having a blast doing all sorts of trick plays that are completely unnecessary, considering how weak Boston's defensive line is, but he even ran in one touchdown himself, then threw to his running back, only to rush to the endzone to catch the second touchdown.

"He's such a showoff," Hope says to Savannah and Adeline.

"Eh, he's having a good time." Adeline smiles down at the field. "There's nothing better than doing the thing you love and doing it well. Especially when your family is around to watch."

Savannah beams. "Well, you would know."

"I can't wait to watch you again," Hope says.

Head snapping up, I frown at my cousin. "Huh?"

"We'll have to update the readers of the column this week. They're going to be so excited when they find out the girl looking for love is the first female goalie in the NHL," Savannah squeals.

"What's she talking about?" I say to Adeline.

With apology in her eyes, she takes a step toward me. "I wanted to tell you myself, but Aunt Sara has a big mouth and announced it to the girls five minutes ago."

My heart stumbles a little. "Announced what?"

Those brown eyes of hers are full of caution when she murmurs, "I'm not going to be your coach anymore."

My lungs seize up. "No. You aren't fucking quitting because that asshole is coming to play. I'll fucking quit before that happens."

Inhaling sharply, she shakes her head. "No. Dirk—no. I'm not going to be coaching because I'm taking Sidney's spot on the team."

"What?"

Her lips twitch, the first sign of true excitement from her. That flicker of competition that used to flare between us. "Yup, so you better watch out, Hanson. Competition's back."

True joy rocks through me. I wrap my arms around her and spin, reveling in her squealed laughter. When I set her down, it's impossible to release her. So with my hands on her hips, I stare into those gorgeous brown eyes. "It was never a competition, Adeline."

She laughs. "Oh. Because you're the best?"

"No, because you are," I say without hesitation. "Welcome to the team, baby. We are so goddamn lucky to have you."

Blushing, she averts her gaze. "Thank you."

The click of a camera cuts through the moment, and the two of us turn.

Savannah's phone is aimed in our direction and she's grinning at the screen.

"What are you doing?" Adeline asks, squinting at her friend.

With an innocent shrug, Savannah pockets her phone. "So you're still on for your date with Scott tomorrow, right? *This* won't change that?"

The *this* she's speaking of could be the way I'm currently holding Adeline. Or maybe it's her new position on the team.

But then my mind catches up to the other part of her statement. *Date.* She's going on another date with Scott?

My body goes taut. "Date?"

Adeline stumbles back, breaking contact, and forces an awkward smile. "Uh, yeah. Date number two."

I don't fight her on it. In fact, I keep my mouth shut completely. Because even if she has a date with someone else tomorrow night, things are looking up. She's no longer my coach. That means there's one less issue keeping us from being together.

CHAPTER 36

Addie

THE THING about big moments is that they're generally fleeting.

After the Olympics, athletes are expected to return home and go back to their regular lives.

Or worse. In my case, after that night with JJ, after we told each other we loved one another, the bubble we found ourselves in didn't even make it twenty-four hours before it burst.

So despite the feral excitement my family showed in response to my news, when Monday rolls around, I expect things to go back to normal. Well, as normal as they can be when I'm walking into a locker room filled with men who are now my colleagues.

JJ goes first, telling me to wait so he can make sure everyone is dressed. With the door wide open, he yells, "Listen up."

A few guys grumble greetings, but they all settle quickly. "From now on, there's no dick in the locker room."

I close my eyes and groan. He is absurd.

"Ah, Cap," Bobby Dean whines. "Tell JJ I can't help it. This thing just wants to be seen."

If I had to guess, he's humping the air aggressively. Neanderthals. Every last one of them.

Brayden appears next to JJ and waves me in. "Hanson is right. Our new goalie is here."

I step forward and give a little wave. The lot of them are all dressed for practice, and thankfully, there's not a dick in sight. As they take me in, I wait for their faces to drop. For the glowers and concerned mumbles and disappointment.

Bobby steps forward first, and I brace myself.

"Shit," he shouts. "Addie Langfield is gonna be a *Bolt*?"

"Fuck yeah." Royal saunters across the room and slaps my hand. "Can't wait to take the ice with ya."

"Angles, Angles!"

Bobby starts the chant, but soon the entire locker room is shouting my nickname at a deafening volume.

I take in the scene, unable to breathe. The guys are all smiling. But no one as brightly as JJ.

Told you, his eyes say.

My stomach flips over. He did. When it comes to this career, he has always believed in me.

He waves his arms, and when the chanting dies down, he says, "She's got her own locker room."

I jolt back, blinking. What?

"But we're going to make sure she can come hang with us in here before games. Clothes, men." His jaw hardens as he scans each of them. "No dicks out. I'm serious."

"What are you talking about?" I choke out.

Demeanor softening, he looks my way. "Your dad didn't do the honors?"

I open my mouth, only to shut it again when no sound comes out. Finally I just shake my head.

He reaches for my hand, but he catches himself quickly and then slips it into his pocket instead.

I'm not the only one who catches it. Bray is watching him, eyes narrowed.

JJ clears his throat. "Come on, I'll show you."

I follow him out the door and across the hall to the door that leads to the film room. Inside, the space is unrecognizable. Where the huge screen used to be mounted, there's now a mirror and two sinks. The white marble of the vanity is oddly similar to that in the bathrooms in the brownstone.

I chuckle. When my dad likes something, he sticks to it.

To the right is a spacious shower, and to my left is a bench and four stalls in the same design as the equipment in the men's locker room.

Four stalls. Enough space for three other players. A thrill shoots through me. It's suddenly easy to imagine a time when another woman will join me in here. When I won't be the only female on the team.

The best part has been stored inside one of the stalls.

It's my goalie gear. Complete with my new uniform.

I snag it, spin it around, and suck in a breath. *Langfield*. I admire the way my last name—the last name of the man who gave me everything, of the family that has never once not shown up for me—is emblazoned across the shoulders. But the next part makes my heart stutter. "Thirteen. But that's—"

"My number." My Uncle Brooks appears out of thin air, leaning against the open doorframe.

"I don't understand. Your number was retired. You're—Brooks Langfield." A manic laugh bubbles out of me. "Number Thirteen. Greatest of all time."

He grins. "There's not another person in this world who could wear that number, Addie. Do it proud."

I blink back tears and turn to JJ "Did you know about this?"

Smiling, he dips his chin. I so badly want to rush into his arms. I want to hug him. Crash against his chest and celebrate this wrapped in his warmth. Instead, I simply suck in a breath and nod at my uncle. "It's perfect. Thank you."

"Get dressed. We've got a lot of practice ahead of us."

That statement ends up being the theme of the week. Despite the exciting media signing my Aunt Sara organizes and my own eagerness to play, Brooks and Gavin keep JJ as our goaltender for every game over the first two weeks. Jarred and I practice as if we'll be playing, but it isn't until the second week of November that I'm given the green light.

"You're on tomorrow night."

Jarred, JJ, and I are all seated across from Brooks, going over tomorrow's game plan after watching film.

I peek over at JJ, apprehensive about his reaction.

But I should have known better. I should have guessed he'd be smiling.

"You're ready," he says.

My shoulders sag in relief. This man always knows what I need to hear.

Of course, I'll never let him know that. "Obviously."

"Fuck, this is so cool," Jarred says. He's like an excitable puppy. About every twenty-five seconds, he interrupts, reminding one of us of a highlight from our career.

It's sweet. I'm touched, really, that he knows so much about mine.

He has this funny habit while in the crease of making noises every time he blocks a shot.

Boing. Ding. Bing.

Like he's a pinball machine. It's oddly entertaining. Like those ridiculous ASMR videos my little sisters love so much.

But he's good. And young. He's got the time and the talent to become great. And working with the three of us? We'll make sure it happens. It's fun. Molding players. I can see why Gavin enjoys coaching so much.

I, however, am thrilled to be back in the crease.

"Make sure you get some sleep tonight." With that, Brooks releases us.

The second we're in the hallway, Jarred is bouncing by my side. "Are you excited? You must be so excited. Your first game in the NHL. This is huge, Addie. Huge!"

Joy washes over me. His excitement is contagious. "Yeah, I am excited. Thanks, Jer."

He rubs his hands together. "Doing anything to celebrate? You guys have a pizza tradition, right?"

Brows furrowed, I eye JJ How does this kid know about that?

"He talked about it during one of his first interviews," Jarred says.

"You did?"

"You don't remember?" he teases, acting affronted.

I'm smiling. I can't stop smiling. Today is a good day. Hell, any day is a good day lately. I spend my days playing hockey with JJ, and at night…we're…doing okay. We have dinner as a family. Not just JJ and Avery and me, but the whole crew. Even my brother. He's around all the time now that his season is over. The Revs didn't make it to the world series, though Finn isn't as heartbroken about it as I thought he'd be.

We were in California on Halloween, which killed JJ But the two of us FaceTimed with Avery, who carried Vivi's phone the whole time she was out trick-or-treating with the rest of our crew.

JJ and I sat side by side on the bed in his hotel room, so close our thighs touched, with my iPad propped up. We went for the bigger screen to get a better view of Avery's costume. The two of us ate so many Twizzlers while we watched her that I had a stomachache that night.

The pain turned out to be a good thing.

Otherwise I don't know that I could have left JJ alone after we said good night to his little girl.

He was struggling. Wearing a fake smile while talking to Avery while his body language screamed devastation. I can't imagine the stress he's under as Avery's only present parent. It kills me that she doesn't have a mother who would do anything for her like mine does for me. But she's got JJ, and if he could clone himself so he could work and be with Avery at all times, he wouldn't hesitate.

If Sidney had been healthy, he could have made both work. He could have taken a red-eye after tucking Avery in and been back in time to dress for the game. But without Sidney, JJ's presence on the ice has been mandatory, and traveling overnight like that would be too much of a risk.

It's a relief knowing he shouldn't have to face a situation like that again for the rest of the season.

Because he's got me.

I'm practically bursting with excitement. Like there's firecrackers in my chest, erupting in reds and greens and—who the hell am I kidding? The only color it's shooting is Bolts blue. I was meant for this team. Meant to wear this color. And tomorrow, I get to do that on the ice.

"I don't remember every interview you ever gave," I say flippantly. Though there was a time I hung on his every word, so I probably saw it and was positively giddy when he told the press about our little tradition. "But pizza is for after games, not before." My phone buzzes in my pocket as I explain to Jarred.

"Let's do something else to celebrate, then," JJ says.

Smiling, I peer down at the notification on the screen, but when the words register, my stomach sinks. The smile falls right along with it. "I, uh, actually have plans."

"Oh," JJ mumbles.

Head lifted, I force a smile. "With Scott."

That's another thing I've done a lot of the last two weeks. Talked to Scott. I've been on two dates with him as well. He's...sweet. And funny. And he does absolutely nothing for me.

When it comes to Scott, I wish I felt the kind of fireworks I feel for hockey. Or the butterflies I feel for JJ.

But it's still new. Maybe that will change.

JJ nods, his dark hair a little unruly, his expression unchanged. Easy. Smiling. Fine. "Right. We should get home, then."

Those simple words cause an ache in my chest. Now that I'm not his coach, I was sure he'd make his move. That he'd try again.

And maybe he would have, if not for Tabitha. The whole marriage thing is kind of an issue.

While my feelings for Scott are practically nonexistent, the thought of JJ's marriage summons a lot of strong emotions. None of them good. It makes me sick. And sad. And it makes me wish for something that I can't change. A past we didn't get.

But if I take a chance, if I believe enough in the both of us and will it to be true, could we maybe rewrite a little of our story?

Could we have a future?

CHAPTER 37

JJ

SMIRKING, I pocket my phone, focusing on my father.

"Thank you for letting her stay," my dad says as he follows me to the foyer.

He and Mom suggested they keep Avery for the night, and while I normally refuse to spend a whole night away from her when I'm in Boston and don't have a game, my father reminded me that it's important to have a life outside of work and parenthood. That I need to live a little too. It was similar to the sentiment he made when I told him I was marrying Tabitha. That I didn't always have to do the so-called right thing. That I could be selfish sometimes and still be a good person. So tonight, I said yes. My hope was that this would be my chance to put it all on the line. To tell Adeline my plan. And maybe finally take her out on that first date we never got.

But she's going out with Scott. Again.

My parents offered to pick Avery up, but I didn't want to be there when Adeline left. It's always a production. Savannah and Josie and sometimes a camera crew come over to document while she gets ready, asking her to talk about her thoughts about the last date and hopes for the next one.

It's a lot.

And it's killing me.

I'd really like to be a dick and beg my mother to shut the damn thing down. She owns the magazine. She has the power to do it. I've had to fight the urge to rip the pages from the magazine where Adeline talks about how funny Scott is, how sweet he was when they went to the movies, how he held her hand and bought her favorite candy.

Not Twizzlers. She only eats those to make me feel better.

God, Adeline has done far more than anyone should have to in order to make life easier on me. I figure getting out of her way is the least I can do in return.

Now I need a distraction. If I don't find something to focus on, I'll lose my mind thinking of her out with him.

"She's excited. You guys don't mind keeping her till Tuesday, though? And bringing her to the game?"

Dad laughs. "Mind? Your mother is ecstatic to wear a new jersey. Did you hear they bedazzled jerseys this week at *Jolie*?"

I frown. "What are you talking about?"

His lips twitch in amusement. "Hanson is out, buddy. Hate to break it to ya, but everyone will be wearing an Addie jersey to the game."

That makes me unreasonably happy. "Really?"

"Yup. Your mom is going to have Avery help her bedazzle her own tonight so she'll match all the Langfield women and her Mimi."

I almost want to stay so I can see that in person. "That's great," I say, voice tight.

My father slips his hands into his slacks and rocks back on his heels. "So you, uh, gonna make your move? Or did Beckett scare you off at the football game?"

I cough out a laugh. "I don't know what you are talking about."

He stares me down, blue eyes piercing. He's not buying what I'm selling.

I don't back down. There is nothing going on. No matter what I wish were happening.

"Listen…" He ducks, shaking his head. When he looks back up at me, his face is a mask of regret.

It's an emotion I recognize. One I feel all the way to my soul.

"I wasted so much time thinking I was doing the right thing for your mother. Believing I knew what she needed. I stayed away for years, and because of that, I missed out on her pregnancy. I wasn't there for her or my little girl the day she was born. I missed out on the first eleven years of Chloe's life…" His chest falls with a defeated sigh. "You don't get that time back. There's no rewind. I know she isn't Avery's mom, but"—he shakes his head—"she's the love of your life and she loves your little girl."

My heart lodges itself in my throat. "I know that."

He scowls like he can't believe I'm aware yet still being so obstinate. "So what are you waiting for?"

"Maybe it's just too late for us." I rough a hand over my face, fighting the heat building behind my eyes. "She's dating someone else. And I still haven't resolved this shit show with Tabitha. Knowing her, it won't go smoothly even when I finally serve her with divorce papers. She's going to try to ruin everything in my life. It's what she does. And I don't want that to touch Adeline."

With a heavy sigh, he shakes his head. "Leave Tabitha to me. You —" He blows out an aggravated breath. "Try chasing your happiness for once, rather than worrying. You've been doing it since you were a boy. Trying to make things easier for everyone else. And I get it, your mother's battle with cancer meant you learned a lot earlier than most that life isn't fair. But your mom never stopped fighting. So why the hell did you?"

Your mom never stopped fighting. An hour later I'm still rolling those words around in my head. Why did I give up the fight?

When I get home, the house is quiet. Finn, Winnie, and Hope took the kids out for dinner and a movie.

Finn texted, inviting me along, but I quickly declined. Why would I want to endure the chaos of dinner out with a bunch of kids if my own isn't even there?

In the silence, I'm wondering if I should have agreed. Or maybe I should drive over to Bray's and talk him into giving me another tattoo. I'd do just about anything to distract myself from thoughts of Adeline and her goddamn date.

I need a shower. A reset maybe.

I pull my shirt over my head and toss it onto the bed. Then I snag a pair of shorts from the dresser and shuffle to the bathroom.

When I push the door open, I stagger back. Because the room isn't empty. No, Adeline fucking Langfield is standing at the sink wearing nothing but her jersey.

Jesus, I thought the sight of her in *my* jersey would be the stuff of fantasies. But seeing her in hers has me losing all goddamn sense. Her toned legs are bare, the pale skin mouthwatering. Immediately, my attention is drawn to the freckle behind her knee I discovered it when we were seventeen and at the beach together for the first time.

Fuck, this woman is my goddamn dream come true and she's getting ready for a date with someone else.

Will she sleep with him tonight? That thought makes my stomach roll. Will he treasure her? Please her? Treat her the way she deserves to be treated?

I blow out a breath, forcing the thoughts from my head. "Sorry, I thought you'd already left. I'll use another bathroom."

"JJ."

I'm still staring at that freckle when she spins around. The movement is what I need to break from the trance I'm in. I drag my attention up and find myself face to face with her. Beautiful honey eyes, red lips, soft skin.

Her lips twitch. "Two truths and a lie."

"What?" I tug at my hair, groaning. "I don't want to play a goddamn game right now, Adeline. I don't want you to go on this *fucking* date."

One side of her mouth hitches in cocky amusement at my spiraling.

It's sexy as fuck.

She holds up a thumb. "I'm not getting dressed for Scott." Her index finger. "I actually have no interest in getting dressed at all." Her middle finger. "I'm not your coach anymore, Hanson."

The flirtatious, raspy tone pulls at something deep inside me, making it hard to breathe.

"I don't know which one is the lie."

Her eyes flare, humor swimming there. "None of them are."

My heart rate quickens and hope floats right up my throat. "You're not going out with Scott?"

She shakes her head.

"And you don't want to get dressed?"

I take a step closer, and of its own volition, my hand reaches for her jersey. I tug her closer and grasp her waist.

When she doesn't pull back, relief cascades through me.

"Nope," she says, voice soft, pupils dilated.

I swallow audibly. "And you're not my coach anymore."

She grins, her tongue peeking out. "No, I'm not."

"Fuck, Adeline. Tell me to stop, because I'm one breath away from fucking you against this door."

She bites down on her bottom lip. "There's a perfectly good bed in either of our rooms."

That's all it takes to break me. My mouth crashes against hers and it's like I've finally been set free. Her lips are soft, but her whimpers are loud and unapologetic. Her fingers dig into every inch of me she can find. She scratches at my bare chest, the moan escaping her enough to make my head spin.

I cup her cheeks and hold her still for a second. "Addie, baby."

She smiles. "Thought you only called me Adeline."

I lick her lips and her eyes roll back. "Shut up for two fucking seconds, please."

The sound of the giggle she lets out goes right to my goddamn dick. Fuck, I love this woman. And I want her more than anything, but I need to know this is more than a hookup. More than her scratching an itch.

"Adeline, I'm hanging on by a thread here."

Smile softening, she reads me like only she can. "I'm yours, JJ. Call me whatever the fuck you want, just know: I'm yours."

That's all I fucking need to hear. Our mouths fuse together again, and this time I'm the one desperate to touch every inch of her body. I slip a hand beneath the jersey, and when I find nothing but skin, I hiss. "Adeline fucking Langfield, you aren't wearing any panties."

She grins against my mouth. "Seemed pointless."

With my face lifted to the sky, I groan, and in French, I praise the heavens above for her perfection.

"Tu es mon paradis," she whispers back to me. *You are my heaven.*

I smile at her words. At the way she learned French because of me. For me. I was so fucking foolish, not realizing what I had all along. Not seeing that I could never get over her.

Grasping her ass, I pick her up. Then I carry her into my room.

"Finally," she says, the word an echo of my own thoughts. The sheer relief in those three syllables sums up what I'll never truly be able to voice.

With her legs wrapped around my waist, I settle on the bed and hug her to my chest.

"What are you doing?" she murmurs, amusement tinging her tone.

"Savoring every freaking second of this."

Hands on my cheeks, she pulls back and holds my gaze. "I'm not going anywhere, JJ. Rush, go slow, do whatever feels right, because we aren't running anymore."

Eyes falling closed, I press my forehead to hers. "I just—" I inhale, straightening and drinking her in. "I've been so fucking scared that I'll screw it all up again. For years all we've had are moments. Snippets of time I clung to during the days I wasn't near you. First when we were teenagers. You saved me when my mom was going through chemo. Do you know that? I lived for the few moments we had together before we'd fall asleep. Your head on the pillow beside mine. Your eyes the last thing I'd see."

I blow out a shaky breath, brushing my thumb over her cheek.

"I'd wake up extra early to watch you sleep. To listen to you breathe. When I got into the NHL, I'd wait for your calls, Adeline. If I'd known—"

I shake my head still so goddamn angry at myself.

"If I'd had a fucking clue that you felt for me what I felt for you, there would never have been anyone else. I just—"

My body shudders as I inhale deeply.

This woman is perfect. Even now, she's silent, listening, allowing me to find my words.

"I'm so glad I have Avery, but I hate that I lost you because of it. That we only had one moment in time. And I'm scared that I'll screw this up again. That I'll get tonight and that by the time dawn comes around, it'll all be taken away again."

She licks her lips, her eyes glassy. "I lived for the moment you'd look up from the net and catch me behind the glass. You'd light up. There could be hundreds of people watching, but it mattered to you that I was there."

I huff out a laugh. "You were the person I wanted there most." I shrug. "I missed you. I looked for you. Even after everything."

"The thing about moments is, they're what we remember," she murmurs. "And in every moment that truly mattered, you were there. And I really tried to be there for your big ones too."

"You were."

We may not have been speaking, but she attended every birthday party we threw for Avery. My little girl loves Adeline because even though she wasn't with me, Adeline never disappeared completely. She could be counted on. Our families spend holidays together, so I saw her plenty, even during the bad times. It was torture. I don't know whether I was the one not talking to her or she wasn't talking to me. Either way, we didn't speak. But she was there.

And I was there the night she played her last game in the PWHL just like I'll be there for her first game in the NHL.

But if we're going to do this right, I need to tell her everything. I don't just want moments anymore. I want everything. So I take a deep breath and garner the strength to open up. "You were there for all the big ones, but if I hadn't fucked up so badly, you would have been there for more. I'm sorry. I'll never stop regretting marrying Tabitha."

She winces.

"I don't want to talk about her, truly." I sigh. "But I'm not sure that we can move forward until I say this."

She nods without argument.

"It was never a real marriage. Not like..." I consider moving on. She doesn't need to know this, but I want to clean the slate. Fuck it, "Not like we would have."

Her eyes flare, but before she can freak out about it, I go on.

"I never touched her. We were roommates, raising a child together. That was *all*."

Adeline's entire body seems to go still and she squeezes her lips tight.

"It's only been you since I've known how you felt, baby," I whisper. I made a promise to her the night we spent together years ago and I want to her to know I kept it. Even if I broke so many others. "Still," I continue, knowing that remaining celibate doesn't atone for everything else I did wrong, "even a piece of paper connecting me to her is too much. I'm doing my best to make it right. I've been trying to serve her with divorce papers for weeks. So not only are you not my coach anymore, but soon I won't be married anymore either. We can be together, Adeline. As soon as the divorce is final. We don't have to be a secret anymore."

Ducking, she shakes her head. "We can't tell anyone about us."

My stomach somersaults. "What? Why?"

"I just signed my first NHL contract. I'm the league's first female goalie. Ever." She stares at me, emphasizing the point. "I don't want the world focusing on my personal life. I want my career to stand on its own, and if I'm just another female hockey player who's fucking one of her teammates, *that* will be the story."

Pain radiates through me. Fuck.

She splays a hand over my cheek. "We know that's not our story," she says softly. "*We* know who we are to one another. That's all that matters. Right?"

"And what am I to you?"

"You're my best friend."

I try not to let those words hit me like they do, but they're like a knife to the heart. Yes, she's my best friend too, but I want so much more.

"Adeline, I don't want to just be your best friend."

Her smile lights up her face. "I never said *just*."

"Then what else am I to you?" I'm begging, but I'm not the least bit ashamed. I'm bursting at the seams with anticipation. Desperate to know whether this is as real for her as it is for me.

Her eyes glitter as her smile grows. "Our relationship can't be defined by any one thing, because you are everything to me. You're the person I want to spend my time with. Compete with. You make me better. You make me laugh. You make me happier than anything else ever has. You also annoy the hell out of me."

A surprised bark of laughter bursts out of me.

"And you're the man I love. The one I always have and always will love."

My heart thuds against my sternum. "What?"

"I love you. You have to know that." She says it so simply, like it's always been obvious. And maybe if I'd been paying better attention, I would have known. I wish I had.

"You already know I love you," I tell her. "That I'll always love you."

"As much as I'm loving all this communication," she says with a pretty smile, "I'd really like to do something else for a little while."

I chuckle, the sound dark, as desire courses through me. "You feeling needy?"

She tips up her chin for a kiss. "So needy."

I press my mouth to hers. Where words might fail us, this doesn't. I tell her with each kiss that she's it for me. That things will be different this time. And she responds, telling me she knows. There's a newfound trust, a choice in every brush of our lips.

Splaying her hands on my chest, she pushes me back against the bed. Long chestnut waves create a curtain as she leans against me, her jersey bunching at her waist. "Fuck, Adeline." I run my hands up and down her warm thighs, reveling in the sight of her bare cunt.

"You've got quite a few tattoos," she whispers, perusing the expanse of my chest.

A few are obvious. Standard, I guess. The symbol for the Boston Bolts. All the guys have that one. It's a Bray special. Five yellow stars, just like my dad has inked on his skin. He started with three: one for him, one for my mom, and one for Chloe. Later he added one for each of us boys. There's a shooting star among them, a symbol that represents Avery, because she's my magic.

Adeline traces each one, and I relish every touch, my heart beating for her, need and comfort mingling in my chest.

"What's this one?" she whispers, moving closer to the small triangle on my ribs. "JJ." She lurches back, her focus darting to my face.

Silently, I smile. She's smart enough to figure it out.

"Say something," she begs, her voice strained.

"Kiss me anyway." The words are in script and form a triangle.

For Addie Angles.

"Why?" she whispers.

I blink up at the ceiling, swallowing back emotion. "It's a reminder that no matter what, it was worth it. That trying is always worth it." Tilting my head, I study her, wiping at the tear that rolls down her cheek. "You will always be worth it, Angles."

She rolls her lips together. "What if I want it to work out? What if I don't want to just try? What if I want it all? What if I know it'll be hard and that we're going to be put through it, but I can't fight it anymore?"

A smile creeps across my face. "Kiss me anyway."

She angles in, and with her lips against mine, she murmurs, "I was hoping you'd say that."

The skin beneath her jersey is warm and so damn inviting. I smooth my palms over her hips and abdomen, and when I brush the underside of her breasts, she sucks in a breath.

"God, I want to fuck you in this jersey, but I'm so damn desperate to see all of you."

She makes up my mind for me, grasping the hem and pulling it over her head.

Fuck.

She's more beautiful than I remember. Her breasts are heavy, nipples pebbled in anticipation.

Arching up, I suck one into my mouth, eliciting a moan from deep within her.

When she grinds against me, I flip her onto her back, needing to be as naked as she is.

She watches me with hungry eyes as I slide down my joggers and boxers in one go, then kick them across the room. I press one knee into the mattress, then the other, but before I get too far, she reaches out and strums her fingers across the barbells lining my dick.

"I could feel them the last time we were together, but I didn't get to look." She shifts, popping up on her knees too. "Lay down for me."

Fuck, this woman. She'll be the death of me.

I obey quickly. I'd do just about anything she asked except walk away from her.

"Do they hurt?" she asks of the three piercings that make up the Jacob's ladder lining my shaft.

"No."

She rolls them between her fingers, tugging a bit, and a bolt of electricity shoots through me.

Eyes closed, I exhale. "They feel pretty fucking incredible right now."

"Are there ways I can use them to make you feel even better?"

She strokes me, her grip tight, and my vision fades in and out.

"I—fuck, Adeline, don't stop. Please," I breathe.

Humming, she drags her tongue across her lips. She shifts again, and then her warm breath ghosts over me. Pleasure lances through me and pours out my tip, making me shudder.

"I wonder how it will feel when I do this." She rolls her tongue over one piercing, then the next, starting at the bottom and working her way up.

"Fucking hell." I groan, awash with ecstasy.

She peers up at me, the hint of a pleased smile playing at her lips. "That good?"

With one hard nod, I cup her cheek. "So good, baby. You're so good for me."

Her cheeks go pink, but mischief flashes in her eyes. "I thought you were the one who was going to be good for me? Wasn't that your line? *I'll be a good boy?*"

"I will be a good boy," I insist, my voice rough. "I'll do anything you fucking want if you just wrap those perfect lips around my cock and suck. Please, Adeline. Put me out of my goddamn misery and let me have you."

Her eyes don't leave mine as she opens her mouth wide and waits for me to thrust inside her. And, fuck, the second I hit the back of her throat and she gags, my soul leaves my body.

"Again." I pull out and thrust back in.

She gags again, but she doesn't pull back. Instead, she closes her eyes and takes me deeper.

I slide back, and when I pull out of her mouth completely, she rolls her tongue over my crown.

"Again," I warn. I give her a second to prepare, then I push into her mouth. This time I know I'm in trouble. My spine tingles and my balls grow impossibly tight. "Fuck, baby, I'm going to come."

I squeeze my eyes shut, desperate to hold back. But the woman doesn't let me. She hollows her cheeks and sucks, holding me captive at the edge. When she cups my balls and squeezes, I lose the battle and fuck up into her mouth until I explode, bliss making my vision hazy.

She pops off me with a pleased sigh, licking her lips. "That was fun."

I cough out a surprised laugh. "Jesus, fuck, Adeline."

She giggles. "What? Pretty sure I just set a record. I should get an award or something. Best blow job, maybe? Actually, don't tell me. I don't want to know."

Rolling over, I pull her warm naked body beneath mine. "Adeline Langfield, you're the best I've ever had of everything in my life. There's no fucking competition."

She pouts. "But I love competitions."

"Fine." I brush my nose along her neck and nip at her ear. "Want to see if I can get you off quicker than you just got me?"

Those brown eyes that I'm a goner for flare. "Now that is a competition I can get behind."

"Yeah you can." I push up, giving her space. "Ass up, baby."

Her face falls. "What?"

"Did I stutter?" I arch a brow. "Turn over. Ass up. Now."

She rolls her lips like she's considering arguing with me, but in the end, I think she can tell I'm not fucking kidding, so she shifts onto her stomach.

When she doesn't get on her knees, I smack her ass lightly. "I said up."

Groaning, she pops her ass into the air.

"Fuck." I bite my fist. "You're a beautiful woman, Adeline. I love staring at your face, but this pretty pink hole is really doing it for me right now."

She drops her head and giggles. "Gross."

I suck on my thumb, getting it nice and wet, then slide it down her crack.

"What are you doing?" she whispers, her breath going short, her muscles tensing.

"Relax for me. I'm going to make you come like I promised."

"That's the wrong hole," she mumbles.

I circle the puckered skin, pressing lightly on it, relishing the resistance. "No, baby, it really isn't."

"Oh god," she whines.

"Can I have this ass, sweetheart? I promise it will feel good. You'll come harder than you ever have."

"I—um." She peers back at me, her lip caught between her teeth. Then, with her eyes squeezed shut, she exhales, her body relaxing. "Okay. Yeah, yes."

I chuckle. "Oh, baby, you won't regret this. I promise." I move in, not wasting any time now that the clock is ticking.

When my tongue finds her delicious hole, she squeezes her thighs together.

"What are you doing?" she hisses.

I lick the soft flesh and hum. "I'm making you come, baby. Now shh. I'm on the clock." With my thumb, I drag my saliva around her hole. Then I slide inside her.

In response, she squeezes tightly. Fuck, it will feel so good when she's squeezing my cock like this.

I work my thumb out and back in, then lick at her again. I alternate until she's a crying mess, her legs shaking, her pussy spasming, searching for something to fuck. God, it's heavenly to watch. With my free hand, I stroke her clit, keeping the rhythm in time with the work I'm doing on her ass. In a matter of seconds, she's coming undone.

"JJ, please. Oh god. Fuck, shit, fuck. That's not right. Oh my god." Moaning, she grinds her pussy against my hand, the move making her ass swallow my thumb. Then with a scream, she comes.

When the spasming stops, I drop down beside her, grinning. "Pretty sure I won."

She slumps, covering her eyes. "I hate you."

Amusement rolls through me. "No, you don't."

She shakes her head, a smile on her pretty face. "No, I really don't." Sighing, she shifts, taking me in. When her attention drops below my waist, she bites her bottom lip. "You're hard again."

"You just came all over my tongue and fingers."

Her laugh is loud in my quiet bedroom. "And?"

"Adeline." I huff. She still doesn't get it. "My absolute dream girl just moaned about how I was a god while squirting all over my bed. Of course I'm hard."

She snorts. "I did not call you a god. And I didn't squirt."

I push her over and swipe at the wet spot on the sheet, then hold up my finger. "Oh no?"

Hands on my chest, she pushes me back, hard. Then she jumps on top of me, her strong thighs squeezing my hips tight. "You're such an ass."

I dip my chin. "Who's obsessed with your ass. Yes. That's me."

"Oh my god. You're going to be so annoying about this, aren't you?" She tosses her head back, her hair cascading around her shoulders.

She's so goddamn beautiful, even when reprimanding me.

"So annoying," I promise.

She squeezes her eyes shut and huffs. "Fine. I guess I can accept that."

Laughing, I clutch her hips. "Oh, really?"

"Yeah, considering I like you and all—" She rolls her eyes. "I guess I just have to accept this is who you are."

I take her in, my heart near bursting. "No, Adeline, you don't just like me."

She bites her lip, her eyes darting away.

"Say it," I demand.

"What?" She plays dumb.

"Adeline."

"Jesus, JJ." She groans. "You're so damn needy."

Laughing, I arch a brow.

"Fine," she grouses. "I love you."

"That's good. Because in about two seconds, I'm going to fuck you, and I'm going to be really annoying after I make you come three more times."

Eyes heating, she bites down on that plush lip again. "Oh yeah?" She rolls her hot, wet cunt over me, groaning. "Oh my god, the barbells feel so good like this."

I bite down on my tongue, stars dancing in my vision. "Yes."

"Can I have you? Like this?" she asks, hands falling to my abs as she adjusts her hips, stopping when my tip is pressed to her entrance.

I groan, fighting the urge to stab into her. "You can have me however you want," I rasp. "And Adeline?"

Her eyes meet mine.

"I love you too."

Her smile softens and she sighs. "I think I could get used to this."

"Good," I murmur, zeroing in on where we're connected. The way she's hovering above me, just my tip inside her.

She rolls her hip again. I slip out of her, my piercings hitting her clit.

When her eyes roll back and she lets out a breathy sound, I decide that I'll make her come this way first. I want to watch her take everything she needs.

With my hands on her hips, I shift her, moving her slowly over me again.

She sighs this pretty, content sound. "Oh, that feels good," she tells me, almost surprised.

I lick my lips, studying her every reaction.

"Again," I tell her.

She allows me to roll her up and down and up and down. Her tits shake with the movement, and in seconds, her mouth falls open and she cries out. I slide her up and push inside her in one quick movement, gritting my teeth as she pulses around me, riding out her orgasm. A pretty red flush rises up her neck as I fuck up into her. God dammit. It's hard to believe that this beautiful woman is finally mine.

With every orgasm she grows slicker, and I revel in her warmth.

"My turn," she murmurs.

Shit. I'm fucked. The two of us are so goddamn competitive that we'll just keep trading orgasms. We'll keep pushing to pleasure one another, making each time better than the last.

So when she has my toes curling forty-five seconds later, I curse.

Because there's no goddamn way I can stop.

Then again, why the hell would I want to?

CHAPTER 38

Addie

WHEN THE LOUD ringing of a phone interrupts Gavin's pregame speech, he glares at JJ. "What are you doing?"

Sighing, JJ pulls it out of his cubby. "It's Avery." He holds up the device as proof. "She didn't get to see Adeline today. She just wants to wish her luck."

My uncle grunts, his expression hard, but rather than shut him down, he says, "Make it quick."

JJ puts Avery on speaker immediately and says, "Hi Aves."

Before my favorite girl can respond, the rest of the team joins in, hollering "Avery."

My heart thumps as I beam at the group around us.

I spent years worrying that I wouldn't actually belong in a locker room like this and that all the players I encountered would treat me like Dirk did. But every day, this group of guys proves me wrong.

"Hi," Avery chirps. "Addie, are you there?"

Laughing, JJ pushes the phone toward me.

"Hi, Avey girl."

"I'm wearing your number. Auntie Sara said number thirteen is lucky, right, Mimi?"

Cat replies, "Yes, because it used to be Uncle Brooks's number."

I'm smiling so hard my cheeks hurt. "You make me feel so special," I tell her. "I can't wait to see you."

"I can't wait to see you. Mimi says I have to sleep at her house tonight because you will be busy after the game, but I really want to come home with you guys. Can I?"

"Avery," Cat chides.

I look at JJ, my expression pathetic, I'm sure. Because as nice as it was to have a whole night to just the two of us, I already miss her fiercely.

Lips kicking up, he gives me a single nod.

Holding back a little squeal, I say, "I've been given the okay by Daddy. If you can stay up and wait for us, we'll take you home after the game."

"Yay. You're the very best, Addie. I love you."

My heart swells. "I love you too. I'll see you soon."

"Okay. Remember: kick some hockey player butt."

The group around me laughs, the atmosphere in the room light.

"I'll try."

Gavin gives us a look. "Can I continue now?"

JJ says a quick goodbye to his daughter, then stashes his phone.

"As I was saying," Gavin continues, "tonight is a big night. With our new goalie playing, there will be more eyes on us." He scans the guys, standing tall. "That means tonight is the perfect opportunity for every single one of you to go out there and show the rest of the league how we play this game. Show them the type of team we are. How hard it will be for our opponents to pull off a win. Play like all eyes are on you, and not just our goalie. And that's the last thing I want to say. Because that's who Addie is. She's your goalie." He finally meets my eye. "She's our goalie."

I nod, my chest tight with pride.

"Now go have fun. I have a feeling it'll be one of those games we'll all remember."

Jarred, always one to get pumped up, slaps my back and chants "Angles, Angles."

Grinning, JJ joins him.

Bobby stands, bouncing and waving his hands, summoning

everyone to join in. Bray shakes his head, but he nods at me, a hint of a smile on his face, and joins in as well.

JJ's full focus is on me, his face split with happiness.

I can't help but wonder if everyone in the room is thinking what I'm thinking. He looks like a man in love.

Maybe they can't see it. Maybe it's because I know he is.

Cheeks burning, I throw my arms up and wave them once. "Okay, *enough.*"

"Ya heard our goalie. Let's go," Brayden yells.

By some miracle, they all obey our captain. As the guys file out, I stand and collect the rest of my gear. When I join the procession, JJ is at the back of the crowd, waiting for me.

"You ready?"

I cringe. "Not when you're looking at me like I have something to be nervous about."

His face lights up with amusement. "You're going to be amazing. Don't even try to tell me you don't know that."

"I know." I do, even if the butterflies in my belly are going wild. "I'm excited. This is it." I suck in a shaky breath. "This is the moment I've been working toward my entire life."

"And here I thought last night was something special," he murmurs, voice teasing.

God, this man gets me. He's not insecure about my work ethic or talent. He knows what this game means to me because it's just as important to him.

"Last night was amazing," I say, "but that's because we both scored, multiple times. Tonight will be better because no one is scoring on me."

He drops his head back, laughing, and heads for the door. At the threshold, he turns back and winks. "Until tonight."

I follow him toward the ice. But the moment I step out of the tunnel, my thoughts are drowned out by the noise.

JJ turns around, giving me an encouraging smile.

If only I could freeze this moment. It's another special moment in my life, and of course JJ is here for it. The cheers are deafening. While the majority of the noise is probably coming from my family and friends, that isn't the most meaningful part.

It's the sight of Avery, Dec, Beck, Gracie, Mari, and Emmy Lou all pressed up against the glass, held up by various family members, waving aggressively to get my attention.

I skate in their direction, and the noise grows even louder.

As I approach, the adults turn the kids around. Every one of them is wearing a number 13 with *my name* emblazoned on it, and all the girls are rocking rhinestones too.

Laughing, feeling like I'm floating off the ground, I rush toward them. Avery is practically bursting at the seams, smacking the glass and calling out to me.

I lift my helmet so she can see me better. "Hi."

"We're matching!"

Giggling, I nod. "Yeah, but yours is sparkly."

"Aunt Sara should make yours sparkly too. That's her job, right? She owns the team."

"Aunt Sara does oversee the team," I explain. My father would definitely argue that she doesn't, in fact, own it. Then again, he probably would also disagree that she runs the team. If he has one flaw, it's taking credit when he hasn't earned it.

When I spot him a few feet back, I suddenly feel like Avery. Like I want to bang on the glass and get his attention. I want him to pay attention to me. To be proud of me.

As if he can feel me watching him, he shifts and his eyes are on me. Instantly, my worry seems ridiculous. Because his entire face lights up. And it's not because I'm in hockey gear or playing in the NHL. It's because he loves me. And he's proud of me. Always. I suck in a rough breath and mouth "Hi."

He nods. "Hi, Little One."

I laugh as tears fill my eyes. "I'm taller than you," I mouth, motioning to my skates which give me that extra height.

He responds the way he always does. "You'll always be my Little One."

I nod and collect myself, reining in my emotions. Helmet pulled down, I give one final wave. Then I head toward my net. It's time to kick some hockey player butt.

"It's not every day that a goalie ends their first game in the NHL with a shutout," one of the male reporters says.

I glance at Gavin and my aunt Sara, who are standing in the corner of the room watching the postgame interview. Then I look at JJ, who's got a hat pulled down low, hiding in the back.

There's not a thing anyone could say in this moment that would truly ruin my night, because yeah, I blocked every damn puck that came at me during my first game in the NHL.

More importantly, we won 3-0. The Bolts' offense was on fire, working together so seamlessly it felt like the season hadn't just started. And the defense rarely allowed New York to get anywhere near the net. But the few times someone slipped through, I blocked the shot with no problem. I was in the zone; loose and prepared.

And we dominated.

"You don't have anything to say to that?" The reporter scans the room, laughing like he's proud of himself.

I tilt my head, expression flat. "I didn't hear a question."

"Well," he stutters, his expression going sour, "what are the chances you can do that again?"

There's no point tempering my smirk. "Considering I pulled it off through an entire Olympic series, I'd say chances aren't horrible."

Sara beams. Gavin closes his eyes, his shoulders shaking as he chuckles, and a few of the female members of the press laugh.

"Obviously, being a woman makes this job a bit harder," the man follows up, clearly digging in.

"Well, there are thirty-two teams in the NHL and two to three goaltenders per team, and like you've pointed out, I'm the only female, so I guess you'd have to ask the other eighty or ninety goaltenders in the league if they think that because I'm a woman, my job was harder than theirs tonight."

He frowns. "That's not—" He shakes his head, his face turning red.

With a hand out, motioning to his chair, I say, "You can sit now." When he drops into his seat, I smile at him. "Good boy. Who's next?"

JJ chuckles loud enough to be heard from the back of the room, threatening to crack my composure. It takes effort, and I have to hold my lips together to keep from giggling, but I manage.

"Congratulations," a female reporter says, taking the proffered mic. "I'm Lizzie Stevens, Channel Ten, and I think I speak for every woman to ever play hockey when I say it's about damn time."

Warmth blooms in my chest. "Thank you, Lizzie."

"It's a big night. Are you going anywhere special to celebrate?"

My eyes find JJ's in the back of the room again and I grin. "Yeah. You could say I have a little tradition to uphold tonight."

"And what is that tradition?"

I stand a little taller and focus on her again. "Greasy pizza with my best friend."

CHAPTER 39

Addie

"DADDY." The tiny voice sounds awfully loud this morning. But not as loud as the knock that follows.

"Shit," I hiss, ducking under the covers.

JJ pulls me back up and presses a kiss to my shoulder. Then he bounces out of bed with far too much energy. I'm sore from the game and exhausted from staying up far too late after we ate pizza with Avery—it was fun including her in on our tradition even if it was way past her bedtime—and plain worn out after lots of delicious sex. I should have snuck back to my bedroom. I still could.

I eye the door, gauging how long it would take me to get to the bathroom before—

"Addie," Avery squeals, darting for the bed.

Looks like it's too late to escape now.

"Did you sleep with Daddy so he wasn't lonely?"

"Nah, she was the lonely one," JJ teases, plopping down beside her.

Her pajamas are light blue with yellow ducks on them and her blond curls are a beautiful mess.

Her little face scrunches in concern. "Do you have to go to skate soon?"

JJ pulls her onto his lap, snuggling her tightly, and a wave of envy hits me. Not because he's holding her but because they're right in front of me, and yet they still feel so far away.

But that's my doing. It's time to remember that. And I don't have to do it anymore.

So I hold out my arms. "No skate this morning. Come give me snuggles too. Your daddy's right. I was super lonely this morning, and I came looking for you to snuggle, but all I found was stinky Daddy."

"Daddy's not stinky." Laughing, she leaps out of his lap and runs across the bed toward me, stepping on my legs in the process.

Pain shoots through me, but I bite back a wince as she pulls back the covers and snuggles into my side. Thank god I put clothes on after we cleaned up last night.

Sighing, I run my fingers through her silky curls. "Maybe not, but he doesn't smell as good as you." I press my nose to her head and inhale her. "Why do you smell like sugar?"

Her giggles light me up inside. "You're silly. I'm no sugar. I'm Avery."

On the other side of the bed, JJ wears a soft smile, watching us.

God, I love him so much. This moment is everything we've been missing. Everything we could have had. Everything we still could.

I'm trying not to get ahead of myself. We can't go public with our relationship, so it's best if we keep it a secret, but it's impossible to do that around his little girl. I need her in this little bubble with us.

This isn't just sex. This isn't a fling. JJ and I are building a life together, and Avery is an integral part of that life, so while we lay the foundation, it's important that she's right there with us.

But our girl has a big mouth, so I have to be careful. I can't have her telling my father or any of my uncles that I've been sleeping with her daddy again.

"Adeline and I have to go to the arena this afternoon for a meeting, but maybe we can make pancakes and bacon before we go," JJ says.

Avery peers up at me. "Do you like pancakes? I love pancakes, and Daddy always lets me put all the things in mine."

My lips curl up at the sweetness in her voice. "And what are all the things?"

She flattens her lips, giving me a serious look. "Can you keep a secret?"

I peer over at JJ, who nods, so I do the same.

"Good, because this is really special. No one knows but Daddy and me because we're the dream team. If we tell you this, you'll be on the dream team too. Do you want to be on our dream team?"

The way she says it, like it's a revered position, is so damn special.

And yeah, I've wanted to be on a few teams in my life, but never have I wanted to be part of one as much as I do now.

Voice cracking, I say, "I'd like that very much."

Avery bounces up and jumps on the bed. "You hear that, Daddy? She wants to be on our team." She throws herself into his chest.

He hugs her tight. "Of course she does, Aves. We're the best team." Though he's smiling for his daughter, his eyes are flooded with emotion.

He never hides the way he feels. I don't think he even tries. If I'd allowed myself to believe that years ago, then maybe I would have seen that it was all right there in front of me from the beginning. He's been looking at me the same way for the last ten or so years.

Standing in his lap, Avery spins, drapes an arm around him, and tips her head against his shoulder. "So first we use chocolate chips—"

She rattles off the secret ingredients, which I discover quickly are necessities for a basic chocolate chip pancake recipe.

But the belief she has that there's something magical about them fills me with affection. Of course she believes it. Because that's what JJ does. He makes even the simplest things feel magical.

"God, I could eat pancakes like that every morning." Finn tilts back in his chair, rubbing his abs. He makes sure to lift his shirt so we all have to see them. Idiot.

The twins ate their weight in pancakes and then ran outside. It's freezing, but not one of us stopped them. After all that sugar, they need the movement.

Winnie left for work before we made it downstairs, and Vivi is suspiciously quiet in the corner of the room, picking at her pancakes.

I don't think Hope has gotten a bite in yet. As quickly as she cuts into one, the baby beside her in the highchair devours it.

Finn, to my surprise, cut up pancakes for Gracie and Mari before anyone else had gotten settled, allowing Hope to focus on Emmy Lou.

"I still don't understand why you're always here." I peer over at Hope, who's focused on the baby, then zero in on my brother.

He drops his shirt with a sigh and heaves himself forward.

JJ chuckles under his breath. He's probably been watching the idiot make a fool of himself as well.

"Don't you have to meet Savannah at the arena soon?" Finn snaps.

Frowning, JJ sets his fork down. "Why are you meeting her there?"

"She's taking pretty pictures today." Avery tilts her head up and grins at me, a smear of chocolate across her chin. "Right, Addie?"

I cringe, picking up my water glass. Shit. I'd totally forgotten about that. "Oh yeah. I guess I am."

"At the arena?" JJ asks, his words measured. He's trying to keep his cool, trying to hide his annoyance about the article, and he's failing spectacularly.

"They want to get some shots of you on the ice, right?" Hope asks, finally looking up.

I shrug, going for nonchalant.

"She also mentioned girls' night," she says, lips twisting.

"You should come." I snatch my phone off the table and check my calendar. The pink notation on the 20th of November tells me that I don't have a game and we're apparently going pole dancing again. Lips pressed together, I survey her. "But I have to warn you, it was Savannah's choice this month and she always picks the same thing."

Laughing, Hope peers over at Finn quickly before looking back my way. "I heard."

"Why did you say it like that?" Finn asks, squinting at her.

JJ shakes his head. He knows exactly what Savannah always picks. I've told him before. "Little ears," he reminds Finn.

He throws visual daggers my way. "What could you possibly do on girls' night that little ears can't hear about?"

I make a twirling motion with my fingers to signify spinning on a pole.

"Magical snow?" he guesses.

JJ scowls. "Why would you guess magical snow?"

"Isn't that what Elsa does to summon the snow?"

"Elsa! I love Elsa. Can we watch her?" Gracie says.

"Elsa," Mari squeals.

Vivi picks up her plate and stands. "Come on, girls. I'll put the movie on for you."

All three big girls jump up and rush toward the back room where my dad set up a movie screen. The place is brimming with all the toys he's bought for his grandkids.

Before Vivi passes me, I reach for her wrist. "You okay?"

She nods. "Just feel a little off."

"You weren't feeling good yesterday morning either," Hope points out. "Maybe you should go to the doctor. It is flu season."

Vivi shakes her head, her face a sickly pale color.

"I agree."

"If I still don't feel good this afternoon, I'll call," she promises.

I sigh, studying her, looking for clues about what could be wrong. "Okay."

The moment she's gone, Finn starts in again. "So what's this spinny thing you do?"

Hope giggles. "It's pole dancing, Finn."

My brother stares at her. It's like she's put him in a damn trance by saying his name. Or maybe it's that she's finally looked his way. Or maybe he's imagining his best friend pole dancing.

I shudder. Shit. I don't want to think about what that would do to him. With a shake of my head, I focus on Hope. "Anyway, you should come."

She shrugs, her fairy-tale red hair dancing around her shoulders. "I'll see if my mom can watch the kids—"

"I'll watch them," Finn blurts out.

She gives him a soft smile. "You already do so much. I'm sure you have better things to do."

"Yeah, Finn. You really do a lot here," I agree, smirking. "When was the last time you did something for yourself? Like go on a date?"

He glowers at me. "Not all of us are Boston's Bachelorette, you know. How are thing with Scott, by the way? Didn't see him at the game last night."

I kick out beneath the table, aiming for him, but hit nothing but air. "I ended it with him. Wasn't feeling it."

My brother chuckles. "Right. So who's next?"

"What do you mean who's next?" JJ's brows pull low as he looks from Finn to me.

"I think I'm going to get the baby cleaned up," Hope says, her eyes darting around the room.

"I'll help you," Finn says, apparently ready to walk away from the fire he just started.

JJ stares me down from across the table while I start stacking plates. "We should get this cleaned up. I have to go soon."

"Right." He stands, his chair scraping harshly against the floor. "For your bachelorette spread."

"JJ." I huff, glowering at him.

His scoff is laced with disgust. "Excuse me if I'm not thrilled that my girlfriend is going on dates with other guys."

I cough out a laugh. "Girlfriend?" With a shake my head, I stride for the kitchen. "Unbelievable."

He storms in a moment later and drops the plates onto the counter beside the sink. "What the hell did I say wrong now?"

I spin to face him, scrub brush in hand. "You didn't even ask. You just assume I'm your girlfriend."

"We love each other and we're sleeping together. Hell, we even live together. What else would I call you?"

A sardonic laugh bursts out of me. "Oh, JJ, don't be this dumb, please."

He balls his hands into fists at his sides. "I don't see how I'm being the dumb one here."

"My brother was baiting you," I say with a sigh, suddenly exhausted. "And you walked right into it. You know we need to keep this a secret for the time being. I can't be your girlfriend when you still have a *wife*."

Eyes darting between mine, he grits his teeth.

I press my lips together to stop myself from smiling and grasp his wrist. "I love you," I remind him. "This dating thing is just for the magazine. I agreed to the series. You know this. But I'm not your girlfriend. Not yet. We may not like the situation, but until you're officially divorced, we have to keep it to ourselves. You get that, right?"

His chest rises and falls rapidly, his breathing labored, as if he's been on the ice all morning. But when I rub my finger gently across his wrist, he sighs. "Yeah, I get it." He pulls me into his arms. "I don't have to like it, though, right?" He presses a kiss to the top of my head.

Sighing, I tip my head back and rest my chin on his chest. "No, I guess you don't. And for the record, *you* are someone else's husband. That is far more annoying than any fake dating dog and pony show could ever be. Just like you have no interest in that title, I'm not too fond of being the Boston Bachelorette or whatever it is their calling me. It means nothing. We know what we are to one another. And we know what we want. We're the ones with a real future here. Okay?"

Angling in, he presses his lips to mine. "Fine. I love you."

I smile up at him. "I love you too. And I hate to do this since you cooked, but I've got a photoshoot to get to, so you'll have to do the cleaning too."

CHAPTER 40

JJ

Theo: It's looking more and more likely that I'll be back in Boston come this March.

Finn: Probably sooner. You guys aren't making it to the Superbowl.

Theo: Ass.

Me: He truly is.

Theo: Ouch. What did you do to JJ, Finn?

Finn: He's just pissed because Addie is going on another one of her dates. The dumbass still refuses to tell her how he feels. I legit lobbed that ball to you, JJ. How the hell did you not use that to push her to go out with you?

Me: You're really saying that's what this morning was about?

Brayden: Have we all forgotten that JJ is MARRIED?

Theo: Ah, it's a piece of paper. Which you're taking care of, right?

Me: Yes.

Me: And she's not our coach anymore, Bray.

Finn: Is that your way of saying you're finally
gonna grow some damn balls?

Me: My balls are just fine. Fuck you very much.

Bray: She may not be your coach anymore, but
I'm at the arena right now, and I've got to say,
the new assistant coach seems very friendly
with her.

MY GUT LURCHES. What the fuck is he talking about now?

CHAPTER 41

Addie

"YOU REALLY THINK THIS IS NECESSARY?" I balk as the hairstylist holds up the can of hairspray for at least the fifth time since she finished doing my hair.

I'm in my uniform, pads and all, standing in front of the net, but my hair and makeup are over-the-top.

"You look gorgeous," Savannah says from the bench.

"You realize I don't wear my hair like this during a game, right? It's normally hidden by my mask."

"As is your face," she argues. "And we can't have you on the cover of *Jolie* with a mask covering that gorgeous smile."

Stomach sinking, I throw a hand up and groan. "I never agreed to a cover."

"Right, but this is huge. You're the first female goalie the NHL has ever seen. Cat wants to celebrate you."

I was told this was a photoshoot for the New Romantics article. Apparently they didn't deem it necessary to inform me that my face was going to be on the cover of a fucking magazine.

My life feels like it's spiraling out of control a bit. Ever since Sidney got hurt, I've been barreling forward and I haven't had time to consider how this will all work.

The conversation with JJ this morning only reinforced that. I'm tempted to stop playing this part in Savannah's series, but she's so excited, and I'm the one who offered to be her New Romantics girl. How do I let her know that I no longer want to date a bunch of random men when I can't tell her that I've already found my forever man because he's married?

God, that sounds so bad.

It is bad.

And if I didn't know the truth about their marriage, maybe I'd feel badly for stepping in like this. But I do know the truth. Tabitha didn't marry JJ for love. She used him. Not even for her daughter like she told me that day in the hospital. No, she used him for his money, and now that he's cut her off, she's stopped even attempting to have a relationship with her daughter.

She's awful.

But I'm not stupid enough to believe that ours is a love story anyone would celebrate.

So I'm stuck standing in front of the net, goalie stick in hand, trying to look like a serious hockey player while also apparently looking like a sexy woman who is deserving of love.

I'm pretty sure I just look exhausted.

"You almost done in here?" Gavin calls as he enters the arena.

"Yes," I yell.

Savannah, though, is louder. "Just a few more minutes."

"Savannah," he growls.

My best friend spins and gives him her megawatt smile. Honestly, between her curves, her smile, and her sassy attitude, Savannah tends to get what she wants. And if she can't use any of those features, her sexy fiancé steps in and makes sure it happens. But Gavin was Camden's coach too, so he's not afraid of him like most people would be.

"Two minutes." He rolls his eyes and turns around. "Fucking beauty pageant on the ice."

I wince. "Sorry, Coach."

As he's waving me off, Brooks, Brayden, and a man wearing a ball cap appear and walk toward him. The man is familiar in a way I can't place, but from here, I haven't gotten a good look at his face.

The photographer calls for my attention, so I push that thought aside, force a smile, and hope they get the damn shot.

Five minutes later, as I'm finally skating toward the bench, I realize why the man in the hat was so familiar.

"Ryan?"

"Addie." My old Olympic coach breaks into a big smile, arms held out for a hug.

"What are you doing here?" I pull out of his hold and take in his familiar brown eyes. Ryan was my coach in both Olympic appearances, and we kept in touch, though since the season started, I've been too distracted to keep up with what he's been up to.

I can barely keep my own head on straight.

"This is why I wanted to meet today," Gavin grouses. "I was going to wait until Jarred and JJ got here, but seeing as how you were playing Barbie on the ice, I guess we'll do this twice."

I hold up my hands and take a step back. "Talk to Cat and your sister. They arranged for this."

"Don't you worry. Sienna will be hearing from me," Gavin says.

His youngest sibling also happens to be the creative director for *Jolie*.

"Brooks," he sighs, "can you call the guys and find out what's taking them so long?"

"You look great," Ryan says, stepping closer.

I grin. "So do you. What are you doing here?"

He looks over his shoulder at my uncle, and when I follow his line of sight, I discover Brayden is watching us very closely, his brows drawn together.

I wave at him. "Hey, Bray."

He nods. "Figured JJ would be here with you."

I shrug. "Nah, they didn't ask him to pose for the cover. Then again…" I grin. "Ya think I can convince him to swap and put on the lipstick?"

Ryan laughs, but Brayden only grunts. For him, that may be the closest thing I'll get. Or maybe not, since his expression is still dark and his focus is still fixed on Ryan.

A tendril of unease flows through me under Bray's scrutiny, so I step back to put a little space between myself and my former coach.

"And who are you?" Savannah appears out of thin air, pushing her hand forward toward Ryan.

"Ryan Hobbs. The new assistant goalie coach for the Boston Bolts."

My jaw drops. "Really?"

He breaks into another bright smile. "Yup. Looks like we'll be working together again. I'm really excited about that."

"Oh that is very exciting," Savannah echoes.

"Ry, come here for a second," Brooks calls.

"It was nice meeting you," Ryan says to Savannah. Then he turns to me and winks. "I'll see you in a few."

"Well, he wouldn't make a bad future ex-boyfriend," my ridiculous friend coos the moment he's gone.

I glare at her, suddenly sweating under my gear. "Oh my god. He's my coach." Which is so fucking weird, by the way.

"And you were JJ.'s. And that hasn't stopped him from looking like he wants to kill the new coach."

Huh? I turn, scanning the people in the arena. It only takes a moment to spot him walking through the doors, jaw set, eyes narrowed on Ryan. He doesn't even see me. Fuck.

"I'm not JJ's coach anymore," I mutter as he stalks toward the group of men.

Shit, I should probably go over there.

"Does that mean you hold a different title now?"

Savannah's question forces me to look away from the disaster that's about to go down. "Huh?"

"If you want to talk about JJ rather than some other man for the series, I'm game."

"No. I'm not—" I blow out a frustrated breath. Fuck. "I'm not talking about JJ in the magazine."

Her lips kick up on one side. "Whatever you say. But you do have to go on another date, and if it's not with JJ—"

"Could we keep doing this if I didn't identify the person I dated?" I hedge. "If there was someone I was interested in, that is."

"Hmm." She taps a red nail against her chin. "We could make that work. So long as we were getting the full story."

Relief washes over me. Maybe it's a possibility.

I peer over at JJ again. Ryan has a hand held out to him, and he's glaring down at it. Yeah, this is not going to be good. If I date another man, even if only for show, things will only get worse.

Sighing, I turn back to Savannah. I need to put out this fire before it turns into an inferno. "Let me think about it."

"Don't think too long. We need November's cover article ready for press by the end of next week, and the readers need at least a little information about what our New Romantics girl is up to."

I swallow. Dammit. I'm in too deep to stop it.

This plan of mine better not blow up in my face. I don't have a great track record in that department, though, when it comes to JJ.

JJ

WHEN VIVI'S name flashes on my phone's screen, my stomach drops.

Avery was not thrilled when she found out both Adeline and I would be gone for another week. She cried herself to sleep last night, her tears breaking my damn heart. This morning we took her to breakfast, and I told Adeline to head to the airport without me so we weren't both leaving at the same time.

Unfortunately Avery fell asleep while watching a movie, and I thought maybe it would be better not to wake her when I had to leave. I second-guessed that thought the entire way to the airport, and I have a feeling this call is going to confirm I made the wrong choice.

"Hello," I say as I check the console to confirm I'm not leaving anything important in the car.

"Daddy, where are you?" The sadness in Avery's voice pierces my heart.

"I have to go to work, Aves. We went over this. Vivi has all sorts of fun things planned for you and your cousins. You won't even miss me."

"I already miss you," she says through broken little tears.

Fuck, I don't know if I can do this. I force myself to climb out and pop the trunk. Then I stare at the suitcase and consider turning around. I can't keep doing this to my kid. It's not fair.

"Aves." I blow out a breath. What the hell do I do now? How do I make this okay?

"JJ, I got this," Vivi says in the background. "Avery, what do you say we go check on the raccoons? I think Uncle Beckett left some treats for them."

"I don't want the raccoons. I want Daddy," Avery sobs.

Jaw clenched, I close my eyes and run through my options. "What if I called Mimi?"

"Do you think…she'd want to…hang out with me?" Her soft voice breaks every few seconds as she tries to suck in little breaths, but there's a hint of hope in her tone.

"Let me call her. If she's around, I'm sure there's nothing she would want to do more."

"Do you think she'll want me to stay the night?" Avery hedges, my little negotiator.

I chuckle. "I'll see what I can do. But Aves, I gotta get off the phone to call her, okay?"

"Okay. I love you, Daddy. I'm sorry I'm not so brave."

My gut clenches, nearly making me double over. "You are the bravest girl I know."

"So I can still be on your team?"

The fissure in my heart, the one that showed up this morning when I left her, opens up. "There is not a thing in the world you could do that would keep you from being on my team. You don't have to be brave for me. Okay?"

She sniffles. "Okay, Daddy."

"I love you and I'll talk to you soon."

"Love you too."

As I pull the phone away from my ear, Vivi tells Avery that she found the raccoon treats. When my little girl squeals, apparently changing her opinion on visiting the raccoons, my muscles relax a little. I grab my suitcase, shut the trunk, and lock the car. Then I dial my mother.

She quickly agrees to pick up Avery, offering to keep her for the entire week if that's what Avery wants. It's not a permanent solution, but I don't have any other choice. I really don't think bringing Avery on these road trips is the right way to go either, but maybe that would be better than constantly breaking her heart. Maybe I should just hire a full-time nanny to travel with us.

I blow out a breath. I should discuss it with Adeline. Get her thoughts.

Feeling a little less like I'm going to crack a tooth but still like my heart is in my throat, I hustle through the airport. I'm late, so when I get to the gate, the team has already boarded.

I offer an apology to Gavin, but he only shakes his head. "I remember those days."

I raise a brow.

"Avery having a tough time letting you go? Vivi used to scream and cry when I'd leave. What I'd do to have those days back," he says with a wistful smile. "Now it seems everything I say is wrong."

I grimace. Damn, that's got to hurt. The Vivi I know is sweet and kind. I hope they figure it out.

He sighs. "She traveled with us until she turned five. Some of those days were rough, even with Millie's help. Don't be so hard on yourself."

I'm an empath, there's no doubt. I feel things deeply, but I rarely let the painful emotions show. But I'm so goddam overwhelmed right now. I feel like I might just break. Tears blur my vision, but I press my tongue to the roof of my mouth and nod. If I try talking right now, I'll lose it. So I squeeze his arm and head down the aisle. He cuffs my shoulder, stopping me, and when I turn around, he holds my gaze. "It's okay."

I take a deep breath and let it out slowly. "I'm good."

With a nod, he lets go.

Head down, I head straight to the back. The second I spot Adeline, a rush of relief hits me. For the first time in an hour, I'm hit with the urge to smile.

That evaporates quickly, though, when I realize the seat beside her is taken.

By Ryan fucking Hobbs.

I approach, standing a little too close to him, and say, "Aren't you supposed to be sitting up front with the coaches?"

He darts a look at Adeline, then looks back my way. "I wanted to run a few things by Addie."

"Should I sit here so we can all discuss?" Brow raised, I point to the row across from them. It's occupied, but the guys are watching me like they're ready to hop up the second I ask. Maybe it's the expression on my face. Murder. That's what it probably says. I want to murder this guy. And anyone who gets in my way. I'm just...today is not the fucking day.

"Oh, I wouldn't want to bother you. Go rest. Addie and I have this covered." He smiles again, dismissing me.

I lean to one side, assessing Adeline.

The look she gives me in return begs for me to listen.

Bray calls out to me from two rows back, probably sensing that I'm on the verge of losing my shit. "Hanson, I wanted to talk to you about something."

With a grunt, I head in his direction. I slump in the seat beside him quickly and put on my seat belt. I've held up the entire team long enough. I may be pissed, but I'm not a complete dick.

My best friend turns my way, silently examining me.

I shake my head, facing forward. "Not in the fucking mood for your commentary, Cap."

"I wasn't going to say anything."

I scoff. "Right."

"He's her coach, just like she was yours," he reminds me. "Nothing is going on."

"Yup."

"Listen, I—"

"Seriously, Bray, I can't do this right now," I grit out. "My kid is having a meltdown because her mom hasn't called in three fucking months. I can't find the goddamn woman to serve her with divorce papers, and the woman I'm in love—"

I swallow down the words and shake my head. Then I remove my headphones from around my neck and pull them over my ears. Every step forward feels so precarious. I'm not sure which one is hiding quicksand. Which will do me in, stealing all I've built over these last few weeks—things I've spent years praying for—as I sink.

Bray squeezes my knee. I don't move. I can't even accept his sympathy. So with my jaw locked tight and breathing through my nose to hold back the tears, I close my eyes and tune everyone out.

Hours later my mood hasn't improved, but after a FaceTime call with Avery and my mother, my heart doesn't hurt so much. My girl was all smiles and my mom promised that she and Dad were thrilled to have her for the week.

I swear I have the best parents in the world.

I'm brushing my teeth when a knock sounds on my door. Assuming it's Adeline, I stride over to it and pull it open so she can get in quickly.

Sneaking around. Always fucking sneaking around.

She sighs, her shoulders sinking. "I know you're pissed about Ryan, but—"

"I don't give a fuck about Ryan," I say around my toothbrush. I head for the bathroom and spit into the sink. After rinsing out my mouth, I set the toothbrush down and turn, only to find that Adeline has me cornered in the bathroom, blocking the door, so I prop myself up against the counter and cross my arms.

"Please, I know you aren't thrilled that he's our new coach."

The chuckle that works its way out of me is dry and annoyed. "Do you blame me? The guy was obsessed with you years ago, and now here he is again, eye-fucking you every chance he gets."

She folds her arms, her expression hard. "He's our coach, nothing more."

I blow out a breath. Fuck. I don't want to fight. "Seriously, it's not about Ryan. I'm just—I don't think I'll make good company tonight."

Head tilted, Adeline frowns. "You want me to leave?"

"It's Avery." I pull on my neck. "She freaked out this afternoon. She's taking Tabitha's disappearance so damn hard, and I just—I can't fucking find her. Or get her to pick up the goddamn phone and talk to her daughter." My heart thunders, and I can feel my blood pressure rising. "And until she's served and I get custody arrangements in place, I can't tell Avery a thing. Hell, even then I don't know that I can." I tug at my hair. "If I knew Tabitha would be gone for good, I could prepare Avery for that. But what if she comes back? Then what do I do? What if she finally gets served, only to fight for custody? I just—I don't fucking know what to do, and every time I walk out that door, I feel like I'm failing my daughter."

Adeline steps forward, concern written all over her face. "Tabitha couldn't just come back, could she? I mean, she abandoned Avery."

"That's what my attorneys will be arguing," I mutter. "But that's the point. I'm still fighting for my daughter. And until I work that out—"

Her eyes widen and her lips part. "Oh." She takes a step back. "I can go. I didn't mean to make things harder on you."

I grasp her wrist, dragging my thumb over her soft, warm skin, soothing myself. "I'm just—I wanted you to know where my head was at. I didn't mean I wanted you to leave. I never want you to leave. I want you to be part of this." Forcing my head up, I admit, "I just don't know if that's fair."

Eyes narrowing, she steps closer, standing taller. "Fuck fair, JJ No matter what, I would want to be here for you. But the way I love that little girl? I want—" She flattens her lips and takes a deep breath. "I want to be whatever I can be for her. As much as you're comfortable with. Like Beckett was for me. He may not be my biological dad, but he's more of a father to me than mine ever was. It still hurts knowing that my biological father chose not to be part of my life, and Avery will experience the same kind of pain, no matter how much we want to protect her. But we can show her that not everyone leaves. That the people who truly love her will always show up. I want to be that person for her. If you'll let me."

As always, I'm blown away by this woman. By her heart. And for the first time in a long time, I don't feel so alone in all of this. Adeline giving me a second chance was a long shot, but her loving my daughter the way she does is the dream.

Looping my arms around her, I pull her into my chest, and for the first time today, the pressure behind my ribs eases. I press a kiss to the top of her head and breathe her in. "I love you. You know that, right?"

She nods against my chest. "I love you too."

"And Avery loves you." With a sigh, I add, "I think she'll be okay."

Face tipped up, she gives me one of her soft smiles. "We'll make sure she is."

I press my mouth to hers. I need to be closer to her. Because today has been painful and this woman always makes things better.

She hums softly against my mouth, like she feels the same way.

Wrapping her arms around my shoulders, she pulls me closer, deepening the kiss.

Grunting, I settle my hands under her ass and pick her up. With her snug against me, legs around my hips, I walk into the bedroom and straight to the bed, where I fall on top of her.

"Need you," I tell her between kisses.

I drag her onto my lap and pull on her top, fumbling and desperate. She helps me by tugging it over her head and then undoing her bra. While I struggle to remove her pants, she grasps the hem of my shirt. She loses her balance and almost falls off my lap. And as we break into laughter, I toss her onto the bed, stand up, and pull my pants down. I'm done playing games.

Licking her lips, she kicks her leggings into the corner of the room. And then she backs up on the bed until she's lying against the pillows, naked, complete perfection.

"Fuck, I adore you." I crawl up her body, kissing every spot I pass, only stopping when I make it back to her lips.

"I need you inside me." She wraps her fingers around me and strokes.

I'm already hard. How could I not be when my literal dream girl is naked in my bed? She easily lines me up against her warm cunt. "No games, no foreplay," she breathes. "Just fuck me. Please."

I drink her in. My beautiful best friend. The woman who makes everything better. This is no different. The moment I sink into her, my worries and concerns dissipate.

"Shit," she gasps against my mouth.

"Too quick?" I pull back, hovering above her.

Head shaking, she grasps my ass and pulls me deeper. "Better."

With a grunt, I bury my hand in her hair. I can't get over how much I love her. How right my life is when I'm with her. "Perfect," I murmur against her mouth. "Fuck, baby, you're so perfect. You make everything better. Please, please don't ever leave me again."

She smiles up at me, eyes glassy. "Will you go on a date with me when we get home?"

Surprise rockets through me, and I break into a grin. "Are you asking me to be your next bachelor?"

She shakes her head. "Savannah told me I could keep the person I'm dating a secret. So I'm not asking you to be my next bachelor. I'm asking you to be my secret boyfriend. Fuck the piece of paper that says you're married or magazines that say I'm single." She hesitates for only a second, and then she gives me that soft smile that I'm beginning to believe is just for me. Just like she is. "Be mine, JJ, because I'm yours and I'm so tired of pretending we're anything other than that."

"I'm yours, Adeline." I press a kiss to her lips. "Always." I shift my hips, then sink deeper. "And yes, I'll be your secret boyfriend. And one day soon, the rest of it will be nothing but a memory. I promise."

CHAPTER 43

Addie

FOUR CITIES OVER NINE DAYS. By the end of the trip, I'm delirious and extremely ready to get home to Avery. Every night JJ and I FaceTime her, and every night at least one of us ends up a little teary eyed. Always Avery, but often JJ too.

Seeing this man who can be such a force on the ice turn into a puddle for his little girl only makes me love him more.

It's getting hard to hide in public. And it's hell keeping my physical distance when we spend nearly all our time together. It's natural to gravitate toward him. To want to reach for his hand when we're standing beside one another, to want to lean in and kiss him when he smiles at me.

It kills me that I can't comfort him when he's dealing with unwanted press, like right now. The press normally abides by a well-known set of rules. But everyone with a phone thinks they're media these days, and tonight, while the team is out celebrating a big win in Seattle, a guy has pushed himself into JJ's space while his friend holds up his phone and records. I was coming back from the bathroom when I noticed. Before I could approach, JJ looked at me and shook his head.

So I'm hanging back. Bray is with him, looking like he might explode, but JJ's calm, silently telling his friend to cool it. Fighting on camera with some low-life idiot won't do him or any of us any good.

I stop a few feet away and lean against the bar, waiting for them to get this dog and pony show over with.

"I'm Brent Jennings with Pub Stop Sports, and I'm here with JJ Hanson of the Boston Bolts. Hi, JJ."

JJ gives a singular nod.

"Tonight was a big win for Boston. Congrats."

Another nod, then a grunt. "Thanks."

I choke back a laugh, garnering JJ's attention. Instantly, his expression warms.

"The loss of Sidney Howe so early in the season must have been tough. But Addie Langfield seems to be meshing well with the team. Are you concerned at all about your spot with the Bolts next year?"

Unease curls through me. Where is this guy going with this? JJ is one of the top goalies in the league.

"I'm only focused on this season."

"But your contract is up and Howe's isn't. Correct? So if Langfield keeps playing as well as she has been, she's in contention for your spot."

Another grunt and a nod.

"Are you at all concerned? She's a legacy. That's got to be intimidating. What are the chances that the Bolts organization gets rid of one of their own?"

I roll my eyes. The idea that anyone, even my uncles, would consider signing me over JJ is ludicrous.

JJ's body goes taut and his jaw goes hard. Fuck. They hit a nerve.

Before I can step in and temper the situation, he smiles.

"I've been competing against Adeline my entire life," he says, his tone firm though his anger less obvious. "If management signs her next year, it will be because she's the best damn goalie we've seen since Brooks Langfield played. And it will have *nothing* to do with her last name."

I miss the rest of the interaction. My heart is thundering too loudly in my ears, and my head spins. Because I know JJ better than I know anyone in the world, and he believes every word of what he just said. No one has ever believed in me more, and that's saying a lot, considering the Langfield men all have my back.

But fuck, how didn't I realize that JJ's contract is up next year? And what does that mean for us? When Sidney comes back, my spot disappears. Which means I'm back to being the coach…and no longer living in this dream world where I have the perfect man and get paid a lot of money to play my favorite game.

A cheer goes up at the table, pulling me out of my thoughts. When I blink to clear my vision, I realize the camera is gone so I head over. "Everything okay?" I ask as I join the group.

Bobby waves a bartender over.

Shit. I know exactly what comes next.

"We're doing shots to celebrate six straight wins."

Bray shakes his head. "You're going to regret that when coach is knocking on your door tomorrow morning."

We're playing in California in two days, so we're traveling tomorrow, meaning we have the odd night off. It's nice not to have to get right on a plane or on a bus after a game and to t let loose for a night. So I shrug. "I'll do a shot."

JJ eyes me, his look saying *I was hoping to go back to the hotel to celebrate. Why are you engaging with them?*

But I only have a year with this team. A year in the NHL. And I want to enjoy every minute of it before I go back to coaching.

"Ya know," Bobby says, the glint in his eye making me nervous. "If you really want to celebrate, Langfield, I've got an idea."

Interest piqued, I lean in. "And what is that?"

He eyes JJ "Don't ya think we should make her an official Bolt?"

JJ groans. "No."

I smack him in the chest. "What, can't handle a little competition, Hanson?"

Sighing, he shakes his head. "It's not that kind of competition."

"Yeah, but every player on the first line has done it. What do you think, Cap?" Bobby practically shouts. "You think she has it in her?"

For the first time in a long time, Brayden actually smiles. It's not a smirk. It's a goddamn jubilant grin, and it's glorious. "Yeah, man. Angles has been playing just as much as Hanson has. Why shouldn't she do it?"

"Yeah, why shouldn't I do it?" I echo, focus fixed on JJ.

He slams his eyes shut. "Don't say I didn't warn you."

And suddenly I'm a little nervous. What the hell did I just agree to do?

"A tattoo shop?"

Bray, JJ, Jarred, Bobby, Royal, and Maxim all came along with me to partake in this madness. The rest of the guys were more interested in the women circling our table than in witnessing whatever Bobby was challenging me to do.

"Okay, Adeline isn't comfortable. I'm going to walk her back to the hotel," JJ grouses.

Head tilted, Bray eyes me. "You uncomfortable, Angles?"

I glance up at the dancing rabbit on the shop window. It's kind of cool. And I don't like backing down from a challenge. "I'm fine," I say, steeling my spine. "So I'm getting a tattoo?"

"Fuck no," Bray snaps.

Bobby snorts. "Like Cap would let anyone else tattoo you."

JJ crosses his arms, shifting so he's partially in front of me. "No one is tattooing Adeline."

"Oh my god." With a shove, I push him out of the way. "You aren't my goddamn bodyguard. I can do what I want."

He glares at me, his blue eyes dark beneath the shitty parking lot lights.

I lift my chin. He may be my secret boyfriend, but he's not in charge of me, and if he keeps pushing, he's going to give us away.

Finally he sighs, running his hands through his hair. "Fine."

"So if I'm not getting a tattoo, what am I doing?" I ask Bobby.

He smirks, his face lit up with mischief. "Every player on the team has a certain piercing."

I have to work extra hard not to let my jaw drop. Oh fuck.

JJ's laugh is low.

"What kind of piercing?" I squawk, thankfully remembering that as far as these guys know, I'm in the dark about JJ's hardware.

Bray shakes his head. "Just a piercing. Any kind you want. It's tradition. Everyone on the first line has one."

Bobby huffs. "That's not—"

Brayden shakes his head. "Just because you idiots were all convinced to pierce your goddamn dicks doesn't mean she needs to follow suit."

"She doesn't have dick," Maxim says in his thick Russian accent.

"Thanks for the anatomy lesson, Loob," I mutter, though my throat has gone dry.

JJ only has the Jacob's ladder. Does that mean every single one of them has their penis pierced? Is that really a thing?

Suddenly Savannah's text about the OG Bolts team surfaces. She mentioned that the guys all had them. Which includes my uncles. I slap a hand to my mouth. I'm going to be sick.

"I warned you," JJ murmurs, standing a little too close. His breath is warm on my neck, grounding me in this moment.

"Oh shit." Jarred clutches his junk. "I don't think I want to be on the first line."

"You're safe for now," Royal mutters.

He and Sutton have been dating for almost a year. How did she not share this little tidbit with us? I'm going to kill her.

"So you want me to"—I swallow past the lump in my throat—"pierce something?"

Without my permission, my attention drifts down Bobby's body.

Just as I reach the buttons of his jacket, JJ nudges me. "Don't."

Bobby just grins. "I'll show you mine if you show me—"

Brayden swats the back of his head before he's finished the sentiment.

He ducks, rubbing at the spot. "Fuck. Stop being so sensitive."

"She's lady," Maxim says, eyes severe. "Do better."

His stony expression is too much. A laugh works its way out of me, and my apprehension fades.

The guys join in, laughing and hooting. Even JJ relaxes a little.

With a deep breath, I step toward the door. "Okay, boys. Let's go see what this lady can get pierced."

The whole group of them are staring at me when I step out. JJ looks like he's ready to lunge across the room and take me far, far away from here.

I have to hide my giggle.

Jarred is bouncing on his toes. "What'd you get, Angles?"

JJ scowls. "Don't answer that."

"Cool it," Bray coughs out.

Bobby jumps to his feet and rubs his hands together. "C'mon. We've all seen each other's."

JJ full-on growls. "I will literally pull your eyes out of their sockets."

I snort. "No one is being violent. And none of you are seeing what I got." I grin. "But don't worry, I'm officially a Bolt now."

"Not quite. Bray's gotta tattoo you first," Royal says with an easy shrug.

"I'm down for that," Jarred says.

"You not official yet," Maxim says matter-of-factly.

When Jarred's face falls, I wrap an arm around him. "It's okay. I'll wait and we can get ours done together."

His little puppy dog face lights up as we wander toward the street.

"Are we going out for another round?" Bobby asks, pulling out his phone, probably to see where the rest of the guys ended up.

"No," Bray, JJ and I say in unison.

Bobby shrugs. "Your loss. Who's coming with?"

Maxim shrugs, and Royal and Jarred nod, so we say our goodbyes, and when they go left, we go right, heading back to the hotel.

Beside me, JJ's movements are stiff. He so badly wants to ask what I pierced, but knowing him, he doesn't want to say anything in front of Brayden.

"Are you excited to get back home?" I ask Bray when I can't stand the silence anymore.

He shrugs. "Doesn't really matter to me where I am. Home, here. Either way, I'm playing hockey and that's all that I really care about."

"But you like the tattoo thing?" I hedge.

He nods. He's got a baseball cap pulled low on his head.

Even though he's been playing pro for more than a decade, he hasn't quite adjusted to the fanfare that comes with a career like ours. I barely notice the press because I grew up surrounded by the media and attention the Langfields attract. JJ's almost had it worse. While my dad is well-known in Boston, JJ's mom's name is known worldwide. She's the biggest fashion icon of the last, like, four generations. Our fame has nothing on that of our parents.

But Bray didn't grow up in the circus the way we did.

"You think that's what you'll do when you retire?"

He whips his head to the side, glowering. "I don't want to think about that."

JJ snorts. "Hockey is Bray's entire life."

"And it isn't yours?" his best friend scoffs.

JJ's eyes catch mine in the moonlight and he smiles. "No. Not anymore."

My stomach flips and my heart rate picks up a little at the implication there.

We're silent for the rest of the walk, each one of us preoccupied with our own thoughts.

Bray gets off the elevator a floor below us, and the moment the doors slide shut, JJ turns on me, caging me in against the wall. "What did you get pierced?"

I grin up at him. "Two truths and a lie."

His eyes fall shut but his lips twitch in amusement. "Fine."

"I could have lived a very well-adjusted life never knowing that Maxim Loob's cock is pierced."

Reeling back, JJ practically combusts with laughter.

I shrug. "Is good piercing," I say, trying my best at Maxim's accent.

"That's definitely a truth."

My eyes dance. "You can see my piercing right now if you look close enough."

His eyes dip to my breasts.

I fold my lips together to keep from laughing.

"What's the last one?"

"I already have a tattoo."

He chuckles. "Now that's the lie."

"Oh, you think you know all my secrets, Hanson?"

He hovers close again, his lips brushing against mine. "No, but I know every inch of this body, Adeline, or at least I did up until an hour ago." He nips my lip.

I stick my tongue out, defiant, and the bastard sucks it into his mouth, pulling a whimper from me.

The elevator dings and I push him back.

He stumbles and groans as he holds the door open for me. "Jeez."

"We could get caught," I whisper as I pass him. There's something thrilling about that.

Not that I actually want to get caught. But the sneaking around, just for the moment, feels hot.

I glance over my shoulder to make sure he's following me and find his eyes filled with heat. "Then I guess we'll have to be careful. Gavin's rooms next to mine. We should go to yours."

My eyes dance. "Ryan's room is next to mine. Do you think you can be quiet, Hanson?"

He catches up to me, and with his front pressed to my back, he leans down and murmurs in my ear. "If you think there's a world in which I'll ever let Ryan Fucking Hobbs know how you sound when you come, you've lost the fucking plot, Adeline."

A shutter rocks through my body at the feel of his hot breath against my neck, and I lean back against his chest as I hand him my key card, allowing him to open the door and guide me inside. The second the door shuts, he's on me, spinning me around and scanning my body. "Where is it?"

I laugh. "You're going to have to find it."

He tugs at the tie around his neck and drags it from his collar, then wraps it around his fist as he stalks toward me. "Lose the top."

Chin held high, smirk in place, I lift my blouse over my head and toss it at him.

He snatches it with one hand and pulls it to his nose, inhaling, his attention still on me. "Bra too."

I shrug. "Whatever you say, JJ."

I snap the back of my bra and let it fall to the ground.

A sigh escapes him, his eyes roving all over me.

I look down at my unpierced nipples, then grin at him. "Disappointed?"

He bites his fist. "With you? *Never.*"

Then his gaze drops to my pants. "Show me."

Biting back a smile, I push down my pants, making sure to kick them toward him when I'm done. "Is that what you wanted?"

"Adeline," he warns, damn close to losing his patience.

I dig my thumbs into my panties, toying with the black lace. "Is this what you want?"

Jaw hard, he grunts. I take pity on him and shimmy my panties down slowly. I can't help but to tease him even when I'm obeying.

His eyes narrow like he's searching for a sign he's missed.

I slap a hand over my bare cunt. "On your knees."

Without hesitation, he goes down, hitting the floor with a thud.

I'm giddy with power. Turned on over the control.

Those stunning blue eyes of his lift to mine. "Now what?"

I bite my lip, a thrill zipping up my spine. He'd do anything I ask right now. Anything at all.

"Crawl."

His eyes flare for one singular moment, war raging there. He almost fights me on it. Almost. Instead, he drops his hands to the floor, and like a goddamn predator, he prowls to me.

Shit. Suddenly, I'm no longer in control. I'm the prey. And this man is going to eat me alive.

When he reaches my feet, he lifts his head, running his nose between my thighs. "Fuck, Addie baby. You smell incredible."

I can barely breathe over my desire.

"See anything new?"

Sliding his tongue between my thighs, he parts my lips, searching. I moan and my hand falls to his head, my fingers digging into his hair. God, that feels good.

He hums against my sex and then sucks my clit into his mouth. "Nope. Tastes the same too."

I grab his hair and pull, forcing him to look at me. "And how do I taste?"

He grins. "You taste like mine."

He buries his face again, forcing my legs apart, then returns to licking and sucking until I'm a quivering mess. Until I get too loud, moaning his name. Then his hands are around my hips and his mouth is pressed to mine, swallowing all my sounds.

Without breaking away, he carries me to the bed. He drops me onto it, then quickly undresses. "You gotta be quiet, baby. Gotta promise me I'm the only one who gets your sounds."

"Only you," I vow.

He sucks in a breath and pauses like my words are grounding him. But then he's on me, his weight settling over me. Then he presses inside me in one thrust.

My toes curl into the bed, searching for purchase as he steals my breath. "So good," I mumble. "So fucking good."

"Where's the piercing, Adeline?" he rumbles as he lifts his chest up, still seated deep inside me but no longer pressed against my hot, needy skin. He scours the space between us, as if he somehow missed it before.

"Do you really think I'd get my tits pierced mid-season? Can you imagine the chaffing?"

He chuckles and pulls out, leaving just his tip inside me, and studies the place we're joined. His abs ripple under the strain as he holds himself still. "Not your clit either," he murmurs.

A surprised laugh escapes me. Did he really think I'd do that? Lips twitching, I pull my hair back. "I got my cartilage pierced. Jesus, Hanson."

The man lights up as he studies the small silver triangle I picked out because it matches his tattoo. "I like it," he mumbles.

"I like you." I grip his ass cheeks and pull him against me now that he's properly explored all the space between us.

"But I wouldn't be opposed to any other piercings you might be interested in during the off season," he says, thrusting deep.

I smile, moaning. "No?"

Looming over me, he ghosts his lips over mine. "No. Then again, I like everything about you, Adeline Langfield. Pierced, unpierced. Dressed, naked. On top of me, below me…"

"That's good," I say as I wrap a leg around him and flip us so I'm on top. "Because I'm not going anywhere. Now do you think you can be quiet so I can finally fucking come?"

When he lets out a loud laugh, I slap a hand over his mouth and then roll my hips, fucking him slowly and forcing him to take every orgasm without making a goddamn sound.

Yeah, this sneaking around thing might just be a little bit too much fun.

CHAPTER 44

Addie

JJ: Excited for our first official date, Angles?

Me: Feels like cheating calling it that…like we're rewriting history or forgetting a big chunk of it.

JJ: Nah, I'm keeping every moment I've ever had with you.

I SQUEEZE my eyes shut as the biggest smile spans my lips. Things have been so good since our last tour of away games. It's so much easier when the two of us aren't sneaking down hotel hallways and dodging teammates.

That Jack-and-Jill bathroom I was cursing a few months ago has become my salvation now.

No one even questions why we spend so much time together. We work together and we've known each other our whole lives. We share similar hobbies, and Avery is always begging me to hang with the two of them.

When she's awake and I'm home, I can usually be found with her and the rest of the kids. It's been fun, and I've really gotten to see each of their little personalities. I guess my mom was right when she said this would be good for all of us. Winnie seems a little less stressed, the boys are much better behaved because my sister has support and because JJ and Finn are always gently correcting them in the way a second parent would.

Finn is here a lot. It's possible he's moved into the basement, but considering I don't want him digging into my secrets, I haven't pointed out that the guest bedroom down there looks lived in.

Vivi seems anxious, though. Or tired maybe. I feel like been a bad cousin and friend because I've been in my bubble of joy and I haven't checked in nearly enough. With the holidays coming up, though, I really do hope she and her dad work out whatever the issue is. My uncle adores her, and she's not a bad kid at all. I have faith that they'll make amends eventually. For now, Vivi doesn't know what she wants in life, and in a family of overachievers, I can imagine that is a hard pill to swallow. But she's been great with the kids, going above and beyond most days, which JJ often mentions to Gavin.

Hope hasn't attended her first girls' night yet. We had to postpone, so technically it's my month to choose the activity. I saw the coolest video of people playing tennis on the ice. It'd be a blast setting something like that up on the pond behind Savannah and Camden's house, but it hasn't been cold enough to skate outside yet, so we're sticking with pole dancing next week.

It's physically painful keeping JJ a secret from them. Confiding in each other is the part I love most about girls' night. With my travel schedule, I miss out on so much of their lives, no matter how dedicated I am to calling and texting. But the moment we're all in the same space, all the little details get spilled. Thoughts and ideas, moments we've missed, big things that we forgot to mention, or, you know, felt weird mentioning. Savannah and Josie have no filter, but Sutton isn't quite as open, and now that she's in New York performing on Broadway, we don't see her nearly enough and we miss out on so many of her wins.

I hate it. Hence, girls' nights.

"Who are you texting?"

At the sound of my father's voice, I jump, and my phone clatters to the kitchen counter, knocking over the protein shake I just made. "Shit."

Eyeing me warily, he reaches for the paper towels, then picks up my phone to wipe it off.

My stomach churns. Shit, what if he sees JJ's name?

Heart racing, I try to snag the paper towel out of his hand. "I can do that."

He chuckles, but he doesn't let go. "I'm not going to look at your messages. You're not twelve. You can have secrets." He cleans it off, hands it back to me, then turns to the sink and picks up the sponge.

"What are you doing here?" I say awkwardly.

He glances over his shoulder, brows furrowed. "What's going on with you?"

Instantly, I feel properly chastised. It's silly to act this way, but my father is not going to be happy when he finds out about JJ and me, and I hate disappointing people. It's the competitor in me, mostly, though there are other factors, I suppose. The whole abandonment thing for sure. I never want to give my dad a reason to leave me the way Drake did.

Shame hits me a second after that thought does. Beckett isn't Drake, yet I can't help but worry that one day, he'll tire of me.

Why do I allow what one person did years ago dictate so much of my life and shape my personality? I doubt the man has so much as thought of us in years. Why does he get to consume so many of my thoughts?

"Can I ask you something?" I say instead of answering his question.

Face softening, he walks over with the sponge and works to clean the rest of my mess. "Of course."

I take a deep breath. "Was it, um—" I twist my lips, searching for the right words. "Was it hard to get us kids to open up to you when you first came around? Like...did we struggle asking for..." I huff a breath. "When did things get easier for Finn and Winnie?"

He studies me, his green eyes full of curiosity.

When he doesn't respond right away, I start to ramble. "The kids in this house...they all, well, they're kind of like we were." I don't know why, but my eyes fill with tears. "Half families. With parents who walked away. Who didn't choose them. Not Dec and Beck, I guess. But the girls."

I swallow thickly and clear the emotion from my throat. "I want to make things easier and I thought you might know how. Because you're you, so you must have figured it out. And, well, I don't know. How do I do that? How do I help Avery not feel like there's something wrong with her because her mom won't call her back?"

Dad drops the sponge onto the counter, leaving the mess as it is, and pulls out the stool beside me. As he angles my way, I swear his shoulders take on my burden. Like he's feeling it with me. Helping me carry it. Then he shakes his head. "I don't think you can fix that. And I certainly couldn't fix it for Winnie and Finn. Especially Winnie." He sighs. "But I want to be very clear about this: I'm a selfish man, Addie. I loved your mother so much. For a very long time. Probably longer than was appropriate."

I let out a surprised laugh. "Really?"

He nods, his mouth curving into a wistful smile. "Had I known how badly she struggled and for how long, I wouldn't have hesitated to break up their marriage." He shrugs, grimacing a little. "I was a bit obsessed."

My smile grows. That's not new information. He loves my mother fiercely. She loves him completely, but there's something extra in everything my father does.

"My point is," he starts, hands on his knees, "I didn't want Drake in the picture. I had come in and everything was going well, but I knew that I couldn't just replace him." A shock of pain flits across his face. "I wasn't their father. I could step in and raise them and love them, but they'd always have the scars he left on them. So your mother and I gave him another chance. But only one. He had a choice. Be in your lives or be out. Because the coming in and out whenever he chose would have been catastrophic to them."

I nod.

"I say I'm selfish because I wept the day he told us he'd give up custody completely."

I frown. This part of the story is new to me. They never said a word.

"And they weren't tears of sadness, Little One. They were tears of joy. Because I could finally be their dad."

"You keep talking about them, but that's me too," I choke out.

He straightens, his eyes widening. "What?"

"He didn't choose me either. I-I wasn't enough. Or maybe I was the *too much*. I was the third child, and I was barely more than a baby when he left. So maybe it wasn't them. Maybe it was me."

His eyes fall shut and he shakes his head. For the first time in my life, he mutters a legitimate curse in front of me.

"Fuck." The word is so quiet that I could almost make myself believe he said *duck* if he hadn't emphasized that *F* sound.

"I'm sorry. You…" God, I sound like an asshole. Our father has given us everything, and here I am telling him I'm broken up about some man he had to step in for. A man who left a mess for him to clean up. "This was silly. You're right. Avery is better off. We'll all figure it out together."

Clearing his throat, he grasps my hand. "You were the first person to ever call me Dad." He offers me a tight smile, a little bit of moisture gathering in his eyes. "I guess I didn't lump you in with Winnie and Finn because he never got that. *I* got that name. You and I shared a bedroom when I moved into the old brownstone, did you know that?"

I nod. I've heard the stories many times.

"You were the cutest thing I'd ever seen. Sweetest little girl. You were two, and you were the first person in the house to take to me. Even before your mother or Finn. You were always happy to be in my arms. You never cried, and you were never fearful of this strange man who showed up one day. We—" His throat bobs. "We always had a special bond."

Tears fill his eyes in earnest now, and I can't help but tear up too.

"I don't put you in that category with your brother and sister not because I love them any differently than you or the twins. All five of you are mine. Have been since the day I met you. But you were my first. You called me Dad and you made me a dad."

He presses his tongue into his cheek, like he needs a moment to compose himself.

"So, Adeline, don't you ever think you were not enough because some man didn't choose you. Instead remember that this man has always chosen you. And I will choose you every day for the rest of my life. You tell Avery *that*. Or better yet, show her that she's surrounded by all kinds of people who love her. So what if she only has one parent? Your uncles and aunts have loved you fiercely since day one. Family is not who you are born into; family is who shows up."

With tears streaming down my cheeks, I suck in a hard breath. "I'm sorry, Daddy." I throw my arms around him, practically knocking him off his stool, but he catches me. Because he always does. He always has.

And he always will. It's time to stop wondering why a man I don't even know didn't choose me. Because two wonderful men have.

My dad squeezes me tightly and presses a kiss to my head. "You don't ever have to apologize for having feelings. I have a lot of them," he says with a wry laugh.

"You are the best man I know," I tell him honestly. "I'm so glad Mom found you for us."

He tilts his head back, trying to keep from crying.

"Let's start over again," I say, trying to lighten the mood. "Hi, Dad. What brings you here today?"

He looks at me, eyes shining, a smile on his face. "Holiday Skate is today, remember? I'm taking the boys so Winnie can relax."

"And family always shows up," I breathe out in understanding.

He nods. "Yes, they do."

CHAPTER 45

JJ

"BUT WHY COULDN'T ADDIE COME with us?"

Antsy, I drum my fingers against the wheel as we pull up to a stoplight. I'm excited for time with my little girl and for family skate with all the guys, old timers and current players alike, along with their families. But Adeline and I have big plans tonight, and it's hard to focus on anything but that. I'm desperate to make every detail perfect. I have to get at least one fucking thing right. We deserve this. We've earned this.

I glance in the rearview mirror at my little girl. She's wearing her pink Langfield jersey over a white turtleneck. Her blond curls are in two braids that I'm damn proud of. I perfected the style after watching Adeline do them for years after practice. "She's picking up Josie. She told you that." And I've told her the same thing at least four times since we left the house.

Arms crossed, she looks out the window, pouting. "She's supposed to be on our team, not Josie's."

I chuckle. Avery is just as possessive of Adeline's time as I am. It's adorable.

She absolutely would have come with us if we weren't trying to hide how very much we're settling into being exactly that: a team. We've taken Avery skating a few more times over the last week so that she's prepared for today, and I'm pretty sure she likes skating with Adeline more than me.

Honestly, Adeline has become such an integral part of Avery's life that it makes sense that she'd be confused about why she isn't with us. I wish she was with us just as desperately. I've reached for her across the center console at least three times, only to find air. It's like she's a ghost in the passenger seat. We're both missing her.

But we'll see her in less than a half hour, and then tonight, I'll have her all to myself.

"Are you excited to sleep at Mimi's tonight?"

My parents will be at Holiday Skate, and then they'll take Avery home with them after. My dad helped me with tonight's arrangements, so he knows what a big deal it is. He did something similar for my mom years ago, and Mom still gushes about it.

I'm just so damn excited to see Adeline's reaction.

"Yeah, they're coming to see me skate, right?"

"Yup. They can't wait."

"And you'll record it and send it to everyone else?"

I look at her in the mirror again. The hope in her blue eyes hits me straight in the chest. "Yes, Aves, just like I always do."

She nods, content with my answer, and peers out the window. She's stopped asking about Tabitha. Maybe it's a bad thing, but for me, it feels like a step in the right direction. She shouldn't be tormented by a woman who doesn't care enough to even call her own daughter, but I still worry. When it comes to Tabitha, it's always better to worry.

Avery asks me whether Adeline is here twice on the way from the car to the rink. I remind her that she had to stop at Josie's, so she couldn't have beat us. She isn't thrilled with that answer and sticks close to my side as we approach my teammates.

When Bobby spots us, he gets down low. "Hey Aves, whatcha wearing?"

She frowns up at me, her little hand tucked into mine. "Can he not read?"

Bray throws his head back and roars. "Dammit, I don't want kids, but I love yours."

Avery beams at him.

"I can read. I just thought maybe you'd want another one." Bobby twists at the waist and procures a gift bag from behind him, then holds it out to her.

I eye him, laughing. What an idiot. "You bought my kid a jersey?"

He shrugs. "She's the team's kid. She should have all our jerseys."

Avery shakes her head, her little lips turned down. "Nope. I'm only on Daddy and Addie's team."

Bobby looks up at me, eyes widening. Then he gets to his feet and leans in so only I can hear him. "Nicely done, JJ. Didn't think you had it in you."

"Avery, say thank you for the gift," I remind her, ignoring his comment.

"Thank you for the gift. However, I only wear Addie's jersey, so unfortunately this will just sit in my drawer."

Bray coughs out another laugh. I swear the guy has laughed more in the last two minutes than he has in the last year. "Brutal. I fucking love you."

I glare at him. There's no way I want him getting on board with the ducking bullshit, but I'd appreciate it if he'd at least try not to curse *at* my child.

He holds up his hands, cringing. "My bad, Aves. You're a cool one."

"Thanks," she chirps. "But I'm not wearing yours either, Cap."

He just laughs harder.

"What's all the noise about?" a deep voice says from behind me.

Bray straightens and his smile grows. "Hey, Dad."

I'm not a small guy by any standard, but being in the presence of this legend instantly makes me feel like a little boy standing on the other side of the boards watching Tyler Warren play hockey. He was a presence. An attitude. A leader. Covered in tattoos like Brayden, he could absolutely pass as his biological father, when in reality the two share no DNA.

He's in a black long-sleeve Boston Bolts shirt and he's wearing his hat backward like Bray, his smile bright. "JJ, Bobby, and Avery." He kneels in front of my little girl and thumbs toward us. "These guys giving you trouble?"

"They don't understand that I will only ever wear Addie's jersey from now on and I'm not on the team." She huffs like the idea is ridiculous. "I only just now learned to skate."

War's eyes jump up to me. "Did you? Does that mean your dad will bring you down to my house to skate on the pond? I even have pretty string lights set up, and my wife loves to bake this really good French toast casserole that's the perfect breakfast at dinnertime."

Avery looks up at me. "Can we, Daddy?"

I squeeze her shoulder. "Sure thing."

"You just tell me a date," War says, focused on me now. "I'm sure Josie and Scarlett would love to host a whole family night at the house. Between Cam and me, we've got enough bedrooms for everyone."

"Thank you, sir."

He shakes his head. "Forget that nonsense. We're Bolts. I've told you to call me War."

I know and I do it in my head, but it's so intimidating to say out loud.

Bray chuckles low again. He knows exactly what I'm thinking.

And I prove him right as I stutter out a "Yes, sir. I mean War, sir. Thank you, sir."

I roll my eyes at myself.

"How's coaching going?"

War coaches his other son's high school team, and word is that he and Daniel Hall's son are entering the draft next year.

He shifts, sticking his thumbs in his pockets.

Instantly, I can feel Avery staring at his fingers. They're covered in tattoos.

"Daddy," she whispers.

I shake my head.

"But Daddy." She tugs on my pants. "He's got drawings on his hands. Can I get drawings on my hands?"

Brayden and War let out matching chuckles. "Your kid's a riot," War says.

I roll back on my heels. "Don't I know it."

"Coaching is good," he says. "It's my last year, so I'm soaking it all in."

"What are you going to do next?" I ask.

With a shrug, he scans the arena. "It's hard to come back here and not want to just come home. Then again," he says, what looks like wicked delight flashing in his eyes, "it'll be the first time in eighteen years that my wife and I have had the house to ourselves. We might just hang out *naked*"—he mouths that word, and Avery doesn't notice, thank fuck—"all day and night."

Brayden groans. "Come on, Dad. I'm at work."

Chuckling, War throws an arm around his son's back. "Let's go find your brother. He wants you to take him around again."

As the two of them disappear, Avery squeals and runs toward the door.

I don't have to look to know who she's spotted. But I do anyway, eager to set my eyes on her myself. And when I do, I nearly stagger back. Adeline's black pants are so tight they're molded to her long athletic legs. Her white sweater looks soft to the touch, and those lips I love to obsess over are painted red. Her long dark hair is down and blown out, probably in preparation for tonight.

She looks like a fucking Charlie's Angel walking our way.

"Jesus, Addie Langfield cleans up nice, huh?" Bobby mutters under his breath.

The guys aren't used to seeing her like this. While she dresses in suits after games just like the rest of us, she keeps her hair braided.

Right now she looks like a runway model. My fucking runway model.

"She certainly does," I agree.

Bobby waggles his brows. "So you and her?"

I clap him on the shoulder and squeeze. "Now's not the time to figure it out."

Then I head toward my girl, hoping like hell I can make it through the next few hours without giving us away. But damn, those red lips might just be my downfall.

love anyway

"Look at you."

Avery does the smallest of spins, showing off what she and Adeline worked on the other day. The two of them are surrounded by Josie, her sister Scarlett, Savannah, and Vivi, and they're all cheering Avery on.

"I appreciate your help getting her here," Gavin says, smiling.

When he asked me to mention the family skate to Vivi, I told him I thought it would probably mean more if he actually invited her. He said he already had but she'd been noncommittal.

I get that he wants the chance to see her in person to work on their relationship, so I agreed. It's a good plan. But he'd have to move away from the boards to enact it, and so far, he's only stood here watching.

"She looks like she's having a good time."

"They all do," my father says, coming through the gate. He sidles up next to me and surveys the scene. "Adeline's so good with her," he says softly.

Gavin doesn't miss the comment. Leaning forward, he scrutinizes my dad, then me. "Something I should know?"

Dad, always my hero, answers for me. "It's just nice that Avery has a female in her life who cares so much. Her mother—" With a low growl, he shakes his head. "Anyway. Adeline is a good influence on her."

Beckett skates up to the other side of the boards with Dec and Beck in tow. They're both pretty good on the ice.

"Why you all over here?" he grouses. "This is a family skate, no?"

Before I can respond, the most beautiful laughter floats across the ice. Adeline has Avery in her arms and she's skating backward quickly, making Avery laugh hysterically.

My heart hammers at the sight of them. It squeezes tight and then grows ten sizes. That's my family right there.

"I'm going to—" I point.

All three of them are smiling, watching as well.

"Come on, Gav. Take Dec and we'll go get your girl to skate with us," Beckett says.

My dad wanders away too, looking for Mom.

I head toward my girls, taking off quickly and building up speed.

Adeline spots me, and her smile grows, the competitive side of her flaring to life. "Look Avey, it's Daddy. You think he can catch us?"

Avery throws her head back, cackling. "No, girls are faster!"

I love that she thinks that. Adeline is going to give so many little girls like her that same type of inspiration.

But right now, I need to get my arms around them, so sadly, I'm going to have to prove them wrong.

"Maybe sometimes, but this daddy is itching for a hug from his daughter because she's about to leave. I'm going to use my super-powers to beat Adeline this time."

Laughter bubbles out of Adeline. "No fair."

I speed up, ensuring that we're headed to a mostly empty part of the rink. While I trust this woman with my life, she's skating backward with my kid in her arms, and I don't take chances with Avery.

She slows slightly, no doubt thinking of Avery's safety too, so I catch up to them quickly. Locking eyes with Adeline, I nod, and we both slow. Then I wrap my arms around them both.

"Caught you," I yell. The hug is quick. I make a big show of the moment so that it looks like this is just part of the game rather than an opportunity to brush my nose through Adeline's hair and inhale her for one perfect moment. Or squeeze her hip gently, telling her *hello* and *I'm excited for tonight* without uttering the words.

The connection only lasts a moment. But I live for our moments.

"You sure did," Adeline says, almost breathless.

"Can Addie sleep over with me at Mimi's?"

"No, baby." Chuckling, I press a kiss to Avery's cheek. Then I hold my arms out.

Adeline stretches her arms out, passing my little girl to me. She's not so little anymore, really, so skating around with her for the last two hours, mostly carrying her, much to Avery's delight, has probably been exhausting.

I'll make it up to her tonight. I'll massage every inch of her body. And then kiss every spot.

"But why?" She sticks out her bottom lip, pouting at Adeline. "Do you want to sleep at my Mimi's with me?"

With a soft smile, Adeline presses a hand to her back. "I always want to be with you, Avery, but I have plans tonight."

"You do?" she says, voice filled with almost wonder.

Adeline's eyes meet mine for a second, full of affection, then she focuses on my daughter again. "I do. I'm going out with my best friend."

My little girl perks up in my arms. "Who's your best friend?"

"So many questions," I say. "Come on, say good night. You'll see Adeline in the morning, okay?"

"You promise?"

Adeline cups her cheek, moving in a little closer. "I will always come back. Okay? You and me and Daddy, right? We're a team?"

Avery's little body relaxes in my arms. "I told everyone that. I'm not a Bolt. I'm Adeline and Daddy's."

Adeline's eyes widen, and for a moment I worry she's freaking out, but then her lips quiver and tears form on her lashes. She wraps her arms around Avery and presses a kiss to her cheek. "You sure are my girl. I love you. Have a good time with Mimi and Pops."

It takes another half hour for Adeline to say goodbye to our friends, then she heads out. I wait about ten minutes, chatting with the guys a little longer, planning to meet her down the street so no one sees us leave together.

I'm so damn anxious for the rest of the night to get started. I can't wait for her reaction. In a rush, I take off down the hall toward the elevator. I'm about ten feet from it when a loud whimper echoes off the walls.

"You bitch," a deep voice growls. "Thought you could ruin my career."

My head snaps toward the locker room. I'd know that voice anywhere. What the fuck is Dirk doing here?

I throw open the door and storm in, and when I find Adeline pinned against the wall, Dirk's hands around her throat, a blinding rage takes over.

CHAPTER 46

Addie

DAMMIT.

I'm not normally this weak. Fuck, am I irritated. I was too distracted. Too happy. I didn't even consider that it could be Dirk when I heard a man call my name from the locker room.

I walked in like a complete idiot.

But this room is normally filled with my teammates. My family. I felt comfortable here. Safe.

"It wasn't bad enough that you took the spot that should have been mine, you greedy bitch, but then you brought the rookie up? Made me the laughingstock of my team."

Dirk is still whining. His ego is bruised because I'm playing in the NHL and he's not. He's been going on about this for a solid five minutes.

At first he was just raging. Not violent. Though he stood between me and the door, trapping me in here.

When I brushed him off, telling him he didn't deserve to be called up, he lost it. He yanked me by the arm and shoved me against the wall. And now his hand is on my neck.

I glare at him. "Can't answer your questions. Can't breathe," I grit out.

He doesn't loosen his grip.

In reality, I can breathe. But I'm irritated that I let myself get into this position. I tried clawing at him, but digging my short nails into his arm didn't faze him, and he's standing back a bit too far for me to gouge him in the eye. Not that I want him any closer. He reeks of alcohol and body odor. His eyes are bloodshot and he's unsteady on his feet.

That gives me hope. I can take him. But first I need to get a grip on him.

"All because we fucked once. Couldn't handle the rejection."

Bile works its way up my esophagus, and an onslaught of memories hits me. *He didn't touch me*, I remind myself. *I had myself checked out. He didn't touch me.*

"You bitch. Thought you could ruin my career," he jeers. He tightens his hold on my neck.

Fear lances through me. Okay, I need to get out of here. I—

"Get your fucking hands off her," JJ shouts.

One moment I'm pinned against the wall, and the next JJ has Dirk by the hair and Dirk releases me.

Stumbling, I rub the spot, soothing it. "*You* ruined your career," I scream at the asshole. "And I didn't willingly go into that room with you, so fuck you very much."

"Eh, you were begging for it," he slurs.

JJ pushes him against the wall, bringing his knee up between the asshole's legs, rendering him a sputtering mess. "The fuck did you just say?"

"I said," he groans, "she was begging for it." He sucks in a breath and spits at me. I jump back, barely getting out of the way in time.

"I wouldn't beg for anything from you," I say, my blood pressure skyrocketing.

His chuckle makes the hairs on the back of my neck stand up. "You know how it is," he says to JJ, like they're friends. "I didn't even do anything to her. I could have. Bitch was begging for it like a needy whore. She really wanted the hockey dick, you know what I mean?"

JJ tightens his hold on Dirk's throat and leans in close. "You know what mobsters do when they want to take their time killing someone?"

Dirk's eyes widen and his mouth falls open.

"Little breaths. So you can feel everything. So you don't pass out. So take a deep breath."

He releases his neck, but Dirk just stares at him.

"I said take a deep breath, motherfucker."

"You're insane." The asshole glowers, but he inhales.

JJ clutches his throat again, squeezing. "I am. Now tell me, what the fuck did Adeline mean when she said she didn't go into that room with you willingly?"

"JJ—" I say, panic rising inside me.

He shakes his head and turns to me, his eyes going soft. "Baby, you did nothing wrong. I want him to tell me what he did to you."

But I'm not sure *I* want to know what he did to me. And I don't want JJ to know how weak I was after he broke my heart. It's pathetic, but when I showed up in Vegas and found a familiar face, even if it was Dirk, I accepted his apology. He said he'd been a stupid kid and asked if he could buy me a drink to make it up to me.

I remember that first drink, and maybe another. But I have no memory again until I woke up the next morning naked with him in my room.

"I didn't do anything. You were begging," Dirk sneers.

"Don't look at her; look at me," JJ warns. When he doesn't listen, he clutches his cheeks and yanks his head so he's facing forward. "You don't get to look at her." With a growl, he reels back and slams his fist into Dirk's eye. "There, that'll fix that. Now keep going."

Dirk screams in pain. "You're sick."

JJ cuffs his neck again. "Yup. Now tell me what you did to Adeline."

"JJ," I plead. Things are getting out of hand, and I'm scared he might actually kill the asshole.

Teeth gritted, he shakes his head. "No. He doesn't get to breathe easy after causing you to live in fear for years. He's going to tell me exactly what he did to you, and then he's going to apologize. Isn't that right?" He pushes harder against Dirk's windpipe.

Choking, Dirk forces out a "Fine."

JJ lets up a little, head tilted, waiting for the confession.

"I drugged her and took off her clothes. Made her think we were together. But all I did was take the videos of you two from her phone. Got a bunch of stills made and put them up in the locker room. Stupid whore had it coming," he taunts, his lip curling. "Oh," he adds, looking my way, "and I jacked off while you whined in the bed. Such pretty whimpers for a hockey player."

I wrap my arms around myself instinctually, feeling dirty all over again. Like I did that day.

JJ slams his fist into Dirk's stomach.

He grunts, flailing like he's trying to escape, with no success. "I did what you asked. Told her everything. Why you hitting me?"

"I said don't look at her." JJ slams his fist into his other eye.

"*Enough,*" I scream, body trembling and heart hammering.

"He's going to apologize," JJ says, his tone strangely soft. "Then we'll go home, okay?"

Eyes closed, I take a deep breath. "Fine."

"Now apologize," JJ grits out.

Dirk responds by laughing.

Growling, JJ punches him in the gut again.

"Stop, please," Dirk finally begs.

Dark laughter pours out of the man I love. "You want me to go easy on you? Seriously? Fuck, you're dumb. You were so focused on her family connections all these years that you never bothered to look into mine. You'll regret that later."

"What does that mean?" the asshole asks, his eyes widening.

"Say you're sorry," JJ grinds out. He squeezes his windpipe again, then releases it. "Take a breath and apologize."

Dirk doesn't bother with a comeback this time. Instead, he inhales quickly and looks at me. "I'm sorry. I'm so sorry."

JJ puts his hand on his throat again, his whole body taut with anger.

Dirk's eyes widen like he didn't expect it. I didn't expect it either.

"JJ," I cry again, clutching his arm. "You need to let him go."

He shakes his head, but he won't look at me. "See, I don't think I do. I think—"

The door to the locker room swings open and Gavin strolls in, head down.

"Coach," I shout, maybe in warning or maybe in desperation, hoping my uncle can stop JJ from doing whatever it is he's going to do.

Gavin snaps up straight, eyes widening when he takes Dirk in.

Both of Dirk's eyes are swollen, and his head is lolling to the side, his face nearly purple.

"What the hell?" He lunges forward, trying to get between the guys, but JJ keeps a firm grip on Dirk.

"I found him with his hands wrapped around Adeline's neck." His tone is perfectly calm. It's terrifying, really.

My uncle spins, giving me a once-over. "Are you okay?"

I nod quickly. "He just took me by surprise. I'm not normally that weak."

Shoulders falling, he rushes to me and pulls me into his arms. "You aren't weak. Being attacked like that doesn't mean you aren't the strongest woman I know." He tightens his grip on me and rubs my back.

At the comforting touch, my walls crumble and my nervous system crashes. My body, already trembling, shakes in earnest now.

He almost killed me. He might have if JJ hadn't found me. He took advantage of me years ago. Drugged my drink. Stole my private pictures. Plastered them to walls for a whole team of men to see.

I can't breathe. It's too much.

"It's okay. It's okay," my uncle murmurs as I suck in deep, shuddering breaths and cry against his chest. "What else did he do to her?" Gavin's tone is laced with pain and fury.

"He took advantage of her. Four years ago. It's why she didn't play in that NHL game. He drugged her and put private photos of her all over the locker room."

"I need you to take her. Can you do that for me?" Gavin says. "I need you to get her home and take care of her."

My heart cracks at the desperation in my uncle's voice.

Stop being weak, Addie. You are strong. You can do this. I take a long breath and step back, forcing my shoulders to straighten. "I'm fine. Sorry, I just needed a minute."

I swipe the tears from my cheeks, but more pool in my eyes, making the scene before me a blurry mess.

JJ drops Dirk, who falls in a lump onto the floor. Then JJ's scooping me into his arms, cupping the back of my head. "Oh, Adeline. I'm so sorry." He hugs me tight and I bury myself in his chest. "I just—"

I shake my head. "If I'd found you the way you found me, I'd have done the same." I let out a bitter laugh. Because I'm not this weak. I could have protected JJ.

"Of course you would have. You're the strongest person I know."

"Can you get her out of here?" Gavin says, staring down at Dirk, who is moaning on the floor.

JJ cups my cheeks, looking at me with so much love in his eyes. "Want me to call the guys so they can create a distraction before we head out?"

I blink, my mind spinning. Considering. It takes a moment to understand why he's asking. There's always press around the arena. It may not be a game night, but because it's the Holiday Skate, a few local stations are here.

"You trying to tell me I look bad or something?" I try to tease.

He gives me a pained smile, swiping the tears from my cheeks. "You look beautiful, like always."

I drop my forehead to his. "I can do this."

"Of course you can."

I straighten again, and he presses a kiss to my lips.

As if he's imbued me with some of his strength, I nod and take another breath. Then I head toward the door. I don't look at Dirk. He doesn't deserve another ounce of my attention.

JJ opens the door and steps to the side. At the threshold, I stop and peer back at him, holding out a hand.

His brows tug together as he studies it. "Adeline." He swallows. "The press is out there. And our teammates."

I nod. "Take my hand anyway."

"Everyone will know." The words are rough, like he won't allow himself to hope that I want that.

"Take my hand anyway," I repeat, meeting his gaze.

"This changes everything," he says, giving me one more chance for an out.

I smile. It's bright. It's filled with hope. Because yeah, I'm ready to shake it all up and change everything.

No more being scared. No more hiding.

I stick my hand out farther. "Take. My. Hand. Anyway."

With a sharp breath in, he snags my hand and tugs me into his chest, tucking me beneath his arm and pressing a kiss to my forehead. "I love you."

"I love you too. Let's go home."

With a smile on my face and my head held high, I walk through the halls, my hand firmly locked in JJ's, past the press and past our teammates.

The secret is out. And I couldn't be happier.

CHAPTER 47

JJ

I CAN'T STOP TOUCHING Adeline. Seeing Dirk's fingers wrapped around her throat was the most terrifying experience of my life. Had I left the rink a minute later, I could have lost her forever.

The rage is there, of course, but the fear is what makes it hard to breathe. Makes it hard to keep my hands off her.

"I'm not going to disappear," she teases, voice soft. We're lying in her bed. The perfect date I had planned didn't happen. I won't tell her that I hired her favorite band to perform on a rooftop in Boston. A private show just for the two of us. So we could dance beneath the stars. I sent a text apologizing for the no-show, but there was no way we were making it there after what happened.

Adeline is too proud to voice what she's feeling, but she's spooked.

Of course she is. He had his hand wrapped around her throat. He violated her. Tonight and years ago.

I hate myself for the way I behaved when I found him in her room back then. Fuck, I was so damn weak. She thinks she's the one who's weak, but god, she's the strongest person I know. How she got up that next morning and moved forward without telling a soul is inconceivable.

"Just let me hold you, please." I press a kiss to her temple.

She shifts, those beautiful brown eyes of hers finding mine in the dark. "I'm sorry our date got ruined."

I shake my head. "I'm exactly where I want to be." Face buried in her hair, I inhale her, skating a hand down her arm, strumming again. Her warmth a comfort.

"What do you think happens now?" Her voice drips with uncertainty.

"With?"

"Us? Dirk?" She leans back, studying me. Cautious.

This girl. She still doesn't get it.

"Us? We're together. And I don't ever want you to say that asshole's name again. He doesn't deserve another second of your time."

"*JJ*," she chides.

I shift onto my side, facing her. "I don't care what we have to do to make this work. Nothing matters but us and Avery. I'm done worrying about everything else. I love you and I want this. It's that simple."

Her lips curve up. "Yeah?"

I press my mouth to hers in answer.

Her hands wander and dip beneath my shirt, then her palm is pressed against my chest.

I hiss at the sensation. I'll never get enough of her.

She rakes her fingers down my abdomen and smiles against my mouth. "Need you."

"I'm yours." I lean back, allowing her to take control.

Her gaze roams over me like she's soaking in those words.

They've always been true. I've been Adeline's for as long as I've known that life outside of hockey exists. Since the first night we lay down in this bed all those years ago and she offered me comfort in my darkest moment. I think I fell in love with her right then and there. I had a crush before that, but when my head hit that pillow, I was a goner.

She pushes my shirt over my head, and I tug hers off too. We undress quickly, silently knowing exactly what we both need. I'm already hard, and the second she straddles me I feel how wet she is for me. With a firm hand, she pumps me once, twice, and I hiss out her name. "Adeline, please."

A wicked smile plays at her lips. "Love when you beg for me."

"Then you'll be a very happy woman for a long, long time, because I'll be begging for you for the rest of my life." I hold her hips, guiding her up to her knees.

When she shifts down, taking me completely, my whole world shifts. Everything is right.

"Fuck, Addie baby."

"Yes, Jonathan?"

God. When she says my name like that—the sexy rasp of her voice, the teasing—I feel whole but also undone. She rewires my insides. Fixes it all.

"I love you so goddamn much." I squeeze her soft hips.

In response, she rolls them over me, stealing my breath.

Then she leans down and presses her mouth to mine, her breasts settling against my chest. "I love you too. Now fuck me. Help me forget everything else."

Arms looped around her, I hold her to me as we make love.

She puts on a good front most of the time. And she really is fucking strong. But that small admission that she's not okay is everything to me. Because Adeline isn't hiding from me anymore. And the two of us aren't hiding from the world.

By some miracle, Adeline fell asleep in my arms relatively quickly. But my mind is still spinning. It only takes one minute of contemplation before I send the text.

Me: I need a favor.

Uncle Frank: Anything.

I slip out of bed and tap his contact, then bring the phone to my ear. This conversation can't be in writing. I'm Jonathan Francis for a reason. I wasn't lying when I said Dirk should have looked into my family. Had he done just a little digging, he'd know about my family's connection to the Irish Mafia. And I know without a doubt that my uncle will handle Dirk in the only way the man deserves.

CHAPTER 48
Addie

Savannah: Hi, hello. Um, what the hell is this?

Josie: That looks like a picture of our sweet
Addie holding hands with JJ Hanson. Addie,
dear, do you have something to tell us?

Sutton: Oh my god. I'm missing out on
everything! Addie! JJ?!

I GROAN and take in the man lying next to me, snoring. It's oddly endearing, really, that this beautiful, always put-together man does something so totally annoying. He never snored when we were kids sharing a bed. Then again, he always snuck out of my room before I woke up, so maybe he did and I slept through it.

Unsure of how to respond to my friends, I click on the link. I should probably figure out what they're talking about before commenting anyway. While JJ and I walked out hand in hand last night, ready for the world to know, I'm not sure what's being said or what images they captured.

When the page loads, I groan again, this time dropping my head back against my pillow. Shit. That is such a bad picture of me. Sure, I'm smiling at him, but my eyes are bloodshot from crying and my hair's a mess.

It's on ESPN, though. Not a gossip rag.

The headline reads *Adeline Langfield and JJ Hanson: More Than Teammates?*

We knew this could happen. Now we just have to brace for the fallout. Which…fuck, I have no idea what that will look like. I'm kind of terrified to read the article.

An alert pops up on my phone before I can read any farther, and my eyes narrow as I take in every word.

Local Hockey Player Dead in Pedestrian Accident.

Fuck. What?

I click on the link and suck in a breath when I see Dirk's name. Clutching JJ's arm, I shake him awake.

His eyes flutter open and he yawns. "Morning, baby."

I squeeze his arm, then slap at his chest. "JJ….Dirk, he's…" I can't even say the words. Oh my god.

Shifting, he frowns. "Dirk's what?"

Rather than try to explain, I shove the phone in his face.

His eyes narrow as he reads the headline and then his lips lift just a little. "Ah, you don't say?"

"JJ." My heart lurches. "He's…he's *dead*"

His smile only grows.

"*JJ.*"

He presses his lips together, effectively hiding the expression. "I'm sorry. Yes. I see that. He's dead."

The smile returns. What the hell? Heart in my throat, I snatch the phone from him.

"I'm sorry, baby. I know it's shocking, but honestly…fuck." He shrugs. "He got what he deserved."

I hate the way my stomach flips at his words. How my heart rate settles. How my own lips tip up.

"You don't have to worry about him anymore, Adeline."

"Did you—" I shake my head. Never mind. I don't want to know.

He pulls me into his arms and hugs me tight. "I love you."

"I love you too," I mumble, still a bit numb.

I can't believe Dirk is dead. That…he can never hurt me again. JJ did that, didn't he? Head tipped back, I study him. He's already smiling down at me. Yup, he definitely did.

Why doesn't that bother me? Why do I think it's hot? Unable to stop myself, I lean up to kiss him. My lips are just brushing his when there's a knock on my door.

"Addie."

Vivi's concerned voice sends my heart racing.

I pull away from JJ and snag a shirt from the floor. Then I rush to the door and peek out into the hall. My cousin is clad in pajamas, her brown curls a mop on top of her head.

"Oh my god," she says, her face a mask of panic. "Did you see the news?"

"About Dirk?" I frown.

I'm surprised Vivi has heard, let alone is this upset.

She shakes her head and thrusts her phone in my face. "No. It's Tabitha. She's gone to the press."

CHAPTER 49

"LOOK at the bright side here. At least we can serve her now," my father says as he settles on the couch in our living room.

By the time we were dressed, there was a swarm of reporters outside the brownstone.

I pace the living room, feeling trapped. We can't even leave our damn house. Aiden snuck in through the back and got Vivi and the kids out of here. Avery is still with my mother. Thank fuck. Winnie and Hope are in the kitchen with Adeline, trying to keep her from freaking out.

Because yeah, this is bad.

Tabitha is using the photo of us last night as proof that I breached the fidelity clause of our prenuptial agreement. She seems to have forgotten the dozen or so affairs she's had over the years. Never mind that we're fucking separated so I can do whatever the fuck I want.

God, I hate the woman. It's been months. She couldn't find the time to talk to her daughter but somehow got a publicist and an attorney to fabricate this ridiculous story that Adeline and I have been having an affair for years.

She's using pictures from the Olympics, alleging that she and I were already engaged and that while she was giving birth to our child, I was gallivanting around with Adeline. It's absurd. But there's just enough of the truth to push the narrative, and the narrative isn't fucking good.

Fire burns in my veins. "I don't want her served; I want her dead."

Dad arches a brow. "You've done enough of that for now."

I whip around, a strangled sound escaping me.

He merely chuckles. "You think I don't keep tabs on you?" He shakes his head. "I would have done the same thing if someone hurt your mother." He shrugs, nonchalant. "Hell, I did. But we're not involving Frank in this."

I close my eyes and pinch the bridge of my nose. "I just want her gone. Avery doesn't even ask about her anymore. And Adeline doesn't deserve this."

"We can certainly agree on that." Beckett stalks into the living room, and my heart rate skyrockets.

Shit. When did he get here?

In a button-down shirt, without a tie, and a pair of dark slacks, he's all business, and he looks pissed.

He nods at my father in greeting before turning his glare on me. "Sit."

"Beckett—"

"Sit," he growls.

Exhaling, I drop to the couch beside my dad.

"You told me nothing was going on," he says. His tone and his expression leave no room for stretching the truth.

"Nothing was going on when I told you that. But I've always had feelings for Adeline," I say. "I think you know that. But she wasn't open to anything so long as she was my coach."

He drops his head back. "Fucking hell, it's been going on that long? Tell me there's no truth to what Tabitha is saying about the Olympics."

I grunt, my lip curling. "I didn't even know about Avery until after the Olympics. Tabitha and I never even dated." I inhale, reining in what little control I still possess. "I only proposed to her after I thought Adeline had moved on."

God dammit. I'm still so fucking angry at how stupid I was. How reckless. Mean.

I tried to punish the only woman I've ever loved by marrying someone else, and I fucked everything up.

Dad pats my knee, his touch soothing me just a fraction.

"Fine. Good. We'll craft a statement denying everything. And you'll move out," Beckett says evenly. "Today."

"What? No." I launch myself to my feet.

He's lost his mind if he thinks I'll give up Adeline that easily.

Glowering, he angles forward. "What part of my statement sounded like a question? This isn't up for discussion." He shakes his head. "This is a mess, and you won't take Addie down with you. You'll end it. You'll stay clear of one another. And you'll get your divorce wrapped up. Focus on your daughter. I'll worry about mine."

My instinct is to yell. To tell him to go fuck himself. Adeline is mine. But my father squeezes my leg, and I tamp down on my anger. Beckett is only looking out for his daughter. I got us into this mess. It's up to me to find a way out. Without giving up Adeline. That part is nonnegotiable.

"Daddy."

The three of us turn at the sound of her voice.

She's standing in the entryway to the living room, her brows furrowed, her eyes red and heavy with exhaustion. Her hair is a mess since it hasn't seen a brush yet today. She slipped on one of my over-sized Bolts sweatshirts after her shower and we crawled back into bed so I could hold her.

Beckett walks toward her. "Are you okay?"

As he approaches, she holds up a hand, stopping him. "I'm fine."

He studies her, forehead creased like he doesn't believe it. "Gavin mentioned—" He shakes his head and glares at the floor. "Are you sure you're okay?"

She zeroes in on me, her expression full of pain. Heartbreak. But when she looks back at her father, she stands taller and gives a quick nod. "JJ got to me before he could hurt me. JJ loves me, Daddy. And I love him."

Beside me, my father clears his throat and shifts. "I agree with Beckett."

I jolt, a sense of betrayal slapping me in the face. Dad knows how I feel about Adeline. He's privy to all I've been doing to make this work.

I look at him, my heart cracking in two, unable to speak.

His eyes soften. "She's going after everything, JJ. Without the prenup, it's all up for grabs."

I throw out my hands. "She can have it. I don't give a fuck about money. I want Avery and Adeline. That's it." I drag my hands down my face. "She can have everything else. I don't care about it. I don't need it."

The money, the houses, the cars, none of it means anything if I don't have my daughter and Adeline. That's all I ever was to Tabitha—dollar signs. And she used our daughter in her schemes.

If she wants my money so badly, she can have it. But only if that means she stays away from Avery.

"Fine, but what about Adeline's career?" Beckett asks, turning my way. "Because if she stays with you, everything she's worked for comes into question. Dating a teammate? It's messy. It looks bad."

"Right, but it's not unethical," Adeline points out.

"It doesn't matter." He sighs, focusing on her like he thinks he can get through to her. "The press will still destroy you. In the eyes of the media, you stole Tabitha's husband. It's a tale as old as time. I'm not saying it's fair, but this has always been your dream. Are you really willing to throw all of it away?"

I stand and stride across the room. "No, she isn't."

Beckett's nostrils flare, his jaw ticking. "If she stays with you, she is."

I shake my head, a sense of peace washing over me. "No. I'll retire. Then she's not dating a teammate."

Adeline lets out a disbelieving scoff. "You'll what?"

I tug her closer and press a hand to her cheek. "I don't want it if I can't have you."

She searches my face, brow creased in confusion. "You can have me. This is ridiculous. Tabitha already ruined things once. I won't let her do this to us again."

I stroke her cheek. "She won't. But Avery has to come first. And she doesn't have a mother who gives a shit—"

"Right, but I care."

A genuine smile plays at my mouth. But deep in my soul, I know this is the right decision. "I know you do, and I'm so thankful she has you in her life. But this is my responsibility. Avery has to be my number one priority, and while she needs me, the Bolts *don't*. They have you. And you deserve this time to shine."

"*JJ.*" Voice breaking, she shakes her head.

"Either way, I planned to announce it at the end of the season. Avery is almost five. She's starting kindergarten next fall. She needs stability and I want to give her that."

Adeline's shoulders rise and fall with a bewildered sigh. "I hate this."

I press my forehead to hers. "I know. And that's another reason I love you. You always have my back. But I'm not upset," I promise her. "I can't wait to cheer you on from the stands with our girl at my side. Can't wait for you to show her what a strong woman can do. You're such a good role model and we're both so lucky to have you. I won't do a thing to tarnish that. You deserve this career, Adeline. Like I told you years ago, you're going to be a legend in the NHL and I am going to be your biggest fan."

Eyes filling with tears, she wraps her hand around my neck and presses her lips to mine. Lost in the feel of her, I swipe my tongue into her mouth and settle my hands at her waist.

Only when a throat clears beside us do I remember we're not alone. Jolting backward, I rough a hand down my face. Fuck.

"Sorry, Daddy," Adeline says sweetly, but rather than release me, she turns and settles against my chest so we both face her father.

With a shake of his head, he lets out a heavy sigh. "No one is retiring."

"Beckett, it's what he wants," my dad says before I can formulate a response. "We've been planning this. He knew he couldn't remain her player, so as long as she was a coach, this was the plan."

Frown deepening, Adeline turns to me.

I nod, eyes locked with hers. "I told you I was figuring it out. You and I were always the plan, baby. And I'm serious. This is what's best for Avery."

"Fine," Beckett says, like he has any say in the matter. "But after the season is over. Like you said, Avery goes to kindergarten next year. You're not retiring midseason because someone isn't getting her way. We'll figure it out."

Adeline throws her arms around her father. "Thank you, Daddy."

He hugs her tight. "I'd do anything for you," he tells her, voice choked.

If the way his eyes mist over is any indication, he knows what happened with Dirk last night.

I don't blame him for being emotional. For coming in here guns blazing. He only wants to protect his little girl. Even if she's nearly taller than he is.

"But how will we deal with the press?" Adeline glances back at me.

"We go with the truth," Beckett says matter-of-factly.

Adeline's brows tug together. "The truth?"

Smiling, he looks from his daughter to me. "Yeah. And fortunately, we have access to a magazine article that'll help us do it."

"The New Romantics," Adeline whispers, turning to me. She sighs, her body deflating. "But it's been focused on me dating other people."

"Yeah, but the world loves a love story," he reminds us. "Even if it's a messy one. Especially when it's about two people who have been best friends all their lives. Tell them the truth," he says. "Tell them how you fell in love. About your shared love of the game and how it brought you closer. Tell them the truth." He puts his hands in his pockets and eyes my father. "Seemed to work for both your father and for me. We both made a mess of things before we got it right, wouldn't you say, Hanson?"

My dad dips his chin, a hint of a smile breaking through.

Beckett nods in return. "We'll help you get it right."

Adeline searches my face, a thoughtful frown marring hers. "What do you think?"

"I could talk about why I love you all day long," I tell her, grasping her hand. "It'll be an easy story to sell."

Face turning pink, she takes a deep breath. "Okay, let me go talk to Winnie and Hope. And I should probably call Savannah and Josie, see what they think. Maybe they've got ideas for how to spin for it."

She leans in and presses a kiss to my cheek, her mind working.

I can't help but chuckle. She's already focusing on this next project, and I guarantee that by the end of the day, she and the girls will have a damn good plan for how to handle it.

Pretty sure our money is wasted on publicists and attorneys. That group of women is full of better schemers than any expert we could pay. And they have my girl's back.

I don't care how I look when it's all said and done as long as Adeline and Avery are protected, and I have faith that Savannah will make sure of it.

I've never been so thankful that my mom owns this magazine. She wouldn't publish anything that could hurt either of us.

Once Addie has disappeared through the doorway to the kitchen, I turn to Beckett. "I thought you didn't want me with your daughter."

He eyes me, his mouth turned down. "Were you really willing to give it all up?"

Of course I was. But it's not a hardship the way he thinks it is.

I give him a rueful smile. "A wise man once told me that he'd give his life for the ones he loves. I'm not giving it all up, sir. I'm gaining everything."

Beckett nods. "That's why you're the right person for my daughter." He holds out a hand.

I step closer, sliding my palm against his.

Rather than shake my hand, he pulls me in for a hug, slapping my back hard. "Welcome to the family, son."

CHAPTER 50

Addie

"ONE MORE OF you two standing back to back," Josie begs.

I groan, but JJ only chuckles. I'm glad one of us is enjoying this.

"Stop being so difficult," Josie yells as the photographer points and clicks. "The people are eating this up. Especially JJ's point of view."

"Who would have known so many women would love hearing a man's opinion?" I grouse.

Tugging on the back of my jersey, JJ skates backward, pulling me around the ice like an idiot. "They only want to hear about the great Adeline and how she came to be such an amazing player." He stops and holds out a gloved hand. We probably look absurd decked out in our uniforms, minus our masks, as he guides me like we're damn figure skaters.

"We have a game to get ready for," I remind him.

His eyes dance. "You have a game. I'm on the bench tonight, baby."

I shrug, though I doubt he can see it beneath all my gear. "Not my fault I'm better than you."

He chuckles. "Ryan likes you better."

Scoffing, I roll my eyes. "Are you saying our coach is giving me special treatment?"

Hovering closer, he kisses me. It isn't easy with all the padding, but he tugs me by both sides of my jersey until we're as close as we can get and presses his mouth to mine. When he pulls back, we're both breath-less. "Nah, he just knows who's the better goalie. And that's you, Adeline Langfield."

"You are such a suck up," I tease. "And yes, because you said that, you'll be getting all the sex after tonight's game."

"Ah, perfect," Josie squeals. "The readers are going to eat up these pictures!"

With a groan, I drop my head back. Shit. I'd already forgotten about her and the photographer.

I can't be too annoyed, I suppose. Not after all she and Savannah have done for us. For a week after Tabitha's ridiculous press confer-ence, we walked around holding our breath. Freaking bodyguards showed up to escort me to and from the arena to keep the press at bay. When I called my father to give him a piece of my mind, I discovered it wasn't his doing, but JJ's. The two of them are more alike than I'd care to admit.

By week two, the first article had run. Savannah agreed with my dad's suggestion to start at the beginning, so the first article covered our time at hockey camp when we were fourteen. The summer before we played together for the Boston Eagles. It was interesting reading JJ's perspective of that time. While I assumed he embellished a bit for the story, he swore it was an accurate representation of how he felt all along. He was enamored by me. A little intimidated, but mostly just happier when I was around. It was eye-opening to see how his thoughts and feelings shifted that first night after he came to stay with us.

I also finally found out what he said to me on prom night. I *knew* the words he spoke in French sounded like a love confession.

For the last six weeks, the magazine has published article after article detailing memories from each of our points of view. Everyone loves a love story. And reliving it is a blast. Even the messy bits. Because it got us here. With Avery. Together.

"You two done modeling? We've got a game tonight, ya know," Gavin grumps from the bench. His arms are folded and he looks prop-erly annoyed.

"Sorry, Coach…" I push back from JJ and dig my skates into the ice, heading for the locker room. As fun as going down memory lane has been, I'm ready to focus on my other greatest love: hockey.

"Is everyone decent?" I step into the locker room, one hand over my eyes and trying not to trip.

"Is safe. JJ would kill us if not," Maxim says from somewhere deep within the large space.

I drop my hand, and when I find the whole lot of them dressed and ready for the game, I grin. Over the last few weeks, I've seen Bobby's ass a few too many times, though I'm pretty sure that was by design. The kid is ridiculous. And in the grand scheme of things, it could be so much worse. As long as they aren't swinging their junk in my face, I'm good. I'd still rather not see him naked. Even if he does have one of the better asses in hockey. No hair; no tan lines. I definitely teased him about that. Then Bray told me the guy gets spray tans, and I about lost it.

Fuck, these guys are weird. But they're my weirdos now and they took the news of my relationship with JJ in stride. It's all I can hope for, especially because the media asks questions about our relationship, no matter who they're talking too. They've all started answering the way Maxim does. "Is love. Who doesn't love *love*?"

The coaches enter the locker room, and the team settles quickly, waiting for Gavin to give one of his rousing speeches.

"It's January, boys—" His eyes dart to me. "And girl."

I drop my head and give it a shake, and a few of the guys laugh.

"I hope you all had a great holiday, but now it's time to focus."

Christmas at the brownstone was magical. Hope was worried about her daughters' first Christmas without their father—he didn't even call—but my brother was there playing Santa and keeping the kids distracted all day long.

We didn't hear from Tabitha either, which wasn't a surprise. For a hefty two million dollars, she agreed to give JJ sole custody. But the agreement requires her to answer her daughter's calls every night. Avery doesn't ask to talk to her often, but when she does, we want her to be able to reach her mother. If Tabitha doesn't pick up, she's in breach of the agreement and has to pay the money back. It's definitely motivated her to pick up the phone when it rings.

My favorite part of Christmas was the moment Avery appeared at JJ's door, asking if she could snuggle with us before we opened presents.

The girl didn't run down the stairs to see what Santa brought the second she woke up like my nephews did, instead seeking out extra snuggle time with her dad and me. That's just one more reason I love her so much. She's a special soul, and those twenty minutes snuggled up with her reminded me of all the times my mom and dad did the same with us kids. All five of us piled into their bed on Saturday mornings. It's a tradition I want to start with Avery.

I may not have ever wanted kids of my own, but there's no doubt Avery was always meant to be mine.

"What my brother is trying to say is—" Aiden interjects as he hops up onto the bench surprisingly easily for a guy his age and sways back and forth. "It's time for a little Bolts edition because we are fucking winning tonight."

The energy in the room skyrockets. It's not often that Aiden breaks into song anymore. When he played, it was part of the pregame tradition. Now, he's selective about when he'll treat us.

When he launches into his own version of "Paper Rings" by Taylor Swift, I can't help but smile and dance to the catchy tune.

The mood is high
Cause Addie Langfield's 'bout to take the net
With Maxim Loob and Banksy on defense
We're 'bout to put New York to bed
Bobby Dean is fire
As is our entire fleet
Hawke, get the puck for a goal or two or three
I'll be on the sidelines watching with glee

Score one goal and it'll be a good night
Oh. Give us another and please no big fights
A hat trick would be really nice
(one, two, one, two, three goals)
The Bolts like shiny things, and the Cup is better than a ring
Uh-huh, that's right,
Stanley, you're the one we want

The second time he sings the chorus, we join in, singing along with him, and by the time he's finished, we're all pumped up and ready to take on New York.

God, I love being a Bolt. And I really love being a Langfield.

JJ and I are the last to take the ice. Even though he's not set to play tonight, there's always a chance he'll have to sub in, so the warm-up is important. Loud music pumps through the speakers as we enter. The arena is dark save the blue lights dancing around the ice. The energy is high, but it ratchets up a level when we come out.

With a nudge, JJ points to a group of girls holding up signs that read *I want to be Addie Langfield when I grow up!* and *#13 is my SHE-ro.*

I bark out a laugh. "I'm definitely no one's hero."

He shakes his head. "You still don't get it, Angles. To all these girls, you're a fucking inspiration. You made it to the NHL. You're a legend."

I shake it off. While I appreciate the sentiment, I've yet to earn recognition for tonight. I've got to block pucks to do that. Being a woman doesn't make me a legend. Winning games will, though.

Even so, all the pink jerseys with my name on them do something to me. After pictures of my aunts and Avery wearing them trended online, our social media accounts were flooded with so many requests that Aunt Sara had a giant rush order put in. They sold out in hours.

I swear every person who bought one is here tonight. The whole arena is pink. I'm partial to Bolts blue, but it makes Avery happy.

After warm-ups, I skate over to the girls who are waving to me from behind the glass and smile for a picture for them. Then I head to the net. Time to focus and earn that title everyone keeps throwing around.

CHAPTER 51

JJ

FOR MOST OF MY LIFE, I believed there was no greater feeling than the one that took over when I was on the ice. In the crease. Crouched down, blocking, in the zone.

I was wrong. Turns out nothing compares to watching Adeline do that.

As the clock runs down and she's thirty seconds from a shutout, my body buzzes with an electric energy that only hits me when she's the one in the net.

That feeling only solidifies my decision. Retiring at the end of the season is the right thing to do. The thrill of watching her is more than enough for me. Especially when I turn around and catch Avery's smiling face as she screams Adeline's name from her spot on Vivi's lap.

Adeline's aunts and my mother are at tonight's game. Even Chloe, who's in Boston for the holiday, showed up.

Bray nudges me. "I still can't believe you're giving this all up, but fuck are you leaving us in good hands." He just came off the line, and with a score of 3-0, it's probably safe for him to relax. He scored two of the goals and assisted Bobby with the third. Not quite a hat trick, but the light in his eyes tells me he's feeling good. He's been on fire lately. We all have been. And I'm enjoying the hell out of my last season.

"The best hands," I say as Addie blocks one more shot and the buzzer sounds, announcing the end of the game. "A fucking shutout." I hop the boards and skate across the ice to celebrate. I pull my helmet off and toss it to Bobby, who's already had his chance to hug Adeline and congratulate her.

"Stupid boys. You should know now to protect your helmets," she mutters. With a smirk, she takes her own mask off and hands it to Bray. "Can you hold this for me?" Then she skates closer to me, mischief in her eyes.

"What are you doing?" I ask as she gets close.

She bites her lip, but there's no stopping the smile that blooms on her lips. "Didn't you hear? I just played another shutout. I think I deserve a kiss from my fiancé."

My heart flips, but I try not to get ahead of myself. Did she really just say what I think she did? "Your fiancé?"

She nods, her eyes bright under the stadium lights. "Yeah."

"You know I'm broke, right? Lost all my money in my divorce settlement."

She grins. "Yup."

"I don't even own a house. I live with a bunch of wild family members. It's a bit chaotic."

Her smile grows wider. "That's okay, I kind of love that chaotic family."

"Me too," I rasp, heart hammering in my chest. "After the season ends, I won't even have a job, though."

She cups my cheeks. "It's a good thing I'll be working, then. I'm happy to float you."

I shake my head, a wave of embarrassment washing over me. "I'll figure something out, I swear. But I have to do this. Avery needs me."

Adeline's expression softens. "JJ, the last thing I want you for is your money. But I do want you. Hell, I'd marry you with paper rings. You're all I need."

I frown. "Did you just…." I search her eyes, looking for any hint of apprehension but finding none. "Adeline, are you serious? Did you just ask me to marry you?"

She bites her lip, the color of her already flushed face deepening, her nerves finally coming through.

"Adeline Langfield." I adopt that chiding tone she likes to use on me.

She shakes her head.

"Adeline Langfield, did you just propose to me? Are we going to have to change the name on your jersey to Hanson?"

She scoffs. "Oh my god, I'm not taking your last name."

Amusement courses through me. "That's fine, I'll take yours."

"JJ," she says. There's that chiding tone I love so much.

"Were you serious?" I ask, my heart in my throat. "Would you really marry me, rich or poor? Job or jobless?"

"JJ, I'd give away the last pennies I have to marry you. I'd give all this up for you and Avery. So yeah." Her eyes widen like it's just hit her. Nodding along in shock, with a big smile on her face, she drops to the ice. Still in full gear, face flushed and hair a mess, she looks up at me. "Jonathan Francis Bouvier Hanson, will you marry me?"

"Oh no. You aren't beating me to this," I say, dropping down in front of her.

The crowd around us goes wild.

"Two truths and a lie," I say.

She smiles. "Today is the best day of my life. You are the best thing to ever happen to me. I won't miss you at all when you retire."

I laugh. "We both know you'll miss me like crazy."

Her eyes dance. "Your turn."

"I was put on this earth to be your husband and Avery's father. You're already my best friend. And you're my favorite person in the world. And the best goalie I've ever competed against."

She chokes on a laugh. "That was a lot more than three, and I don't think any were lies."

"You're right. It was a proposal. Marry me, Adeline Langfield. I want more moments with you. I want an eternity."

Tears crest her lashes and fall in streams down her cheeks. "I love you."

"I love you too, baby," I murmur, my voice barely audible over the raucous crowd. "Is that a yes? Are we really doing this? Because, fuck, do I want to."

Lips pressed together and teary eyes shining, she nods. "This changes everything."

I grin. "Good. Now kiss me."

"There's no going back," she taunts. "You kiss me now, and it's for life. I'm keeping you forever."

I cuff the back of her neck and pull her mouth to mine. "Kiss. Me. Anyway."

With a hum, she brushes her lips against mine. "You were almost right about everything."

I want her mouth so badly, but I want to know her thoughts more, so I pull back a fraction. "What did I get wrong?"

"I'm not the only legend, Hanson. We did this together. *We're* what makes us legendary."

I kiss her hard, reveling in the feel of her. She's right. Adeline Langfield is the love of my life and if this is the end of my career, then what a fucking way to go.

Epilogue

Addie

"YOU'RE GOING to get us caught." I push against JJ's chest and spin in his arms to face the sink. I've been trying to collect all the glasses people keep putting down around the house, but every time I take another step, I find one more.

"Right." Finn lets out a sarcastic laugh as he steps in through the back door in an Olaf costume. He was all excited when Hope's girls asked him to join in on their family costume until he realized they didn't want him to be Kristoff to Hope's Anna, but rather the dopey snowman. He still dressed up, of course. He'll do anything to make her girls smile. "Because no one knows you're together or that he's always got his tongue down your throat."

I roll my eyes at my older brother and focus on the sink. "Are the kids ready to do the piñata? It's freezing outside."

It's Avery's fifth birthday, and because we missed Halloween, JJ suggested her party be Halloween themed. My father, of course, took it up a notch, and because virtually everyone who lives on this street is part of our family, we all went trick or treating, giving JJ the chance to recreate the missed Halloween with his daughter. My dad really is the best.

They all are. Every one of my aunts and uncles here tonight is dressed up and playing along.

When we got back, the kids begged Finn to take them out back to play with the raccoons, and Finn can never say no to any of them.

The past month has been the perfect combination of chaos and complete joy.

Our team is on fire, JJ is enjoying the hell out of his last season, and I'm reveling in every moment I have with both him and Avery.

"Yeah, that's why I was coming inside. Win wants to know if you want them to do it outside or if you're setting it up in here."

I survey JJ, deferring to him. He's the parent, after all. I still feel slightly lost when it comes to the parenting stuff, but between Hope and Winnie, I've got two wonderful role models who can show me the ropes. And when they aren't around, my own mother is only a phone call away. Not to mention about half a dozen aunts in the neighborhood.

JJ shrugs. "If they aren't too cold out there, let's set it up outside."

I set the clean glass on the drying rack and pat my hands with a towel. "Okay. I'll run up to the kids' room and grab the piñata, then."

JJ grabs my hips. "I'll help."

Finn snorts. "Right. Help. Don't take too ducking long. Dad's outside, you know."

"Race you." I push past JJ and rush toward the stairs. The two of us are as competitive as ever.

JJ snags me around the waist. "Cheater," he breathes out against my ear.

I'm giggling when he sets me on my feet. "On your mark," he warns. "Get set—"

I scream "Go!" and rush up the steps, laughing as he whines from behind me about cheating again.

I'm laughing and out of breath when I reach the top of the steps, but before I can celebrate my win, JJ's got me pinned against the wall, kissing me again. I melt into him, my hands slipping beneath the hem of his Dream Team T-shirt. That was Avery's requested costume. The three of us are dressed as superheroes for her dream team.

JJ clutches both my wrists in one hand and pushes them above my head, kissing my neck. "Don't start something you can't finish."

"Who said I couldn't finish? Bet I can make you come in thirty seconds, Hanson."

Chuckling, he presses one more kiss against my lips. "I'm sure you can, but guess what?" He drops my hands and rushes toward the kid's bedroom at the end of the hall, leaving me in the dust. "I'm gonna win."

A shocked squeak escapes me. "And you call me the cheater," I yell as I run after him.

When his hand hits the knob and he pushes it open, thereby beating me, I groan. But the sound dies on my lips quickly.

Because inside the bedroom, Brayden has Vivi pressed up against the wall, in a very similar position to the one JJ just had me in.

"Coach is right downstairs!" JJ growls.

The two of them jump apart, though Vivi looks a hell of a lot more guilty than Bray. His tongue goes to his cheek and he glares at JJ. But before he can open his mouth to speak, a loud bang on the door cuts him off. "You two better be dressed," Finn yells from the other side.

Vivi spins toward me, her eyes pleading.

I give her a quick nod, telling her I'll cover for them. "Come on, JJ." I point at the piñata and candy. "Let's go get this set up."

His focus is still fixed on Brayden. They're having some type of conversation with their eyes.

I grab JJ's shirt. "Let's go." Then to my brother I yell, "Don't get your panties in a snowball. We're coming."

"That better not be a sexual joke," he hollers.

Finally JJ snaps out of it and grabs the candy and piñata. "Better go downstairs before you see your sister's panties."

"Gross." His feet pound loudly against the hardwood floors of the hall, the sound growing fainter as he descends the stairs.

"You've got five minutes," JJ warns them. Then he shakes his head at Bray. "After all the shit you gave me." But he's coughs out a laugh when he says it and Bray's eyes twinkle.

"I'm sorry!" Vivi calls out as we head for the door.

I glance back and see Bray leaning down and giving Vivi a soft smile. "You've got nothing to apologize for Vi." Then he presses the gentlest of kisses against her lips.

I spin quickly and flatten my lips to stop the squeal.

Vi? Damn, he's got a whole nickname for her and everything. How the hell did we miss this for so long? I shake my head. It's none of my business. So with a smile, I say, "I'll see you downstairs."

The moment we close the playroom door, I spin to JJ, "How long do you really think that's been going on?"

He rolls his neck and glances at the door. "I saw something a few months ago, but I—" He shakes his head. "Fuck, he made me think I was nuts for comparing him sneaking out of Vivi's room to me sneaking out of yours."

Snorting, I smack him in the chest. "You caught him sneaking out of her room and you didn't tell me?"

Her presses his tongue to the inside of his cheek. "I really didn't think it was anything."

I blow out a breath. "Well, you were wrong. Hopefully we make it through the season without coach killing him."

JJ chuckles. "Not our monkey, not our circus."

I grin. "I don't know, Hanson, I'm pretty sure we're all in the circus together."

His expression softens and the frustration he was feeling over the lie Bray clearly told him eases. He wraps an arm around me and guides me toward the stairs, all the piñata stuff in his other one. "You're right, babe. And I wouldn't want to be doing it with anyone else."

Fifteen minutes later Vivi walks outside wrapped in a jacket by herself. I don't notice whether Bray comes out too. I'm too focused on the big smile Avery is wearing as she swings the plastic bat, missing the piñata completely.

To no one's surprise, Dec hits the piñata with precision, breaking it wide open and sending candy flying to the ground. Avery snatches my hand and pulls me toward the mess of candy, begging me to help her collect the most. She clearly inherited her dad's competitive streak.

It takes over an hour for bathtime that night. There's dirt and grime beneath the kids nails and Avery ended up barefoot, chasing the raccoons at some point, so the bottoms of her feet are black.

Still, I'm smiling when JJ and I settle beside her on her bottom bunk to do our typical good night routine.

"Can we call Mimi?" Avery asks.

JJ sighs, but he's smiling. "She just left, Avey girl."

Our girl pouts. "What about Aunt Chloe? She wasn't here. Can we call her?"

JJ strokes her silky hair. "Baby, she's sleeping. It's after two in the morning in Paris."

She slumps back against her pillow. "Fine."

"Want us to tell you a story?" I coax.

Her blue eyes light up. "Oh! Can you tell me the story about how you fell in love again?"

Her father's matching blues meet mine and his lips hook up in a smile. "Well, the first time I realized I liked Adeline more than as a friend, we were out on the ice."

Avery reaches for my hand as the two of us focus on her daddy's every word.

"She was the best skater, and I just knew one day she'd be the best goalie in the NHL. I even told her she'd be a legend that day."

Smiling, I murmur, "I remember the moment like it was yesterday." Then again, I remember them all.

ACKNOWLEDGMENTS

Thank you so much for returning to the brownstone with me. Whether you are a first time reader of mine or someone who knows every ducking character and all of their inside jokes, I appreciate you. This book poured out of me. I couldn't type it fast enough because I just wanted to know JJ and Adeline's story and I hope you enjoyed it as much as I enjoyed writing it.

Just like it takes a village to raise kids, I have one hell of a village when it comes to writing books. First and foremost to Jillian Arly, Amanda, and Samantha for your help with all things hockey, female hockey players and THE OLYMPICS. Your feedback was invaluable.

A special thank you to my beta readers Sara, Sarah, Phoebe, Emily and Jill and to my incredible editor Beth. A huge thank you to Glav, Courtney, Mackenzie, Andi, Nicole and Kylie, the lovely ladies who help create content and spread the word along with my street teams and content teams.

Thank you to Jenny for this beautiful cover and Elen for the illustrations throughout the book.

And a huge thanks to Tiffany for handling the audio production. You are a gem! And to my author besties, Jenni and Daphne, you make this all a little less lonely.

As always a huge thank you to Sara. Not only could I not do this without you, I would never want to. You make work fun, even when we're both going a little batty. I'm glad we got to bring back our favorite character, Jay Hanson.

If you want to follow along on my writing journey and have sneak peeks into all the characters in my world, follow me on Instagram, join my awesome Facebook group Britt's Boozy Book Babes, sign-up for my newsletter and follow me on TikTok.

ALSO BY BRITTANÉE NICOLE

Bristol Bay Romance

She Likes Piña Coladas

Kisses Sweet Like Wine

Love and Tequila Make Her Crazy

A Very Merry Margarita Mix-Up

Boston Billionaires

Whiskey Lies

Loving Whiskey

Wishing for Champagne Kisses

Dirty Truths

Extra Dirty

Mother Faker

(Mother Faker is Book 1 of the Mom Com Series, but is also a lead in to the Revenge Games alongside Revenge Era. This book can be read as a Standalone, or after Revenge Era and before Pucking Revenge)

Revenge Games

Revenge Era

Pucking Revenge

A Major Puck Up

Boston Bolts Hockey

Hockey Boy

Trouble

War

Playboy

Beauty

Snow

Standalone Romantic Suspense

Deadly Gossip

Irish

Hope Harbor

Darling Daffodils Farm

Monhegan Summers (Co-Written with Jenni Bara)

Summer People

Dad Coms (Co-Written with Jenni Bara)

Who's Your Daddy

Better Daddy